A YOUNG PIONEER'S JOURNEY IN 1851

JEFFERY PAUL PEDERSEN

A YOUNG PIONEER'S JOURNEY IN 1851

This is a work of fiction.
Names, places, characters, and incidents are either a product
of the author's imagination or are used fictitiously.
Any relationship to persons, living or dead,
is purely coincidental.

ISBN-13: 978-1-940354-75-0

Published by
New Friends Publishing, LLC
Lake Havasu City, AZ

Visit New Friends Publishing's website at
www.newfriendspublishing.com

Printing history
First edition published in October, 2021

ACKNOWLEDGEMENTS

I have felt inspired to write this book for many years. It seems as if an internal void could not be filled until I accomplished this task. The true-life lessons of my grandparents and ancestors on both sides of my family and their contributions cannot be forgotten.

I would like to thank my maternal grandparents Calvin and Dorothy (Stallings) Gardner, the inspiration for this book, for teaching and showing through example what it means to be a descendant of pioneers.

I would like to thank my Danish ancestors Peder and Nelsine Mariane (Sorensen) Pedersen, who migrated and landed in Idaho Falls, Idaho, in 1901. Soon after settling, Grandpa Pedersen started the Sportsman Association in 1911. The Association was a leader in wildlife conservation, and in part, assisted in making it possible for many to enjoy hunting, fishing, and conservation in the Western United States.

Thanks to my neighbor and friend Gary R. Lowell EdD, Director at Seminaries and Institutes of Religion in Rock Springs, Wyoming, for the initial text and doctrinal editing.

My deepest gratitude to Layne and Anne at New Friends Publishing for helping make a dream become a reality.

SOME OF MY FAMILY'S PIONEER ANCESTORS:

Elias Gardner

Pioneer Trail Companies:

    Heber C. Kimball Company (1848) Age 41

    Richard Ballantyne Company (1855) Age 48

    Rescue Companies (1856 Martin Handcart Company) Age 49

Born: 2 April 1807 Vernon, New York, USA

Death: 15 February 1891 Annabella, Utah Territory, USA

Buried: 17 February 1891 Glenwood, Utah Territory, USA

Joseph Stallings

Pioneer Trail Company:

    Stephen Markham Company (1850) Age 36

Born: 26 August 1813 Annapolis, Maryland, USA

Death: 27 August 1893 Eden, Utah Territory, USA

Buried: Eden, Utah Territory, USA

Thora Thurston

Pioneer Trail Company:

    William Snow/Joseph Young Company (1850) Age 30

Born: 20 July 1819 Buskerud fylke, Norway

Death: 14 November 1895 (76) Annabella, Utah Territory, USA

Buried: Annabella, Utah Territory, USA

John Killian

Pioneer Company:

    Unknown (1851) Age 55

Born: 25 April 1796 Lincolnton, North Carolina, USA

Death: 10 November 1858 (62) Killian's Canyon (Emigration Canyon), Salt Lake County, Utah Territory, USA

Memorial Marker. Buried in Killian's Canyon (Emigration Canyon), Salt Lake County, Utah Territory, USA

Thomas Killian

Pioneer Company:

    Unknown (1851) Age 30

Born: 30 April 1820 Lafayette County, Missouri, USA

Death: 15 September 1862 (42) Parowan, Utah Territory, USA

Buried: Parowan, Utah, Territory USA

INTRODUCTION

I was about eight years old when my grandpa started taking me with him to work as he traveled the vast open spaces of western Wyoming. Part of his job was making sure troughs had water for the antelope, elk, deer, feral horses, as well as cattle grazing in the area.

As we traveled the two-track dirt roads, some were barely visible, Grandpa would stop, get out of his work truck, grab a shovel, and walk to a spot in the ground. I would climb out of the truck and walk over to Grandpa as he straightened rocks and removed weeds from what looked like a grave.

"Who is buried here?" I asked.

Grandpa replied, "A pioneer."

"How do you know?"

Grandpa pointed to a two-track trail some yards away. "That is the Pioneer Trail."

Over the years, we stopped at many, many graves. We arranged the rocks that cattle or other animals had kicked around and removed weeds that were starting to grow. I asked him if he knew any of the people. He replied, "No, but they are pioneers."

I did not appreciate what Grandpa was doing until I became older. Taking care of pioneer graves was not part of his job description, but for Grandpa, this was personal. His grandparents were some of these pioneers. His grandfather had made two trips and participated in the Martin Handcart rescue in 1856. I still remember some of the stories he would tell me about our family and their journey as we traveled the dirt roads in southwest Wyoming.

As I researched my family's journey across the plains, I discovered some of them traveled in 1848 and 1850, and most of them traveled in 1851. Other than their names and a few journals, there is little information about the company my family belonged to as they made the trek in 1851.

Historians ponder the high death rate along the trail between 1848, 1850, and 1852 and so on. What happened in 1851? As you read this book, you will understand why the death rate during 1851 was very low. In addition, there were two major events that occurred in 1851, which made the death rate rise again in 1852 and thereafter.

Today, as I get into my truck and pick up my grandson and granddaughter, we travel and camp on the same two-track dirt roads of western Wyoming where Grandpa had taken me. I want them to know who my grandparents were, who our family is, and the sacrifices they made for us. I want them and others to know and remember what it means to be sons and daughters of Pioneers.

Although this is a fictional book, it is a compilation of true experiences and events from journals of those who traveled in 1851. The names, characters, and businesses are either the products of the author's imagination or used in a fictitious manner. The purpose of this book is to let the reader experience the day-to-day travels from Kanesville to the valley of the Great Salt Lake. Experience what it is like to travel the trail and appreciate what it is like to be a pioneer.

Join with me as we follow the daily events of a thirteen-year-old pioneer as he travels the trail in 1851. Follow him as he tries to make sense of his world through his trials, loss, and confusion, as well as his happiness, shyness, fun, and responsibilities on his journey to the valley of the Great Salt Lake, and into adulthood.

Jeffery Paul Pedersen
Rock Springs, WY

CHAPTER 1
LET ME INTRODUCE MYSELF

December 1867 Manti, Utah.

Pa stopped by again on his way home to Parowan after attending meetings with the brethren in the area regarding Indian troubles. As always, Pa brought treats for the little ones, like Grandpa did with us when we were little, as well as Christmas gifts for everyone. Every time Pa visited, he walked over to one of the wagons I kept, which now sat by a barn a few yards from the house. Pa walked over and inspected the corner brackets he'd made. He examined the wheels made by my brothers and looked at the reinforced leaf springs he'd made especially for this wagon. Pa quietly walked around the wagon, stopping at the back, removing the old grease bucket from the hook, holding it for a minute, looking over his shoulder, and replacing it back on the hook. Pa then solemnly walked over and patted me on my back with a little hug. "Thank you for keeping and taking good care of her."

It had been sixteen years since we had made the journey, and not a day went by that I did not recall some events or memories of our journey. I could still hear Captain Walton yelling, "Come on men, put your shoulder to the wheel. Push, push!"

Although our journey had taken twelve weeks, I felt like I had grown up on the trail, and the foundation for my life had been developed during those twelve weeks. I was now twenty-nine-years-old and had little ones of my own, running around the house as I wrote and compiled my trail journal entries. Pa said it was time for me to share our trail experiences with others. I reckoned our story of traveling the trail was much like so many others who had traveled, filled with happiness and hardship. I still remembered the words of our trail captain, Captain Reed, as we had started our journey. "Good and bad qualities will be revealed and intensified on the trail."

Here is my story, written from memory and journal entries, written as if I were thirteen years old again.

* * *

Hello, my name is William Phillip Killian, everyone calls me Willy. I would like to share with you our story about my family's experience traveling from Kanesville, Iowa to the valley of the Great Salt Lake in 1851.

For me, my journey started in September of 1850. I remember a lesson I learned in church from Brother Thorston. He taught us that President Young said it was important to keep a journal for our benefit and the benefit of our families in the future. Brother Thorston said that this was a unique time in history for our people and our country. He taught us that people would remember our lives, journeys, and experiences for a long time. When we eventually gathered to travel west, every company should have a person assigned to keep a journal of events. He taught us it was important for us to keep a journal so we could remember what we did and how we overcame challenges. Brother Thorston said our journals might someday be used for the improvement and teaching of others.

I will start my story with our life in Kanesville 1850.

In my family, we have:
Father: Elias Killian.
Mother: Irene Batchelor Killian.
Sister: Rebecca age 23, married to James Coons. They have a son, James, Jr. 15 months. They live with us.
Brother: Benjamin Ezekiel age 21.
Brother: George Elias age 20.
Sister: Sarah age 18.
Sister: Dorothy Ida "Dottie" age 16.
Brother: Joseph Samuel age 15.
Me - Willy – age 12.
Brother: Edward (Eddy) Francis (died at 18 months).
Sister: Isabella "Izzy" age 10.

Last year, Pa was asked to care for a widow, Julia Rene'e Lee. She had been married to Henry Francis Lee. A Missouri mob had killed Brother Lee, along with their eleven-month-old daughter Gabriela. We called her Mama Julia. Mama Julia had a son, Gabriel Henry "Gabe" Lee age 7, and a daughter Catherine "Cate" Lee age 5. Mama Julia had come from France. She talked with a heavy French accent and used funny words like, "La-Va-Che (Holy Cow)," and "Zut-Ah-lores (Darn it)," when people could not understand her. When we were clumsy or silly, she would say "mal-a-dwah." She was always happy, but strict, and very busy all day. I liked being around her.

Our family had moved several times during my short lifetime. I was born in Kirtland, Ohio, September 25, 1837, moved to Missouri one year later, and then to Nauvoo, Illinois in the fall of 1840. March of 1846, we moved to Winter Quarters to help with preparations for those moving to Great Salt Lake Valley. Our stay in Winter Quarters was short and full of sadness and death. Winter Quarters was on Indian land, and the government ordered us to move east of the Missouri River to Kanesville. In April 1847, we settled near the Missouri River about a mile north of Elm Grove and about two miles from Kanesville to again help with preparations for those moving west. We were happy to move to Kanesville because Grandpa George and Grandmother Dorotha Killian lived in Kanesville. Grandpa and Grandmother Batchelor moved from Ohio to take care of the farm in Montrose. They did not want to move out west because of Grandmother Batchelor's health.

After Eddy's death at eighteen months old, Mother was not the same. Mother did not want to leave her parents, but Grandpa and Grandmother Batchelor told her she must stay with her family. Soon after we moved to Winter Quarters, Mother spent a lot of time in bed or sitting in her rocking chair. Grandpa Killian said Mother suffered from melancholy or a depressed spirit. I hoped and wished Mother would get better. I remembered when she had been happy and busy like Mama Julia, but now she slept a lot and didn't eat much.

When we arrived in Kanesville, Mother always said, "Why are we always on the wrong side of the river? Why can't we be closer to friends?" Pa would remind her it was the place assigned to us to help the others prepare for their trip out west.

Rebecca would help with the cooking and cleaning, even after she had married James Coons. James was a veteran of the Mormon Battalion during the Mexican American War. We all liked James. He was tall and stout and looked like he could pick up a large bull. He went into business with Pa and my brothers, making wagons and learning to be a wheelwright. While in the Mormon Battalion, James had made the journey all the way to California. We enjoyed listening to his stories at suppertime. He and the battalion did not fight in any battles; the closest incident to a dangerous skirmish was a cattle stampede through their camp. James said the journey to California was very difficult. He said that many times they did not have much water and the territory sometimes was very hard to travel. He very seldom talked about the bad experiences. The only person James would talk to about these bad times was Grandpa Killian. I reckoned because Grandpa experienced some of the same things in the second British war.

Pa was a blacksmith and a master wainwright. My brothers Ben, George, and James were good wainwrights and wheelwrights. Sam was learning blacksmithing. They were all very good at their trades. I was learning the trade as well, while helping around the shop. I helped measure and cut the wood and cleaned around the shop. I always enjoyed working in Pa's shop, listening to the rhythm of the hammer striking hot iron on the anvil, the rhythm of the "ten pound ten." Pa would say that, as babies, Mother would bring us by and, if we were fussy, the singing of the hammer and anvil would calm us. I was always reassured and comforted by the ring of the ten pound ten.

We built our wagons from hickory and oak because they were very sturdy and hard woods. Pa reinforced corners and other parts of the wagon with iron braces. Pa and Grandpa said many of the wagons made in St. Louis were shoddy. They began to fall apart by the time they arrived in Kanesville. Pa would sell these unfortunate travelers his wagons at reduced rates in exchange for their shoddy wagons. Some of the wagons that came from St. Louis were so bad, the only thing we could use them for was firewood, and they fared poorly even at that. It was a wonder they even made the short trek to Kanesville.

I would help Pa clean out the forge, remove the ash and clinkers, and bring in coal, charcoal, and other things, depending on what Pa was making. The shop created a lot of sawdust and shavings. I cleaned up the sawdust into bags and took them to the icehouse to use as insulation. We built an icehouse on the edge of the Missouri river. In the winter, we cut large blocks of ice out of the Missouri River and placed them in the icehouse and covered them with sawdust. We also filled barrels a little more than halfway with water and let them sit in the icehouse in the winter until they froze solid. We put a lid on the barrels and covered them with sawdust. We could have ice into September.

In our spare time, we trained and broke the horses and oxen Grandpa Killian traded from the "greenhorns," very inexperienced people moving out west.

Many people from the old states heard about the gold in California or the opportunities in Oregon and wanted to travel there without experience. They would read popular books and magazines, then go buy animals and goods from people who claimed to have what they needed. Once they traveled a few hundred miles with untrained animals or poorly made wagons and supplies, they were almost ready to give up. When they reached Kanesville, Grandpa was there to trade their trouble-stock and supplies for more suitable creatures and supplies. Sometimes, newcomers just wanted to sell everything and go back home because of the hardship they endured just getting to the border of the States and Indian Territory.

The shop was busy six days a week during the travel months. Hundreds of wagons would come during the months of March to August. Pa said the trail from Keg Creek to Kanesville was good for business and good experience for the travelers. People who were new to driving overloaded wagons down steep hills often applied too much brake or not enough. This usually damaged the wheels or other parts of the wagon. We were there to fix or replace broken or worn-out parts.

Grandpa and Pa leased 2500 acres of land northwest of Kanesville near Indian Creek. We held 200 head of cows, forty oxen, and sixty horses. We also owned the timber rights for a few years. We lived on sixty-four acres where we had six milk cows, three pigs, a dozen or more chickens, and two quiet cow dogs. Izzy, my little sister, said she had two cats, but Pa said no one could own a cat. Cats were too dispassionate to own.

A couple times a week, Grandpa took us out to practice pushing the cows, horses, and oxen around. Grandpa had done the same training for Pa. He had done the same when my brothers and sisters were younger, too. Grandpa said it was important to learn how to "steer the steer." Grandpa said he had read too many letters and stories from people traveling west and had seen too many people not able to handle their stock. Because people did not know how to handle their stock, the stock ended up stampeding and causing injury. Grandpa said most of the damage and injury that happened on the trail was because people did not know how to "steer the steer."

Grandpa always had forty to fifty well-trained Justin Morgan cow horses for sale to people who knew how to use them. He said there were other good breeds of cow horses, but he preferred Mr. Justin Morgan's horses. Grandpa and Mr. Herbert purchased highbred horses from a man who lived in the Ohio Valley by the name of Mr. James Smith. Grandpa said James Smith was one of the only breeders in the area who knew what he was doing and who Grandpa and Mr. Herbert trusted. I had met him a couple times. He was a nice and honest man with a sense of humor and wit that fit right in with Grandpa and Mr. Herbert. Grandpa preferred bay and chestnut cow horses.

I had bought a beautiful bay gelding from Grandpa a few years back. I had given the horse the Latin name Acer because he was energetic and smart. Acer liked to show off his bucking and prancing skills, which he had started shortly after foaling. As he got older, Acer calmed down a little and was becoming a good cow horse. Acer was quick and turned instinctively with a stray bull or calf. He was beginning to corral without me on his back.

According to Grandpa, there were six basic steps to prevent stampedes and other potential problems:

> *1. Before starting the trek, combine all stock that are traveling with you and spend a day or two, if you can, moving them from one place to another. Create minor disturbances from a barking dog or a bolting horse. From this, you can see which animals will go their own direction or become too skittish and panic. Remove these animals and put them in yokes to pull wagons, sale, or trade to Indians along the trail, or totally remove them. The difficult ones create stampedes.*

> *2. At the beginning of the trail, stay a safe distance from the stock to avoid startling. The stock will settle and will adapt to traveling after a few days. Have at least two or three good cow horses on each flank to help herd the stock. Have the lead person weave methodically back and forth, so the leaders in the stock can always have them in view. Develop a whistle or yelp. This will save you from losing your voice, and it reassures the stock.*

> *3. At night, always have at least two people on horseback always guarding the stock with at least two quiet cow dogs with the herd. A barking cow dog will do more harm than good most of the time. Horses help you*

travel more distance quicker; this is very important in Indian country to avoid Indians from trying to steal or stampede the stock. Indians are more likely to steal or stampede if they see someone sitting around or one person just walking around.

4. At night, always sing or talk to the animals in a low tone. This is especially important during storms. If the stock can see and hear you, they are less likely to stampede. This will also keep you and your partner awake.

5. If your stock stampedes, do not try to cut them off; just try to steer them in a circular direction. This usually keeps them together and has them running in circles until they settle down. It is inevitable that a few will scatter away from the herd. If you have time, find them. If not, leave them for others to use. If you keep chasing the same problem stock, you will lose time and they will eventually cause more problems.

6. If you can, always drive your stock away from buffalo. For some reason, cows especially like to think they are buffalo and try to join the herd. This is always short lived; cows cannot keep up with buffalo.

If people followed these simple steps, they and their stock would arrive safely.

CHAPTER 2
GRANDMOTHER AND GRANDPA KILLIAN

If there were heavenly angels on earth, one would be Grandmother Killian. I had never heard her raise her voice or speak an ill word about anything or anyone. She had been a schoolteacher until a few years previous. Sometimes, Grandmother would help our schoolteacher, Miss Watkins. I was always on my best behavior when Grandmother was helping Miss Watkins. I never wanted to disappoint Grandmother. I did not know if it was possible to disappoint Grandmother, but I never wanted to.

There was this one time when Grandmother was helping Miss Watkins, and Grandmother gave me a sour look. My friend Sylvester (we all called him Vess) had found a large flea on his head from one of his cows he was milking that morning.

You see, every morning, I went the barn and milked the cows. Sometimes, I tended to close my eyes and kinda nap while milking, and that was how I got fleas. I sat on my one-legged bench and milked the cows. I preferred the one-legged bench because it allowed me to move when the cow moved. We had one of those three-legged stools, but I could not move with the cow. Dotty complained so much about the three-legged stool that Pa solved the problem by making a stool with one leg, right in the middle, so we could sway with the cow. Anyway, if I leaned my head against the cow, sometimes fleas jumped from the cow to my head. So, sitting in school, I would feel my head itch and, sure enough, there were a couple of flees.

We then had fleas to race. With Vess sitting next to me, I would make a string circle on my desk. We would put the fleas in the circle and start tapping on my desk until the winning flea jumped out of the circle. I knew this was a bad idea because Grandmother was in school with us, but I knew I had a winning flea, so I decided to do it anyway. We made our circle, placed our fleas, and started tapping. Vess' flee won, again.

We then heard a familiar voice behind us, "I see a couple young men not only playing games in school, but sleeping while milking cows."

We both turned and there was Grandmother.

Grandmother told us to go to the front of the classroom. Vess and I slowly walked to the front of the room, and Grandmother asked us to tell the class what we were doing. We both hemmed and hawed, then I finely told the class we were racing fleas.

Grandmother tapped our heads. "So, where did you get these fleas?"

"From our heads," we replied, getting more embarrassed as we stood there.

Grandmother grinned. "And how did you get them on your heads?"

We both explained we rested our heads on the cows as we milked them, and fleas jumped from the cows to our heads.

Then, we heard a giggle and Izzy called out, "I told you—boys have fleas!" All the girls in the school started laughing.

Miss Watkins brought school to order and told us to return to our seats. As Vess and I began to walk back, Grandmother stopped both of us, gave us each a kiss on the forehead, and said, "Now boys, you know better."

Grandmother could grow anything. If she came across a tree, shrub, flower, vegetable, or fruit she wanted to grow, she would kindly ask the owner, if there was one, if she could take a sprig or start. Grandmother would take the start, put it in a jar of water until it started roots, then plant it. It would grow every time. Grandmother always had little jars of starters all around the house and some in Grandpa's shop.

My earliest memory of Grandmother was helping her make bread. Grandmother had a large dough box with legs and a lid. She mixed all the ingredients in her large dough box, put the lid on the box, and used it as a table to shape the dough into bread, biscuits, piecrusts, or other items. I remember Dottie and I would watch or run around the dough box while she made the dough. Our mouths would be open, like little birds, waiting for a piece of dough. Grandmother always fed her "little birds." Grandmother then put the bread into the oven Pa had made for her in the hearth. Once Grandmother put the dough in the oven, it seemed to take forever to bake. The smell of fresh baking bread only lengthened the time before it was finished, it seemed. Sometimes, Grandmother would make figures from the dough like, fish, turtles, horses, cows, and of course, us! Grandpa always laughed when he looked at her creations. He said it added to the taste.

One of my favorite memories was lying on Grandmother's lap as she read to me or while she was mending clothes or darning socks. She would reach her hand up my shirt and scratch my back in always the right places; she would often put me to sleep by scratching my back.

Grandmother would often take us to Herbert's Mercantile, where Grandmother and Mrs. Herbert would talk for a long time. In fact, that was how Izzy got her job working with Mrs. Herbert.

Grandmother said that Grandpa had a humorous disposition. Grandpa was always happy and laughed often. Grandmother said he was not always like that, but age and grandchildren quieted his soul; but he still had a wandering spirit, always wanting new adventures. I lived at Grandpa and Grandmother's house almost as much as at my house. Pa did not mind and neither did Grandpa or Grandmother. Grandmother made bread daily and Grandpa and I would sit at the table, break the bread, and put it in small wooden bowls. We used the bowls as cups also, but for Grandpa and me, it was our bread bowls. We filled our bread bowls with bread, milk, and sugar. We tried to portion our milk and sugar to equal parts. Grandpa had a very large sweet tooth. Grandpa always ate the ends of the bread because, as he said, the ends were not good for little boys. I later found out that the ends were Grandpa's favorite part of the bread.

Grandpa would tell Grandmother and Pa he was taking me to do chores. We loaded the wagon with tools to mend corrals or get wood for making wagons. However, we would end up at the river fishing. I did not think Grandmother believed that we were only going to do chores, because she would send a small basket lunch, which always included worms for fishing. Grandmother always said Grandpa had a Colt's Tooth. I asked Pa what "Colt's tooth" meant. Pa said that meant Grandpa liked to play more than he liked to work, and sometimes, spent too much playtime with a young man that should have been working. Then Pa would give me the glare that would make my blood run cold. I knew Pa would never hurt me more than a twitch on the backside, but those glares would make me think twice about going with Grandpa. Of course, Grandpa would always talk me into it. Most of the time, Dotty, Izzy, and Gabe went with us to "do chores."

I asked Grandpa why he did not blacksmith like Pa. He said it was too hard of work. "One time, I tried to replace the shoes on a horse, and I did such a bad job that the horse was no good to anyone until a man from West Virginia bought the horse. As it turned out, the horse was a great mountain horse because one side was a foot taller than the other side. The horse could only walk around on the mountain slope in the same direction."

"Oh, Grandpa, that is silly." I laughed.

Grandpa continued, "So, I figured I could sale, trade, and train horses and stock better than working with my hands."

I asked how he could tell which people he could trust and were telling the truth.

Grandpa looked down and sighed and made a large frown. Grandpa always made a large frown when he was thinking. His frown was so large the corners of his mouth almost touch his chin. We kids were practicing making large frowns like Grandpa.

Anyway, Grandpa made a large frown and said, "Most people are honest, good people. However, you will always find some bad apples in the barrel you need to watch for. The stories they tell or the names of people they say they know can tell you a lot about that person. The people that are too willing to drop a name or are quick to tell you how good of a person they are, that usually means you need to put your guard up."

I looked over at Grandpa. "What about the people in the Church?"

Grandpa was still frowning, but then his left eyebrow went up and his right eyebrow had a scowl. "Remember in the Bible, Jesus said, 'Beware of the Scribes?' Scribes were opponents of Jesus's Church. A member of the Church who is quick to tell you how good a member they are, how righteous they are, or to boast of a position they hold or held to gain your trust—you should not walk away from, but run from dealing with them. Actions and deeds say more about a person than what they say or want you to hear. By their fruits, you shall know them."

On Sundays after church, we would all get together at Grandmother and Grandpa's house for supper. "Grandmother makes the best food you have ever tasted," said Grandpa. Grandpa said Grandmother was a cook for General Washington, and that was why we won the war, and that was how they met.

Grandmother shook her head. "Now, Grandpa, quit telling stories."

We all knew Grandpa was telling stories. "Ohhh, Grandpa!" we all said. Sometimes after supper and after everything was cleaned and put away, we would sit in the big room and read or listen to stories from James or Grandpa while James Jr. would crawl around Grandmother's braided rug. That little guy would start in the middle and follow the braid to the end, turn around and follow it back. He did this until he tired himself out and would fall asleep in the middle of the rug.

Grandpa always liked to tell tall tales. He would often start a serious conversation and end with a tall tell. For example, one Sunday we were in the big room. Grandmother, Rebecca, Dottie, and Mama Julia were darning socks and James Jr. was doing circles on the rug when my brother George asked Grandpa what he thought we would do when we got to the Great Salt Lake City.

"Well, George," Grandpa said, talking to us all, "the letters I am getting from those now living in Great Salt Lake City is that the valley is growing and Brother Brigham wants to start expanding south and west to California and north a couple hundred miles. I am sure it will be like when Grandmother and I settled in Missouri and here in Kanesville. We lived out of our wagons until we built our cabins and cleared at least forty acres. Grandmother and I will start farming and raising, buying, and selling livestock as we are doing now. Elias and you boys will start up your smithing and wheelwright business, and I'm sure we will do just fine."

"What about Indians?" George asked, "Think we would have trouble with Indians?"

Grandpa nodded his head as his frown appeared. "We have always got along just fine with the local Indians, wherever we've landed. What most people do not understand is that the Indians were here for hundreds of years, and they are protective of their land, game, and resources. They are as protective of their game as we are for our stock. It is okay if we kill and use what we need, but do not kill more than we need and do not waste game or resources." Then Grandfather leaned forward, making sure he had all our attention. "Our Indian neighbors may kill one or two of our stock, if needed for food. As they see it, if we kill one of their animals for food, they can kill one of ours if game is scarce. This is what most people do not understand. They want what we want, a fair deal. Occasionally, you do get a bad apple among Indians as you do with anyone else, and you deal with them accordingly."

Grandpa sat there with a frown on his face shaking his head. "One day in Missouri, we did have a run-in with a few problem Indians. Do you remember that Grandmother?" As Grandpa looked up at Grandmother, Grandmother gave him a puzzled look. Grandpa continued, "It was a few, maybe ten or twelve Indians came on the farm to steal and do harm and drive us out. When they came, I was pondering on important things with my eyes closed."

We all yelled, "Napping!"

"Anyway," Grandpa continued, "Grandmother didn't want to bother me so she, 'hammer and tongs' struck out, armed with that big darning needle," pointing to Grandmother, "set off after them. She bravely poked each one in the behind at least a dozen times before they decided they better skedaddle, and they never came back again."

"Oh, Grandpa," Grandmother said, holding up her needle. "Come over here and I'll teach you not to tell tall tales."

We all laughed.

After a long pause, Grandmother, still concentrating on the work at hand said, "There were at least fifty Indians!"

"Oh, Grandmother," we all yelled, laughing. Grandpa and Pa just sat there in awe because that was the first time Grandmother bested Grandpa in storytelling.

Grandpa and his partner, Mr. Bernard Herbert, owned a livestock company. Mr. Herbert was not a member of the Church, and Grandpa called him his Falstaffian friend. Mr. Herbert was almost as round as he was tall, and he laughed very much and very loud. He swore and drank often. "Too much for his and Grandpa's good," said Grandmother. Grandmother liked Mr. Herbert, but Mrs. Herbert and Grandmother were the best of friends. Grandmother called Mr. Herbert a harmless tease. Mother and Mama Julia called him a vile man, and they would not let him in their house. They tried to avoid him as much as they could.

Mr. and Mrs. Herbert did not have any children. Mother said he was too bad of a man, and God would not allow innocent souls to be in their house. Mother warned I must always, always, stay away from him. Little did Mother or others know, except Grandpa and Mr. Herbert; Izzy and I spend a lot of time with him. Mother would faint if she knew Izzy would visit Mr. Herbert more than I did.

Mr. Bernard Herbert had a brother, Elias, who owned a general store a few shops down the street. A couple times a month, Mr. Bernard Herbert would give me a note to take to his brother Elias. Mr. Herbert told me that he used notes to talk to Elias because his brother would hit him with a stick if he got close to him. I would take the note to his brother, and Mr. Elias Herbert would take the note, scowl, and ask the same question each time, "How is that scoundrel doing?" I would reply he was doing well. Mr. Elias Herbert would give me a note to take back. Upon returning, Mr. Bernard Herbert would read the note, go to the vault, and take out a big bundle of cash, put it in a bag, and tell me to take it back to his no-good, mean brother. When I did this errand, I would get a nickel or some candy for my services. Sometimes, Izzy would join me on my messenger services. Mr. Elias Herbert's wife really enjoyed Izzy and would have her stay and help around the store until I returned.

After about eight months of this, I asked Grandpa what this was all about and why the Herbert brothers hated each other.

Grandpa laughed, "They are the closest brothers can be. You see, William, the note Bernard sends is the amount of money he could give to the needy families in the area. The note that Elias would send back is the families that needed help and how much he would need. And the bag would be the money Elias asked for." Grandpa told me the Herbert brothers helped many, many families get what they needed for their journey to Oregon, California, Great Salt Lake Valley, and other places, as well as local Indians who also needed help.

"Why not let others know what they are doing and why not correct those that think badly of them?" I asked.

Grandpa just laughed. "To them, it's a game. If people knew how generous and how much money they have, people would be pounding their doors down asking for charity. When they are asked for handouts and do not wish to give, they use each other as a reason they cannot give. They would say, 'My ornery brother will not allow me to give.' They use each other to protect each other." Grandpa said that Bernard even teased him, saying he would get to heaven before Grandpa because he was buying his way to heaven. "The Herbert's don't believe in a single god, heaven, hell, or religion. They believe men should be more godlike to each other, and they practice it. So, William, let's continue to keep this a secret, okay?"

"Okay," I replied, nodding my head. Grandpa said it would really hurt and disappoint them if this got out. I repeated, "Okay!"

Earlier in the year, the Church called Grandpa to be a teamster for a party leaving in late July. Although it was a late start, he, Grandmother, and my brother George left for the Great Salt Lake City. George went to provide help to Grandmother and Grandpa. The real reason, and everyone knew it, was because George liked Ruthann Thorston, daughter of Brother Thorston. Brother Thorston's family was traveling with the same company as Grandpa and Grandmother. I asked Grandpa if I could go with them, but Grandpa said I better stay and help my Pa and look out for my brothers and sisters. Grandpa said he would make a special place for all of us and would see us soon. I would miss them very much.

CHAPTER 3
LIFE ON THE PLAINS 1851

We had many daily chores all year. Our morning and evening chores were almost the same: milking the cows, feeding the chickens, gathering eggs, slopping the pigs, going to the river to get water to fill the troughs, and loading the wagon with hay to feed the horses, cattle, and oxen. We also fetched water for household needs, cut and stack cordwood, and did other things that needed to be done before going to school. We lived almost two miles from town and school, so we needed to do our chores quickly to walk to school and be on time.

School was not my most favorite. I did okay, but I was not at the top of my class. When my mind thought too much, I had the yearning to go fishing, and I started to daydream about fishing with Grandpa. Sometimes Vess, or an obnoxious girl by the name of Hanna Hart, would hit me and bring me out of my fishing daydream. Hanna knew everything, or she thought she knew everything, and she would tell me she did. Hanna and her family would be traveling with us when we were to leave in about a month. Hanna had a brother, Herkimer. We all called him "Herk." Herk was the same age as Izzy and, sometimes, they did things together. Herk was a very nice boy and not a "know-it-all" like his sister. I was glad school was out for the summer.

In the summer, we had another chore . . . weeding the garden.

We had a very large garden that grew almost everything we needed for a year. That year, we would use what we could for our journey west. Everyone under the age of fourteen had to weed and hoe the garden. So, Izzy, Gabe, Cate, and I had our sections to work. It would usually take about three to four hours a day, six days a week, to stay on top of the weeds. No one really enjoyed it, but it needed doing. Sometimes, Mama Julia would help Cate because she was only six years old, but she had hers to do as well.

Occasionally, we would find a snake in the garden. Most of the time they would be harmless, and we let them be. Izzy did not; she would always pick up the snake and throw it as far as she could. When Izzy came across a rattlesnake, she would beat it to death with her hoe. She would leave it for other snakes, as she would say, to show other snakes what would happen if they came around. Izzy was not afraid of snakes or most anything else. She sometimes would catch a rattler by waving her red handkerchief with one hand and grab it near the head with the other hand. "The best time to catch it is when it strikes the handkerchief," she would instruct me. She would cut off its head and hang the body on our fence. Yes, my little sister was a snake killer and always carried around the pocketknife Grandpa gave her to remove the heads. Sometimes I wondered about my little sister.

Every morning in the summer, Izzy would get out of bed and walk around doing her chores, whispering, "I hate weeds, I hate weeding, and I hate hoeing." All morning long, same chant, same tone. Even after she was done with her weeding, same chant, "I hate weeds, I hate weeding, and I hate hoeing." Sometimes, Izzy would put a tune to it and sing the same words while we walked to town. She would stop her chant as soon as she got to the door of Mrs. Herbert's store, where she worked every day. I say "work." It was more like hanging out and giving Mrs. Herbert companionship. Of course, Izzy stocked and cleaned the shelves and did general errands. Mrs. Herbert would pay Izzy two cents a day for working.

Izzy had a pet as unusual as she was. A very calm, medium-sized steer with one horn. Izzy gave it a Latin name for one horn, "Unicornis." Unicornis followed Izzy almost everywhere she went. Sometimes Izzy rode Unicornis to town. She would get many reactions from people, from fear for safety to laughter. Mrs. Herbert always made Izzy tie Unicornis out back. Keeping a steer tied in front was bad for business, Mrs. Herbert would say.

One morning, as we started our daily weeding, Izzy was not singing or chanting her weed-hating chant. After a while, I asked her if she was feeling well. Izzy said she had never felt better. When it was time to start our weeding, we each picked up our hose and buckets and went out to the garden. When we arrived at our garden spot, I noticed a young boy, Donncha McDonough, one of Izzy's friends. Donncha's family had come from Ireland earlier that year. He had a very thick accent and was hard to understand. They were living in a tent until they could build their house.

Izzy started talking to Donncha, then she handed him her hoe and started showing him how to hoe and clean furrows.

I walked over and asked Izzy what she was doing.

Izzy said, "I am going to pay Donncha to do my weeding and hoeing."

I scowled at her. "You can't do that."

"Why not?" replied Izzy.

I walked closer to her. "Because that's not how it's done around here."

Izzy rolled her eyes at me. "Well, this is my way, so you go back to your area and get back to your weeding. Those weeds aren't going to pull themselves."

I angrily went back to my area and went to weeding. All the while, I heard and noticed Izzy teaching Donncha how to weed: What days to weed, what areas, and how to follow-up and maintain furrows.

After about four hours, she handed Donncha something.

He tipped his hat and said, "Aull bea seyon yah tomarr."

"Okay," said Izzy, and she went to the house to wash up to go to town.

I walked over to Donncha and asked him why he was doing Izzy's weeding.

Donncha always had a crooked smile to match his crooked hat. Donncha replied, "Ae be mad as a box of frogs not to, so long as I keep me noodle capped. Ya se, back home, we were so hungry we could have ate a reverend mother. Now, I can tuill me a copper or two and besides, Izzy might give me a snog." Then, he let out a snorting laugh.

I just stood there, dumbfounded, looking at him. I had no idea what he had just said. I tipped my hat and wished him a good day.

Donncha just grinned, nodded his head while tipping his hat.

It was going to be a long few weeks in the garden until we left.

I finished up, emptied my weed bucket, and cleaned my hoe. I checked up on Gabe and Cate. They had since scampered off doing their own things. After I cleaned up, I hurried down the lane to catch up with Izzy. When I caught up with her, I asked her what she was doing.

Izzy picked up her pace. "Walking to town."

I stepped out in front of her. "No, about the garden and Donncha."

Izzy went around me. "Oh, I hired him to do my hoeing and weeding."

I raced in front of her. "How much?"

Izzy hurried her pace and went around me again. "Half-a-penny a day."

By now, we were almost running. "Does Pa know about this?"

"No, only us. Besides, why should he? I'm getting my chores done."

We slowed our pace to almost a walk. "I don't think it is right. You need to do your own work," I demanded.

"I am, through Donncha," she again proudly replied as she started running again.

I was becoming more irritated with Izzy and her lackadaisical attitude regarding her role and responsibilities. I caught up and stepped in front of her. "Well, I'm going to tell Pa and Mrs. Herbert what you are doing."

Izzy shoved me, almost knocking me down. "Go ahead, I don't care."

That made me mad. We got into town and went into Herbert's Mercantile.

"Ah, William," said Mr. Elias Herbert, "a message from my brother?"

"No," I said, "I am here to tell Mrs. Herbert what Izzy is doing with the money she is giving her."

Mr. Herbert gave me a puzzled look while Izzy glared holes into me. Mrs. Herbert came in from the back with a basket of thread bobbins and Mr. Herbert said, "Young Mr. William here has a grievance to take up with you regarding the monies you are paying Izzy."

Mrs. Herbert glanced over to me as she put the bobbins away. "Oh, is that so?"

"Yes," I insisted. "Izzy is paying a newcomer boy a half-a-penny a day to do her weeding and hoeing in our garden."

Mrs. Herbert continued putting the bobbins away and not looking up. "Do you think the pay is too much or too little?"

I walked over by Mr. Herbert's desk. "What? No," I said. "It is not the amount. It is the fact that Izzy is not doing her work."

Mrs. Herbert still rearranged the bobbins in colors. "Are the weeds being rid of and the furrows maintained?"

"Well, yes," I replied. "But that is not the point. It is her job to weed and hoe."

"Well," said Mrs. Herbert as she turned to Izzy. "Is that true?"

"Yes, it is," Izzy proudly replied.

"Do you think he will show up every day and do a good job?" Mrs. Herbert asked Izzy.

"I hope so," said Izzy. "Or I'm sure there are other poor kids that would like to make a half-a-penny a day."

Mr. Herbert burst out a laugh and almost fell off his chair. "Remind me again, Izzy, how old are you?"

Izzy gave him that scowling condescending look God gave women and replied, "You know how old I am. I am eleven years old."

Mr. Herbert took out his handkerchief and wiped his eyes chuckling. "Just making sure. I thought for a moment I was listening to a small version of Mrs. Herbert. And then on the other hand, perhaps I am."

Mrs. Herbert finished putting away the bobbins according to colors and walked over to me. "So then, William, what seems to be the problem?"

I stammered to reply, knowing I had lost this argument. "I guess it is all right, for it's like Izzy hired someone to do her chores. But Izzy thinks Pa and Mother named her after Queen Isabella. I told her they just liked the name."

Izzy looked up with a scowl. "No, they did not! Mother and Pa named me after a famous Queen." Then Izzy seemed to grow a couple feet taller.

Both Mr. and Mrs. Herbert chuckled. Mr. Herbert said, "Yes, indeed they did, Izzy, because you are a queen around here."

I let out a deep sigh because I knew I had lost this battle as well. "I reckon I better get along to Pa's shop and do my work there. Have a good day, and I am sorry if I offended."

Izzy called out, "You may be excused from this court."

Mrs. Herbert tapped Izzy on the head to remind her that her majesty had work of her own to do. "Yes, ma'am," said Izzy as she went to work, and I left the store.

After work, we loaded the wagon, went to Herbert's store, and picked up Izzy. Pa and Mr. Herbert had a short conversation. Mr. Herbert handed Pa the revolvers Pa had purchased from him.

Earlier in the month, Pa, James, Sam, and Ben had purchased Colt revolvers from Mr. Elias Herbert at a very good price. According to Pa, Mr. and Mrs. Elias Herbert's freight company had the contract of providing provisions to the Dragoon Regiment stationed at Fort Leavenworth. One of the provisions was the Colt revolver made for the Dragoon Regiment called the Colt Dragoon. Mr. Herbert had ordered additional revolvers to sell to his friends.

They shook hands, Pa got in the wagon, and we headed home. Izzy was staring at me, and I pretended she was not there. I was still stewing inside. I knew at supper that I could get others to see the error of my little sister's ways.

That evening, as we sat around the supper table eating, it was time I let Pa and the others know of the great injustice going on in the garden.

"Pa, did you hear what Izzy is doing with her chores in the garden?" I proudly stated, hoping to get Izzy into some trouble. I looked over to Izzy.

She gave me this smug look of, "Go ahead. You are going to lose again."

Pa looked up. "No, William. What is Izzy doing in the garden?"

"She hates weeding, so—" I started to say when Mama Julia interrupted me,

"William, don't use that word 'hate.' That is such a hurtful word."

"Yes, Mama Julia." I continued, "I'm sorry, Izzy really dislikes—"

I was interrupted again, this time it was Izzy. "No. I'm sorry, I hate, hate, and hate weeding and hoeing. I do hate it!"

Mama Julia gave Izzy a disagreeable look. A look! Izzy got a look, but I got a reprimand. I should have known at that point that I had lost the battle again as I had done earlier that day.

Izzy took a big bite of bread and began to speak when Pa scowled at Izzy. She chewed and swallowed her bread. Then she blurted out, "Why are we tending and weeding the garden anyway? We will not be here when the garden produces. We do all the work and someone else gets all the rewards. It's not fair. It's stupid."

"Now, Izzy, you know better than that," Pa said while also speaking with bread in his mouth and receiving a half-mean and half-laughing look from Izzy.

Then, Mama Julia gave us history lesson. "Izzy, you know the history about the olive oil that you sell at the store?"

"No!" replied Izzy defiantly, followed by another scowling look from Pa.

"A long, long time ago, the Greeks were an up-start country trying to compete in trade with the Egyptians and others in the area. They sold beautiful pottery, but they needed something else. They came up with the idea of planting and harvesting olive oil. Do you know how long it takes to grow olive trees that were ready for harvesting olive oil?" she asked as she surveyed the table.

No one replied.

"At least two generations." Mama Julia continued, "The grandparents planted and tended to the trees. When their children grew up, they would tend to the trees and cultivate them. When their children, the grandchildren grew up, they would harvest the olives and press out the oil, making olive oil. It took three generations to finally produce olive oil for the market.

"Our garden and this trip we are about to take are much like the olive oil. We planted and tended the garden so others will have something to eat. We are making this journey so our children and grandchildren will have a better and safer life," Mama Julia finished.

While everyone pondered on what Mama Julia had said, I thought it was my chance to get Pa's and my brothers' perspective on Izzy's great crime in the garden. I was sure they would see the terrible injustice Izzy was doing in the garden as much as I did. I sat up in my chair and cleared my throat to get everyone's attention. "Well, anyway, Izzy hired a local Irish boy, Donncha McDonough, and paid him one-half-cent a day to do her weeding and hoeing."

Pa nodded his head. "I know of the family. Good people, just starting out. I am thinking of selling them our farm when we leave to go west." He looked at Izzy. "Did you instruct him on how to weed properly?"

"Yes, Pa, I did," replied Izzy.

"Does he know he needs to come here every day?" Pa continued his line of questioning.

"Yes," Izzy said, "I taught him what rows to weed and hoe on what days, and how to properly maintain the rows."

"Good. Did you show him how to clean and put away the hoe and bucket?" Pa asked.

Izzy rolled her eyes and seemed to become more annoyed. "Yes, Pa, I did."

"Do you think you can rely on this young man?" asked Pa.

"I do, Pa." Izzy confidently replied.

Seeing I was about to lose the debate, I asked, "What if you did not work for the Herbert's? How would you pay him then?"

Izzy gave me that scowling look. "I have enough money to pay him and two others to do my chores for a year."

This declaration surprised and impressed everyone at the table, including Pa. It was not so much of what she said, but the boldness, conviction, and near haughtiness of how she said it that made everyone at the table look at her approvingly.

Trying not to smile too much, Pa said, "Okay that is fine, but remember, that part of your garden is still your responsibility."

"Yes, Pa," Izzy replied.

"Very well," Pa said, ending the conversation.

I looked at everyone at the table. "Very well? What do you mean 'very well?' It is Izzy's job, and not some townie kid. We all must do our part, and Izzy is getting out of doing her job. She must do her own weeding."

Pa, looking down, dabbed butter on his bread. "Why do people come to us to have their horses shod or wagons fixed?"

"Because they do not know how," I replied.

"Because, William, they either do not know how or do not want to do it themselves. That is what keeps shops and stores open. Izzy does not have the desire to tend to the garden and has enough money to hire it to someone who wants to tend garden for a fair price. That is commerce. That is what keeps us and others in business." Pa looked up and gave me that Pa-look. "So, William, is this topic of conversation over?"

"Yes Pa, I reckon . . . this . . . topic . . . is . . . ," I stuttered.

Pa took a deep breath of annoyance. "What else is Izzy doing that is annoying you?"

"Izzy said you named her after Queen Isabella. Is that true?" I asked.

A united giggle waved across the table. Pa looked up, surveyed the expressions of his older daughters, and then met the eyes of Mama Julia. He cleared his throat, took a deep breath and a long pause, and said looking at Izzy, "Yes we did."

A very satisfied smile unanimously sat on every female face at the table.

"Ha!" Izzy busted out, "Told you so." Sitting up higher in her chair and mainly looking at me, she continued, "You do not have to address me as queen. Princess will do just fine."

A loud laughter shook around the table.

Pa sat in silence, looking down at his plate and trying to conceal a big smile while shaking his head, knowing he had just contributed to the creation of a monster.

Mama Julia spoke up. "You all are princes and princesses in your own right. I am honored to be amongst such nobles."

My sisters all exclaimed, "We are honored to have you as well."

At that point, the door to Mother's room opened and Mother came out of her room, still dressed in her nightgown, carrying her plate of supper with hardly any food missing. "What is all the commotion about?" asked Mother.

Pa looked up and said, "Izzy is set out to conquer the world."

Mother set her plate down, walked over to Izzy, kissed her on the head, and said, "Of course you are, and of course you will." Mother then walked toward her room and said, "It is very important to have dreams." She opened the door, stepped into the dark room, and said, "Without them, your world is a very dark place." She shut the door behind her.

There was not another word said. The joyous mood was gone. We finished our supper and commenced with our evening chores.

CHAPTER 4
PREPARATIONS

For the past year, Mama Julia, Rebecca, Sarah, Dottie, and occasionally Mother, were busy sewing clothes, and other items for our trip. They made bonnets for the wagons, tents, special tablecloths and many other items, including bags for all sorts and sizes of supplies. Bags were made that would hold from 125 pounds of flour to very small ones for various spices and medicines. Bags for seeds, bags for plant starts, bags for dried fruit, bags for fresh fruits, bags for dried vegetables, bags for fresh vegetables, bags for sugar, bags for rice, bags for cornmeal, bags for beans of various kinds, bags for crackers to put in cans to catch the crumbs for cooking, bags for toys, bags for ammo, bags for nails, bags for clean clothes, bags for dirty clothes, bags that would "breathe" and sacks that would not "breathe," bags for bags. Truly, bags for everything.

They sewed pockets at the end of each wagon bonnet for individual belongings or "treasures." Izzy, Gabe, and Cate wanted four pockets sewn into their dresses and trousers.

When Izzy asked Mama Julia and Rebecca to sew four pockets on her dress, they told her, "It is unbecoming of a young woman."

Izzy protested, "Perhaps, if I ever become one of those ladies, I probably will not have pockets on my dresses, but for now, I want many pockets and a special pocket for my knife."

They knew if they did not sew pockets on it, she would sew them on herself.

Although it was Izzy's idea, I also liked the idea of having pockets, so I asked if I could have pockets on my trousers. They agreed. Once they made trousers with pockets for Gabe and me, we wore them all the time. When Pa, Ben, Sam, and James noticed the convenience of these pocket trousers, they each wanted pocket trousers. I think I noticed Rebecca and Dottie sewing pockets on their dresses under their aprons.

We all had three pairs of every article of clothes, including button boots. I doubted Izzy and Gabe would wear any shoes on the journey, but they had them if needed.

They made tents and wagon bonnets with heavy material, doubled to hold up to the wind and rain. Izzy, Gabe, and I would often sleep in the tents to try them out. Sometimes Mama Julia and Dottie would join in the adventure. Even the tents had pockets. They had made three tents. One for Pa, Mother, Sarah, Dottie, Izzy, and me; another for Ben, Sam, Mama Julia, Gabe, and Cate; and the third for Rebecca, James, and little James.

Pa and my brothers made three special wagons for our journey. The first wagon would carry most of our household items and Mother's and Mama Julia's special things, like Sunday dishes, mother's portable melodeon, spinning wheels, rocking chair, mother's feather bed, some food supplies, and medicine and medical items. Pa made the first wagon with heavier leaf springs to protect the breakable items. Mother, Cate, and James Jr. would ride in the first wagon.

The second wagon carried most of our food supplies, butter churn, wash tubs, scrubbing board, soap, and cooking items, including two smaller versions of our sheet-iron stoves and two reflector ovens Pa had made.

The third wagon carried Pa's smithing tools and small forge, my brother's woodworking tools, plows, and more tools. All wagons carried extra tongues, a tree, yokes, skeins, hubs, and other wagon parts, and a dozen caged chickens.

Pa and my brothers made folding tables for each wagon using Hager hinges, attaching one table to the wagon and the other table hinged to the first table, making one long six-foot table when opened with legs on the end and in the middle. The tables were made of thin boards, so when doubled, they were a little thicker than the boards on the rest of the wagons. They did not weigh much.

For the comfort of the adults, my brothers made chairs with four legs, square leather seats, and an iron ring to hold the legs together. They made eight of these chairs in case guests came visiting. Special tablecloths were made for these tables to have at least "civilized meals on our journey," said Mama Julia.

CHAPTER 5
THE JOURNEY

Wednesday, July 2, 1851.

Before the start of our journey, Pa sold his timber leases and business to Donncha McDonough's family. Of course, Izzy was involved in the negotiations, making sure Donncha and his brothers and sisters knew how to take care of the garden and the snakes.

Mother was still troubled and did not talk much, just mumbled. I felt sorry for Mother. The doctor kept giving her medicine to help her, but it just made her tired and sleepy. Pa and Mama Julia had everything ready for the trip. Mother would ride in the wagon. Sarah wanted to stay. She would not say why, but we all knew she liked a young man named Isaac Kessler. Pa reminded Sarah she needed to go to help take care of Mother.

To our surprise, Pa asked Isaac to join us. Isaac was happy to go. We later found out that his family had planned on going with our company all along. Pa and Brother Kessler thought it would be a witty surprise. We all thought it was a funny surprise, except for Sarah and Isaac. I asked Mama Julia why Sarah and Isaac did not think it was funny. Mama Julia said they were in love. Someday I would understand, but I still did not get it.

Mama Julia was really keeping the home and family together. I was very glad she was part of our family. Dottie and I were excited to get going. Dottie would read us letters from Grandpa about all the graves along the way, especially within the first three-hundred miles. Nearly two hundred graves within three hundred miles on the south side of the Platte. Perhaps that was why we would be traveling on the North side of the Platte River. Dottie read stories to us, as well, and they were full of adventure. I hoped no one from our family or company would die. That would be sad.

Thursday, July 3rd

Pa received a letter from Grandpa and Grandmother from Great Salt Lake City. They were well and doing fine. They were busying themselves in preparing for our arrival, but Grandpa thought our stay in the valley would be short. Brother Brigham wanted to protect our welfare by establishing settlements all the way to California and up north. Grandpa also sent counsel to Pa, Ben, James, and Sam regarding taking positions in the wagon companies. He told them to leave the leadership to those that desired positions of esteem. Grandpa wrote that, while Pa, James, Sam, and Ben would be excellent captains of the whole company or of tens, Grandpa said he had learned from experience making the trek. It was better to serve as councilors and not leaders.

Grandpa wrote: *There is too much division and too much strife happening along the trail, even among the saints. Elias and the others should be the strength behind the leaders in supporting them and keeping order. Prudent counsel is better to come from peers in support of leadership. This will increase the chances of a safe and harmonious trip across the plains.*

Grandpa commended Pa, James, Ben, and Sam on earning and maintaining the respect of many of the saints and people of Kanesville in general. Grandpa and Grandmother were looking forward to our reunion and missed us all very much. He added that, if anyone was interested in fishing, the fishing was good at several places along the trail.

Izzy, Gabe, and I giggled, knowing he was talking to us.

Friday, July 4th

July 4, Independence Day. We spent the day finishing preparation to begin our journey in two days. Pa and my brothers loaded up all their shop equipment in our third wagon: Pa's billows, anvils, tools, and a small forge that Pa had made along with fifty pounds of coal. James, Ben, and Sam loaded their wood-working tools, templates, and such. Mother, Mama Julia, Rebecca, Dottie, and I finished loading the first two wagons. We had many things to do and were excited for the celebrations that night. Izzy and I went into town to say good-bye to Mr. and Mrs. Herbert at the store and to Mr. Herbert at Grandpa's shop.

As soon as Izzy walked into the store, Mrs. Herbert started to cry.

"Oh, darling, I am going to miss you so." She knelt and gave Izzy a long, long hug.

This made Izzy cry and they hugged each other for a few minutes.

When they composed themselves, Mr. Herbert gave Izzy a long hug, then turned away. "I need to get something we have for you," he said as he cleared his throat. "One moment please," he said as he went into the back room.

After a few minutes, he returned, carrying a small leather pouch. He wiped his eyes. "I must have some dust in my eyes."

Mrs. Herbert let out a little chuckle. "He is going to miss you very much, as well."

Izzy was nervously shaking. "Oh, what is it? Can I open it?"

"Go ahead, let's see what's in it," said Mr. Herbert.

Opening the pouch, Izzy looked in and let out a gasp. "Oh, no, no. It's too much." Izzy emptied the pouch on the counter and out came two twenty-dollar gold pieces.

They gave us both a big hug. We cried a little, and Mrs. Herbert reminded Izzy that when she turned eighteen, the gold would help her start her own mercantile. Izzy promised and said she was looking forward to seeing them again soon. They gave us another big hug and shooed us to our next stop.

As Mrs. Herbert patted both of us on the backside, she said, "Someone is waiting for you at your grandfather's shop."

Mr. Herbert cleared his throat and wiped his eyes. "Be sure to be careful around my brother. He is a terrible fella and still could lead you astray." We all giggled, but suddenly, Mr. Herbert turned exclaiming, "I have some more dust in my eyes."

Mrs. Herbert kindly rubbed his arm. "Run off now, you two. Remember to be safe and write often."

"We will and we promise," we said as we headed to Grandpa's old shop.

As we opened the door, Mr. Bernard Herbert had his back to us as he quickly shoved a small whiskey bottle into his desk drawer. "Oh, something for this cough," he said.

Izzy and I just looked at each other.

"Well, come in, come in. So, you are off on your journey to the great unknown."

Izzy ran over to him.

I walked over to his desk. "Well, it looks like it," I said.

"We sure had a great time, didn't we, William?" he said as he reached out and placed his hands over Izzy's ears. "Although we never caught any of those handsome gals walking around, we sure had fun trying," Mr. Herbert said, laughing as he took his hand off Izzy's ears.

"I heard every word you said," said Izzy, wiggling into her comfortable place on his big chair as she often did when she sat with Mr. Herbert.

Mr. Herbert made room for Izzy on his chair. "I'm sure you got the lecture from those other people you just came from. 'Be sure to be safe. Be sure to write. Be sure to change your unmentionables, blab, blab, blab.' "

We both snickered. Izzy said, "Yes, we got all that from them."

"Well, I sure am going to miss you. You have brought a ray of sunshine to all of us," said Mr. Herbert as he took out his handkerchief and wiped a couple tears away. "Be sure to say hello to your grandparents from all of us, and take good care of them."

"We will," I said.

Mr. Herbert held Izzy as he leaned back in his big chair. "When I find a big enough carriage that will carry my generous derrière, we will come out and visit. Who knows? Maybe they might have those monstrous traveling train machines they have back east that will go out west. Then we can ride out to visit. Or, maybe I'll hire one of those hot-air balloons to take us."

Izzy started laughing and poked his big belly. "Oh, I don't think they make one big enough."

Mr. Herbert let out a belly-shaking laugh. "Well, aren't you cuter than a bug's ear. I am going to miss your honesty, my sweet child," he said. He drew me in and put an arm around me and hugged us both. "Now run along. Don't want those mothers of yours thinking I am leading you astray."

We said our goodbyes and, as we walked to the door, Mr. Herbert said, "Oh, wait, I almost forgot. There is something in my top drawer for you, William."

As we walked back to his desk, Mr. Herbert opened the drawer and pulled out the bottle of whiskey. "Oops, you're not old enough for that yet," he said as he shoved the bottle back in the drawer. He fiddled around in the large drawer. "Oh, here it is." Then Mr. Herbert tossed me a leather pouch like the one Izzy had received. "The pretty ones do not get all the treasure." I opened the pouch and in it were two gold pieces, like Izzy had received.

"Oh, Mr. Herbert, I can't accept this. I didn't earn it."

Izzy grabbed it from me. "I can," she teased.

Mr. Herbert laughed as he walked over and wrestled it from Izzy. "Yes, you have, my young apprentice. Indeed, you have. Now, run along," he said, reaching for his handkerchief to dry the tears from his eyes.

As we reached the door, Izzy stopped, turned, and ran back, giving him another hug. "We love you," she said.

Mr. Herbert put his handkerchief to his mouth and cried as he stood there watching us leave. He muffled out, "We love you, too, our sweet angels. We love you, too."

We walked back to where our families were preparing for the festivities. "How were your visits?" asked Pa. Izzy and I showed him our pouches and told him all about our visits. "That is a lot of money. Do you want me to keep them safe for you?"

I gave Pa mine, but Izzy said she wanted to hold on to hers for a while longer.

"Alright, for now," said Pa, "but make sure you give it to me before the day's end."

"I will Pa." Izzy slowly walked off, clutching the pouch against her chest.

Evening finally arrived. We all gathered around to hear Brother Mayes give a speech on the sacrifices that had brought independence to us as a nation and about the sacrifices that had been made by those who brought religious independence to the saints. Afterword, many of us sat around the large campfire. It was a good time.

I gazed into the fire as it crackled, thinking of all the fun times we had in Kanesville. I took a deep breath and sighed. "I wish Grandpa was here to tell us about his stories of him and General Washington and how they ran the British out."

Pa abruptly turned, almost falling off his stump, gave me one of his Pa-glares, and asked, "What?"

I repeated what I had said and how I wished to hear more stories of Grandpa and his adventures with General Washington.

Pa, my brothers and others busted out in belly laughs. Pa said, "Oh William, your Grandfather never served with General Washington. Grandpa was not even born then."

I looked up at Pa with a puzzled look.

"True," Ben said, "he did serve in the second British war, but not with General Washington."

I was horrified. "But Grandpa said he did."

Pa chuckled. "I'm sure he said that." As Pa looked at all of us sitting around the crackling fire, he explained, "Your Grandfather likes telling all of you stories. But most are, as most of you know, tall tales."

Ben jumped in. "Grandpa tells us stories to make us interested in history, so we will appreciate what those who went before us did, and the sacrifices they had made for us so we can have a better life."

I sat there, looking around the fire, then my eyes met Pa's. "What about him and Tecumseh, the Indian chief, being friends and Grandpa trying to talk him into keeping peace," I asked.

"No," the others said together, laughing.

"What about giving Jim Bowie his famous knife? Or killing the raccoon for Davy Crockett's hat?"

Again, they all laughed, and Pa said, "Sorry, William, another of Grandpa's tall tales."

Pa spoke again, taking time to look at each one of us around the fire as the sun settled in the red clouds beyond the trees, "Your Grandfather loves you all very much and wanted to pass on to you something he always taught us." Pa paused, kicking the dirt with the toe of his boot. "One of Grandpa's favorite quotes comes from a line from one of his favorite statesmen, Patrick Henry, in his 'Give Me Liberty or Give Me Death' speech. 'I know of no way of judging the future but by the past.' According to your grandfather, if you know the past, the better your decisions will be to guide you in the future."

Noticing I was struggling with the newfound truth, Pa looked at me and placed his hand on my shoulder. "You okay, William?"

"Well, that makes a little more sense. I once asked Grandpa, if he had done so much to help Lewis and Clark make it through their tough expedition, how come I had not read his name in the history books? Grandpa told me, 'Because, Willy, I was the one writing the journal. It would be rude to always mention my name.' "

"Oh, that Grandpa," Izzy said, and we all laughed.

Saturday, July 5

We started our trip to Great Salt Lake City early in the morning. We said goodbye to those that would follow in the months to come. We made a bed for Mother in the wagon and set off. As we passed through town, the people were wishing us well, and we all looked forward to the time we would all be together again.

We followed the trail for about two miles as it dropped along the Missouri River bottom. Looking across the river, I could see our home we had just left with the garden, icehouse, and corrals. It was just a few years before when we had cleared the land and helped Pa, Grandpa, and my brothers build our house. I remembered how big our garden had seemed as we had cleared the land. It seemed like our garden would go on for miles. I remembered helping to sow the seeds for our first garden. I remembered our first harvest, using the trees we had cleared from the garden to build the icehouse and cutting ice from the river in the winter.

I remembered the many times fishing on the banks with Grandpa, hiking and sitting on the edge of the river, listening to Grandmother read us books. I remembered Grandpa saying, "When you build your first homestead, you will always have the knowledge and confidence that, wherever you go, you can always do it again. You will never be without a home. Success builds on success, and nothing can ever take that away from you. You just build on it all your life."

The staging area was scattered and disorganized because of the tardiness of many of the families coming with us. Finally, at two o'clock, the organization of the people and wagons took place.

I attended a meeting with Pa and my brothers. This meeting was to appoint a company captain: captains of fifty, and captains of ten. In confidence, Pa informed the leadership that he or his sons would not accept leadership positions. Pa explained his position to the leaders, and they thanked him for his wisdom and agreed to his request. Pa did this because of the warning Grandpa had given him in a letter.

They chose Brother E. D. Reed as company captain. Captain Reed then walked through the men gathered there and asked if any among us who would be willing to serve as a captain of fifty, a captain of ten, or as company scribe. Most hands went up. I noticed Pa and my brothers were not raising their hands.

Captain Reed then asked if there was anyone among us, for whatever reason who wished to decline to serve as a captain of fifty, a captain of ten, or a scribe. A moment of silence went by with no hands raised. Then Captain Reed, looking at Pa and my brothers, began to speak. At that point, Pa and my brothers raised their hands.

A unified muttering arose through the ranks. Captain Reed looked at

Pa and my brothers and said, "As you wish. Everyone here knows you have earned your right, for whatever reason, to decline service."

Our company was assigned to Captain Walton's company of fifty and Captain Manus's company of ten. I knew of Captain Reed and believed in his abilities. I also knew of Captain Walton and Captain Manus. I would reserve my judgment of these two men to see what the trail revealed.

Then Captain Reed read notes of wisdom he said he had learned on his travels.

"This is my third and, I hope, my final time making this journey. New trails have opened the last couple of years, which avoid many dangerous river crossings and cut days of travel off the old trail. We will be traveling some of these new trails. These trails are not easier; perhaps they may be harder, but they are safer. This trip that we are about to take will try every person to the very core. Good and bad qualities will be revealed and intensified on the trail. You will be made aware of human nature in all its different dispositions, both good and bad, over our journey.

"We will have designated hunters that are instructed to kill only what we need. It is a sin against God, nature, and man, to kill more than what we need. On this journey, killing game for sport is strictly prohibited.

"There will be times that, for whatever reason, we must leave behind animals that are weak or worn down. This does not mean you lose your claim over your animals. If another traveler comes upon you having an animal you had left behind, and you can prove it belongs to you, you have the right to take it back as long as fair compensation to the finder for their troubles is made.

"This rule applies to any animals that you might take in and nurture along the way. This is the basic of the Golden Rule. Live it.

"Please remember to sustain, respect, and honor the laws of the nation, including those ordained and endorsed for our good and safety while crossing the plains. Thank you, and may our Heavenly Father keep and watch over us."

After his speech, Captain Reed informed us we would delay starting that day due to Indian problems and the slow start of many of the families coming to the staging area. Captain Reed called for each captain to gather, organize, and ready their companies for an early beginning in the morning. Captain Reed released the crowd. He then asked Pa and my brothers to meet with him. I went back to our wagons with the others.

While waiting for Pa, I went exploring around to see what I could find among the many items left behind by those who had traveled before us. While I explored, I came across Brother Stoot. He asked if I could help him find the grave of his beloved wife Elizabeth.

"You see," he said, "because of the heavy, heavy rains this year, the grass and weeds have covered her headstone."

I agreed and we began our search. As time went on, Brother Stoot became more and more distressed and started secretly calling out to his late wife. It is hard to see a big, strong man like Brother Stoot cry softly as he crawled on the ground, rapidly searching for his Elizabeth's grave.

Cate came running up and asked, "Whatcha doing?"

I picked her up. "Have you told Mama Julia where you are?"

She said yes and that Mama Julia told her I was here and needed her help to find treasures. I told Cate what we were doing, and she began looking around as well.

After what seemed all afternoon, Cate called out to Brother Stoot, "Is this where your wife is sleeping?"

Brother Stoot ran over, removed the weeds, and cried, "Yes, yes, it is!" The big man picked up Cate, gave her a bearhug as tears rolled down his face.

Cate looked at me with a little confusion.

I took Cate by the hand and said, "Let's go and find more treasures," as we walked away to give Brother Stoot some peace.

When we had walked a distance, Cate asked why the big man was sad when he had found what he was looking for. I explained to Cate that Brother Stoot thought he had lost her sleeping place and would never see her sleeping place again. "Do you remember when your rabbit Stewart died, and Pa made a sleeping place for him by the barn?"

Cate looked up. "Uh-huh."

"And then the next year, when you couldn't find Stew's sleeping place? Remember how sad you were?"

"Uh-huh. But we did find it."

"Yes, we did, after looking around a long time, remember?"

"I remember." Then she paused, "Oh, that is why he was crying."

"Yes, he was both happy and sad."

"Okay," Cate said and began searching for treasures.

I always kinda felt bad for not telling Cate the truth about Stewart. He was not buried but made a fine meal of Stewart rabbit stew.

After that time, I wondered what Pa would do or how he would act if Mother died. I was sure it would be hard on Pa, but he then might marry

Mama Julia. I did not know why Mother would not let Pa marry Mama Julia as other families did.

One day, I had asked Pa why he did not marry Mama Julia. He had turned and given me a stern look and said, in a very annoyed and forceful tone, "Such matters do not or should not concern you or anyone else. This matter is between your Mother and me and God. No one else. No one else!" He then turned and went back to working the iron in the forge.

Cate and I went back to the wagons and had supper of beef, corn soup, and biscuits. Izzy, Dottie, Sarah, and I stayed back at the corrals until the guards came. I offered to stay with the stock at night, but Pa said no. I was very excited to leave the next day. I did not know if I could sleep. We sat around the fire until ten o'clock, then Pa told me to go to bed. Izzy, Gabe, Dottie, and I did not sleep in the tents, but under the stars. After the third time Pa told us to go to sleep, a warning of a switch soon followed.

I remembered the last time I had gotten a switch to my backside. About three years before, I had spoken to mother with a harsh tone. To my surprise, Pa had been standing behind me. "William, apologize to your Mother and then go get a switch."

I apologized and went behind the house, cut a very thin long willow and removed the leaves, and brought it back.

Pa took it from my hand and looked at it. "Are you sure you want me to use this?"

"Yes."

"Are you sure?" asked Pa again.

"Yes," I replied with more confidence. The bigger ones hurt so I thought a small thin one would not be as painful. I was wrong, very wrong.

Pa only hit me once with the thin willow. It opened the skin, cutting into my behind. Pa and I spent the next little while tending to my behind, stopping the bleeding, and bandaging me up.

During this time, Pa and I had a good talk about respecting others. I remembered this lesson each time I sat down for a few days afterwards. Although it had been my choice in switches, I knew he had been sorry he had hurt me. After that, Pa always threatened us with a switch, but he never spanked or hit any of us again. The looks he gave us were enough to get us in line.

Mama Julia would hold up a large wooden spoon, but she never used it. It was hard to take Mama Julia seriously when she held up a spoon with a big smile on her face.

When Pa told us he would use a switch if we did not go to bed, we knew he was getting to the end of his tether. We quieted down and went to sleep.

CHAPTER 6
BECOMING ACCUSTOM TO TRAVELING

Sunday, July 6: Day 1

We awoke at five o'clock. Got dressed and started our chores as we did at home: Milking the cows, feeding the pigs and chickens, gathering a few eggs, and soothing the stock.

We gathered for breakfast. Mama Julia and Sarah cooked breakfast while Rebecca and Dottie tended to Cate, James Jr., and Mother. After breakfast, we all helped load the tents, blankets, and clothes in the wagon along with the food and cooking items. Pa and my brothers yoked the oxen, saddled their horses, greased the hubs, and helped Izzy, Gabe, Sarah, and me in preparing the stock for travel. Pigs did not need preparing. They just followed.

At 7:45, we were to gather for daily prayers and instruction. My initial judgments of Captain Manus, regrettably, were coming clear. He was late in calling the company together. I could not believe we were starting late. I was so excited. I thought everyone would be excited and ready to go, too. The little children were running around as the men were yoking the oxen and the women were packing and securing items in the wagons.

The words I heard most often were, "I thought you packed it," or "I do not know where it is. You last had it."

"It is an exciting organized chaos," observed Mama Julia.

While our family and five other families were ready to get on the trail, we were still waiting for others.

Unfortunately, many of the other companies were as slow in getting started as we were. Captain Reed rode up and asked Pa what the delay was.

Pa simply took off his hat and pointed towards Captain Manus, who was trying to get his and another family loaded and oxen yoked.

"What is the delay, Captain Manus?" yelled Captain Reed.

"None of your affairs," Captain Manus snidely yelled back.

"When you are holding up my entire company, it is my affair, so I suggest you either ready yourself right now or stay in Kanesville. The choice is yours, Captain Manus. We are heading out in ten minutes . . . with or without you." Captain Reed rode off to another company, and we heard him yelling the same command to all the other companies. The ten minutes passed and we hit the trail.

It was nine o'clock when we started. Some of the other families were still trying to load on the move.

I looked over to Pa. "This is no way to start our journey."

"Never you mind, boy. Just make sure your stock does not spook and run. Keep 'em close together. Keep 'em in tight."

"Yes, sir, we will, Pa," I replied as Pa rode to our first wagon. He tied his horse to the wagon and walked on the right side of the yoked oxen that were pulling the wagon. Mama Julia walked on the left side. Mother, Cate, and James Jr. rode in the first wagon.

Ben and Sam had their saddled horses tied to the back of the second wagon and walked alongside the yoked oxen.

James had his saddled horse tied to the back of the third wagon next to his rifles, pistols, long knives, and swords in the wagon. Because James was a sharp-shooter in the war, he was one of our hunters. He and Rebecca walked with the yoked oxen of the third wagon.

Izzy and I and the others were in the back, herding the stock. We would ride our horses and Unicornis for the first couple of days to keep the stock together and bring back the strays.

"Hy-yoo," came from Izzy, who was at the right front of the stock riding Unicornis.

"Veloz," came from Gabe, who was at the left front, riding his chestnut gelding Sancho. Gabe named him after Don Quixote's squire. Don Quixote was the last book Grandmother read to us before she had left.

"Hee-upp," was my call as I rode Acer with my whip in the back of the stock on the right side.

"Cheee-yaa," came from Sarah and her whip on the left, back of the stock with her horse Bell. Bell was a chestnut mare and had a bell-shaped marking on her forehead.

A beautiful calming hum, song, and sometimes whistle came from Dottie as she gently do-si-do'd in front of the stock on her bay mare, Dottie. Yes, Dottie named her horse Dottie.

The trail was hilly and difficult in some places. Occasionally, a stray would wander off into the thick woods that lined the trail on both sides, and we would run them back. We traveled along ridgelines, climbed up and down hills. The day was hot and seemed long. Pa would hang back, check on us, and then quickly walk back to his position. Izzy kept asking what time it was, and if we were almost there. Pa came back and told us the traveling at first would always seem longer than it was because the trail was new to us. Pa asked Izzy if the nearly two-mile walk to town had been long and hard.

"No, not at all. I could run it."

Pa said, "The road to town was easy because you were used to walking it. This trail is new, and it will seem longer at first until we become accustomed to walking the trail every day. Then, it will become easier and time will go quicker."

We traveled about six miles and nooned at a creek with good grass. As soon as we stopped, people sat or laid down on the ground removing shoes and boots and rubbing their feet and legs. After almost an hour, we were back on the trail. The trail had the same steep hills and hollows, until we traveled another four miles and came upon a familiar but sad site. Our old home of Winter Quarters. It brought back many memories, mostly sad ones of sickness and death.

Dottie became silent as we passed through this dreadful place. Even the stock became silent as we passed. The trees had started growing back, but it was still a barren place. We could see where our cabin and tents once stood. Others must have used the logs and posts from the cabins for other purposes. I could still see the outline of our gardens and corrals, as well as the remains of other makeshift barns and cabins. Some structures were barely standing among the graves, but not many. We did not have to chase any cattle or horses back to the herd as we traveled past this dreadful area. It seemed the stock too felt the dark feelings coming from the area.

I remembered, one time when we had lived there. It was January. The frozen ground had prevented us from digging graves. Mother had walked out of our cabin and wandered around in the cold among the dead bodies. Mother was not wearing a coat or shoes. She just walked around talking to her dead friends, caressing their cheeks, until Rebecca brought her back into the cabin. So many deaths in a short period. It was a sad place with mostly sad memories.

The many happy memories we had made at our homestead were a big difference from the memories of our home in Winter Quarters. I had hoped to never see our home in Winter Quarters again, but I was also very sad I would probably never see our home in Kanesville again. Although I was excited to see Grandmother and Grandpa again very soon.

The trail went back up into the hills, trees, and hollows as we traveled another mile, and then we encamped near a creek. My brothers helped us gather the stock from the other companies of ten. With all the trees around, it was easy to tie off a corral. As we finished the corral, it began to rain and the stock became restless. Dottie and I stayed with the herd. After a while, Izzy and Gabe took our places so we could get something to eat and put on our rain clothes and hats on for the night. Pa came over, checking to see if we had what we needed for the night.

He nodded his head in approval. "If you need anything throughout the night, let me know."

"We will, Pa," said Dottie, and we went back singing to the stock.

It rained most of the night. We kept occupied by eating dried fruit, making up silly songs to sing, reciting Longfellow, Shakespeare, and the Bible. We made a game of trying to find each other's hoof prints as we rode around the stock.

Around half-past three, Pa came out. "You have about two hours to get some sleep. I've got it from here."

He gave us a hug as we passed him in silence to our wagon.

Monday, July 7: Day 2

Shortly after going to sleep, a loud commotion outside awakened Dottie and me. We got dressed and went out to see what was going on. As it turned out, we were able to get a little over an hour of sleep.

About thirty wagons of Oregon Emigrants were returning to the States. They told us that on Saturday, a herd of buffalo ran through their camp, which caused their cattle to stampede and join the herd of buffalo. They recovered a few of their animals, but not enough to make the journey. They said they did not know if they would continue or just go home to eastern Ohio. Pa looked over to Dottie and me, gave us a wink, and went about his business. We were very glad Grandpa took the time to teach us how to take care of our stock.

Having the Oregon Emigrants passing through caused some in our company to rethink going on this trek. We had a few murmurings, especially among mothers of two families in our company of ten, but we all were ready to hit the trail at eight o'clock.

The trail was the same as the previous day: hills, hollows, and trees. The trail was wide enough for two, maybe three wagons traveling next to each other, if needed. However, there were many stumps still in the ground away from the main trail. As the trail went through the wall of tall overhanging trees, it looked like we were going through a cave in some areas. The shade gave relief from the sun, but it was still hot, even in the shade.

We traveled for about eight miles, and then the trail turned flat and sandy for another two miles. The trail took a turn and we were again climbing hills, hollows, and trees until we came to a large creek called Pappea. Pappea Creek was about nine feet wide and three feet deep with high banks.

At three o'clock, we encamped. The banks along the creek were high and full of foliage. The company stopped, and we herded the stock north along the creek until we found a place where we could drop down to the creek. We corralled the stock near the creek so they could water and feed as needed. The stock traveled closer together today without us having to chase more than a few back to the herd. The ones we did chase were those that did not want to climb any more hills. I could not blame them.

The bridge over the creek was in bad condition. Captain Reed ordered all wood workers and craftsmen to work on the bridge while the others cut and boarded logs. Many in the company were lying or sitting down, complaining about feet, leg, and body sores, while others were moving slowly at cutting the wood and working in general. This made Captain Reed angry. He called a meeting with all the captains. I do not know what he said, but we all could hear him yelling.

Soon, all men and boys fourteen years and older were busy cutting and making boards and working on the bridge. Dottie, Sarah, Izzy, Gabe, and I stayed back with the stock.

A company of twenty-five wagons heading to California came upon us. Not wanting to wait or help with the bridge, they decided to hire a shoddy ferry operator with a very suspicious-looking ferry. The ferry was about 300 yards down the river. About a dozen wagons made it across before the ferry gave out and sent four wagons tumbling with all their contents, oxen, and passengers into the river. This was a frightening sight as people and stock tried to make it to the edge.

Although the water was only three feet deep, the river was very swift. I did not think everyone made it out. The other wagons of that company traveled down the Pappea to find a fording site. As they traveled down, they tried to help gather the stock and people that had made it out of the water. What a very sad and terrible sight. The ferry operator made it out unharmed, and I was sure he would be in business again. I hoped he would be more careful next time, but I did not think so.

At about half-past six, the bridge was finished. We all crossed safely, and a little after seven o'clock, we encamped. Ben, Sam, and I gathered all the stock from the rest of our fifty and corralled them with the others. We had supper, did our chores, and made beds in the wagons because it looked like it was going to rain again. After supper, Ben, Sam, and I went over to Captain Manus to ask who among the company of ten he wanted to watch over the stock during the night.

Ben walked over to where Captain Manus was lying down and asked, "Excuse me, sir. We need two guards to watch over the stock tonight. Who do you recommend?"

Captain Manus sat up, and as he put his boots back on, said, "What foolishness are you talking about?"

"We need two guardsmen to watch over the stock," Sam explained.

Captain Manus finished buttoning his boots and stood up. "Why, what's wrong with them?"

Ben shook his head. "Nothing is wrong with them, sir. Do you remember the company from Oregon that passed us this morning?"

"Of course, I do. Do you know who you are talking to? I'm the captain of this company of ten and I demand respect, especially from young hooligans like you three."

"We mean no disrespect, captain," Ben replied, "but the reason they are returning home is because their stock stampeded, and they could not find enough stock to continue the journey."

Sam joined in the conversation. "We want to prevent such a thing from happening to our stock."

Captain Manus walked around, looking at the company. "Well, I think it is foolishness, but go tell Mr. Laroy and Brother Carter that I order them to stand guard."

Ben and Sam looked at each, and then Ben gave Captain Manus a puzzled look. "Mr. Laroy just got off the boat from England headed for the gold fields in California. He knows nothing of managing the stock, and you want him to stand guard?"

"Are you questioning my orders and my authority? I can have you banished from this company," said Captain Manus.

"No, sir, but may I suggest that I watch with Mr. Laroy, so I can teach him how to watch over our stock?"

"Oh, so now you are giving orders?" Captain Manus shook his head and kicked up some dirt. "I suppose that will be all right. Now go do as you are told and get out of my sight."

I started walking away when I heard Ben and Sam say, "Yes, sir."

We went to the wagon of Mr. Laroy and informed him about the duties and job of guards. Mr. Laroy got very excited and turned to his family, saying, "I am going to become one of those American frontiersmen we read about back home." Mr. Laroy ran over to us, put his hands on Ben's shoulders. "Do I get a rifle?"

Ban and Sam tried very hard to conceal a laugh. "No, that is not necessary, but it looks like it will rain, so please bring some rain clothes."

After Mr. Laroy gathered his rain clothes, he and his family met Ben by the corrals. Mr. Laroy was given Sam's horse to ride. Sam's painted gelding was a well-trained cow horse.

The Laroy's had come from a place called Bristol, England. Mr. Laroy said that after the riots, many had decided to leave. He said that although the riots happened twenty years before, things never "felt right" after that. When Mr. Laroy heard of the gold fields in California, he thought that, since he had experience in the coal fields in Bristol, he could easily find gold looking at rocks in California.

Mr. Laroy had never ridden a horse. It took seven attempts for Mr. Laroy to sit on the horse without falling off. At first, he was getting frustrated because his family came to see the show. Of course, they laughed each time he fell off, but soon he started laughing as well. Ben told him to keep his shoulders even with the horse's shoulders for balance. Each time Mr. Laroy fell off, Sam cringed as he held his horse in place.

Finally, Mr. Laroy was able to stay on the horse. He looked so proud and his family watched with pride. Sam patted his horse on the neck and wished him good luck. Mr. Laroy thanked Sam for saying that. Sam said he was talking to the horse. That made the Laroy family laugh. I knew Sam. He did not find that to be funny. Sam was concerned about his horse.

Later, we could hear Mr. Laroy singing to the stock. He had a remarkably good singing voice. I was sure the stock was in good hands.

Soon after we had prayers, Dottie and I climbed into the wagon and quickly fell asleep. Occasionally, the rain and thunder would wake me up, and I would hear Ben and Mr. Laroy whispering and Mr. Laroy singing. It put me back to sleep. It rained most of the night.

Tuesday, July 8: Day 3

I woke up at five o'clock the next morning, got dressed, and went on doing my chores. I noticed Ben and Mr. Laroy bidding good-bye, and all the stock was safe and rested.

At eight o'clock, we hit the trail. We were not riding our horses but walking. The stock was traveling together. We kept our horses saddled, just in case. The trail still had hills, but not the steep hills and hollows of the last few days. There were not as many trees around either. The trail was sandy, but not difficult. We traveled about five miles and at about ten o'clock, we arrived at the Elkhorn River ferry crossing. Pa and my brothers helped with the departing and arriving on both sides of the river. Around eleven o'clock, ten Omaha Indians rode up. They tried to take control of the ferry. Captain Walton and several men managed to retake the ferry. The Indians started yelling, placed a traditional red blanket on the ground, and demanded pay to cross the river.

Pa, noticing the commotion, approached the Indian men. The leader recognized Pa and they had a conversation. Pa led the leader to our herd and gave him two cattle and a horse.

The horse was a fine horse, but the two cattle were troublemakers, and we were glad they took them. After all, that was why we brought them.

The leader was satisfied and they left. Everyone went back to doing their jobs. While we waited to cross, we helped Mama Julia and Rebecca pick mulberries that seemed to grow all around the river. By the time it was our turn to cross, our stomachs were full, and we had enough mulberries to last a few days. We also had purple-stained fingers that would last a few days.

Eventually, we all crossed the river safely. As we swam the stock across, the resident swallows seemed annoyed that we were coming close to their homes. The swarm took turns diving toward our heads and flying back up high into the air, preparing for another assault. The birds did not touch us, but they wanted us to know they were there and not happy.

Once we safely crossed, we traveled about a mile and crossed another creek with a good bridge. We followed the trail along the flat river bottom. Travel was sandy, but good and quick. Little reddish-purple flowers, tall white flowers, and small blue flowers with tall stalks, lined the trail. If it were not for my fishing daydreams, I probably would have learned the names of the flowers. I knew Hanna Hart knew the names of the flowers, but I was not going to ask her about them. She would get too much satisfaction in telling me something I did not know, but should know.

Her favorite response was, "Daydreaming about fishing when you should be learning." Then she would not tell me until she was ready to tell me. That's why I was content in describing the flowers and not providing the names.

At half-past four, we encamped by the Platte River. It had good grass, wood, and water. Someone must have told the mosquitoes we were coming because they welcomed us in swarms. The stock was restless due to the pesky biting of these bloodthirsty devils.

The stock was traveling together without any of them wandering off. I thought they might be getting used to traveling together. As soon as we stopped and set our wagons in formation, most of the people laid down exhausted and complained of soreness. Some in the group passed around a bottle of whiskey and many gladly accepted.

Pa did not allow us to participate in neither the laying down nor the whiskey; I reckoned because we did not need it. We were not any better than anyone traveling with us, but we did do a lot of walking and heavy chores. I thought that helped prepare us for the journey. We did our chores, ate supper, had evening prayers, and slept in the wagons again. Pa informed Captain Manus that Brother Jackman and Sam would guard the stock.

Wednesday, July 9: Day 4

We awoke again at five o'clock and began the day with the same routine.

After we finished breakfast, we loaded up the wagons, yoked the oxen, greased the hubs, and met for prayer. We were ready to leave, but some were still sleeping, including Captain Manus.

At half-past nine, we hit the trail. We traveled for about two miles and came upon some mounds to our left. Pa said they were Indian graves. The trail was rocky and hilly. The wagons shook at every step. The shaking made some items fall off the wagons like water ladles, unsecured grease buckets, or items sitting on the inside ledge of the wagons unsecured. Of course, others in our group picked up the items and returned them to their owners.

Unsecured water barrel lids were the most common problem. If they fell off and were not picked up quickly, the oxen or wagons that followed would run over them and break them into pieces. A water barrel without a lid would end up with drinking water that had trail dust and bugs in it, and it would lose a lot of water over the bumpy trails.

It rained a little that morning, but then settled into a hot day by the afternoon. The mosquitos were upon us again as we traveled. The trail turned into a slough and made traveling slow. The slough got everything wet, and once we were wet, it took a long time to get dry. It was bad for the feet.

After our nooning, a company of twenty wagons heading to Oregon passed us. They told of Indian problems they had not far away. Someone in another company of ten had lost one of his horses during the night. The owner of the horse hunted for most of the day, but he could not find his horse. Some were saying that one of the Pawnee Indians took the horse.

We traveled fifteen miles and encamped at four o'clock near some ponds and a creek. There was good water, grass, and wood. There were fewer people lying down as we made camp, but still the majority were lying down. Wagon owners brought their oxen, and we corralled the stock along the creek where there was good grass. The moon was waning and still bright, but we built fires at each end of the corrals for safety.

After corralling the stock, we did our chores and ate supper. We were all starting to become more tired, until we became accustomed to the traveling. Pa said that soon the routine would become a habit and energy would again be with us. That day was the last day of saddling our horses. We walked our horses and Unicornis, and the stock stayed together.

After supper, we picked berries and rhubarb. As we picked fruit, we heard a scream. Herk Hart came running, screaming, and crying. People rushed to him, and as soon as they reached him, they backed away laughing. Herk had a meeting with a skunk. He did not get the full contact but only a slight hit of the skunk's spray. Still, it was enough to make him sleep alone under their wagon. Izzy, of course, had to get her teasing in. Izzy's teasing only made Herk laugh, which frustrated Izzy, so she quit teasing poor stinky Herk. I was glad Herk thought it was funny.

Mosquitoes were our constant companions, making sure they reminded us that they were there. We started a fire to try to keep the pests away, but they still hung over us like a plague of old.

"Pa, why did Heavenly Father create mosquitoes? Do they do no good?" asked Izzy.

"To teach children what it is like for parents to have children: pests,

pests, pests." Pa laughed.

Izzy simply stood up, walked over to Pa, and pushed Pa off his small stump. "Buzz, Buzz," she said, and everyone laughed, including Pa. No one else but Izzy could knock Pa off his seat without getting in trouble. In fact, Izzy got away with most anything.

Captain Manus came to our wagons and asked, "So, Mr. Stockman, who do you want to stand guard tonight?"

James said, "I'll do it."

"Do you think you are qualified?" snarled Captain Manus.

James quickly stood up to confront Captain Manus when Pa stood up, put his hand on James's shoulder, pushing him into his seat.

Pa then walked over to Captain Manus, grabbed him by the vest, and demanded, "Harvey, get over here."

Although Captain Manus stood about eight inches taller and was a bit huskier, he followed Pa around the wagons.

"Listen, Harvey," Pa commanded, "we will get along just fine if you never come near my wagons again or address any of my family without my permission."

They were on the other side of the wagon, but we could still hear what they were saying.

Pa continued, "From now on, I will decide who will stand watch. Do you understand?"

"But I am the captain," Captain Manus sheepishly insisted.

"Yes, you are, and I will sustain you so long as you lead by righteous example. You think being a leader is to have power over others, but it is not. Being a leader is to serve others by example, not have others serve you. A leader brings everyone along safely, physically as well as spiritually. Be that type of leader, and I will sustain you."

"I will lead however I want! The guards are your responsibility for now, Mr. Stockman. Make sure you do your job, or I'll have you removed. Good night," said Captain Manus as he huffed off.

Pa returned and asked James to go see if Isaac Kessler was up to watching with him. Then he added, "While you are there, ask Isaac's father if he could watch tomorrow night with me."

"Yes, sir," said James. After a while, James and Isaac returned and prepared for the evening.

Of course, Sarah was there to help Isaac saddle his horse. They lingered for a while.

Pa walked over and said, "If you need anything tonight, just let me know."

"Yes, sir," said both James and Isaac.

"Oh, James, watch these two." Pa said pointing to Sarah and Isaac. "Make sure she does not stay all night, distracting Isaac from his duties."

"Oh, Pa," exclaimed Sarah. Both Sarah and Isaac blushed.

"Keep'n my best eye on 'em," James said, winking, looking through his rifle sight eye.

We did our chores, had supper, sat around the fire until we said prayers, and then went to bed.

CHAPTER 7
"BUFFALO POOP PIES"

Thursday, July 10: Day 5

I woke up at five o'clock, did chores. The milking and eggs went well. Packed up the tents and blankets, had breakfast of mush, salt bacon, and biscuits. We finished loading the wagons, said prayers, and hit the trail at half-past eight.

The trail was sandy and slow. Some of the sand had been blown into drifts, and the wagons sunk deep into the loose sand up to the hubs. The oxen bellowed as they pulled with the men and women pushing from the back. We traveled about six miles and passed an old Pawnee village. I could see where the huts had once stood, plus the garden spots. I wished I could go exploring, but because of the heavy and slow trail, we could not stop.

After we nooned, the trail became easier and our travel was faster. At about three o'clock, I noticed wagons coming upon us. They did not overtake us but kept a safe distance behind. Dottie no longer needed to stay up front, so she came back with me, taking Sarah's place. We had lost Sarah the previous day from our camp due to love. She was now traveling with Isaac's family. At least we still had her horse to flank the stock. From now on, it was Dottie, Izzy, Gabe, and me herding the stock.

At five o'clock, and after traveling another six miles, we encamped along the Platte River at a place with good grass, good water, and enough wood for cooking and fires. The mosquitos and biting horse flies were our companions. We gathered and corralled the stock where they could water and feed as needed. We gathered wood, enough for fires on each end of the corrals.

As we were unpacking, the wagons that were following us came to our company and spoke with Captains Reed and Walton. As it turned out, they were four wagons of saints and four wagons of Oregon settlers wanting to join our company. Captains Reed and Walton assigned one of the Oregon settlers, the Bradshaw's, to our company of ten. They seemed like nice people and very able to make the journey.

After supper, Captain Reed called a meeting. Pa and my brothers attended. I went along with them. Captain Reed announced that, starting the next day, we would leave no later than seven o'clock in the morning and make camp later in the evening. He said that, at the current rate of travel, we would run out of provisions three weeks before entering the Great Salt Lake Valley.

Platte and Loup River

There was some grumbling among some of the captains of ten and others present. Captain Reed instructed the captains to return and inform their individual companies of the new schedule and then added, "We are close enough to Kanesville that those who wish not to travel with us may leave at this point."

We returned to our wagons, and Captain Manus informed everyone of this new schedule. Captain Manus said he thought the decision was unnecessary, and he said we would not run out of food, but he would "listen to ol' Cap Reed, for now."

I noticed Pa shaking his head as we headed back to our wagons.

We did chores, pitched our tents, and prepared our beds. Then Pa, looking at the clouds, told us to dig a trench two feet deep and two feet wide around the tents to catch the rain if it did start raining. We had supper of dandelion greens, ham and beans, cornbread, and mulberry rhubarb cobbler.

After supper Gabe, Izzy, Dottie, Herk, and I went down to the Platte to fish. Of course, Herk stayed downwind. During an hour of fishing, we caught fourteen good-sized catfish. Herk caught two that weighed over seven pounds each. I wondered if it was the smell of skunk that made him catch the largest ones. We brought them back, skinned, cleaned, and salted them.

We sat around the fire for about a half-hour, said prayers, and went to bed.

Sure enough, around midnight, a huge thunderstorm brought rain and a lot of it. The thunder was clapping all around and getting close. Pa and my brothers and some of the other men went out to settle the stock.

I heard Pa yell, "James, picket those wild-eyed ones there and there. Ben, Sam, get some hobbles on those there and there." Brothers Carter and Ward, along with Misters Laroy and Bradshaw, came running over, asking how they could help. Pa asked them to secure the rope and add another rope around the corral.

I got out of bed and ran up to Pa. "Do you need any help?" I asked.

Just then, a giant lightning bolt hit a few yards away from the stock. The sound was deafening, and it lit up the area as if it was day. To my amazement, the stock just stood there, unable or unwilling to move. Then, as I lived and breathed, I witnessed something that made me stand in amazement. Just as the lightning had struck, the horns of the cattle began to glow an eerie blue-green glow. The stock shook their heads and bellowed in annoyance as the glow danced about their heads. This lasted for about a half-a-minute.

Pa put his arm around me and pointed at the cattle. "Isn't it a wonderful sight? I've always liked seeing this happen."

"You've seen it before?"

"Oh, many times. They call it St. Elmo's Fire. I can never get enough of it."

Seeing Pa standing in the rainstorm with a look of a kid wanting to see another magic trick, gave me the assurance that everything would be just fine.

Just then, another bolt of lightning hit right over the stock and the blue-green glow returned for a few seconds as the stock bellowed and shook their heads. Some of the horses started to buck and frightened the cattle, but there were enough men around to calm them and calm the rest of the stock. All the stock stayed in the corral as the thunder moved away, but the rain continued to pour down on us.

After a while, with the stock secured, we went back to our tents and fell asleep, listening to the rain hitting the tent and making its own kind of music. I always liked sleeping when it rained.

Friday, July 11: Day 6

I woke up a little before five o'clock, and the rain had stopped, but the ground was very wet. The trench around our tents worked, and the ground where we had slept stayed dry. All our stock was secure. However, four horses and a milk cow were stuck in a slough covered with weeds and mud with only their upper bodies, necks, and heads sticking out. We rescued four of the five animals, but one horse panicked and moved so much that it sunk deeper into the slough and died. Pa and my brothers removed the pickets and hobbles, and we went about doing our chores.

We received word that we would not get an early start because stock in the first company of fifty had stampeded because of the storm. We discovered that three of the finer horses in another company of ten, in our company of fifty, had their ropes cut and were missing. Unfortunately, due to the hard rain, we could not find their tracks. I hoped the captains of these companies would learn from this and be more careful in their guard duties, or at least bring their horses and corral them with the rest of the stock.

At half-past eight, we hit the trail, which was very muddy, making for hard, slow traveling. James and the other hunters mounted their horses and went hunting, but with no success. Although he had seen a few deer, he could not get close enough to take a clean shot. Small rolling hills had covered the area with few trees to use as a hiding place.

We traveled about four miles and came to the confluence where the Loup River ran into the Platte River. We followed the trail up the north side of the Loup River. The river was on my left and rolling hills with very few trees on my right. After traveling another hard, slow ten miles, we made our encampment. We had good water, grass, and wood. The sky was clear with no chance of rain, but a very good chance of mosquitos.

We gathered and corralled the stock, unpacked the wagons, did our chores, had supper of catfish and corn bread, and played a game of hide-and-seek in the tall grass with some of the other kids in our company. The night was still and calm with an occasional cry of coyotes and wolves. As I went to bed, I could again hear the people in other wagons whispering softly as mothers and fathers sang soft lullabies to their children trying to get them to sleep. Then I heard a chorus of snores. I went to bed around ten o'clock with another chorus of mosquitos buzzing. I put my head under the blanket and went to sleep.

Saturday, July 12: Day 7

Pa woke us up a little before five o'clock. I got dressed and commenced on daily chores. Milk and eggs were good. We had breakfast of salt bacon, biscuits, and berry-spread. We struck the trail a little past seven o'clock and made good time in the morning. About half-past nine, a company of nine wagons headed for California passed us.

The afternoon turned very hot and muggy. The stock was quiet as we traveled along. None of them wandered off but seemed content to follow the herd. Occasionally, we got one that wanted to take a break before we stopped at noon. The dogs or the cow-horses or we shooed them back into place. We kept up our individual calls, keeping the stock in line. The stock did not need any prodding. I supposed that they, like us, were getting used to the routine of just walking.

The trail was sandy, rocky, and a little slower. Rocks on the trail shook the wagons with every bump. Wagon drivers tried to avoid the larger rocks, but at times there were too many, and they really rocked the wagons when they hit them. These large rocks were about the size of a loaf of bread and they could cause damage to the wagons and the wheels. The day heated up very quickly, causing the stock and people to get tired quickly. We nooned and then continued.

Around three o'clock, about forty Pawnees visited us. They wanted to trade blankets and skins for horses or cattle. They were mostly unsuccessful in trading as they passed each company. Pa gave them one of the troublesome horses and an equally troublesome bull. We knew Pa could not help but be generous to these people. I believed Grandpa and the Herbert's had taught this to Pa and all of us. The Indians said they needed more horses because the Pawnees were at war with the Sioux.

They offered Pa some blankets and skins, but Pa said no because we did not need them.

It seemed the Sioux were at war with everyone after having been driven out of their homelands near the Great Lakes area. Whatever the reason, they were a cantankerous bunch. The Sioux were the ones that had given Lewis and Clark a hard time on their journey.

Another company of nine wagons heading for Oregon passed us. They were made up of Swedish immigrants who spoke very little English. They had smaller wagons with teams of three sets of yoked oxen pulling each wagon. They seemed to be in a very great hurry.

We crossed Looking Glass Creek. I believed people called it "Looking Glass" because it was very clear. The water was cool and clean, and the stock and people took drinks as we crossed. It was difficult to find cool springs or creeks this time of the year. The ice in our water barrels had almost melted.

We traveled another five miles and crossed Beaver River. It was about twenty-six feet wide and almost two-and-a-half-feet deep. The banks on all the rivers and creeks we had crossed were particularly high, and we were taking great care so wheels, trees, and axels did not break. We also crossed very carefully because of the swift water. Our company of fifty had three minor accidents crossing the river. Two wagons had almost tipped over, but the men had caught them in time to keep them upright. The other had been a wheel breaking as the wagon went down the bank into the river. They had quickly replaced the wheel, and we all made it across safely.

We turned at Beaver River and followed it. Around four o'clock, we encamped by the Loup River. There was good water, good grass, and good wood where we stopped and more trees a little way up the river. We corralled the stock. The next day was a full moon and there would be enough light so fires would not be unnecessary. We did our chores, had supper, and sat around the fire talking about times back in Kanesville. As we sat by the fire, Captain Reed called a meeting that Pa attended.

Pa came back and announced that we would be staying the next day. Pa informed my brothers that they needed to repair wagons and do some smithing. He turned to the rest of us and said, "There is no need of getting up early, except you, William. We need you to help us tomorrow."

"Yes, sir," I replied. I was a little disappointed because I was tired and wanted to sleep later. However, I was also excited because, for now, I was one of them. Pa turned to my brothers. "There is still daylight. Let's unpack the tools, and forge."

My brothers, Pa, and Brother Kessler went to cut firewood. Mr. Laroy and his thirteen-year-old son Charles, along with Brothers Carter and Hart, came and asked if they could help. Pa thanked them for coming and said, "Of course, we could use your help. We need at least thirty good-sized dead trees to burn with the coal we brought."

"Oi, we will cut your trees," Mr. Laroy proudly exclaimed.

Pa patted him on the shoulder. "I'm sure you will. I have no doubt."

Charles, I, and the other men went to the grove of ash trees nearby. Within a few hours, and as the sun set, we had gathered all the wood we needed. Pa asked Mr. Laroy if his son could dig a two-foot by two-foot by two-foot-deep hole for the used coal and wood to fall into as he was smithing. Within no time, Charles had dug a very square box with sides and edges so precise it seemed like he had used a carpenter's rule.

Mr. Laroy helped Pa and Ben move the forge from the wagon and place it above the hole Charles had dug. Mr. Laroy then told Pa that he had some experience in smithing back home in England. Pa and Mr. Laroy talked for some time while they set the billows and finished the forge.

Throughout the night, a chorus of wolves' and coyotes' howlings accompanied us.

Sunday, July 13: Day 8

We woke up at five o'clock. I began to do my chores when Pa stopped me. Although it was the Sabbath, we needed to work and do repairs.

"Izzy and Gabe will do your chores today. We need you and Charles to help unload the tools and help around the shop area like you did at home."

Charles and I looked at each other with big smiles on our faces. "Yes, sir, we will."

Pa told us to go get some breakfast and be ready to start in thirty minutes.

By half-past six, my brothers had their tools sawing, planing, and drilling, with Pa in the background setting the rhythm with that reassuring, confident, and familiar sound of the ten-pound-ten. The ringing, singing, sound of the ten-pound-ten bolstered me out there on the prairie that all was well.

Charles and I kept the work area clean, running to the wood and coal piles and bringing more wood and coal, emptying the used coal so the forge could breathe. Pa occasionally sat down throughout the day while Mr. Laroy welded and forged the iron into whatever was needed made or mended. They made a good team, and my brothers were amazed that Pa took a break. Of course, when James, Ben, or Sam tried to sit, Pa would give the Pa-look and they would be right back to the job.

While we mended wagons and shod horses, the women washed clothes and made bread and food items for our trip the next day. The whole camp was busily preparing and rearranging contents in wagons. It seemed those first seven days were a trial run. People took the lessons learned from the past few days to secure and re-secure, pack and repack, tighten, fasten, mend, and prepare to continue our trek the next day. We all checked, double-checked, secured, and mended the wagons. We stretched the bonnets tighter. The trees, tongues, and yokes were re-secured. We checked the tires, rims, hubs, skeins, and spokes, making sure they were tight and securely mended. All the wagons looked ready for the trip again. Around three o'clock, all the wagons, wheels, rivets, and other sections that needed repairs had been completed, and we began putting Pa's and my brothers' tools in the wagons.

We cleaned and washed up and attended our Sabbath meeting where Brother Hart turned his sermon into a play. Apparently, he had planned this many days before. He had five of the sisters in the company play the role of women in the Bible: Eve, the wife of Adam and the first woman; Sarah, the wife of Abraham and the mother of Isaac; Jochebed, the mother of Moses, Aaron, and Miriam; Elizabeth, the wife of Zacharias and the mother of John the Baptist; and Mary, the mother of our Christ.

Each of the sisters played the role of these noble women very believably. They told about their lives, hopes, and their children. The sisters were very convincing, and by the end of Mary's part, there was not a dry eye in the company. The sisters talked about the joy of being mothers and wives and how the sacrifices they were called on to do was almost unbearable, how they wished it were someone else called to carry their sacrifice, but in the end, it was love, faith, and commitment that carried them through their sacrifice. It seemed that the spirit of the women of the Bible spoke through the sisters. There on the prairie, on that trail, I attended the best Sunday meetings I had ever attended, and I learned so much.

We went back to our wagons, did chores, had supper, and sat around the fire talking about the meeting we had attended. We went to bed around ten o'clock.

Around midnight, we were all awakened by wolves. We had heard wolves every night, but these were close. Very close.

Pa and my brothers got up and, armed with rifles and pistols, went out to make sure our stock was secure.

With a full moon lighting everything up, Ben whispered to Pa and pointed to four Indians that had wolf skins over them, crawling up to the stock. Pa, Ben, Sam, and James each fired a volley, aiming just in front of them. This kicked up dirt in their faces. This scared the sneaky thieves, and they jumped up and ran off. It also quieted the wolves for a time.

The gunshots made all the men in the company come running with their guns and swords, all except for Captain Manus. Pa told them what was happening and said it should be safe for now. They all turned in with their guns close by.

Pa told the guards on duty about what was happening and to be extra vigilant.

Monday, July 14: Day 9

We awoke at five o'clock and did our chores. The chickens were doing a good job laying eggs, and the cows' milk was about the same. Fleas and those pesky mosquitos seemed to sleep in. After the chores, we had breakfast of ham and biscuits, finished loading the wagons, yoked the oxen, had prayers, and hit the trail at seven o'clock.

The trail was sandy and rocky, but not as rocky as before. The traveling was quick. We traveled about four miles and hit deep sand, which slowed our travel and created strain on the oxen. The men and women pushed while the oxen pulled for about two miles until we reached Plumb Creek, a shallow creek. We did not have any difficulty crossing over except for the high banks on each side. As we waited, we collected more mulberries and rhubarb that grew near the creek. I believed I would have purple fingers for the rest of my life. It was worth it, because those berries were very sweet and good.

As we crossed, we came upon traces of an old Pawnee mission next to the creek at our right. After traveling another couple of miles, we crossed Ash Creek. This creek was about thirteen feet wide and a foot deep and swift , but we managed to cross without troubles.

After crossing, we climbed out of the river bottom and came across an old Pawnee village that, according to Brother Hart and the trail guide he read as we traveled, the Sioux burnt the village to the ground. The trail was sandy, rocky, and slow traveling. We followed the trail until we came to a deep ravine. As the third company of ten in the first company of fifty went down the ravine, a gunshot rang out. It seemed that, during the commotion of last night, one of the men did not take the cap out of his rifle. He placed it in the front of his wagon as he went back to bed. He forgot about it, and when his wagon went down the ravine, the rifle slid out of the wagon. When the rifle hit the tree, it caused the rifle to fire. The 53-caliber soft lead ball hit his nine-year-old daughter in the arm, and the ball nearly took her arm off below the elbow. The doctor amputated the dangling part of her arm and mended her properly. The poor girl was resting in the wagon as we continued.

Captain Reed reminded all those that possessed firearms to check and double-check to make sure they removed the caps before traveling. It was suggested that they should have another person check firearms, but that suggestion was dismissed.

"We can all take the responsibility of our own firearms to make sure we practice safe and prudent practices," instructed Captain Reed.

We traveled another couple of miles and came to Cedar Creek. We turned north along the creek and encamped near Cedar Creek. We had good grass and water but very little wood. Because of the lack of wood, Izzy, Gabe, and I went around gathering buffalo wood. But Izzy called it what it really was: "Buffalo Poop pies." This buffalo wood seemed to burn hotter than wood and did not add any bad or unusual taste to our meal.

James said that, while he was in the Mormon Battalion traveling to California, they had passed through an Indian tribe that would fire their pottery with sheep poop because it burned hotter than wood. Unlike wood, it did not turn their pottery black. James said these Indians lived on top of three bluffs and were very friendly.

We corralled the stock, did chores, and Izzy, Gabe, Charles, and I went exploring. We went down to the creek, but the mosquitos were very bad so we headed away from the river. We did not see anything interesting except some buffalo skulls and bones, so we headed back.

We had supper of dandelion greens, ham and beans, corn bread and cinnamon bread rolls. Mosquitos were very pesky, and because of lack of wood, we could not build a big enough fire to keep them away. Around nine o'clock, we had prayers and I went to bed itchy. Buzz, Buzz.

CHAPTER 8
OUR FIRST REAL TRIALS ON THE TRAIL

Tuesday, July 15: Day 10

I woke up at five o'clock. We had a rest from the mosquitos for a while. I reckoned they liked to stay up late and sleep in. I wished I could sleep in with them. Did chores, had breakfast of ham, eggs, boiled rice and berries, and milk. Had prayers and struck the trail at seven o'clock.

We traveled back to the trail and began crossing Cedar Creek. The creek was very wide, about 135 feet wide, and shallow. The scouts found a place without deep holes and big rocks. We crossed the creek safely, but the mud was deep in some places, and we used ropes and double-teams to cross all the wagons. Again, while we waited, we found rhubarb growing in large quantities, cut almost a bushel, and collected a couple baskets of mulberries, chokecherries, gooseberries, and currants. When it was our turn, we waded the stock across while being pestered by swallows. I was hoping the swallows would eat the mosquitos, but I thought they were working together in bothering us as we crossed Cedar Creek.

I did not like getting wet in the muggy heat. It took a very long time to get dry again. The trail was soft and grassy. The wheels and hoofs were sinking a few inches, but the travel was not as difficult as the sand. We traveled about four miles and climbed up a ravine where the trail turned sandy and rocky again. After about six miles, we came out of the ravine, climbed a bluff, and followed the Loup River on the bluff for about six miles. We followed the trail down the bluff to the Loup River. Again, the scouts found a good place to cross.

Captain Reed said that because of the heavy rains this year, some of the crossings are more difficult and some barely recognizable from day to day because the swift water and debris constantly cutting into the river banks.

The heavy rains made the Loup River deeper than usual. The leaders decided to float the wagons across the river. The scouts found a safe place where three wagons could safely float the river at once. The Loup River was about three hundred yards wide, three and a half feet deep, and four feet deep in the middle. Because of how wide the river was, it was not as swift but still dangerous. It was the narrow, deep rivers and creeks that we needed to watch for, like the Pappea and the unfortunate accident with the ferry crossing we had seen there on July 7th.

Companies formed lines at their assigned crossing spots. Twenty men crossed the river carrying two ropes for each wagon. For the first wagons to cross, they removed the wheels, secured the bonnets, and tied two ropes to the front corners and two ropes to the back corners. Young children and older people who rode in the wagons stayed in the wagons as men crossed with these wagons for safety. The oxen assigned to the wagons crossed with the wagon, but not attached. Once a wagon and oxen crossed, the men on the other side would help put the wheels on the wagons, yoke the oxen, and move the wagons to a staging area. After about two hours, everyone had safely crossed and we brought the stock across without troubles or difficulty. Again, as we waited, we went berry picking.

We traveled about a half-mile up the Loup River and at six o'clock, we encamped at a place with plenty of grass, wood, and water for the stock. There were about a dozen Sioux warriors on a high bank across the river checking us out. The guards in all the companies were on extra vigilant watch that night. Pesky mosquitos and some thieving Indians were a constant companion so far on our journey.

After we did chores, Izzy, Gabe, Charles, Herk, and I went to the Loup River to fish. Herk had lost the scent of skunk. As soon as we put our lines in the river, we caught fish. After catching eleven large catfish in a short time, Gabe ran them back to our wagon. Mama Julia and Pa were happy to see fresh fish. Gabe came running back and said we needed to catch as many as we could. After an hour, we returned with thirty-one catfish.

We had supper of catfish, bread, and dandelion greens. Mama Julia and Rebecca made a berry and rhubarb cobbler. We sat around the fire until we said prayers and went to bed. I started sleeping under the second wagon because I liked being by myself and I could write in my journal.

We went to bed with full stomachs and itchy mosquito bites.

Wednesday, July 16: Day 11

I woke up at five o'clock and did my chores. For the past few days, I had had a milking apprentice. Cate had decided she wanted to learn how to milk cows. Mama Julia kept a watchful eye over her as I tried to teach a six-year-old how to milk a cow. Her little hands and fingers seemed to tickle the cows, and the cows got frustrated. I found it best to put my hand over hers and proceed in the downward finger crawling motion. This way Mama Julia, Cate, and the cows seemed happier. We packed the tents and blankets, had breakfast of pancakes with berry-spread and salt bacon.

Before leaving camp in the mornings, Mama Julia and Rebecca placed white beans in a large bucket of water and covered them so they would not spill out. When we stopped for supper, the beans were ready for cooking. They always prepared the beans, grains, and whatever food items needed time to soak or soften that way.

Izzy did not like her chore of churning butter. She suggested that we put the cream in a small bucket with a lid securely fastened and secure the bucket on the back of the wagon, then let the trail churn the butter. I told Izzy it would not work. Of course, it did, but not thoroughly. It did cut her churning time down to almost nothing. I loved my little sister, but sometimes I did not like her at all, especially when she thought of clever things to get out of doing her chores. *Oh, Izzy, I do not think the world is ready for you.*

We finished packing the wagons, had prayers, and hit the trail at seven o'clock.

The morning was cool as we started. The trail was sandy and flat. We were heading south towards the Platte River. After traveling about three miles, the trail became very hilly and sandy, making traveling slow and difficult. There was good grass on both sides of the trail and a few trees and bushes at the bottom of every ravine we crossed. The oxen struggled in the sand going up hills. They could not get footing, and the men and women were pushing the back of the wagons. Fortunately, the hills were small, but sometimes the sand got deep. After traveling another six miles, the road was still sandy and hilly, but now the trail was uneven with the wagons leaning to the left, not enough to tip, but enough to put strain on the tongues, trees, and oxen.

After traveling about another four miles, the road leveled out but was still sandy and hard traveling. The oxen, stock, and people were getting tired, but we still had another four miles to go for good water and grass.

We traveled another few hard miles and came to Prairie Creek. The creek was about thirteen feet wide and three feet deep at the deepest part. Captain Reed and the scouts said we could ford the river in many places. We all safely forded the river and headed down the creek for about another half-mile on a soft, muddy trail. At half-past five, we encamped at a place with good water, good grass, and enough wood for cooking. The moon was still bright and with no clouds. Fires by the corrals were not needed. As we put our wagons in formation, about half the people laid down again to tend to their ailments.

Just then, Captain Reed rode up. Noticing people laying down, he yelled, "Get up. Get up now! You can rest when all your stock is secured, wagons unloaded, finished with chores, had supper, and after all else are completed. Then and only then can you lie down and complain about your aliments." Captain Reed continued, "If I witness this abomination of laziness again, you will be sent back to Kanesville. Now get up and get moving." Before he finished roaring, everyone was up and busying themselves, with much grumbling.

We corralled the stock along Prairie Creek. The skies looked clear, so Pa told us not to unload and set up all the tents. We did our chores, collected wood, and had supper of catfish, corn bread, and apple cobbler made from dried apples. After supper, we gathered some of the other kids and played hide-and-seek in the tall grass with the mosquitos.

We had played for about a half-hour when a seven-year-old girl named Polly Carter found a rattlesnake nest of at least twenty snakes near an old fallen tree. Izzy ran back to get her garden hoe, and we all returned to camp. We told Pa what we found. Pa was concerned for our safety, as well as the safety of the stock, so Pa gathered my brothers and some men and they, along with Izzy, went to the nest and killed all the snakes. They came back with the dead snakes, Izzy and others skinned the snakes and prepared the meat for the next day's breakfast.

At nine o'clock, we had prayers and went to bed.

Thursday, July 17: Day 12

I woke up a little before five and did chores. Cate helped me milk the cows, and we gathered four eggs, packed the tents, and had breakfast of snake and eggs, along with the rest of the corn bread we did not eat the previous night. We tended to the oxen. The sand was creating sores on their legs, so we applied salve and wrapped the ones that needed attention. We had prayers and hit the trail at seven o'clock.

The trail was sandy for about three miles, then we went into a slough. As we traveled, the slough became softer and our wagons were sinking into the slough. The mosquitos were constantly swarming us. As we traveled, the wagons sunk up to the hubs and the oxen, men, and women strained as we moved through the slough. I noticed James walk up and talk to Pa. After a short conversation, Pa and James started cutting the tall grass and putting it in the ruts. As they did, our wagons moved easier. Pa mounted his horse and rode up to Captain Walton and then to Captain Reed. By the time Pa returned, everyone was cutting the tall grass and reeds and filling the trail. Cutting the grass was taking time, but it eased the stress on the oxen.

As we slowly traveled, the day warmed up and soon became very hot. This was the hottest day so far on our travels. The heat also dried the grassy, muddy trail, making it hard as rock in some places. This created deep solid ruts. If a wagon did not go straight with the ruts, the spokes would loosen or the wheels would break.

After traveling about eleven hard, slow miles, we came to the Wood River. The banks were again steep and we had to be careful. Eight wagons broke wheels going down to the river causing more delays. I think the trail loosened the spokes, and the hard drop from the top of the bank to the river caused the wheels to break. Finally, at half-past four, we encamped upriver about a half-mile where there were steep high banks, about thirty feet high, on the other side of the river. This created natural corrals, and we positioned the wagons, creating corrals so the stock could water and feed as needed. There was good water, grass, and trees. A very nice place to stop.

As we were tending to the stock and applying salve, Captains Reed and Walton came and told Pa that we were staying here until the next Monday. Apparently, an older brother and sister were ill and needed some rest. Pa said the stop would do the oxen well, and he and my brothers would set up shop and repair the wheels and wagons that needed to be repaired.

Captain Reed called the captains and a few of the men, Pa included, to a meeting. After the meeting, Pa came back and said Captain Reed asked everyone to keep a vigilant watch for signs of cholera and the dumb ague. According to Pa, Captain Reed said the closer we got to the Platte River, the closer we were to the sicknesses that had killed so many on the trail in the last few years. Although we were on the north side, those sicknesses could affect us.

Captain Reed said to be careful where we camped and not camp too close to past campsites. "Avoid picking up clothes or other items, including any sickly animals that others left behind. Do not disturb or camp near burial places. Notify me immediately if anyone appears to have the cholera or the dumb ague."

As we finished tending to the stock, Pa said we should leave the tools in the wagons because it looked like we were in for a storm. We made up our beds in the wagons, had supper of stew, biscuits, and cinnamon bread rolls. We collected more firewood and loaded it under the wagons, built a fire, and put grass on it to try to keep the mosquitos away. At half-past nine, we said prayers and went to bed.

No sooner had we fallen asleep, another tremendous thunder and rainstorm hit us. Again, we got out of bed and made sure the stock was secure, picketed, and hobbled.

Shortly after they came back to bed, it began to hail and a big windstorm joined in. The wagons shook. The stock was bellowing because of the hail. Pa reassured us that we were going to be all right. Cate and James Jr. seemed to sleep through the whole thing.

Friday, July 18: Day 13

I woke up at a little after five o'clock and it was still raining. Pa and my brothers were out taking care of the stock. I went to the corrals, expecting to see some stock missing, but Pa said they were all there. We took the hobbles off and removed the picket stakes. Some of the picket stakes were four feet long and came in handy in this soft ground. The stock seemed to enjoy the cool rain. The river was running high but was not safe. Our wagons were on higher grounds, and the stock had a high place they could go if they wanted. For now, they seemed content wallowing in the water.

Captain Walton rode up and asked Pa if he needed some men to watch the stock. Pa told him that he and his boys would take care of them and said that, once the rain stopped, they would set up the wood-working shop. The blacksmithing would have to wait until the next day. Captain Walton said that would be fine and thanked us for all we did for the company. Just then, Captain Manus came to the corral and demanded to know why Pa did not have his shop set up. Captain Walton told Captain Manus to go back to his wagon. Captain Manus huffed back and climbed into his wagon.

Pa told Ben, Sam, and me to get back into the wagons and dry off. The rain would end soon, and we would begin work. I climbed into the third wagon and used the time to catch up my journal.

It rained hard most of the day, and at three o'clock, the rain finally stopped. Dark clouds still covered the sky. We did our chores and started fires for supper. Around five o'clock, the skies cleared and the sun and mosquitos came out. It got hot very quick.

Misters Laroy and Bradshaw came over asking Pa what he needed to set up shop. Soon Brothers Hart, Pierce, Carter, Terry, Neil, and a few from another company came to help. They helped unload the wagon, cut about twenty dead trees. It took a while for the cook fires to start, but after many piles of broken-up cattails, the fire took and the damp firewood started to burn. Captains Reed and Walton came over, looked around and said they came to offer help but it looked as if we had all the help we needed. The captains then looked over at Captain Manus and Brother Barker trying to start a small fire. They shook their heads and rode back.

At about seven o'clock, the shops were set up and ready for the next day. The ground around us was very soft, and I sunk a couple inches with each footstep. We had supper of ham, rice, and beans with bread. Pa had Ben, Sam, and me set up ropes between the wagons and nearby trees to hang our wet clothes, blankets, and other items that needed drying.

We sat around the fire visiting with the mosquitos and others when Captain Walton came and asked James if he and others would go hunting the next day. James looked over at Pa.

Pa said they had enough help. "So, go ahead."

At ten o'clock, we said prayers and went to bed.

Saturday, July 19: Day 14

I woke up about six o'clock and did chores. Again, Cate helped me milk the cows. Had breakfast of mush and cornbread, had prayers, and started working fixing wagons.

Once again, Charles and I stayed busy cleaning out the forge, getting more firewood and coal, and cleaning around the shop. The greatest need was tightening tires and spokes and making wheels. We had ash trees all around and my brothers used them to make and fix wheels and wagon parts. The shop was busy all day while the women were cleaning, drying, and mending clothes, also baking bread and making other food items for the trail.

Izzy, Gabe, Herkimer, and Hanna were watching the little children in the company. At about four o'clock, all the repairs were finished, but Pa said to keep the shop up for the next day, if any other repairs came along. James and the six-person hunting party came back, each dragging a travois loaded with buffalo meat and the furs. Captain Reed greeted them and thanked them for their services. James said they had killed seven large buffalo not too far away. Most of the time they had spent skinning, cleaning, and cutting poles for the travois. They had used some of the fresh sinew and rope to lash the travois. Captain Reed asked the hunters to keep the travois for future needs. All the families in both companies came and took the meat they needed. There was enough meat for everyone and some left over. James gave the furs to Captain Reed to distribute to tanners in the companies.

Travois

I later walked down to the river. The river widened and gained about a foot in depth. I could see more fish jumping at the flies. It seemed the rains brought them up from the Platte. I went back and asked Pa if Gabe and I could go fishing, but Pa asked us to go ask the other families in our company if they needed any help and to provide help if needed.

Gabe and I helped the Laroys, Neils, and Terrys rearrange their wagons as we had done to ours. We still had time left, so we went to Captain Manus and asked if he needed any help.

"Help with what, you good fer nothing kids?"

I shrugged my shoulders. "I don't know. Just checking to offer a hand."

Brother Barker walked up and whispered into Captain Manus's ear. Captain Manus got a smile on his face.

"We have a job for you," he said as he handed Gabe and me wooden shovels. "Go bury our privy holes and dig other ones a few yards away."

Gabe and I looked at each other, thinking this was a mistake asking Captain Manus if he needed any help.

Captain Manus picked up a large stick and raised it as if he was going to hit us. "Well, are you going to do your job or do I need to use this on you?"

Gabe said, "We are happy to help you in any way." We turned and did what they told us to do. Digging with wooden shovels would have been very difficult if the ground was not wet, but the rain did help us out this time.

When we finished filling the holes they had used, we dug new ones and returned to give back the shovels. "Captain Manus, we are finished. Here are your shovels."

He stripped them out of our hands. "Show me where the new holes are."

We took him and Brother Barker to where we dug the new holes. "Here they are."

Captain Manus raised one of the shovels as if he was going to hit us. "I knew you were good fer nothing, but I didn't think you were stupid to boot." He grabbed the back of my neck and dragged me less than a foot from the holes we had dug and pushed me to the ground. "Here, you lazy good fer nothing kids. Dig here and bury those holes over there. Someone might fall into them and get hurt."

They both started laughing.

Gabe took his shovel and we both began to dig.

Captain Manus then turned to Brother Barker. "You see, Ralph, we seem to be stuck with a whole company of lazy good for nothin's like these boys and their families."

Brother Barker started laughing. "Nothing but good fer nothin's."

After about a half-hour of them making fun of us and saying nasty things about our families and the others in the company, we finished digging new holes and burying the other holes.

Captain Manus grabbed the shovels yelling, "Now get out of here you worthless kids. And don't ever come around our wagons again." As we walked away, Captain Manus hit us in the back with the shovels saying, "Got to get the dirt off them shovels somehow."

We retuned about six o'clock. Pa asked where we had been and why we were covered in dirt and mud.

I told Pa that Gabe and I helped some families dig privy holes and general rearranging of wagons.

"Very good," said Pa. "Very good."

Gabe whispered to me, "Why did you not say anything."

I took Gabe by the shirt and led him away from the others. "What good would it have done but make Pa mad, and then what?"

Gabe's lip started to quiver. "It's just not right. They are supposed to be our leaders and brethren in the Church."

I put my arm around Gabe. "It doesn't matter. Besides Gabe, aren't we grown up enough to handle our own problems without whining to others?"

Gabe wiped the tears with his sleeve. "I reckon so. I reckon there are good and bad people in every place we go, even in the Church."

I put my arm around him again. "Let's go wash up and have supper."

We had supper of buffalo meat, greens, bread, and berry cobbler.

During supper, Mama Julia informed us that an older sister in another company had just died. Mama Julia explained that the woman and her husband had recently come over from Wells, hoping to make a better life in Zion with the saints. Mama Julia said that the husband, Brother Campbell, was not doing well and he might follow his wife in death shortly. This was the first death we had since we had started, and I hoped would be our last. Mama Julia asked if my brothers could make a coffin. Of course, James, Sam, and Ben said they would. I could not imagine what it would be like if someone were to die in our company.

While eating, Pa asked what we were doing at Captain Manus's wagons. I told him that Gabe and I offered a hand. Captain Manus and Brother Barker had a little job for us, and we did it.

Pa made an approving moan.

Sam asked, "So what did Captain Manus want you to do for them?"

Pa looked over at Sam with a disagreeable look. "Never you mind, Sam. I am sure Gabe and Willy completed the chore assigned to them with satisfaction."

We finished supper, helped with dishes, collected firewood, then Izzy, Gabe, and I went and played games with the other kids in our camp. By running around, it helped keep the mosquitoes from biting. James, Sam, and Ben finished the coffin and some sisters lined it with fine white cloth. Pa called us in and we had prayers and went to bed. It was a cool evening and we went to bed itchy.

Sunday, July 20: Day 15

In the morning, after chores and breakfast, Pa and James went with some of the brethren to dig the grave for Sister Campbell who had died the previous day. Mama Julia and Rebecca went to help some of the sisters prepare her body. It was a nice day, but a sad day. We all attended the mournful duty of burying Sister Campbell.

Captain Reed gave some remarks about Sister Campbell, and like her, why we were on this journey. He said, "Death is another part of our journey to reach the ultimate Promised Land and be with God. We can mourn not having her company but should never mourn her loss. She is free from the hardships of this world and dwells with our Heavenly Father. It is we, the survivors that we should mourn, least we stray and not achieve what the Apostle Paul wrote: *'Keep the faith, and finish the race.'* I know how unworthy I am to be a member of His Church, a father, husband, and leader of this company. But my doubts and shortfalls are quickly replaced by the love I have for my Savior and my Heavenly Father, and their love for this unworthy soul, as proven by my Savior's sacrifice in Gethsemane and on the cross.

"Of course, this temporary sacrifice we are currently undertaking pales in comparison to His sacrifice. Yet, we are similar in that we are sacrificing, not for ourselves alone, but for each other. Indeed, we are individuals moving as a whole. Like the parable of the sticks, together we are a bundle, hard, unbreakable, and steadfast. However, as individuals, we can bend and sometimes break. It is to the group and each other that we should dedicate ourselves so we can achieve our goal and dwell with the saints in Zion. Let us be worthy of the sacrifices made by those saints who had lost their lives here, and in Ohio, Missouri, and Nauvoo. Let us be worthy of their sacrifices that brought us here today. I pray each day and night that we here, this group, this company, will be worthy enough to meet with the saints in the Great Salt Lake Valley. Amen."

Captain Reed stood there for a minute in silence. Then his posture and tone took a different, more firm character.

He said, "We have gone but a short distance on our long journey. This is but one of the misfortunes we shall encounter on this journey. There are those amongst us that grumble, cause discontentment, or shirk their load. I am not speaking of any of the families who are not of our faith, but members within the body of saints. I tell you now, as God is my witness," he said, his voice rising, "if this behavior continues, you will be cut off, stripped of your provisions, and left to the Indians, wolves, and elements. You will receive the mark of Cain, so that others will not help you. I will not allow anyone to hurt, disrupt, hamper, or destroy this company."

He paused for a moment and continued in a softer voice. "That is all. Now, go and meditate on these words and humble yourselves before God and prepare to resume our journey tomorrow."

The entire group stood in their places for a few minutes, contemplating what Captain Reed had said, and the way in which he had said it. I believed that, if anyone doubted Captain Reed's abilities or role as leader, he removed that doubt at that moment.

Mr. Laroy started singing a beautiful Latin hymn: 'Nunc Dimittis!'

> *"Now, Lord, you let your servant go in peace:*
> *Your word has been fulfilled.*
> *My own eyes have seen the salvation*
> *which you have prepared in the sight of every people;*
> *A light to reveal you to the nations*
> *and the glory of your people Israel.*
> *Glory to the Father and to the Son*
> *And to the Holy Spirit;*
> *As it was in the beginning is now*
> *And shall be forever. Amen."*

The people who knew the words to this beautiful hymn began singing. They reverently dispersed the crowd, each in their own direction.

After the service, Pa said I could go fishing, because, as Pa said, we could always use dried fish for the trail.

I gathered Gabe, Charles, Izzy, Hanna, and Herk and we went fishing. We were not having as good fishing as we had on the Loup River. I thought the fish had had enough to eat during the fly feast the previous day. We were still catching fish, mainly catfish. Izzy and Herkimer were catching walleye. I tried to figure out what they were doing that I was not. They were playing more than fishing and playing with their poles while the lines were in the water. Soon, they quit fishing when some other kids came, and they went playing. They kept their lines in the water and still they caught walleye. I think the other kids liked having Izzy around because she always had her garden hoe and Unicornis for safety.

After five hours of fishing, we had caught thirty-three catfish and eight walleye. Walleye was particularly prized. Charles always offered to run the fish back to the wagon. As he came back the last time, I figured out why he always volunteered. He came back eating candy Mama Julia gave him. Charles said his and Hanna's family would be joining our family for supper and they had made three kinds of pies.

At six o'clock, we sat for dinner and I ate until I could burst. It felt good to be this full again. After we cleaned and put away the dishes, we sat around a large fire talking and laughing while listening to stories from Mr. Laroy. When his stories started to become improper for children and adults, Mrs. Laroy would slap him on the leg, and he would stop mid-story. That made us laugh harder than the stories he told us.

Around nine o'clock, we had prayer and the Harts and Laroys went to their wagons. Mr. Laroy walked back with a limp.

I went to bed with a full stomach and a big smile on my face.

CHAPTER 9
THE BUFFALO STAMPEDE

Monday, July 21: Day 16

We woke up at five o'clock rested. We did our chores, packed, had a fine breakfast of salt bacon and eggs, and were ready by half-past six. Captain Reed came by, visiting all companies of ten, making sure we were ready to hit the trail by seven o'clock.

The trail was muddy, slow-moving, and very difficult. Mud covered everything and everyone. The trail was mainly flat with a few small hills. The sun heated up and the mud dried, making us look like traveling mud creatures. As we walked, we picked the mud flakes off and tried to do the same to the stock. Pa told us to keep it on the stock to protect them from those annoying mosquitos and horse flies. *What an idea*, I thought to myself. I wanted to jump into a mud puddle, but had to settle on gathering soft mud and applying it to my face, arms, and any other skin that was available to those bloodthirsty devils. Dotty, Izzy, and Gabe noticed what I was doing. They started putting mud to their unprotected skin. Soon, James, Ben, Sam, and even Rebecca followed along.

We followed the higher trail as it went to the high ground overlooking the Platte River. At half-past three and after traveling fifteen miles, we encamped near the Platte River. When we arrived at the camp spot, we were covered in mud again.

Pa looked at us with much chagrin, but after a while, others had the same mud protection. James said we reminded him of a clan of an Indian tribe he had met while marching to California. James said they were the Clan of the Mud Heads. This clan prevented people within the tribe from marrying others who were closely related. If they did not listen to the Mud Heads, their children would look like the Mud Heads or be deformed. I hoped someday I could go there. It seemed mysterious.

We found plenty of trees and firewood. Pa noticed Indian graves high up in a couple of the trees. He said we could go look, but not touch anything. First, we needed to do our chores. After we corralled the stock and did our chores, Izzy, Dotty, Gabe, Charles, Hanna, Herk, and I went to investigate. The Indians had placed the bodies in baskets made from sticks and rawhide. The bodies were lying on their sides, curled up with knees bent. They wrapped the bodies in buffalo robes. Some had bows and arrows. They all had fine ornament handiworks with them. Pa later told us the Indians believed they needed tools, weapons, and handiwork for their journey in the afterlife. We just looked and did not touch. However, Dottie placed fresh flowers at the foot of the trees that had bodies in them.

After we had seen enough of the Indian burial grounds, we headed to the river. The river had a few islands with reeds and some trees. Hundreds of greyish cranes covered the islands and the water around the islands. These greyish cranes had red spots on the top of their heads. As they flew around and landed near us, they appeared to be about three to four feet tall and the wingspan was about four or five feet wide. There were also geese and ducks in great numbers. I had noticed the cranes a few miles back, flying around, but did not give them much thought until I saw them in great numbers. As we stood there watching the cranes, I noticed some on the other side of the river. As I watched them, I also noticed a medium-sized deer come out to the trees and take a drink. I quietly pointed the deer out, and Hanna said some of the cranes were almost as tall at the deer. We just sat watching until we went to supper.

We had supper of fish, biscuits, dandelion greens, and berry cobbler. As we ate, we told everyone about the cranes, geese, and ducks. It seemed only we were interested. After supper, we went back down to the river and sat watching the birds. Soon, Pa and the others came and sat with us. Hanna brought her family. Soon, almost the entire company was sitting on the banks of the Platte River, looking at the birds as they settled in for the night.

As the sun set, we returned to the wagons. Although it was a half-moon, we lit fires at the ends of the corrals for safety. We had prayers and went to bed.

Tuesday, July 22: Day 17

At five o'clock, Pa woke us and we started the day. I did my chores, milked the cows with Cate, gathered some eggs, loaded our tents, and had breakfast of mush and cornbread. We finished packing our wagons, said prayers, and at half-past six, we were ready to hit the trail. Captain Manus was late in getting moving and barely made it by the time we hit the trail at seven o'clock.

The trail was sandy and slow. We traveled about a mile and went up a hill onto a bluff. I could see the Platte at my left and flat land for miles north, east, and south. As we traveled, the wind began to blow from the south. As we walked, the wind picked up. I did not mind the wind because it kept the mosquitos and horse flies away.

We nooned at a small pond off the Platte. We did not stay long. We continued on the slow, sandy trail. As I looked down at the river, the cranes, geese, and ducks gathered because of the wind. The trail remained slow and sandy. We were all wincing and trying to cover our faces as the wind blew sand at us. The stock turned their heads and bellowed, trying to protect their eyes and noses.

At a half-past three, and after traveling a hard, sandy, thirteen-miles for the day, we encamped next to the Platte. The birds were still hunkered down, grouped together as the wind continued to blow. We corralled the stock. Even the stock grouped together to avoid the wind. We did our chores and pitched our tents on the north side of the wagons. We all ate supper, standing up against the wagons. Mother and the little ones ate supper in the wagon. The moon was waning to a new moon, so we built three smaller fires for light and safety. We had to double the amount of wood for the corral fires because the wind made the wood burn very quickly.

We had prayers and went to bed early. The wind howled all night, but my tiredness overtook the wind and I easily fell asleep.

Wednesday, July 23: Day 18

Woke up again at five o'clock and began the day. The wind stopped sometime early morning. Mornings were my favorite time of day because there were no mosquitos or horse flies biting us. We did our chores, had breakfast of mush, biscuits, and salt bacon. We packed our wagons, had prayers, and struck the trail at seven o'clock.

Travel was slow going again. We traveled about six miles through dry ravines past a dry creek bed. At ten o'clock, we stopped across the river from Fort Kearney. There were hundreds of wagons on the north and south of the fort with about a hundred wagons directly across the river from us. Captain Reed said we would stop at this place for the day. If anyone needed to go to the fort for provisions, they could do so. About half the company took the ferry across to the fort. We moved the stock about a half-mile down the river and corralled them near the river where they could feed and water as needed. I only saw a few cranes and other birds. With all the people around, I reckoned they did not feel safe.

It was too early to do chores, so the youth company, which was what we called ourselves because our numbers were growing, went exploring. We went out to trap prairie dogs, but as the Corps of Discovery had found out almost fifty years before, it was harder than we had expected. After about an hour without catching a single prairie dog, we went exploring.

As we explored, we found items left behind by others, like plows, anvils, an old piano, books, lots of books, and other items. We did as Captain Reed said and did not touch the clothes or blankets. We soon got bored with exploring and decided to go swimming. We went back and asked Pa and Mama Julia if we could go swimming. They said yes and sent Sam with us to watch over us. Sam brought his rifle and Colt Dragoon.

We swam for about three hours and went back to the wagons to get dry clothes and something to eat. I took a nap.

After about an hour's nap, I heard the people coming back from the fort. They had hired two wagons to carry all the provisions purchased at the fort. It turned out that the wagons belonged to Brother Arnold. Brother Arnold's family had had a farm between our farm and Kanesville. Brother Arnold's group had left about two weeks before us and followed the southern route. Brother Arnold said their company had had misfortunes along the way. They lost a quarter of their stock to stampedes and theft, as well as other troubles. Some of their company headed back to Kanesville. Brother Arnold asked Captain Reed if they could travel with us, and Captain Reed agreed and sent him to the front of the column to the first company of ten in the first company of fifty. Brother Arnold said he had to go back and get his family and all his stock.

Captain Walton rode up and told everyone to collect firewood for the trail. He said the next couple of encampments would not have firewood. We cut, quartered, and stacked wood in two of our wagons.

It was five o'clock. I did my chores, set up the tents, and prepared for the evening. I asked Pa if we could go fishing. Pa said that would be good. I gathered up the youth company and we went fishing. After about twenty minutes of good fishing, we noticed something in the water coming towards us. It was a ball of snakes crossing the river. Izzy and I could tell from their triangle heads they were rattlesnakes. We all ran back to the wagons, told Pa and my brothers. By the time Pa, Izzy, my brothers, and some men arrived at where the snakes had come ashore, only four or five were there. They killed those snakes, but Pa was concerned that so many had come near our encampment.

We kept a watchful eye as we had supper and built large fires around the stock and in camp. We warned the guards and they seemed a little worried about their guard duty, but said they would be careful.

In addition to poisonous snakes, the coyotes and wolves were howling nearby. They seemed to be coming closer to camp as darkness approached.

We decided to sleep in the wagons due to the danger of snakes at night. Of course, Izzy wanted to stay out all night to kill snakes, but Pa told Izzy to put her garden hoe away and stop her nonsense. Izzy obeyed grudgingly.

We sat around the fire with the uneasy feeling of many snakes all around us. After a while, we said prayers and went to bed. I never did see Brother Arnold come back and join our company.

Thursday, July 24: Day 19

Woke up at five o'clock, did our chores. Cate quit helping me milk the cows in favor of sleeping in and hanging around Mama Julia. Cate not helping did make my milking go much faster. We had breakfast of mush and salt bacon, loaded the wagons, and hit the trail a little before seven o'clock.

Captain Walton gathered the company and gave a few words about how, on this day four years before, Brother Brigham Young and the first saints entered the valley of the Great Salt Lake. He had said, "The Great Salt Lake valley, our new home, will be a safe place where our Heavenly Father has indeed prepared for his people to grow and thrive in unity and safety."

We had prayers and started on the trail. The morning was warm as we hit the trail. We traveled about two miles and the road went into a slough with grass and reeds all around. We did not sink in too much, but the slough did slow us down and put unneeded strain on the oxen.

As the morning turned to noon, the sun got very hot and muggy. A couple oxen in other companies were stumbling with fatigue, and we quickly traded out for fresh oxen from the herd.

When we stopped for our mid-day nooning, Captain Walton

informed us we would be delayed for a time. Apparently, one of the sisters in the first company of fifty, a mother who had recently given birth, wondered off in the morning and was not noticed missing until then. A search party went looking.

After about two hours of looking for the missing mother, we started traveling again.

The trail was hilly, sandy, and slow. We were traveling about the same pace as we did in the slough, but at least we were on dry ground. One of the oxen from the first company of ten that had given out earlier in the morning had died.

As we traveled, the trees were becoming less and less, and the trail had deeper sand to travel in. The entire area had hardly any trees or firewood on both sides. There were willows and we saw an abundance of buffalo pies, which we used for cooking and making hot fires.

We traveled another eight miles and came to Buffalo Creek. The creek was about a hundred feet across and two-feet deep with high banks. We all crossed safely, left the trail, and followed Buffalo Creek for about a half-mile. At three o'clock, we encamped by good grass and water, but no wood.

We corralled the stock near the creek where they could water and feed as needed. I did my chores, set up the tents, and went about gathering buffalo poop pies for cooking fires. We used the wood in the wagons for fires at each end of the corrals. The new moon was coming and the nights were getting darker. The mosquitos and horse flies were very troublesome. The flies were biting the stock so fiercely that blood was running down the poor animals. We gathered mud and covered the stock the best we could.

We had supper of ham and beans, yucca root with dandelion greens, and sweetbread. After supper, we went back to putting mud on the stock.

At nine o'clock, we said prayers and went to bed.

Friday, July 25: Day 20

Awoke at five o'clock and began the day. There had been a light rain most of the night with a heavy dew on the ground that morning. The dew made the many wild flowers in the area deliver a variety of wonderful scents. It seemed to make everyone in the entire company have a more joyous mood and, somehow, gave us more energy than usual. The rising sun brought more colors to our surroundings than I had noticed the last evening. We did our chores.

Mrs. Laroy came over and taught Mama Julia and Rebecca how to make "flapjacks." They were like our pancakes but sweeter and heavier. They tasted good, especially covered in sweet butter. After breakfast, we loaded the wagons, had prayers, and were ready to hit the trail before seven o'clock.

The trail was the same as the previous day: sandy and hilly, we traveled about four miles, went down a small bluff, and passed a tall, long, narrow hill that had a shape of a compass needle. The end area was pointed and the middle was quite a bit thicker.

As we passed the hill, I looked back and Izzy was riding Unicornis.

I asked her what she was doing.

"Removing the thorns from my feet," replied Izzy.

"If you wore shoes, you would not get thorns in your feet," said Dotty.

Izzy kept plucking at her feet. "I do not like wearing shoes. They make my feet hurt."

Dotty chuckled. "Besides, if she wore shoes, she would not have an excuse to ride on Unicornis."

Izzy looked up, gave Dotty a sour look, and returned to plucking thorns from her feet.

I noticed a large dust cloud forming beyond the hills to the north. This was strange because there was no wind, but a light breeze.

The ground started shaking as James mounted his horse and yelled, "Dotty, Willy, corral the stock. A stampeded of buffalo are coming our way." He galloped to Pa.

Izzy jumped off Unicornis and ran for the corral rope. As Dotty and I pounded the picket poles into the ground, Gabe and Izzy tied the rope from one pole to another. As soon as we had corralled the stock, I could see a very large herd of buffalo, numbering in the thousands, about a half-mile away.

It looked like the buffalo were going to pass between the two companies of fifty. We were the last company of ten of our company of fifty, so it seemed we were out of danger, but Pa did not want to take any risks of our stock stampeding with the buffalo. Pa jumped on his horse and rode up to the front.

I heard Pa strongly recommend to Captain Walton that we should make a line of wagons from north to south creating a line or wall. Captain Walton asked him to explain more on this setup.

Pa suggested positioning the wagons with the back of the wagons facing out towards the buffalo. "The lead wagon begins with a twenty-two-degree pitch, thus creating a hook shape. The second wagon lines up on the side of the first wagon, placing the back wheel in the middle of the first wagon. The third wagon lines up the back wheel in the middle of the second wagon, and so forth, creating an inward funnel shape. This will give the buffalo a wider path, while creating a block protecting people and stock."

Captain Walton immediately caught on to what Pa was saying and started to organize the wagons in formation. The first three companies of ten had positioned their wagons at an astonishing pace, creating a protection wall. Because the oxen could not see what was happening, the men of the companies were able to hold them steady. The last two companies of ten kept the same formation in a straight line, just as we had been traveling, keeping everyone safe, including the stock. Pa, James, Sam, and Ben armed themselves with rifles and their pistols and hid behind the last wagon in formation.

Suddenly, the buffalo came upon us. The ground shook. The roar of buffalo calls and thousands of hoofs stomping the ground was almost overwhelming. The dust was thick, and we could barely see a foot in front of us. It was getting hard to breathe. The noise of the stampede was deafening as they thundered by. Occasionally, I could make out the large dark figure of a large, one-ton buffalo, but it quickly faded into the thick cloud of dust.

Dotty, Izzy, Gabe, and I stayed about fifty yards from the buffalo, but it seemed they were right on us. The stock bellowed through the noise and dust, but none of them bolted or spooked. They put their heads down and grouped together in a tight formation. They did not separate into cows and horses, but gathered as one group and huddled very tightly. We kept yelling to one another so the stock could hear us. We could barely hear each other through the noise and our handkerchiefs.

As the herd came to the Platte River, they slowed down, causing a backup. The herd fanned out along the river, away from us. At this opportunity, Pa, James, Ben, and Sam were able to bring down five large buffalo. Because they had positioned themselves so close to the buffalo, they used their new revolvers and all the shots were headshots. They were proud of themselves. They were so proud I had to chuckle at their giddy behavior.

The stampede lasted about twenty minutes. These twenty minutes were the most terrifying and wonderful experience I had ever had. I would never forget this experience, and I hoped I did not ever see it again this close. These were such large, splendid, beautiful animals. It took about thirty minutes for everyone to calm down, clean some of the dust from the wagons, and hold rollcall, making sure everyone was still with us. After Sister Manus reassured Captain Manus it was safe, he crawled from under his wagon, joined the rest of us. We held company rollcall. No one was hurt and no stock was missing from our company.

Captain Reed rode up and said that the first company lost about a fourth of their stock with the buffalo. Their stock was bringing up the rear, and they did not have time to corral them. Captain Reed asked James and my brothers to help track and bring them back.

Of course, they said yes. They mounted their horses and rode out.

Captain Walton came and told us we would be staying, probably for three days. The stock in the first company of fifty was scattered for miles. Also, three wagons had tipped over during the stampede and had some damage. Captain Walton asked Pa if he could help mend the wagons.

Mr. Laroy jumped in the conversation and answered for Pa. "Aye, ya bet cha we will." He slapped Pa on the back with his bloody, dirty hand.

A chuckle came from Pa and Captain Walton. Captain Walton thanked us and rode back to his company of ten.

Captain Reed asked if we had lost any of our stock. Pa looked at Dotty and me, and we said no.

Captain Reed reached down from his horse and rubbed the top of my hat so hard my hat went down over my eyes. "I wish I had these two in my company."

Dotty and I looked at each other with a smile. "Maybe next time," said Dotty.

Captain Reed thanked us. Pa then asked Captain Reed about the missing mother. Captain Reed paused and shook his head in a sad gesture. He said there were no sign of her, then he rode back to the first company of fifty.

Captain Walton brought some men to help Pa clean, quarter, and distribute the meat to everyone. As it turned out, there was more than enough meat for everyone. In this heat, the meat would only last for two, maybe three days, if we could keep it protected. Of course, we could cut the meat into thin slices, cook, and smoke it if we had a few days to smoke and dry it out.

Pa gave the hides to each of the five Captains of ten to distribute to their tanners or those who knew how to tan the hides. After they butchered the buffalo, everyone cleaned up, and we moved on.

Captain Reed led the company a mile down to the Platte where there was good grass and water, but no wood. We could not find a stick for miles. We corralled the stock, unpacked the wagons, and pitched our tents. It was too early to do chores. We helped Mama Julia and the others clean the dust out of the wagon.

After a couple hours of cleaning and hanging the blankets and other items, Pa suggested I get Charles and make a small smoke hut. He said we could use the sod that was all around us in place of rocks and use reeds bundled together in place of sticks.

I ran and got Charles and we started digging a deep large hole about a hundred feet from the wagons. As we dug the hole, Herk and Gabe came and asked what we were doing. We told them what we were doing. They said they wanted to help. Gabe already knew how to cut out sod, so he and Herk went about cutting sod in strips one foot wide and three feet long. Soon, others came with shovels and knives and cut strips of sod.

Within a couple of hours, we had four smoke huts that were twelve feet long and four feet wide and two feet high. We made them this size so we could use the bonnets from the wagons to cover the huts and make the smoking and drying quicker. We made the huts four feet shorter than the wagons so the bonnets could come down on the ends. Pa said we could remove the hoops from the wagons to cover the huts.

The youth company went to the river. We cut reeds three-and-a-half feet long, and we bound three reeds together. We used three reeds to make a pyramid so the reed rods would lay firmly on the sod edges and the strips of buffalo would lay evenly over the reeds. We used strips of reeds as string to bind the reeds together, so nothing would burn.

After we had all the reed rods, we went about collecting dried buffalo poop pies. At this point, we lost half of our youth company. Soon, we finally had enough buffalo pies that we filled the huts with pies four layers deep.

As we made our smoke huts, Mama Julia and some of the other women cut the left-over buffalo meat into strips for smoking and drying.

We unfastened the hoops from our wagons and Charles and I ran to where Pa and Mr. Laroy were working mending the wagons. Charles told Mr. Laroy what we made and asked if we could use the hoops from their wagon. Pa reassured Mr. Laroy he would help put them back on.

Mr. Laroy yelled out, "By god boy, that is a bully of an idea. We are like those frontier chaps we read about back home across the pond. Bully of an idea. Bully!"

I looked at Pa and he was trying to hide a laugh that was ready to burst out. As Charles and I walked back to our wagons, I asked him about the pond.

Charles looked at me with a puzzled look and started laughing. "The pond is the Atlantic Ocean. You Yanks want everything so big, so we have to make everything small to keep you chaps balanced."

I just looked at him, shrugged my shoulders, and said, "I reckon," and we started running back to his wagon.

Once we had all the hoops, we secured them into the ground. Because it was about five o'clock, we would have to resume our smoke hut job the next day. The nights were too moist to try to dry out the meat. We needed a good hot day and, because there was not a cloud anywhere, the next day would be hot like that today. Besides, there were too many predators around to leave the meat hanging unprotected.

Dotty, Izzy, and Gabe collected all the buffalo pies we needed for supper. A few minutes later, Pa came back and said they would finish the next day. Mama Julia said she had invited the Laroys, Carters, Harts, Bradshaws, Neils, and Terrys, to join us for supper. Captain Manus's crew declined to join us. Although Mama Julia was always smiling and seemed happy, she kept looking across the river with a sad look. Something was going on. She was just not herself since we had stopped.

People started coming over, bringing their chairs, food, and most importantly, pies and cobblers. For those adults who did not have chairs, we kids gave up ours. Pa unfolded the tables and they placed all the food on the tables. What a feast.

We had prayers and formed a line with plates in hand. The pecking order was oldest to youngest. I knew there was enough meat, yucca roots, dandelion greens, and other supper items, but I was interested in mulberry cobbler.

When I reached the table, Mama Julia took my plate and made it up for me. "You can have cobbler when you are finished with your plate," she said, smiling.

I slumped my shoulders and said, "Thank you, I will."

She leaned over, kissed me on the head, and swatted my backside as I walked away.

I liked buffalo. It was heavier than beef with less fat. It took a little longer to cook but worth it. As we were having supper, Captain Walton came to our wagons. We gave him a couple bites. Then he and Pa went behind one of our wagons. We could hear Captain Walton thanking Pa, telling Pa that because of him, lives and stock were saved.

Pa thanked him and said that Grandpa taught him the maneuver. Pa said he was impressed how Captain Walton was able to rally the wagons so quickly and precisely. They came out from behind the wagons and Pa shook his hand and told him he was a good leader. Captain Walton thanked us all and was about to leave when Mama Julia asked if there had been any word on the boys gathering the lost stock.

Captain Walton said he had not heard anything yet, but would let us know when he did. Captain Walton turned and bade us good night. As he was walking away, Captain Walton stopped and turned around.

Without saying a word, Mama Julia stood up, removed a clean handkerchief, cut a large piece of serviceberry pie, and put it in the handkerchief.

Captain Walton chuckled and asked, "Can she read minds as well as she cooks?"

We all shouted, "Yes!"

Captain Walton walked away chuckling with a large piece of pie in his mouth.

After we had our fill, we cleaned and put away the dishes, and we all sat around the smoldering fire, talking about what an exciting day it had been. At about nine o'clock, we gathered for prayers and said good-bye to our friends. I went to bed. As I was falling asleep, I heard Pa reassure Mama Julia that the boys were well armed and knew how to take care of themselves.

CHAPTER 10
THE LETTER AND THE GRAVE

Saturday, July 26: Day 21

I woke up at five o'clock, did chores. Milk and eggs were doing quite well. The morning was unusually cool. We had breakfast of buffalo, eggs, and cobbler. I wished all our breakfasts were like this. Well, mainly the cobbler.

As I finished breakfast, Charles walked up and we returned to our smoke huts. We lit the buffalo pies and let them burn the flame down. We went to the wagons and got the meat Mama Julia and the sisters cut. Mama Julia was still looking across the river. I wondered if she was worried about my brothers.

Charles and I put the meat on the reed rods and covered the huts with the wagon bonnets. We put blankets over the front and back of the huts to keep the smoke in. We had to use a spare bonnet because Mother did not want her bonnet smelling of burning buffalo pies and smoked buffalo. I understood.

As we put the bonnets over the huts and covered the ends with blankets, within no time, we could feel the heat and smell the meat. We went and gathered more buffalo pies and kept the fires smoldering, but not flaming. At one time, Mama Julia scolded us because we were checking the meat too often and letting the smoke out. Rebecca came and told us to go fishing or swimming. She and Mama Julia would finish the process. We gathered the youth company and went to a sand bar on the river. The sand bar cut two small shallow channels of running water. The channel was about four feet wide and two feet deep at the deepest. The channel was a good safe place to swim with the younger ones. As we started swimming, I noticed a large group of cranes across the river. At first, some flew away and returned. As the morning went on, they started coming closer to get a better look. Soon, the cranes came so close that the little ones delighted in chasing them. The cranes flew up and came back at almost the same place.

The younger ones also ran around chasing frogs. A little three-year-old girl chased a frog over to a crane. The crane picked it up, tossed it in the air, opened its mouth, and swallowed it. The little girl started screaming and chasing the large bird around, screaming, "My frog, my frog."

We laughed as the large bird simply ran around, just out of reach, and seemed to be teasing the little girl. The larger ones did not mind the little ones getting close and playing around them. Around one o'clock, some of the mothers called us in for something to eat. We ate and I climbed under a wagon for shade and fell asleep.

When I woke up at about three o'clock, I crawled out from under the wagon and noticed Mama Julia looking across the river and holding a piece of paper in her hand. I walked over to her and noticed she was crying.

She quickly wiped her eyes and said, "Oh, William, you must be hungry for some mulberry cobbler." She went to the wagon, got a plate and two forks, went to the deep iron oven, and dished out a large portion and a smaller portion next to it on the same plate. She brought it over and we sat down at the table. As we ate our cobbler, I asked her why she was crying.

She said, "Oh, it is nothing. Do you know what would make this cobbler better? Sweet cream. I will whip some up for dinner." That was the end of our conversation about her. We sat and ate cobbler and talked about other things.

I thanked Mama Julia for the cobbler, she gave me a hug, and I went to check the smoke huts. As I peeked in, a big cloud of delicious smoked meat hit me. I hurried and closed it back up.

Mama Julia called over, "Is it almost finished?"

I replied, "Almost. By this evening it will be ready."

All of a sudden, I heard the familiar sound of the loud crack of a bull whip. Rebecca and Mama Julia almost knocked me over as they ran around the wagons. James, Sam, Ben, and some of the other men led a large herd of stock to the first company of fifty. It seemed everyone ran to them. I noticed Pa removed his hat and let out a sigh. As things settled down and they corralled the stock, my brothers came back to our wagons.

Rebecca and Mama Julia said, "I bet you boys are hungry."

James looked over at Ben and Sam and they laughed. Pa asked James what was so funny.

"Well sir, we would have been here yesterday, but we ran into a

group of Pawnee. They had killed several buffalo, caught our cattle and
horses, and had them corralled when we rode up. After a long meeting,
we were able to communicate with them. They offered to give us our
stock if we helped them skin and quarter their kill. We agreed, and had a
good time helping them. As the sun was setting last night, we went to
gather our stock. They stopped us and said it would be an insult if we did
not feast with them. So, we did."

"James, tell them about you almost having another wife," said Ben,
laughing.

"What?" yelled Rebecca.

James slapped Ben on the top of his head. "Oh, it is nothing. One of
the chiefs wanted me to take his daughter, and the daughter agreed. I told
them I have a wife and if I took another wife, fire and thunder would come
out of her eyes and kill me."

Rebecca reached up and slugged him in the shoulder. "Oh, you wish
I would be so calm."

James said, "The fire comment made everyone laugh. Throughout
the night, when the daughter looked at me, she would make hand gestures
of lighting coming out of her eyes and laugh." He added, "This morning,
we gathered our stock, gave them two horses, and here we are."

Pa looked over at the corralled stock. "How many cattle did the first
company loose?"

James took off his hat and rubbed his beard. "I believe they lost
around a dozen or more cattle and the six horses."

At that moment, Captains Reed and Walton rode up and James told
them what he had just told us. Captain Reed said we were leaving on
Monday.

I went and got Charles and some of the others and went back to the
river to swim and watch the cranes. As we played at the river, I noticed
four Indian men on the other side of the river. Izzy ran back and got Pa
and James. Pa and James said they looked like Arapaho. Pa and James
stood at the banks of the river with their rifles, looking across the river at
the Indians. After about fifteen minutes, the Indians let out a yell and rode
southwest.

At five o'clock, we had supper of buffalo, greens, yucca root, and
biscuits. After supper, Charles and I started taking down the bonnets. Sam
and Ben came, helped, and said how impressed they were with our smoke
huts. We tied ropes between the wagons and hung the bonnets on the
ropes to air them out. Ben and Sam helped Charles and me put the hoops

back on the wagons and gather up the meat. We collected more buffalo pies and sat around the fire, hearing about my brothers' time with the Indians.

We had prayers and went to bed.

Sunday, July 27: Day 22

Woke at six o'clock, did our chores and had breakfast. Mama Julia was not her happy self. I prayed she was not going to get what Mother had. Pa and my brothers went around the entire company with their tools, securing wheels, tongues, trees, and anything else that needed mending. Rebecca and Dotty were washing clothes. Usually, Mama Julia did this chore with them, but she was off walking the riverbed and looking over the river as if she was trying to find something. I did not believe Mama Julia was doing well today.

We attended Sabbath meeting where Brother McNealy gave us a message:

> *Micah 6:8 He hath shewed thee, O man, what was good; and what doth the Lord require of thee, but to do justly, and to love mercy, and to walk humbly with thy God?*

Brother McNealy continued saying that we often used words or superficial deeds to gain favor with God, but it was simple, as the scriptures said.

> *Matthew 6:33 But seek ye first the kingdom of God and his righteousness, and all these things shall be added unto you.*

Follow the golden rule.

As I returned to our wagons, I noticed Pa and Mama Julia talking. Mama Julia was crying. She held a letter in her hand and looked across the Platte River. Pa noticed me looking at them, gave her a hug, came to me, and asked me to gather the family, including Sarah and Isaac and to meet at our wagons in fifteen minutes. I went around telling everyone and went to fetch Sarah and Isaac. When we returned to our wagons, the family was there, along with Captain Reed and a few other brethren.

Pa had asked Mr. Laroy to watch over our wagons, then Pa guided us all down to the river. He then told us that we were going to cross the river, pointed to a little hill, and said we were going there. Mother also was going to come with us.

We hitched Pa's wagon. We all rode across the river at a wide and shallow point. Rebecca and James helped Mother as they climbed the hill. It was about a mile from our camp. As we came to the top of the hill, we noticed a little grave.

Pa said that Mama Julia had a letter to read from her cousin.

Mama Julia opened the letter and said, "My cousin Mary Ann and her husband Frank West sent this letter from Fort Laramie last year and asked if we could find and check on this grave." Mama Julia continued looking at the letter and started reading.

> *"Last July, we were traveling to Zion. Our three-year-old daughter Phoebe, was named after my mother, your Aunt Phoebe. Phoebe was sitting in her friend's wagon leaning forward. They hit a bump and little Phoebe lost her balance and fell out in front of the wheels. The first wheel passed over her as she tried to get out of danger. Her uncle Peter tried to stop the wagon, and as he did, the wagon stopped on top of Phoebe. His uncle Peter and others came, lifted the wagon off little Phoebe and took her out from under the wheel. Little Phoebe was severely bruised. They did all they could for her, but they could tell that nothing more could be done. People left their wagons, gathered around, and all wept for the dear little precious daughter."*

Mama Julia paused to regain herself and continued reading the letter.

> *"When Frank and I got to her, she could not talk and looked up at us. I asked Phoebe if she was hurt. She shook her head no. She closed her eyes for a moment, then opened them again, looking at us. She gave us her big smile and she closed her eyes for her last time. Phoebe passed calmly away and left us crying around her."*

Mama Julia took a break, trying to regain her composure again. Mother stood next to her and put her arm around her, and Mama Julia continued reading.

> *"We dressed our precious daughter in white linen.*
> *They lined a box with white linen and we gently and*
> *tenderly placed her in her coffin. We buried her on a little*
> *hill with two tall trees on the north side of the trail,*
> *between the trail and the river. The grave was consecrated*
> *and then they laid her to rest. They made a nice headboard*
> *with her name, age, and date of her death. This was all we*
> *could do. We prayed often to our Heavenly Father, that*
> *she might rest in peace and that the animals do not disturb*
> *this holy ground, as we had seen many times on the trail,*
> *only to turn away in sorrow and grief.*
>
> *"Please, my dearest Julia, as you come through next*
> *summer, if you could find Phoebe's final resting place,*
> *please attend to it so it was not disturbed. God bless you*
> *and we look forward to seeing you and your new family*
> *next fall.*
>
> *"Very Sincerely, your cousin M.W."*

Mama Julia covered her face with the letter and knelt down on the little grave and said, "My poor little niece. My poor little Phoebe. I wish I could have met you. Be assured, we will meet in the presence of our Heavenly Father."

Pa, Captain Reed, and others cleaned the little grave of weeds and grass and brought in more rocks.

We got into the wagons, crossed the river, and returned to camp.

Mama Julia spent the day cuddling Cate.

Rebecca, Sarah, and Dotty were busy cooking dinner and cobbler. Izzy, Gabe, Charles, and I spent the day at the river. No one hardly said a word. After dinner, we tended to the stock. Had prayers and went to bed just as the sun was setting. For some reason, mosquitos pretty much left us alone.

Monday, July 28: Day 23

I woke up at five o'clock, rested and ready for the day. Did my chores. Milk and eggs were good, I believed because of the good grass and rest. I think the chickens would have been happier if Izzy would have cleaned their cages better and fed them more.

Mama Julia said we would make extra butter and share it with the Kessler family. Although the Kesslers were in another company of ten, we tried to share with them as much as we could. As Mama Julia called them, "Our future in-laws."

We had breakfast of buffalo, eggs, and cornbread, said our prayers, and were ready to hit the trail at seven o'clock.

The morning started warm and the trail was sandy and rocky, which slowed us a little. I could tell the rest did everyone good. The stock and people were walking with higher steps through the sand. The trail went up out of the river bottom onto higher ground. As I looked down at the river, I could see the hundreds of cranes, geese, and ducks looking for food. There were enough frogs and little fish to keep them well-fed.

Around our nooning time, we passed a group of wagons headed for California. This was a small company of seventeen wagons. They said that Indians had stolen four of their best horses and their men went looking for them. James asked what they looked like. They described the Indians that were across the river the last Saturday afternoon. James said they looked like Arapaho and told them which direction to look. He warned them that the Arapaho were hostile and liked a good fight.

As we nooned, Brother Hart walked around talking about the backwards nature of the Indians. He said people that do not try to improve their position in life troubled him. Brother Hart had many things to say about many things. He said, "Two thousand years ago, the Romans had the aqueduct, glass, coliseums. The Chinese had the compass, forge, use of negative numbers. Egypt had the pyramids. They all had written language." His list went on. "The Indians are hunters and gatherers, a step above Stone Age people. Where are their inventions? Where is their motivation to improve?" he asked, then continued.

"Maybe they are content on being content. Maybe that contentment is what will bring about the end of their culture. Maybe it will bring about the ultimate conflict between nature and civilization as described by James Fenimore Cooper's book *Pioneer*: '*He had gone far toward the setting sun, the foremost in that band of pioneers who are opening the way for the march of the nation across the continent.*'

"I can only assume the explorers, travelers, warmongers, inventors, pioneers, and others all had a common trait of being content on being discontent. I suppose most all of us here, on this journey, share some of the contentment on being discontent. Otherwise, why would we be here?

Other than God commanded us, but that is not the point. Whether it be called discontentment, curiosity, a void, necessity, it is all the same: a yearning for something more than what we have now."

He finished his lesson, or rantings, by throwing his hands up. "I do not know. Maybe Adam and Eve would still be in the Garden of Eden if they were content on being content. But they had some discontentment and dared to try new things. I do not know."

Sister Hart walked over, took Brother Hart by the hand, led him to the blanket, and handed him some food. "You think too much, my dear. Now, rest your mind."

I pondered on Brother Hart's little lesson all afternoon. I remembered being the first to break ground on a place and then watching as others came and did the same. I knew what it was like to clear a forest for settlement. We did it in Winter Quarters. By the time we left and moved across the river, there was hardly a tree left close by. I wondered if this was what we would do going out west in Zion. I remembered what Grandpa said about letting Indians kill one of our cattle because we killed deer and other game for food. Could the Indian people quit living the way they live now and still exist?

As Brother Hart said, "I do not know."

The more I thought about this, the more my brain hurt and I got the urge to go fishing. All I knew now was the day was getting hotter and muggier as we travel. The road was still sandy and a little rocky in some places, but mostly sandy.

We followed the trail as it took us south near the river. The closer to the river, the harder the trail. The day was very hot and muggy. Days like today, I felt like I would never get dry. After traveling another mile, we encamped at about half-past three at a place that had plenty of grass, water, and wood.

Catfish in Platte River

After we corralled the stock in a nice grazing area, did our chores, and gathered wood, Gabe, Izzy, Charles, and I went fishing on the Platte. We caught seventeen large catfish and four large walleyes. We took them to Mama Julia. Mama Julia, Charles, and I walked over to the Laroy wagon, and Mama Julia asked Mr. and Mrs. Laroy if they would like to have supper with us the next day. Charles showed them our catch.

Mr. Laroy looked at the fish and gladly said, "Yes, we would be grateful."

Just then, Sister Dawna Barker came up and asked what we were doing bothering these people. "Ya'll aint got no business with these fine folks," she said looking at Mama Julia. "Particularly you, Jezebel. Now, run off."

Mrs. Laroy stepped between Mama Julia and Sister Barker and told Sister Barker that we were their friends and we had invited them to have supper that night.

Sister Barker replied, "Well, I was 'bout to ask you to join us for supper tonight."

Mr. Laroy stepped up and told Sister Barker that his family was not interested in having supper with them and asked her to leave.

Sister Barker stood there for a moment with anger on her face, her lips quivering as if they wanted to say something. Then, Sister Barker turned to leave and intentionally bumped into Mama Julia, almost knocking her down saying, "Watch where yer goin, Jezebel."

Mrs. Laroy walked toward Sister Barker as if to do her harm.

Mr. Laroy grabbed her arm and shook his head. "No!"

As we walked back to our wagon, Mama Julia asked me not to say anything of what happened to anyone. When we got to our wagons, Rebecca said she had seen what had happened and put her arm around Mama Julia.

We had supper, unpacked our wagons, and prepared for the night. We built a nice fire with greenery to try to keep the mosquitos away. I wanted to tell Pa, James, and the others how rude and mean Sister Barker acted, but I promised I would not.

As we went to our tents to go to bed, the company of California travelers who had lost their horses came up and asked if they could corral and camp with us. Pa, noticing some of their stock behaving a little skittish, said it was better if they corralled a little farther back where the grass was better. Pa then called James, Ben, Sam, and me to help build a corral. With the help of the men in the company, we had the corral built and the stock secured in no time.

Captain's Reed and Walton came riding up, asked Pa about the situation. Pa reassured Captain Reed that everything was alright and ready for the night. They said to gather wood for fires because the next few days, wood would be very limited.

Captain Reed turned his horse and stopped. Looking to where Captain Manus and his group were carrying on very irreverently, he turned to Pa as if he wanted to say something. Pa walked up and patted him on the leg, and they both looked at each other.

Captain Reed shook his head and asked, "Does he pull his duty watching the stock at night?"

Pa put his head down with a little smile, kicked the dirt with his boot. "No, Captain. I think he is busy enough as company captain, so I let him alone."

Captain Reed shook his head. "So what you are not saying is that you value your stock too much."

Pa patted him on the leg again, they both tipped their hats, and

Captain Reed rode back to his company.

The California company never did find their horses, and Pa asked the guards to be extra watchful, looking over at our visitors. We lit three fires around the corral because there was a new moon tonight.

I helped my brothers cut and quarter the wood and helped other families.

We said prayers and went to bed.

Tuesday, July 29: Day 24

Woke up at five o'clock and started on my chores. I think I dreamt about buffalos all night. The other day was a day I would never forget.

After my chores and loading the wagon, we had breakfast of mush and biscuits. We had prayers and hit the trail a little before seven o'clock.

We had traveled about three miles when a teamster crew driving their freight wagon with four teams of horses came upon us so quickly, it spooked our stock, but we were able to keep them together. As the teamsters rode on, they came very close to swiping a few of the wagons in our company many times.

The trail was good starting out, but soon we found ourselves traveling in deep sand. Our progress was slowed to about half of what we had been doing earlier that morning. The sand hills made it exceedingly difficult for the oxen, stock, and people.

After traveling about four miles, the road went south around a small lake. We had to stop because of the teamster who had passed us so quickly earlier had broken a wheel. Pa thought the wheel had broken because of the driver's carelessness. We found out that the teamsters were from the Old Bay State and was in a hurry to Fort Laramie to deliver his freight so they could return to St. Louis and head out to the gold fields. I was sure they would not go far with such reckless behavior.

We nooned at the lake and it provided good refreshing water for people and animals. After our nooning, we hit the trail that led us out of the river bottom and the trail became easier. The sun was hot and, after about three miles, the trail went back down to the river bottom. Once again, we were traveling in sand. We had to change out the oxen teams twice by the end of the day. We traveled about fifteen hard, slow, difficult miles. I liked traveling away from the river bottom. The trail was quicker and the mosquitos did not bother us, but those biting horse flies stayed with us. The other good that came from a bumpy trail was the cream had nearly churned to butter.

As we walked between eight to twelve hours a day, the trail got a little boring, so we sang songs such as "Calico Pie."

> *"Calico pie,*
> *The little birds fly*
> *Down to the calico-tree:*
> *Their wings were blue,*
> *And they sang, 'Tilly-loo!'*
> *Till away they flew;*
> *And they never came back to me!*
> *They never came back,*
> *They never came back,*
> *They never came back to me!*
> *Calico jam,*
> *The little Fish swam*
> *Over the Syllabub Sea.*
> *He took off his hat*
> *To the Sole and the Sprat,*
> *And the Willeby-wat."*

This was a favorite song and often had been sung by Izzy and me with our best friends, Amos and Josie Andrews in Kanesville. Amos and his father Enoch Andrews would sing it all the time, while Mrs. Michèle Andrews played the banjo. Mrs. Andrews was always happy and laughed often. They were fun, happy, and always busy. I missed them very much. I hoped I would see them again. We would also sing along with Rebecca and James when they sang church hymns.

The day heated up and the trail was sandy and slow. We crossed a creek about six feet wide and not quite two feet deep. It was an easy crossing. We traveled another few miles and we finally encamped along the river by another lake at about four o'clock. There was good water, good grass, but no wood. We corralled the stock, did our chores, unpacked our wagons, pitched tents, and had supper. We gathered buffalo pies for cooking and used the wood for corral fires.

I was looking forward to going to bed when Pa reminded me it was my turn to watch over the stock with Brother Ward. Brother Ward was from the second company of ten in our company of fifty. Noticing I looked tired, Brother Ward asked Pa if his son Walter could watch in my place. Pa said it was my decision to do or not do my duty. I thanked Brother Ward for his concern, but I would do my duty and keep watch that night.

Because of the new moon, the night was very dark. We made fires on both ends of the corral. It turned out that Brother Ward was an experienced herdsman and did business with Grandpa. Brother Ward asked me if I had seen the four wagons that had passed us coming from Great Salt Lake City headed to Kanesville.

I told him I did not recollect seeing wagons going the other way.

He looked at me with a very puzzled look. "How could you have not seen the wagons?"

I shrugged my shoulders. "What time of the day was this?"

"Around half-past three."

I thought about that for a minute. "Oh, I know how I could have missed them," I said rather embarrassed. "I was in the tall grass taking care of business."

Brother Ward let out a big laugh. "Well in that case, I can see how you could have missed them."

Brother Ward told me that Indians just outside of Fort Laramie robbed these four wagons and had taken their clothes. He said no one was hurt, but it was never a good idea to travel in small companies.

"What about the teamster and the freight wagon that had passed us today?" I asked.

"I believe the Indians know that the freighters and teamsters are well armed and will fight to kill. Plus, that is the property of the fort. Wagons, on the other hand, will not give such a fight and are not property of the United States. They are easier to overtake."

Brother Ward's family was from the upper part of New York by Vermont. His accent was almost as humorous as Mama Julia's accent. When he said, "Lord," it sounded like, "Lard." For Washington, D.C., he said, "Worshington, D.C." When he asked where I was born, it sounded like he had said, "barn," and when he said "barn," it sounded like "born." I had met several people from that area and they all talked the same way.

I believed it was somewhere between midnight and one o'clock, it began to rain. I could not tell the time due to the clouds. Within an hour, there came heavy rains and constant thundering. Pa and my brothers came out to help picket, but noticed the stock were not stirring. Maybe because of the long hard trail. They stayed a while, then went back to the wagons to help those in tents get into wagons. Despite the rains and thunder, Brother Ward and I had a good night with good conversations and the night went quickly.

Pa relieved me at half-past four so I could get a nap.

CHAPTER 11
OUR FIRST DANCE

Wednesday, July 30: Day 25

Woke up at six o'clock. Izzy did most of my chores. Loaded the wagons and had breakfast. We finished packing and prepared for prayers when we learned that, during the night, Indians stole two very good horses from a company of ten at the head of the first company of fifty. The horses were hobbled and feeding near the river. Although guarded, somehow the Indians took them. They thought Omaha Indians stole the horses and believed they were camped a few miles south.

We had prayers and hit the trail at half-past seven.

We crossed Dry Creek and passed the first company of fifty, who were looking for their horses and some stock lost in the previous night's storm. Captain Reed asked Pa if we had lost any stock or horses.

Pa replied, looking back at me, "No. I had a couple of my best men on detail and none were lost."

Captain Reed looked at me with a smile, tipped his hat, and rode out to meet some of his captains. That was a proud moment for me and I was glad I did not give up my duty for a night's sleep.

Because of the storm, the morning was cool and the trail muddy, but good. As it began to warm, the mosquitos and horse flies came out in great numbers. As we traveled, we could see great herds of buffalo in the distance on both sides of the Platte River. I was glad they were at such a distance. Captain Walton sent James and a few hunters out to the buffalo. We finished the last of our fresh meat a few nights before at supper. We still had the meat we smoked but, of course, we preferred fresh meat.

The trail led us away from the river and became easier and quicker. At about ten o'clock, we passed a company of saints that left two days ahead of us. They told us they had had a very troublesome time with their stock running off. They said they had another incident with their stock but this time it killed a young woman.

Captain Harding, the captain of this company of saints, told us that something frightened the oxen pulling a wagon and they started to run. This caused a couple oxen from other wagons for run as well. A young woman was riding in the wagon when her oxen bolted and she jumped out of the back of her wagon. Before she could get out of the way, the oxen and the wagon behind her ran her over. Her brother ran to her and held her as she died. This brother and sister were traveling alone from Ohio to Zion, and now this young man was without a sister and without family. When they had joined the Church, they had left home and headed to Zion to begin a new life. The young man was crying inconsolably, having his sister die in such a devastating way. They made a coffin and dug in the ground as deep as they could. They placed her to sleep in her final resting place.

The young man kept saying, "This is no place for my sister out in a desolate place, where no one will ever know who she was. Over time, her and her final resting place will be forgotten all together."

What a horrible consideration, I thought to myself. *To be buried here all alone, to be forgotten all together. I cannot and do not want to dwell upon such a thought. It troubles me deeply.*

We offered our thoughts and prayers, and we continued with heavy hearts for this young man and for the loss of his sister. I was so grateful for the training Grandfather gave us on taking care of stock. This trail could be so hard and unfair. I felt very sad.

We traveled for another eight miles and at four o'clock, encamped about a half-mile from the Platte River. We had good water, good grass, and plenty of wood. James and the hunters came into camp right behind us with their travois loaded with buffalo. We corralled the stock, did chores, and due to clear-looking skies, we unpacked, set up our tents, and had supper of buffalo stew, biscuits, greens, and mulberry cobbler.

We had prayers early and I went to bed early. I was too tired to care about the mosquitos. I fell asleep, thinking about that poor sister buried alone and then forgotten all together. I was grateful that we believed that we would be together in the next life. I hoped and prayed this belief would comfort the poor brother left alone. I knew the journey we were all making was for our ultimate safety, security, and happiness, as well as the safety, security, and happiness of the saints yet to come. But I had been happy in Kanesville.

I was tired and I was going to sleep.

Thursday, July 31: Day 26

I woke up at five o'clock, rested and ready for the day. Did my chores, packed the wagons, and had breakfast of salt bacon, eggs, and biscuits. We had prayers and struck the trail a little after half-past seven. Our delay was because Captain Manus and his companions overslept.

The morning was warmer than the previous day, and the trail took us out of the bottomland on to higher ground, a little farther away from the Platte River. This distance from the river also put distance between us and the mosquitos, but horseflies kept constant company with us.

The trail was sandy, rocky, but quick. As the day continued, it became hotter, but not as muggy. We nooned a little after midday for about an hour at a place where there was water and good grass. After traveling about eight miles, we dropped back down closer to the river, and the trail became sandy and slowed us down. As I looked to the north, there were miles of small rolling hills with an occasional tree sticking up from a ravine. Of course, to the south was the Platte River.

The remainder of our travel was hot, sandy, and dusty, but a good trail. We traveled another two miles as the trail passed between the bluffs and the river. Traveled another mile and crossed a creek about ten feet wide and about two feet deep.

After crossing the creek, we traveled a few hundred yards and at about a half-past three, we encamped where the creek emptied into the Platte. There was good water, good grass, and plenty of wood. We corralled the stock, did our chores. Clouds looked friendly, so we pitched our tents and had a good supper of buffalo, beans, greens, and sweetbread. After supper, Gabe, Izzy, Charles, and I met up with most of the other kids in our company, played tag and hide-and-seek in the willow trees that grew in large numbers and size along the Platte River.

As we played, I noticed that on an island, there were a few Indian graves in the trees. They looked like very large nests, but we knew what they were because we had seen them before and because some had red blankets. We could not go over to them, so we went back to playing.

They called us in at eventide. Some of the grownups said they were amazed how we could walk for miles and then want to run around and play for hours. I reckoned it was good to be kids.

We had prayers and went to bed.

Friday, August 1: Day 27

Woke up at five o'clock, did our chores. Plenty of milk and eggs. Ready to have breakfast when Captain Walton came to our wagons and said that they had seen buffalo a couple miles to the northwest. He asked Pa if he had a couple hunters who would be willing to go with him and a few other hunters to kill a few buffalo for meat. Pa smiled and turned to James, who was starting to mount his horse. Pa asked Sam if he could handle the oxen while Ben went on the hunt.

Rebecca called out, "Of course, he can, and you never asked me if I could handle it."

Pa walked over to Rebecca and gave her a kiss on the cheek. "I never had a doubt you could." Pa then told James and Ben to load up and saddle up. Before they left, we had prayers and they went off riding for the hunt.

We had breakfast of pancakes and ham. We finished packing the wagons, and at seven o'clock, we hit the trail. The morning was pleasant. There was dew on the ground, which was a good sign of good weather ahead. The wild flowers were in abundance in this area, and the look and smell was very pleasing and made for a good start of the day.

The first two miles, the trail went through a slough, which slowed us up and got us muddy and wet. We soon came out onto higher ground, and the trail was once again sandy and rocky, but quick. As we progressed and the sun began to warm, the mud soon dried.

We traveled about seven miles and nooned by a small creek. After about an hour, we hit the trail again. As we traveled, we again came upon sand and sandy hills, which slowed us down a little. This lasted for about three miles. We came out of the sandy area onto a good trail for about two miles. The trail led us closer to the river. There were plenty of trees along the river. We traveled another mile, and we could see our hunting party about a mile ahead of us. When we arrived, they had killed seven buffalo and almost had them butchered. The company stopped to ration the meat between both companies of fifty. Captain Walton assigned the hides out to those that could tan them.

There was a minor injury among the hunters. According to Captain Walton, Brother Griffiths, a greenhorn immigrant from Wales, talked Captain Walton into going on the hunt for adventure and experience. Once the hunters started dropping the buffalo, Brother Griffiths, in his excitement and thinking he would finish the job, jumped off his horse and pulled out his large butcher knife. The first buffalo he had leapt on was clearly not dead. The buffalo jumped up with Brother Griffiths on his back and ran a short distance before it collapsed and died, lying on Brother Griffiths.

During the commotion, Brother Griffiths lost his large butcher knife and hat. As the hunters rode up to him, they found him lying halfway under the buffalo with a bruised leg, ribs, and arm.

Brother Griffiths was laughing and said, "That was the best time of my life."

That made the hunting party start laughing while they freed Brother Griffiths' bruised body from the large buffalo. He recovered his hat and large butcher knife.

We traveled about a half mile, left the trail, and encamped where the north and south Platte forked. There was good water, good grass for the stock, plenty of wood for cooking and for a fire to keep the mosquitos to a minimum. We corralled the stock, did our chores, and had a good supper of buffalo, rice, dandelion greens, and apple cobbler. While we prepared for the evening, we could hear the cries of wolves and coyotes gathering at the kill area, looking for meat. For this reason, Pa had doubled the guards for the night. We built large fires in four places around the corrals.

After supper, we sat around our fine fire and talked. Mama Julia read us letters from Grandmother and Grandpa. We heard some of the letters before, but we like listening to them again. We had prayers and went to bed.

Saturday, August 2: Day 28

Woke up at five o'clock, did chores. Milk and eggs had increased. Had breakfast of buffalo and biscuits. We began loading the wagons when Captain Walton came to our company and instructed us to take as much wood as possible for the next couple of stops. Wood would be a scarce commodity and it was unknown if we would be able to depend on buffalo chips for fuel. For the next two hours, we quartered wood and stacked as much as we could carry. My brothers and I helped the other families cut and load wood.

We spent most of our time with the Hart family. The Harts were a young family of five. We had become somewhat close to them and provided needed instruction and assistance when necessary. Although Brother Hart and Hanna were very well-read and book-smart, they lacked a little common sense. Herk on the other hand was book-smart, whitty, and had common sense. He had to in order to put up with Izzy.

We hit the trail at nine o'clock and traveled on good trails for about half the day. The sun was not as hot and we made good time. We crossed a shallow creek and continued crossing several deep ravines. As we walked, the wind picked up from the south. The trail was on high grounds. We had small rolling hills to the north, and the North Platte River to the south.

After our nooning, a wagon broke a wheel when crossing a ravine, causing a delay. The trail returned to sand and slowed us down a little. The wind picked up, blowing sand in our eyes. We traveled the slow sandy trail for about six miles and crossed another small creek. The stock grabbed a few licks as we crossed.

We traveled another mile-and-a-half and at four o'clock, we encamped near the North Platte. There was good grass and water, but not a tree for miles. Without trees, we had no shade or wind block. We corralled the stock, did chores, unpacked, and had supper of buffalo stew, cornbread, with greens and wild rose mixed in and cooked together. Captain Walton said we would not travel the next day and observe the Sabbath. Because the moon was almost half-full and the night was still dark, we used some of our wood for the corrals. The wind was still blowing as we had prayers and went to bed.

Sunday, August 3: Day 29

I woke at a little after six o'clock. I did my chores and helped Pa and my brothers tend to the stock. We had breakfast of pancakes and salt bacon. After breakfast, we tended to some repairs on the wagons and helped others if they needed wagons mended. Mama Julia and my sisters washed and mended clothes and straightened the wagons.

Around noon, Captain Reed and the first company of fifty passed us and encamped about a mile ahead of us.

As it turned out, they were able to recover most of their stock that had stampeded due to the thunderstorm early Wednesday morning. They believed that some of the Indians had a hand in not being able to find the lost stock.

At two o'clock, we had a very fine testimony meeting and a good spirit prevailed among the whole camp. Captain Reed announced that, because the days were hotter, we would be leaving at half-past six and taking a longer nooning.

We spent the afternoon resting, reading, writing in journals, writing letters to loved ones, and general chores.

After supper I did my chores, tended to the stock, then I joined the other kids in camp, playing games. We had prayers and went to bed.

Monday, August 4: Day 30

Woke at four o'clock. It was a bit cooler. Did my chores. Milk and eggs were good. We packed the wagons, had breakfast of mush and cornbread, said prayers, and hit the trail at half-past six.

The morning was cool and the trail was good. After about a mile, we crossed a small creek. The banks were high and the two lead wagons in the first company broke wheels as they went down the bank. These wagons belonged to the first company leading the column. The following wagons learned from them and men lined the banks, helping the wagons down until the bank eroded down closer to the creek.

The trail was still near the river, and the trail was sandy and slow going, which gave the mosquitos good opportunities to be the pests that they were. The trail was hard on the stock and people. The wagon wheels would sink down in the sand and the oxen could not get their footing. There were parts of the trail that we had to double-team wagons. The sand was very hard on the oxen as they pulled. The yokes dug into their shoulders. Some were starting to get open sores.

We traveled another four miles and crossed another creek about thirty feet across and a little over two feet deep. The creek bottom had soft deep sand and some wagons sank up to their hubs. Men and women pushed as the oxen pulled the wagons out of the holes. We all made it across safely and nooned on the other side. There were no trees for shade and very little grass in this area.

After about an hour, we hit the trail again and continued on the sandy trail. The sun was hotter than the previous day, not helping our travels. Captain Reed chose to stay on the sandy trail and not go up over the three bluffs just north of us. As we traveled past the second bluff, we continued along the river. We encamped between the second and third bluffs on the Platte River. We found good water, but very little wood or grass. Both companies of fifty were unable to find suitable grass for their stock. We corralled the stock near the river. I did chores, pitched tents, and I helped Pa and my brothers tend to the stock, applying salve to the many that needed salve. We had supper of buffalo stew and cornbread. Mama Julia said there was not a green to eat.

As we finished our supper, we could hear yelling and what sounded like fighting.

Pa and James went to check it out. They returned and informed us that two families in the second company of ten got into a fight over not sharing firewood and chores in general. According to Pa, this fight had been brewing for a couple of days, and the hard days' travel made it surface with guns and knives drawn.

Captains Walton and Reed had to reassign families from the first company of fifty, second company of ten, to replace one of the fighting families in the second company of ten in our company of fifty. It took until about ten o'clock to get wagons moved, stock exchanged, and everyone comfortable in their new order. It was a bad sight to see some of the saints behaving in such a way. But as Grandpa had taught me, we were all imperfect as we strived to become perfect.

We had prayers and went to bed. Mosquitos and horse flies had been very bad.

Tuesday, August 5: Day 31

Woke at four o'clock, did chores. Because of the lack of grass and hard trails, the milk and egg production was low. I helped Pa and my brothers tend to the stock and apply salve to the oxen with open sores. We packed our wagons and had breakfast of buffalo and bread with berry-spread. We hit the trail at half-past six.

We followed the trail along the bluffs. The trail was sandy hard and slow. After about five miles, the trail turned wet and swampy. We hugged the bluffs to try to keep out of the swampy mud. We crossed two small creeks and ravines before we hit the sandy bluffs again. Between the swamp and the heavy sandy trail and hills, the oxen and people were straining.

We had more delays due to wagons breaking trees, tongues, and wheels. Tongues were the most difficult to repair, because they were so long and they carried all the weight of pulling the wagon. Repairs required drilling holes in each of the broken pieces of the tongues, pinning iron brackets to hold them together, and tightly lashing the tongue together. If there had been timber near, we could have made replacements, but because of no timber, we had to make due.

The trees and tongues were breaking for a couple reasons: one was that the wood was not hard enough, and the other reason was the constant pulling pressure caused by the sand. As the oxen pulled the wagons, the sand pulled the wagons down, adding to the pulling stress. Going up a sand hill was not as bad as going down. Going down put pressure on the oxen, pushing the oxen into the sand and, sometimes, buckling the trees and tongues. We were fortunate that the broken trees and tongues had not stabbed or killed the oxen.

While we waited for the wagons ahead, Pa suggested to Captain Manus that everyone should lash their tongues with rope to reinforce them against the stress. Captain Manus said it was nonsense and would take too long. While we waited, we got ropes and began tightly lashing our tongues. As we did, the Laroys, Harts, Bradshaws, Terrys, Neals, and the Carters began to lash their tongues the same way we did.

Captain Walton came to see what was delaying our company.

Captain Manus said, "The delay is because ol' Elias Killian disobeyed an order and persuaded others to disobey as well."

Captain Walton rode over to our wagons and looked at our tongues. Without saying a word, he got off his horse to get a closer look. He closely examined the entire length, stood on one of the wagon tongues, gave it a gentle bounce, then got off. He went to the others and examined their lashings. He rubbed his beard for a minute, mounted his horse, called Captain Manus over, and instructed him to have everyone in the company lash wagon tongues. He went to all the companies and instructed them to lash their tongues the same way we did. This caused about an hour or more delay, but the entire company of Captain Reed did not have another tongue break again.

Once back on the trail, we had deep sandy trails, bluffs, and ravines. Again, this caused great stress on the oxen, stock, and people. We traveled on up what appeared the last sandy bluff, and the trail became easier to travel. We traveled on until we crossed another creek and encamped on grassy lowland. There was enough area for both companies of fifty to camp and corral on cool green grass.

We encamped at five o'clock. We had good water, but no timber or wood in general. We did not have mosquitos or horseflies until we made encampment, but by then, we were too tired to care.

We corralled the stock, did chores, pitched tents, and prepared for the evening. We shared the last of our wood and used it to cook supper. We had a good supper of the remainder of the buffalo we had, with biscuits, gravy, rice, dandelion greens, and berry cobbler. After supper, I helped Pa and my brothers apply salve and bandages to the stock. I was very tired and I wished we could sit around like the others, but we had to tend to the stock. I complained to Pa about this.

He sternly reminded me that the stock was our responsibility. Pa cautioned me against judging people by our own standards. "We are who we are because of who we are. Now, let it be."

I had to think about that statement for a while.

Around nine o'clock, we had prayers and went to bed.

Wednesday, August 6: Day 32

Woke at four o'clock. It was a cool morning. We went about our business of doing chores, packing wagons, and preparing for the day. We had breakfast of mush, salt pork, and biscuits from the previous night. After breakfast, we had prayers and hit the trail at half-past six.

We had good trails and traveled well. About nine o'clock, a group coming from the gold fields in California passed us. Both groups stopped and they told us of how they went through Great Salt Lake City. The city was prospering, the crops were doing quite well, and flour was plentiful and very affordable. This was good news to everyone. We parted with cheerful hearts.

As we traveled, we crossed two creeks and, after traveling only nine miles, we encamped at half-past one o'clock in a grassy area near the Platte River.

Across the river was a large grove of ash trees. Pa said we could use the ash trees to replace tongues and other wagon parts that needed mending. After we pastured the stock, we unloaded the tool wagon and Pa and my brothers joined what seemed every man in Captain Reed's Company across the river to the Ash Hollow.

There were four small islands next to a big island. They used these islands to bring the cut trees across the river. There were no trees on this side of the river. It looked like others before us had cut them down. Across the river was a large barren bluff that stretched along the river for miles. Across the river from us, there was a large hollow cut out of the bluff. This large hollow had ash trees growing from the river all the way up the long hollow, almost to the top.

We were all busy as bees doing our assigned tasks. Gabe, Izzy, Charles, Hanna, Herk, and I were to catch fish. Mama Julia, Rebecca, Dotty, Cate, and little James went to pick greens, fruits, and other edibles that were abundant in the area.

A few hours later, Pa, my brothers, and many of the other men came back across the river with horses pulling plenty of timber for all kinds of wagon repairs. They unloaded the wood, made fires to treat the wood, removing as much water from the wood as they could. They unloaded the wood-working tools and all the wheel and wainwrights that came with their tools, and commenced to do wonders with wood. They made at least twenty tongues and about as many hounds, trees, wheels, wheel spokes, and wheel parts. As one group was making the parts, others went about to repair and replace broken ones. Pa said it was truly a sight to watch what miracles could happen when men worked together without the concern of money or profit.

Captains Reed and Walton rode over to the beehive and sat in awe as they watched master craftsmen at work. They sat high in their saddles with smiles on their faces and pride in their eyes as they watched the brilliance and talent in their company. The captains' smiles quickly faded when they noticed Captain Manus, Brother Barker, and Brother Pierce napping under a wagon. They thanked all the workers and returned to the front of the column.

We found a channel about ten feet wide that passed between a smaller island on the river. It was very deep and had plenty of fish. The banks we were fishing from and the banks of the island had many grassy inlets and holes where the fish liked to hide and find food. There were many swallows, small ducks, and a few cranes feeding in the tall grasses and reeds. Sometimes the cranes chased after the fish on our lines, but we were able to bring them in before they could get them. The swallows were just annoying, just like the mosquitos. Occasionally, we secured our poles and walked along the river, picking and eating mulberries, currents, and chokecherries. As we had fished, we had seen two long columns of wagons on top of the bluff across the river going west.

By five o'clock, we had caught forty-three large catfish and twenty-eight walleyes. We threw back the suckerfish or tossed them across the channel for the birds to eat. Mama Julia, Rebecca, and Dotty made six pies and cobblers from the fruit they had gathered and were baking them in the ovens Pa had made back in Kanesville. They gathered enough greens and other vegetables to last at least five days. This place was indeed an encampment of plenty.

Around half-past five, all the parts had been constructed, repairs had been made to the wagons, and wood chips had been picked up and stored away for future use on the trail. The women in our company combined food they had gathered, along with the fish we had caught, and we had a wonderful feast. We also had enough food for the next day.

Everyone in our company joined in the feast as we sat around a large fire. Mr. Laroy brought out his fiddle. Brother Hart got his guitar. Brother Carter got his harmonica. They began to play tunes. Soon, people were coming over from other companies. Some brought musical instruments and joined the music. People requested songs and started to dance. Captains Reed and Walton came over, ate some pie, and reminded us that we still had to get up at half-past four and head out by half-past six. Having said that, they asked us to please continue and enjoy ourselves.

We kids ran around, causing tomfooleries and friendly mischief. I wanted to dance with Hanna, but I was too shy to ask.

Herk was not too shy to ask Izzy to dance, but he should have been.

When he asked her to dance, Izzy coldly rejected him and said, "I would rather eat poop from a cow than dance with you."

Dotty, noticing the mean rejection Izzy applied to Herk, walked over and asked him if he would like to dance.

Herk accepted and, as they left, Dotty gave Izzy a good openhanded smack on the back of her head.

Izzy just gave her a glare and ran off to play with the others.

We continued until ten o'clock. While everyone was there, Brother Neal offered the prayer, thanking our Heavenly Father for our safe journey thus far, and for this place of replenishment. He asked His blessing to continue to be with us through the rest of our journey. After prayers, we all went to our wagons and went to bed with full stomachs and happiness in our hearts.

CHAPTER 12
CAREFUL WHAT YOU PICK UP ON THE TRAIL

Thursday, August 7: Day 33

Woke at four o'clock and did our chores, packed the tents, had breakfast, and hit the trail at half-past six.

The trail was good as we crossed a small creek. As we traveled, the trail became more difficult because of the sand and rocks. The rolling hills to the north were getting closer and they were becoming rockier. I could see rock formations sticking out of the hills as we passed. We passed some small creeks running from the Platte River. There were no trees. There were, however, a great many birds of many varieties among these wet lands.

As we climbed up a difficult sandy bluff, we noticed a company of eighteen wagons across the Platte River keeping pace with us. Captain Walton sent riders over to find out more about them. The riders returned and reported that the company was from Missouri, headed to the gold fields in California. We had seen other wagon companies, but unlike this company, others did not travel the same speed or keep the same pace.

I had not seen a tree or a bush since we had left our prairie paradise. The landscape changed as we traveled. Brother Hart said the rocks were limestone. *Wow, limestone*, I said to myself. *What was limestone?*

The mosquitoes had been very bothersome that day, although it had been unusually cold until one o'clock. The sun warmed up and soon became hot. The trail soon turned into a nice, quick, and easy trail to travel.

We crossed a small creek, about four feet wide and a foot deep. The creek was swampy and filled with birds of many varieties. We traveled another three miles and encamped near the Platte River. Our companions on the other side of the river made their encampment across from the head of our column of fifty.

Captains Reed and Walton went about our company asking everyone to be extra vigilant due to the presence of our companions to the south.

"Perhaps nothing will come of it, but be vigilant nonetheless," warned Captain Walton.

Mama Julia accidently discovered another cooking shortcut. As Mama Julia, Rebecca, and Dotty unloaded the wagon to prepare supper, they noticed some left-over pie dough from the previous evening was on a box. As they packed, they unknowingly placed another box as well as bags, on top of the dough. When they discovered the dough, it had flattened out to about the thickness of a piecrust.

We used some of the wood we packed from the previous day to build a fire for cooking, but did not have enough for more fires. The mosquitos took advantage of this opportunity.

After we corralled the stock, we did chores, unpacked, set up our tents, and prepared for supper. We had a good supper of stew, biscuits, and berry pie.

After supper, Izzy, Cate, Gabe, Charles, Herk, Hanna, and I went and played by the river and tried to catch turtles. The only one that caught a turtle was Cate, and she had caught it by mistake. As she bent down to pick up a little turtle, the bottom of her dress rubbed the turtle's head and the turtle grabbed on. Cate started screaming. We tried to remove it without tearing her dress or killing the little turtle. Upon hearing the screaming and crying, Mama Julia and Rebecca came running over. They stood there and laughed. They picked up Cate with the turtle still clinging to the dress and took her to the wagon. They convinced the little turtle to let go by putting a little piece of meat next to the turtle's head. They were about the let the little turtle go when Cate started crying, saying, "It is my pet. It is my pet turtle." We now had a turtle to join us on our travel.

Pa doubled the guards. The moon was bright as it was starting to become full. Made for a well-lit corral.

We said prayers and went to bed. With mosquitos, of course.

Friday, August 8: Day 34

Woke at four o'clock, did chores, packed our tents, and had breakfast of salt bacon, biscuits, and some fruit. Just after breakfast, riders from the Missouri wagon company came over to our stock and started poking around. Pa, James, Ben, and Sam armed themselves with the revolvers and went to see what was going on. One of the riders said someone stole five cows and three horses and they knew it was us, "damn Mormons."

Pa introduced himself and James, Ben, and Sam. As they talked, some civility began to rise and Pa said they could look through the stock but would not find any of theirs amongst them. As they looked through our stock, James suggested he go over and look at the tracks to see what direction their stock had traveled.

After the Missouri visitors calmed down, they said they would appreciate any assistance in this matter.

As James saddled his horse, Captain Manus came over with Brother Barker, carrying their rifles loaded and locked.

Captain Manus yelled, "What the hell are you damn Missouri scum doing here?" They pointed their rifles at the Missouri visitors.

Pa grabbed Captain Manus's rifle, knocking him to the ground, and said, "We have this under control. Now, get back to your wagons and prepare to leave."

Captain Manus picked himself up, brushed himself off, and asked for his rifle back. Then he and Brother Barker went back to their wagons mumbling something.

Pa apologized to the Missouri visitors as James and Captain Walton came to the corrals. Captain Walton asked what was going on and Pa told Captain Walton that these gentlemen asked James to help look for some of their stock that went missing during the night. Captain Walton nodded his head in approval and told James not to be too long.

The Missouri visitors shook Pa's hand, tipped their hats, and rode back to their wagons. Pa then handed James his revolver, saying, "Just in case you come across the ones that took their stock."

James took the revolver. Putting it in his belt, he said, "I wish I had been this armed when I went to California."

I had to admit, James looked very fearsome armed with two revolvers, two long knives, and a rifle. In addition to James being a big man, he had a gritty appearance about him, along with a look that he knew how to use the revolvers and rifle.

We finished loading the wagons and started on the trail at half-past six. The trail was good and we made good time. Some places, we hugged the bluffs as we traveled between the bluffs and river. Twice, we had to climb from the bottomlands because the river cut against the bluffs. We nooned by a shallow creek, then resumed a little after an hour.

Just after we hit the trail again, James rode up. He said the tracks that took the Missourians cows and horses were Indian's. He could tell by the human buckskin footprints and the horses had not been not shod. The tracks lead southeast. They followed the tracks for a few miles and found one of their cows slaughtered. James told them he had to return to his company. They offered him some blankets and salt for his troubles. James declined and wished them the best and God bless. They told James that he and Pa were very different from the stories they had heard about what Mormons were like. James told them that most of us Mormons were like that but, like all people, there were good and bad in every group. They thanked him again and said they needed to continue searching for their stock.

We traveled about fifteen miles and encamped in a cove of the bluffs by the Platte River. Very little wood and grass, but the water was good. We used some wood from our stash for cooking food only. We corralled the stock, did our chores, unloaded and set up tents, had supper, and went to bed about nine o'clock.

Saturday, August 9: Day 35

Woke at four o'clock, did chores. Milk was low and eggs were the same. Packed up our tents, loaded the wagons, had breakfast of salt bacon and sugar bread made the previous night. At half-past six, we hit the trail.

The trail was good until we had to cross over a couple very difficult bluffs. These bluffs were interesting formations. They looked like someone or something had cut away the earth around them and left spires and deep ravines.

As we came around a small bluff, Hanna yelled back, "Hey Willy, this bluff looks like you."

People ahead of us started laughing and pointed up. As the formation came in view, it had the face of a giant bullfrog.

I yelled back, "Ha, ha, very funny."

People in front started laughing again. Too bad we were traveling. I would have liked to explore those rock formations.

The trail was sandy and hilly as we started climbing a bluff. It was a difficult trail, and we had to replace two wheels in our company and a few more throughout the entire company, which caused delays. The sun was very warm and the oxen and stock were moaning due to lack of good grass for the past few days.

On the top of the bluffs across the river, we could see another company of wagons traveling. There were about twenty-five in number and they were traveling east. Some said it was a government train, but no one knew for sure. We were seeing groups of Indians traveling west.

James said each group of Indians looked to be from different tribes. Once we made it to the top of the bluff, we could see for miles in every direction. However, we did not see any animals.

There was a strange formation opposite of the river called Ancient Bluff Ruins. Farther south and west, the hills were fading off in the distance to a giant cliff, and then the hills to the south were no more. There was a strange thin rock formation to the west, sticking up from nowhere. I did not ask anyone about it. I was sure we would pass by it soon. As we traveled, we could see a groove cut in the bluffs, which appeared to have good wood and grass. Our scouts and Captains headed in that direction and at around three o'clock, we encamped in this groove.

The groove did have plenty of wood, grass for the cattle, and good water. Due to the isolation and natural corrals, we let the stock graze freely. We did our chores, unloaded the wagons, set up tents, and had some free time until Pa asked me to form a fishing party.

Once again, Izzy, Gabe, Charles, Herk, Hanna, and I and a few others went down to the Platte River and fished. We could tell many groups had camped at this place before. Because of the heavy rains during the year, the grasses grew in abundance and grew tall, covering many of the fire rings. We found at least twenty fire rings walking to the river.

Cate came along for a while and let Gerald, "Stretch his legs," she said. Gerald was the name Cate had given her turtle and *stretch his legs?* I had no idea where she came up with that one.

As we caught a bunch of fish, Charles ran them back to our wagons for Mama Julia and my sisters to prepare for supper. As the day progressed, others lined the river, catching fish until all we could see were people, mainly kids fishing. We prized walleye the most, then catfish, and least of all, sucker. There were some from the old country that liked the suckerfish. Izzy and Herk seemed to be able to catch the most walleye. I think their luck came from not paying attention and always playing with their lines in the water. It seemed Izzy's rudeness at the dance did not trouble Herkimer because they were always playing together when we had free time. By six o'clock, we had caught fifty-two fish.

As we fished, Mama Julia, along with Mrs. Laroy and Mrs. Bradshaw, Sisters Hart, Carter, Neil, and Terry and their daughters, found an abundance of cherries and currants in the ravines a short distance away.

We had a great feast of fish, biscuits, greens, and cobbler. Every family in our company joined us at our wagons, except for Captain Manus, the Barkers, and Pierces. We had a good time.

After supper, Brother Hart asked all the younger people to follow him with sharp sticks, knifes, and hammers. We tooled ourselves and followed him to the limestone at the bottom of the bluffs. He told us that, if we carefully broke apart flat rocks, sometimes we could find fish fossils. Many of the kids did not know what a fossil was, so Brother Hart said they were like pictures. He tried to explain that, a long time ago, water covered this area and fish had lived in that location.

However, the puzzled looks and the silly questions by most of the kids made him just say, "Let's see if we can find fish pictures."

Sure enough, some of us found fish fossils, and we all returned to our wagons to show everyone our treasures. Some of the adults wanted to find some "fish pictures," but it was dark and we needed to go to bed.

We gathered to have prayers when Captain Walton rode up and said that we would be moving on the next day at the same time. A light moan of dissatisfaction rose amongst the group. We then said prayers and went to bed, with mosquitos, of course.

Sunday, August 10: Day 36

I woke up at four o'clock, did chores, packed the tents up in the wagons, had breakfast of mush and cornbread, finished loading the wagons, and hit the trail at half-past six.

The trail was hard-packed and easy to travel. We traveled about eleven miles when we passed the rock formation I had noticed the day before. The tall rock on the other side of the river was called Chimney Rock. Those from the old states said the formation looked like the factory chimneys back home.

I had never seen a factory, nor did I know what a factory chimney was or looked like. I would have to take their word for it. Chimney Rock was a very tall and thin rock formation sitting on a cone base. I think it looked like a tall stick or needle, sticking up from the ground. Chimney Rock had small hills on the west and east side and a large limestone cliff in the background. The thin rock of Chimney Rock climbed almost as tall as the cliff. It was an interesting sight. There were hardly any trees around, but it looked to have good grass.

Captain Reed said there were many people buried near Chimney Rock. When someone died on the trail, their families tried to bury them next to landmarks so if they made it back, it would be easy to find. Or, like Mama Julia's niece, a relative coming along could find the grave.

Chimney Rock

There was an accident in the first company of fifty earlier that day. A little boy, about four years old, was getting out of the front of their wagon when his shirt caught on a nail from the front board. As he fell, his shoulder hit the tongue and both right wheels ran over his arm. The men halted the wagons quickly and pulled him from the ground. He was crying, of course, but upon examination, his arm was not broken. Heavenly Father had been surely watching over him.

We traveled more than twenty miles and at four o'clock, made encampment a few miles east of the Scott's Bluff rock formation. Across from us were six unique rock formations in a row. I thought the largest one on the end to the southwest was Scott's Bluff. Looking north, the rolling rocky hills had left us, and I could see flatlands for miles, with an occasional tree sticking up from a ravine.

We found good grass for the stock and good water. However, wood was scarce. We could have used some of the wood we had brought for cooking, but we found enough buffalo pies to do the job. We corralled the stock, did chores, unpacked the wagons, and set up tents. The road had been good and we had been traveling hard these last few days.

We attended a short Sabbath meeting where Brother Veesey taught about "God's Love."

As we returned to our wagons, we noticed a group of Indians coming towards us. Some were on horseback and others were walking. Pa, James, Ben, and Sam grabbed their revolvers and put them in their trousers behind their backs. Captain Walton, upon seeing them, came riding up.

They had a man with them. He looked part white and part Indian. We could not tell what tribe they were. This part-Indian man started speaking. He could not speak very much English, but enough for James and Captain Walton to understand him.

He said they were Pawnee and they had come in peace and to trade. Captain Walton looked at Pa, and Pa nodded his head, saying yes. He stretched out his hand, making a sign to sit. The Indian interpreter looked at a couple of men. The men looked at the Indian women. The Indian women brought up red blankets to sit on. The dresses of the women were nearly covered with beadwork and very beautiful.

Pa, Mama Julia, James, and Rebecca sat on the red blankets and the interpreter and three other men sat on the blankets across from Pa.

The interpreter asked, "How far walk?"

Pa answered, "Missouri River."

The interpreter nodded his head and asked, "Walk to gold?"

"No," said Pa. "Big mountains Great Salt Lake City."

To our surprise, the interpreter understood where Pa said we were going. The interpreter nodded his head up and down and said, "Mormon, friendly."

Pa had a little smile come across his face and said, "Yes, Mormon, friendly."

The interpreter went on to say that game was scarce for many miles, and they had meat to trade for sugar and corn meal.

Pa asked Ben and Sam to get a small bag of sugar and a small bag of corn meal.

As Ben and Sam stood up and turned around, the interpreter noticed their revolvers. The interpreter quickly stood up, pointing at their revolvers, and angrily said, "Soldiers."

The Pawnee men jumped up.

Ben and Sam stopped, slowly turned around, removed their revolvers, and put them on the ground.

James held up his arms. "Not soldiers. Trade at Missouri River with Herbert."

The White Pawnee looked at Pa and James for a moment. A big smile came over his face. "We know Herbert," pointing at James, "Herbert friend?"

James nodded, pointing to Pa. "Yes, we are friends of Herbert."

The Pawnees sat back down. The Pawnee brought buffalo and antelope meat. They traded them for the sugar and corn meal.

One of the Pawnee men started talking in Pawnee and pointing. We turned and saw Izzy walking around, followed by Unicornis. Unicornis followed every step and movement of Izzy. They all stood up for a moment, watching as Unicornis followed Izzy everywhere she went.

Pa called Izzy to come over.

Izzy came over, followed by Unicornis.

The Indians gathered and talked among themselves. Then the interpreter said to Pa, pointing at Izzy, "Power from Great Spirit."

Pa leaned over, hugged Izzy, and nodded his head yes.

Izzy was confused why she was the topic of everyone's conversation.

The Pawnee men and women slowly came by and touched Izzy and Unicornis. Izzy impatiently stood there, giving them a look of annoyance. When they all had touched her; she turned around, looked at Pa, rolled her eyes, shook her head, and headed toward the river, followed by Unicornis.

The Pawnee stayed for a little while longer as Pa and Captain Walton asked about the trail ahead and any foreseeable troubles. Then, they gathered their blankets and were about to go when Pa noticed a young man eyeing one of Pa's buckskin ponies.

Pa walked over and brought it out of the corral, bridled it with a rope, and handed it to the young man.

The young man shook his head no. The interpreter spoke to the young man. The young man, looking at Pa and Mama Julia, removed a beautiful necklace he was wearing. The necklace was about two feet long, nine inches across. The necklace had six rows of porcupine quills wide, with carved small bones and small clear smooth stones of different colors braided within the quills.

The man handed the necklace to Pa, pointing to Mama Julia. Pa gave Mama Julia the necklace and handed the young man the pony. They shook hands and the group headed northeast.

Pa gave the meat to Captain Walton to give out to those who needed it.

We returned to our wagons, had supper of fish, biscuits, dandelion greens, and berry cobbler. The evening was still warm so we did not need a fire other than to keep the mosquitos away. Because of lack of wood, we did not have a fire. We had prayers and went to bed.

Monday, August 11: Day 37

I woke up at four o'clock, did chores. Milk was still low but eggs were good. Packed our tents and had breakfast of pancakes with berry-spread and salt bacon. We finished packing, said prayers, and had a twenty-minute delay, waiting for Captain Manus's group. At nearly seven o'clock, we hit the trail.

We traveled on hard-packed dirt again, so traveling was swift. After about three miles, we crossed a small creek. A few more miles, we could see Scott's Bluff across the river. It was another giant stone structure, sticking up with other bluffs further off in the distance.

Brother Hart told us that trappers had named the bluffs after a trapper who had lived about twenty-five years ago named Hiram Scott. "Mr. Scott was wounded as he and his companions were fighting with Indians. The companions left him for dead, but Mr. Scott managed to get along many miles until he came to this bluff and died. When others found him, they knew it was him from the things he was carrying when he had died. So, they named it Scott's Bluff and the name stuck."

I think I would have liked to be a trapper, only if Izzy and Unicornis went with me.

We had another accident. Brother Barker's wagon caught fire, which caused a delay for over an hour. From what I could gather, the Barkers, in a hurry to get moving, picked up some of the wood they had used for cooking. A couple pieces of wood still had hot ambers. After a while, the hot ambers grew into a fire, burning some of their blankets, clothes, and other belongings. The fire destroyed their wagon bonnet, so without a bonnet, they would not have any protection from the sun, dust, or rain.

One of the sisters in the company asked Sister Barker why she did not use buffalo pies like everyone else.

Sister Dawna Barker angrily replied, "Cuz'en we ain't heath'ins like ya'll. We be cibilized."

A chuckle arose among the onlookers as she angrily went back to sifting through their belongings, all the while yelling at Brother Barker and her children. I knew I should not hold bad feelings about people, but I really did hope it rained.

We traveled a few miles and noticed groups of Indians encamped on the other side of the Platte River next to a creek called Horse Creek. There were about five groups of teepees, with at least ten to twenty teepees in each group. I could tell each group of teepees belonged to a different tribe by the paintings and markings on the teepees. Apparently, in about a month, an Indian treaty would take place at Fort Laramie.

We traveled another twelve miles and at four o'clock, we encamped by a large bend on the Platte River by two islands. This area created natural corrals for the stock. There was grass, but not in abundance. The same with firewood, but the water was good. We did chores, unpacked the wagons, set up tents, and had a few minutes, so our kid company, which of course, consisted of Izzy, Gabe, Charles, Herk, Hanna, me, and a few of the other little ones, went exploring and gathered fire wood. We went over to the east island and did not notice anything interesting. We then checked out the west island and, again, we could see Indian burials in the trees. The depth and swiftness of the river prevented us from further exploring.

We returned with enough firewood for cooking. Also, to keep the fire going so we could put green grass in the fire for smoke to keep the mosquitos away. It never worked as we had planned, but I hoped it annoyed the mosquitos as much as the mosquitos annoyed us.

As we were having supper, Pa said that yesterday, the first company of fifty came across a woman stranded by the trail in the middle of nowhere. Apparently, a freighter going to California dropped her off. Captain Reed was very suspicious about this woman and her story, and passed the word down among the companies to "leave well enough alone."

In the last company of ten, there was a single guy, Brother Brown from Ohio. He owned his wagon and a good number of stock, including horses.

Pa started chuckling. "Well, Brother Brown felt sorry for this woman and picked her up. When Captain Reed found out, he was ready to banish the entire company of ten, or at least Brother Brown and his stowaway,

Miss Suzanne Paulmus. Some of the men and women in the company of ten talked Captain Reed into having compassion and they would take care of the situation. Captain Reed put the company on notice, and told them if anything happened to create loss of material, stock, or harmony among the company, they would be joining her on the side of the trail."

Rebecca and James chuckled. Mother sat there shaking her head in disapproval.

Mama Julia said, "There is more to this woman than she is letting on. She sounds like a siren and full of trouble."

Pa said we would have to see what happened. We had supper, sat around a smoky fire for a little while, then said our prayers and went to bed.

Tuesday, August 12: Day 38

I woke up at four o'clock, did chores. Milk had increased and eggs were good. All the other animals were faring fine, including Gerald the turtle. We packed our tents and wagons, had breakfast of salt bacon and cornbread. As we ate breakfast, we could hear Sister Barker yelling at her husband and children. We finished packing our wagons and hit the trail at half-past six.

We had a good trail all day. Because of the lack of rain, it was very dusty. We had rolling hills to the north and vast open spaces to the south. The trail was rocky and dusty, but quick.

As we walked, we sang songs. One of our songs had girls' and boys' parts. When it came to the girls' part, we noticed that Izzy was not singing. We all looked over at Izzy. She was riding Unicornis . . . sleeping. Yes, sleeping!

At that moment, Pa hung back as he sometimes did and he noticed Izzy on Unicornis. "Izzy, get off that steer."

Izzy jumped and almost fell off Unicornis.

"What are you doing?" yelled Pa.

"Resting my eyes."

"Resting your eyes? You are sleeping. What if the stock spooked and ran? What would happen?"

Izzy replied in her annoyed voice and spoke very slowly while climbing off Unicornis, "Then I would know where they are going, so I could bring them back!"

Pa looked at her, trying to hide his chuckle. "Be careful and do not do that very often."

Very often . . . very often! I screamed to myself. I looked at Dotty and Gabe, and they gave me the same look I gave to them. We could not believe that Pa had said, "Very often."

Sometimes, I wished I were Izzy. We all picked up small lumps of dirt and threw them at Izzy, but none of them hit her because they were hitting Unicornis and he was getting annoyed.

Just after nooning, we crossed a medium-sized creek. No wagons overturned and all stock and people made it across safely. As we safely crossed, James spotted a herd of deer a ways off to the north. He mounted his horse and rode to them. There were no trees to hide behind, so he could not get a clean shot. He returned without a kill.

As we walked, the sun was getting hotter and our clothes dried very quickly. I noticed that the air seemed dryer. My mouth was dryer, and I wanted a drink of water more often. I also noticed that the sagebrush was taller and made of thick wood, not the soft featherlike sagebrush a few days back. The dust on the trail was becoming very heavy. To make matters worse, a wind started blowing west to east, creating a dust cloud.

We stopped and secured the bonnets to keep the dust out and covered our faces with our handkerchiefs. The only thing we could hear was the occasional bellowing of the stock and Sister Barker yelling at whoever was close enough. We easily climbed two sandy bluffs and passed some interesting formations that came out of nowhere. As we climbed down from the second bluff, I could see high bluffs on the other side of the Platte.

At this point, most of the men and women in the whole company started cheering, throwing their hats and bonnets in the air. I asked Pa why they were cheering.

Pa gathered us together and told us that, from our home in Kanesville to this point, had been the "death area." Hundreds of travelers, from 1846 to this time, had died from cholera and other illnesses in this death area. "Remember in Grandmothers letters, how they could not go a mile without seeing graves everywhere? How she said it was so sad and horrifying it was to pass through? Well, this area, for some reason, is the ending point of the death area."

"Why have we not seen many new graves and had deaths from cholera?" asked Ben.

Pa stood there for a minute, kicking at the dirt as he did when he was thinking. "Well, to be honest, I do not know. I think, for one, we traveled on the north side of the river and not the usual south side. And I think another reason is the heavy amount of rain we have had this year. I really do not know, but let us thank our Heavenly Father for sparing us so we can see Grandmother and Grandpa again."

We knelt down where we stood and prayed, thanking our Heavenly Father. As we got up, we noticed almost everyone else on their knees and thanking God for our safe arrival to this point.

We traveled about sixteen miles and at four o'clock, we found a good grassy area with plenty of wood and good water. As we encamped, the wind died down and the air quickly cooled down. We watered and corralled the stock, did chores, unpacked, and set up our tents. We all went down to the river and washed off the dust from the trail and sat down for supper. We had a good supper of beans and pork, biscuits, dandelion greens, and sweet raisin bread, baked in the oven Pa had made. Throughout the evening, we had two constant annoyances: the mosquitos, and the constant yelling from Sister Barker. We had a fire to keep mosquitos away. I would take mosquitos anytime.

We had prayers and went to bed.

CHAPTER 13
FORT LARAMIE AND LESSONS OF LIFE

Wednesday, August 13: Day 39

I woke up at four o'clock and did my chores. Looked like milk and eggs were up to the normal amount. We were excited for the day. If all went well, we would be arriving at Fort Laramie today. As the trails started to come together, I saw more wagons coming and going. I had no idea how busy the north and south trails were: freight, mail, people going to Oregon and California. We also had people coming from Oregon and California, headed back to the United States.

I finished packing the tents and had breakfast of mush, ham, and the rest of the raisin bread. We finished packing our wagons, had prayers, and were about to hit the trail when a company of the first company of fifty was having difficulties amongst the group. According to Pa, the woman Brother Brown picked up off the trail, Miss Suzanne Paulmus, was causing some sort of commotion.

We hit the trail at almost seven. The trail was sandy but not too difficult. We went a little slower in some places and picked up the pace in others. The mosquitos and Sister Barker were still an annoyance. About four miles later, we met up with some Indians headed to Fort Laramie. Some said they were Cheyenne. Some of the men were very tall, large, and strong in stature. The women were tall and beautiful and dressed in beadwork dresses like our friends, the Pawnee, who had come to our camp a few days before.

There were rolling hills on both sides of the trail in the distance. A few miles more, we came across a camp of Sioux, which numbered over sixty teepees. The Cheyenne stopped at their camp. I hoped we would not have any troubles. Pa said that the Indians would not cause trouble this close to Fort Laramie.

We continued on, crossed Rawhide Creek, and moved on another ten miles and at half-past five, we encamped about two miles from Fort Laramie, next to the river on a prominent point. This point near the convergence of the Platte River and the Laramie River made a natural corral.

Fort Laramie was in a small valley, surrounded by rolling hills. To the northwest, I could see four hills lined together with a few cedar trees around the top. It was an interesting formation. Cottonwood trees lined the river, along with grass and reeds on the banks. Because of all the travelers, there was not much wildlife around.

Fort Laramie was on the other side of the Platte. I could see much going on there. Once we had watered and corralled the stock, Pa asked for double guards for that night. We were on the other side of a full moon, so it was still light at night. This would help the guards. This area had enough grass, good water, and plenty of wood.

Captain Reed said there was enough grass, so we could stay the next day and make any repairs needed. He asked everyone to stay in camp for the night. The next day, those who needed to go to the fort could go. Except for Brother Brown. He had to go to the fort that night and leave his new traveler.

Apparently, some things had gone missing from wagons in their company of ten, and all evidence was pointing to Miss Paulmus. As soon as we encamped, the women took Miss Paulmus aside, stripped her down to her undergarments, and discovered small items of jewelry and other valuables belonging to the company. She confessed, and said she was trying to make it to the gold fields so she could make money.

After this discovery, Brother Brown gave Miss Paulmus a horse and took her to Fort Laramie.

I did my chores, unpacked, set up tents, and went wandering with the youth company. As we went wandering and exploring, Herk, being a townie, wanted a piece of candy. We told him to go ask Mama Julia and she would give him one. Hanna said she wanted one and so did Charles. We all ran back to our wagons.

When we arrived, we could hear Sister Barker yelling at Brother Barker and her children, saying how worthless and lazy they were. She complained about why he made them come on the awful journey, and how she missed her home. She often caused disagreements among other families. Sister Barker always said that she was going to get on the next party heading for the States and leave him to take care of the children and baby alone.

We ran up to Mama Julia and asked for some candy. The first time we asked, she did not do anything, so we asked again. Still nothing,

Herk tugged on her dress, and she turned around and said, "Oh, I am sorry, my angels. I was just thinking of how mean Sister Barker was acting. What is it you wish?"

Herk, Hanna, and Charles yelled out, "Candy."

Mama Julia smiled and reached into her pocket, as if she knew we were coming. She handed us each a piece of candy.

Just then, Sister Barker came and stood behind us, demanding a couple eggs from Mama Julia.

Mama Julia scolded her. "We are tired of you yelling at your husband and children. How lucky you are to have him for a husband. A Missouri mob killed my husband and baby daughter. I know what it is like to have a husband one day and not have one the next day. It is not easy." Mama Julia added, "Your husband is not lazy, and the only lazy person in this company is you."

The more Mama Julia talked, the madder Sister Barker became.

Mama Julia went on. "The best thing that could happen to your husband and children would be for you to leave. In fact," Mama Julia said, "the next party heading for the States. I will personally pay the party to take you."

By then, the other families had come over to see what was going on.

Mama Julia stopped talking for a moment when Herk came between Mama Julia and Sister Barker.

Herk asked Mama Julia for another piece of candy.

Sister Barker looked down at Herk and said, "We grownups are talking. Now, git." Sister Barker hit Herk with the back of her hand, knocking him to the ground.

As Sister Barker turned back to Mama Julia, Sister Barker's nose met Mama Julia's fist. The punch sent Sister Barker to the ground. Mama Julia's punch was not a woman's slap or an around-the-barn-punch, but an all-out man's straight-arm boxing punch.

Everyone cheered and started laughing. Some of the men asked if she was a prizefighter. This loosened the mood a bit.

Sister Barker was still out on the ground with blood coming out of her nose and mouth.

We just stood there looking at Sister Barker when Sister Manus came over and helped Sister Barker up, apologized to the crowd, and helped her back to their wagon.

Sister Barker sat on a chair with a wet cloth on her nose. asking, "What happened? Did I fall down? Was I kicked by an animal?"

Brother Barker walked toward our wagon when he noticed Mama Julia walking towards him. He stopped, turned around, and went back to his wife and wagon. Mama Julia came back to ours.

Some of the adults came over to Mama Julia, asking if she was all right. Mr. Laroy and Mr. Bradshaw asked if she wanted to be a prizefighter because they could set it up for her.

Mama Julia started laughing and raised her fists as if she was going to hit them.

At that moment, Pa stepped forward, grabbed Mama Julia by the waist, and chuckled. "That's enough champ."

They all laughed and went to their wagons.

We had supper of meat pie, bread, and berry cobbler. We finished with our chores and then built a fire.

Before I went to bed, I walked over to Pa as he walked around the stock like he did every night, making sure the guards and stock were set and all was well. We still had almost a full moon and clear skies making it easier for the guards.

Pa asked me what I was doing out and not in bed. I told Pa that I wanted to know what happened to Mama Julia's husband and baby.

"Well," Pa said, "I think you are old enough."

We started walking around the stock and Pa started talking.

"In May of 1848, Mama Julia and her family lived in Illinois, across the river from Missouri with her husband, Brother Henry Lee, son Gabe, eleven-month-old daughter Gabriela, and brother-in-law Milton Lee, who was twelve years old at the time.

They were headed back home after visiting friends that lived a few miles away in Missouri.

"Out of the trees came five men on horses and surrounded them. They were mocking them, saying the governor made it legal to kill Mormons. Brother Lee and Milton started galloping towards home. The mob caught Brother Lee and knocked him off his horse. As Brother Lee fell, Gabriela fell out of his arms. Milton stopped and turned around and rode back to see Brother Lee on the ground. According to Milton, Brother Lee got up off the ground and ran to Gabriela as she was crying. Just then, one of the men hit Brother Lee on the head with his rifle, knocking him back down to the ground.

"Brother Lee was yelling, 'Please do not hurt the baby. For the love of God, please do not hurt the baby.' "

"Another man rode over to Gabriela, got off his horse, picked up

Gabriela, and killed her.

"The man with the rifle started laughing and said, 'This is what we are going to do to all you high-minded, troublesome Mormons.' He shot Brother Lee and left him for dead.

"Milton was unarmed and could do nothing but hide and watch. After the mob left, Milton ran over to Brother Lee. Brother Lee pointed towards a group of trees crying, 'Gabby, Gabby.'

"Milton walked over to the trees and, to his horror, noticed little Gabriela on the ground, covered in blood. He ran back to the horses and found Gabriela's blanket, went back, picked up Gabriela, covered her up, and placed her body on his saddle. Milton then went back to Brother Lee, packed the wound to help stop the bleeding, and helped Brother Lee on his horse. They rode home.

"When they arrived, Milton started yelling for Julia and she came running out. Milton and Julia helped Brother Lee off his horse, then he fell to the ground.

"Julia turned to Milton and asked, 'Gabby?'

"Milton went to his horse, unstrapped the blood-covered bundle, and gave it to Julia. Just then, Brother Lee yelled, 'No, do not look. They killed our baby.'

"Brother Lee reached up, pulled Mama Julia down to him, and told her what happened. As they both sat there crying, Brother Lee died in Mama Julia's arms. That is what happened to Mama Julia's family."

I was sick to my stomach. I just stood there and could not move. This made me mad, sad, and sick.

Pa looked at me, noticing I was crying. He said, "Why are you crying boy?"

"That is very bad and sad what happened to them."

"Indeed, it is, but they are in God's hands. You are a grown boy, almost a man. Crying and tears have never accomplished anything. Be measured, William. Always be measured in laughter as well as tears. You should always be measured."

I used my shirtsleeve to wipe the tears from my eyes. "Alright, I think." I did not totally understand what Pa was saying and looked up at him with a confused look.

Pa saw I was a little confused and I was still very upset. "Think of it like this . . . you only have so many tears or laughs in your life, so you have to use them sparingly." Pa paused for a few moments. "Except the rules do not apply to Grandpa or his friend, Mr. Herbert. Somehow, they acquired too many laughs for their own good."

I giggled a little.

Pa looked down at me. "Are you alright, William?"

I hesitated. "But those men. Those mean and bad men. Where was God?"

Pa gave me a puzzled look. "What are you talking about?"

"Why did Heavenly Father allow it to happen and not stop it?"

Pa replied with a little harshness in his voice. "Heavenly Father nor anyone else will fight our battles for us. Heavenly Father will settle the score in the hereafter. William, I fight my own battles, no one else's. No one else! So, must you."

Pa knelt down so we were eye-to-eye. "William, you will come across bad people, and perhaps you will have to fight. I hope, if you can avoid a fight, you will, but if you cannot, make sure you strike hard. So hard they cannot get up. Never assume someone will be there for you or back you up. Ever! Rely only on yourself." Then he paused. "But always be there when someone needs you, just never expect the same in return."

We started walking back to our wagons and tents as I said, "Alright Pa, but . . . but I can't imagine what Mama Julia went through or is going through."

We stopped and Pa looked down. He started kicking the ground with the toe of his boot. "William, this life is much like our forge and Heavenly Father is the blacksmith. What happens if, while making shoes, we take the iron out before it starts to glow red and we strike it?"

"Nothing much but put dents in the bar."

"Correct. What happens if we keep it in the fire too long and it turns white hot?"

"It burns and becomes useless."

"That is right. Remember the story of Abraham and his only son Isaac? God tested Abraham to the point that Abraham became almost white hot. God then pulled Abraham from the fire by not allowing Abraham to kill Isaac. Abraham was ready for shaping. Heavenly Father will not test us more than we can endure. Life is a series of tests. Tests of pain and sorrow, of both the body and soul. Happiness and prosperity can be tests as well. Without tests we can never become hot enough to be worthy of shaping into somebody worthy enough to return to our Heavenly Father.

"William, we will be tested as far as we can endure, no more. When you become bright red hot, and you feel you cannot take the heat any more, that is when you must dig deep within yourself and find the strength. Then you can welcome the ten-pound ten."

We stood there for a few minutes. Pa looked off into the distance. "We are taught that Abraham was willing to obey God and sacrifice Isaac. What if the test was also intended for Sarah, Isaac's mother, as well as for Abraham? This test must have been as difficult for her as it was for him. She also passed the test by allowing Abraham to take Isaac, but perhaps that would have been her breaking point as well. It's not always so clear."

Pa continued, "I can never imagine what happened to Mama Julia, nor do I want to imagine. She is a very strong woman as we witnessed today. I think that perhaps some of that strength was a result of what she has endured. Never wish for hard times, but never shirk or shrink because of them either."

We began walking as Pa continued, "There are bad, mean people in this world, and people will try to take advantage of you. Be on your guard at all times and in all situations. Seldom will you receive what you think as a fair trade, from man or life, but always give it. And last of all, be grateful."

I looked up at Pa with curiosity.

He looked down at me. "William, ingratitude is the worst sin of all mankind. Let me repeat that again. Ingratitude is the worst sin of all mankind. All other sins derive from ingratitude, like theft, murder, lying, and such. In fact, the Ten Commandments are variations and reminders to be grateful. Grateful to God, parents, and each other."

We arrived at my tent. Pa gave me a little hug, told me he was proud of me, and I climbed into my tent. I heard Pa chuckling to himself as he walked away. "Prize fighter."

Thursday, August 14: Day 40

Woke up at six o'clock, did chores, and helped Pa and my brothers unload the wagons and set up the forge. I went down to the river and noticed large amounts of iron fittings in the river. There were pieces of wheels and pieces of wagons, including tongues broken up along the river. I ran and told Pa. Pa said he already knew about it from a letter from Grandpa.

As travelers heading to California and Oregon reached this point, they discarded items that they did not need or that slowed them down.

Wagons included. Since the fort no longer needed or purchased wagons, they destroyed them, making all parts worthless so, "the Mormons could not use them." We gathered some of the iron and iron parts and used them in mending our wagons.

We had breakfast of ham, biscuits with butter and berry-spread. Then we set to work gathering wood and some of our coal. Mr. Laroy helped Pa, while my brothers set up shop, gathered as many parts that were still usable, and began fixing wagons. Some of the members of our company went to the fort and purchased supplies. Rebecca and Dotty went with Brother Hart to see what dried fruits and greens were available and to purchase more coal to resupply for our journey.

As we worked, other wagon companies came along and asked Pa if he could make some minor repairs for money.

At first, Pa said, "No." But as the repairs on our company was finishing, Pa began working on the wagons of others, both saints and gentiles for a small fee.

A company came up for repairs. They consisted of the most unlikely overland travelers I could imagine. Part of this company came from Maine. It had nine fun, high-spirited sailors. While they waited for their wagons, they behaved silly, making people laugh, including Pa. They referred to noses as "blow holes," as if they were whales.

One went to the wagon and brought out a large rattlesnake he had killed the night before and told us it reminded him of one of his old girlfriends. "This lassie followed me from Maine."

Pa dropped his hammer in laughter.

Pa and my brothers finished their wagon quickly so they could get back to concentrating on fixing wagons. When Pa finished their wagon, Pa did not charge them. He told them the laughter was better than pay and wished them good luck and God bless. They thanked us and, as they left, reminded me to keep my blowhole clean.

Pa said they seemed as mischievous as Shakespeare's "Puck" and just as harmless.

Another company came up with a group totally opposite from the sailors from Maine. One of the wagons in this group had three men lying in the wagon, wounded very badly. They went directly to the fort. While fixing one of their wagons, they told us that some of their companions got into a fight with each other. Two men had been shot dead and left where they had died. During the fight, they destroyed and burned wagons. The three in the wagon were the survivors of the fight and would be lucky if they lived. If they did, there was enough evidence against them that they could be hanged. We quickly repaired their wagon and sent them on their way.

Some paid money for the repairs. Others paid with fruit, greens, or other food items. Pa made repairs on a few and did not charge them because, as Pa said, they scarcely had enough supplies to last them a week on the trail.

Around three o'clock, the Commander of Fort Laramie came to our camp and said people told him of our craftsmanship. He offered Pa, Mr. Laroy, and my brothers jobs. He said he would pay well if we would stay. "We need good blacksmiths and wheelwrights here at the fort."

Pa thanked him for his complements and declined his offer. They shook hands and the commander returned to the fort.

Around six o'clock, we disassembled the shop and loaded everything back into our wagons. We talked to a few more wagon companies as they traveled by. Nothing of interest, but we liked to listen to where people were coming from and going. Some people were rude and called us names, but for the most part, people were friendly.

We had supper of buffalo, which Rebecca acquired at the fort, and cornbread, fresh greens, and berry pies. After supper, we did chores and then the youth company played. Our youth company was growing, and we were having fun playing hide-and-seek, capture-the-flag, and other games. At nine o'clock, they called us in, had prayers, and got ready for bed. However, I had too much on my mind to go to bed.

I again went out to Pa with my questions as he walked among the stock.

As I approached Pa, he looked at me. "What is troubling you this time, boy?"

I shook my head. "Why do people hate us?"

Pa gave me a puzzled look. "What do you mean?"

"Well, what you told me last night about Brother Lee and Gabriela, and people destroying wagons, axes, picks, and other usable things so we Mormons could not use them. Today, folks brought wagons for repair. When they learned we were Mormons, they left with broken wagons. Why are we hated?"

Pa, cleared his throat, started kicking the ground with the toe of his boot, and said, "I wish Grandpa was here to explain this, but he is not. So, here is what I think.

"William, there are many reasons why people do not like us. Our beliefs are strange to many people. People tend to be afraid of things they do not understand. Our way of life, our belief in plural marriage, our ability to live as a unified people, scare people and governments. We are becoming too many, too fast. Our religion is a big change to traditional religions. We believe in Heavenly Father and Jesus Christ and the Holy Ghost, just like everyone. However, when the Prophet Joseph came out of the grove and told the world that our Heavenly Father, His son Jesus Christ, and the Holy Ghost are three separate individuals. That revelation went against nearly two thousand years of Christian teachings and beliefs. This troubled people and even scared them. What if everything you learned about our Heavenly Father from the time you were born until now is not true?

"Something I did not tell you last night was that the leader of this gang that killed Brother Lee and Gabriela was a minister from a church in that area. He relied on the members of his church to support him and his family. If his members left, he would not have money to live.

"Grandpa and Grandmothers' closest friends in Missouri were Reverend Felter and his wife. Sadly, Reverend Felter started losing church members and he began making trouble for Grandmother and Grandpa. Soon, most of the community turned against us, except for the Herbert brothers. That is why we moved from Ohio."

As we walked around the stock, checking legs and shoulders, Pa continued, "That is not the only reason. Some of the reason others do not like us is because of us. We also cause our own pain."

"What do you mean? What do we do that makes people hate us?"

Pa took a deep breath, looking down at the ground. "Remember some of your classmates in school? Was there a difference between the kids that were born in the area and those that came from the old states?"

"Yes, the kids from the old states talked properly and were a little better behaved."

"That is correct," Pa, said continuing. "That is called refinement. You can tell a difference and so can others. Members of the Church coming from the old states, like Maine, New Hampshire, New York, Vermont, Ohio, and other places, came and settled on the edge of the frontier. They are different from those born along the frontier. So, not intending to be arrogant or high-minded, those who moved to the frontier brought finer household items, brought more culture, are more educated, and because we work and exist in unity, we unfortunately and not intending to, excluded those that were here before. I am sure this both scared and angered most of them."

Pa stooped over and applied salve on the lower legs of one of the oxen. "How would you feel if you were born and raised in an area and all your friends, family, and everyone around were alike? Then, a large group of people moved in and were different from you. They had nicer things. They talked proper, and they did not need to associate with you because they had their own people to associate with. And they seemed better than you."

As I handed Pa more salve, I replied I would not like that, because I was there first and I liked my ways.

Pa nodded his head. "Unfortunately, some of the saints did act like they were better than others and were rude and would not let their children play with the local children. In Kanesville, we had seen too many times, members of the Church not wanting to do business with non-members. This caused many to dislike us, as well. Our actions, whether we mean to offend or not, are always watched.

"William, do you remember one of the first letters Grandpa sent to us about one of the brethren in his company that desecrated graves along the trail? Graves who he thought were Missourians?"

I nodded my head yes.

"The company captain scolded him many times, but he continued and caused some members and non-members to leave the company. He continued until there were no more graves within reach to desecrate. That brother and others like him cause as much or more damage to us than a Reverend Felter."

Pa finished applying salve and wiped his hands on his handkerchief. "Our people left the old country to get away from religious cruelty. Here we are again, going west for the same reason. I hope when we, as a people, grow and flourish, we will be secure enough and safe enough to be more tolerant of each other, and of others. I hope we can live how our Heavenly Father would want us to live. The shallow ripple of fear and distrust can turn into a tidal wave of hatred, persecution, and murder.

"William, it is what we do and how we live that makes the difference. Be true to God, yourself, and each other, and we will be okay. That's all I have to say on this. Time for you to go to bed."

I crawled under the wagon and went to bed.

CHAPTER 14
THE NEW NORTH TRAIL

Friday, August 15: Day 41

I woke up at four o'clock, did my chores, and packed the tent in the wagon, all the while thinking about what Pa and I had talked about the last two nights. Had breakfast of pancakes with berry-spread and smoked bacon, had prayers, and hit the trail at half-past six. We had not heard a word or seen much of Sister Barker. All was somewhat quiet in the Manus area.

After about three miles, we came to a part in the trail: one staying north of the river and the other crossed the river and followed on the south side of the Platte River. We stayed on the north trail and continued for about two miles.

The trail was dusty and easy to travel. The stock of previous companies had eaten the grass down to the nubbins on both sides of the river. We were seeing more Indians on the way to Fort Laramie. According to Captain Reed, a large treaty involving about ten Indian tribes was going to take place in a month, affecting future trails going west and the safety of the travelers. This treaty could prevent travelers from using the north trail along the North Platte River.

As we traveled, we could see Laramie Peak way off in the distance to our left. It was hard to know how tall it was, being so far away. After traveling about ten miles, we took a sharp right turn headed up a canyon. This was a new trail people starting using the previous year. According to a letter from grandpa and according to Captain Reed, this new trail, the Childs Cutoff, would cut four to six days off the trip. We wouldn't have to wait at the ferry crossing, and it would save eight dollars a wagon to cross the Platte River.

The trail was rocky and slowed our pace. There were large pine trees along the rocky trail. As we rounded a curve, there were about thirty turkeys about fifty feet away. James and some of the other hunters went after them. We heard about a dozen shots and, soon, the hunting party returned with eight large turkeys.

The road was very rocky and steep in some places. Some in the company were complaining because they had heard the south trail was easier. I thought about what Pa had talked about, getting hot enough to shape.

We traveled for another five miles and at four o'clock, we encamped at a clearing big enough for the company. Once we turned up the canyon, our annoying mosquito companions did not follow. I did not miss them. However, it was strange not having them around.

Child's Cutoff

There was very little grass, some wood, and no water. We used what water we carried for cooking. We had not seen any other animals, except for coyotes and the occasional antelope in the distance. I did my chores. Good milk. I could hear the cries of wolfs and coyotes all around us. We corralled the stock a little closer to the wagon. We had supper of turkey, dandelion greens, biscuits, and cinnamon bread rolls.

The youth company went exploring for about an hour. I found a green rock about the size of my hand. We took it back for Brother Hart to have a look at it. He said it looked like some type of jade, but was unsure. Later we had prayers and went to bed.

Saturday, August 16: Day 42

I woke up at four o'clock, did the chores. Eggs were about the same but, of course, because of our stay at Ft. Laramie and good grass, milk was good. Although we heard wolfs and coyotes all night, the stock was secure. Packed up our tents and loaded the wagons. Had breakfast of turkey with biscuits and gravy. We finished packing the wagons, had prayers, and hit the trail at half-past six.

For the first four miles, we traveled through small canyons. The trail was rocky, but traveling was easy. Then we climbed some rocky hills. The first hill was steep and we had to double team. Everyone made it up and over without harm or injury. Once on top, the land was very different from anything we had traveled thus far. There was very little grass or other vegetation, except an occasional grouping of cedar trees and two kinds of sagebrush here and there. Many people in the company called it desolate, but I liked the new scenery. I could see for miles and the different colors of reddish rocks and dirt mixed with the grey and green of the occasional plants made it a beautiful sight. This land looked like it would require a strong person to live in this wilderness: strong of body, mind, and spirit.

The trail was sandy and very dusty due to lack of recent rains. However, our travels were quick except for the many small hills. The sun was hot, and the stock was bellowing for thirst and feed. Grandpa said cattle can go a couple of days without feed or water, but horses have a hard time. We had to watch our pigs closely because they did not sweat. The heat was very hard on them.

We traveled up and down small hills and ravines throughout the day. The trail was rocky and dusty. I forgot to mention that the entire company got together in behalf of the Barkers and made a bonnet, replaced some of the items lost in the fire a few days before. Brother Barker and Captain Manus thanked the entire company. Sister Barker did not say a word.

We came across a white crusty material that was bitter to the taste. Brother Hart said the alkali was from volcanic ash that fell a very long time ago. Pa reminded us of a letter that Grandmother and Grandpa sent telling us that we would come across this alkali for many miles. Captain

Reed told us that this alkali was not good for man or beast and to be vigilant in ensuring that men and beast did not consume it in this form. Captain Reed said we would come across alkali springs, and if we needed to drink, we must sift it through cloth and charcoal many times. Pa read him one of Grandmother's and Grandpa's letters describing that we could carefully use the thin dried alkali pond crust as saleratus or yeast for baking bread.

We traveled fifteen hard miles and at four o'clock, we found a place that had a little grass but no water. The stock was bellowing. A scout informed Captain Reed that a small spring was located a little over three miles away. We gathered up and continued until we found this spring at half-past five.

The spring barely provided enough water for a stock to get a few licks. The grass was a little better, but not much. The sagebrush offered enough wood for cooking fires. We were in an open area. This openness was good in protecting the stock from the crying wolfs and coyotes that seemed to follow us. We could see them coming a mile away. The moon was a little more than half and provided good light. Captain Reed passed down the message that, due to lack of water and grass, we would be traveling the next day at the same schedule.

We did our chores, unpacked the tents, and had supper of buffalo stew, biscuits, and sweetbread. We said prayers and went to bed. I was tired.

Sunday, August 17: Day 43

I woke up at four o'clock, did my chores, packed the wagon, and ate breakfast of mush and bread with berry-spread. Finished packing our wagons. had prayers. and hit the trail at half-past six.

The trail had many small hills and was very dusty, but easy to travel. After traveling about four miles, we came to a small creek and stopped long enough to water the stock. We traveled around a large canyon that looked very deep. After traveling about eight miles, we descended down and through a ravine that appeared to be a dried-up creek bed. There were grasses but not the kind the stock could eat. We traveled another two miles, and we were once again at the Platte River.

At three o'clock and after traveling a little over fourteen miles for the day, we came to the river flats where we encamped at a place that had wood, grass, and water. Because we were between the river and the bluffs, we did not need to corral the stock. We let them graze and water as needed. We unpacked and set camp.

We all gathered by the river to hear the word of God, along with our brother and sister mosquitos who returned for enlightenment and nourishment.

Brother Kline gave a talk. "What happens when things do not go as planned?" He referred to the scripture story of "Habakkuk Rejoices."

> *Habakkuk 3:17-19:*
> *17 Although the fig tree shall not blossom, neither shall fruit be in the vines; the labor of the olive shall fail, and the fields shall yield no meat; the flock shall be cut off from the fold, and there shall be no herd in the stalls:*
> *18 Yet I will rejoice in the Lord, I will joy in the God of my salvation.*
> *19 The Lord God is my strength, and he will make my feet like hinds' feet, and he will make me to walk upon mine high places. To the chief singer on my stringed instruments.*

We went back to our wagons and did some mending, cleaning, and some relaxation before supper. I walked to the river and I could see clothes, wagon parts, and dead animals stuck among the reeds and willows in the river on the other side.

At six o'clock, we had supper of ham and beans, cornbread, and sweetbread with a sugar glaze. It amazed me what Mama Julia and my sisters could create for meals on the trail. The meals were always good and different. I heard others talk about having the same meal almost every day. I was very grateful I was part of this family.

After supper, we built a fire and sat around talking and enjoying each other's company. Sarah and Isaac came for supper and stayed with us around the fire. We visited until about ten o'clock, had prayers, and went to bed.

Monday, August 18: Day 44

I woke up at four o'clock, did my chores. Not much milk and the eggs were down also. Could be because of the heat. The stock seemed to be doing well. We applied salve and wrap to many of the oxen legs, as we had done for the last many days. Overall, things were well. It was important to change out oxen teams. We had passed too many dead and dying animals in our travels before we had reached Fort Laramie.

We packed our tents, had breakfast of pancakes with berry-spread and salt bacon. We had prayers and hit the trail at half-past six.

We travelled for about two miles, climbed a steep bluff, and descended on a rough and rocky trail. These trails shook the wagons badly. I was glad Pa had put an extra set of leaf springs on our wagons, especially for Mother and the two little ones, and, of course, Gerald the turtle. I could not imagine riding in some of the wagons that did not have good leaf springs. There was an elderly Sister in our company of fifty who had some difficulty walking. She said she preferred to walk than to riding in the bumpy wagon she was sharing with another family.

We finally left the rocky trails and continued to good trails on a bluff. We often lost sight of the river. The area was full of high bluffs on our side of the river and low rolling hills on the south side for miles. There were plenty of cottonwoods and willows along the river, but very few plants away from the river. We had not seen many animals, except a few antelope at a distance on the bluffs. We could see for miles. To the south, we could still see Laramie Peak and some mountains to the west.

We traveled another fourteen miles and we, once again, came back to the river. We traveled another mile and at four o'clock, we found a place with some grass, wood, and good water. We encamped and spread out along the river because there was not enough grass for the stock in one place.

We did not need to corral the stock because of the natural corral created between the river and our wagons. We did not do the usual formation of circling the wagons. The first company of fifty went on ahead for a little over a half mile and stopped. They stayed in formation as they were traveling.

Our company followed and stopped about five hundred yards from the first company. We did chores, unpacked, set up the tents, gathered firewood, and had supper of dumplings and sweetbread. We sat around the fire for a while, talking about the beautiful land we had passed through for the last few days.

I walked down to the river and looked west along the river at all the wagons and the little fires by the wagons. It was an impressive sight.

It was my night to stand guard. However, because of the safety of the area we had encamped, we did not need guards. We then had prayers and I went to bed at the usual time of nine o'clock.

Tuesday, August 19: Day 45

I woke up at four o'clock, did chores. A little more milk, but still a few eggs. We loaded our tents, tended to the stock, and had breakfast of mush and biscuits. I had always liked mush, even in Kanesville. I liked it because it stayed with me longer and I did not get hungry until supper. We had prayers and hit the trail at half-past six.

The trail was good for the first five miles, then we climbed some steep hills. We meandered through hills and lowlands for about a mile, then we came out on the river bottom. We followed the river for about two miles. We had to climb another couple of hills that caused great delays.

Once on top of a bluff, a big thunderstorm came upon us and caused us to hunker down until it had passed. It drenched us, but quickly passed. The trails were very muddy now and our wheels were sinking in deeply. This soil had a lot of clay, so when it rained, we sank down into the mud. When the mud dried, our tracks made deep, hardened ruts that appeared to remain until the next rain. There were times we left the trail for a short distance to avoid ruts made by others. Now, we were making ruts in the trail that we disliked so much, and others would have to leave the trail because of us.

The rain brought out the sweet smell of the sagebrush. I loved that smell. The rain also refreshed the stock. This had been a different kind of rainstorm than the ones at home that had seemed to last a long time. Those rains tended to wear everyone down. These rains were refreshing and seemed to give us energy. We dried out quicker.

We stayed on the bluffs, climbing over hills and down ravines for about five miles. Then we came to some flat lands and could see the river again. We traveled down another dry creek-bed ravine until we came back to the river. The trail along the river was a good trail, and we traveled at a quick pace. We came upon some coal beds in rocks. Pa asked James and Sam to stay behind and see if they could dig out some and see if it would burn.

After a couple hours, James and Sam came riding back, saying the coal was too weathered to fire up. If they had had more time, they could have probably dug some out, but that would have taken a day or two.

As we traveled, we noticed an interesting thing that happened when the ground dried in shallow pools along the trail. The layer of mud on the top curled up. Some had curled all the way around until it had made a circle. When it got hard, it crunched as we walked on it. When we saw a dried pond of curly mud, we raced to see who could crunch the most mud. We had to be careful, sometimes there would be deep mud under the curled mud and could sink to our ankles.

At five o'clock and after traveling about fourteen miles, we encamped at a place where the Platte River split around and created an island.

As I did my chores, Pa told me to gather up my youth company and go fishing. He pointed to the head of the island. "You should have good luck there."

The water was swift and deep. As soon as we put in our lines, we had a heyday. We caught catfish and walleye almost each time we put in our lines. Within an hour, we had caught thirty-three fish. Charles was constantly running back and forth between our wagons and to the river to collect more.

Izzy and Herk explored as they fished. I noticed Herk pick something up and show it to Izzy.

"That is an Indian arrowhead. Do not pick it up because they are bad luck," said Izzy as she knocked it out of his hand, sending the arrowhead to the ground.

Herk picked it back up. "Why is it bad luck?"

Izzy replied in her snooty Izzy-tone, "Because it missed."

Herk looked at her, shook his head, picked up the arrowhead and put it in his shirt pocket. Then they went back to catching fish.

I should mention most every person of our youth company had at least two pockets sewn on their clothes, whether it was shirts, trousers, dresses, or aprons. I had noticed that, when we had free time, many of the young women at camp were busy sewing pockets on every outer piece of clothing for almost everyone. Izzy's idea of pockets was catching on throughout the company.

As we sat on the edge of the Platte, catching fish almost every time we put our line in the water, Hanna said, "I don't know what the big deal about fishing is. It is so easy. Anyone can do it."

I laughed and said it was not always this easy. I told her that it was easy for her because she was pretty.

Just then, I heard Izzy yell out, "Eewwwee. Are you kidding me?

You just said that. I cannot believe you said that!"

That made Hanna and me blush.

Izzy gave us that disgusted Izzy-look and said, "I am finished with this fishing and fishy slimy talk."

Hanna and I continued fishing as Izzy called out to Herk, "Come on, let's go back to the wagons and leave these two alone."

Herk stood there with his pole in his hand. "But I am fishing and catching fish and having fun."

"Herk," demanded Izzy, "let's go to the wagons and maybe you can get some candy."

Herk hesitantly obeyed, dragging a large catfish on his line through the grass and dirt. They went to the wagons and Herk got his candy.

Hanna and I caught about a dozen more fish and went back to our wagons. Mama Julia had Mrs. Laroy, Mrs. Bradshaw, and the sisters help with preparing supper. The Laroys, Harts, Carters, Bradshaws, Neils, and Terrys joined us for a good fish dinner. We sat around the fire, talked, and sang songs. We gathered, had prayers, and went to bed.

Wednesday, August 20: Day 46

I woke up at four o'clock and did my chores. The milk and eggs were increasing. I packed the tents and we loaded our wagons, had breakfast of eggs, salt bacon, and cornbread. Finished packing our wagons, had prayers, and hit the trail at half-past six.

We traveled along the Platte River bottom. The trail was good and made easy travel. We traveled about four miles, climbed a small hill, and traveled along the bluff looking over the river. Looking down at the river, we started noticing bones and dead stock at various degrees of decomposition. We also noticed clothing, pieces of wagons, and large hewed logs washed up along the banks. As we traveled, the debris field seemed to increase. As we passed, looking at all the debris, caused an unsettling feeling to come over all of us. We noticed that our paces had slowed also. Captain Reed rode and visited each company. He explained to us that, what we were seeing and the uneasy feeling we were experiencing, was true and acceptable due to the circumstances.

Captain Reed explained, "This debris is coming from the river crossing about ten miles upriver, close to where we will stop for the day. Travelers taking ferries had some of their stock, wagons, and other items fall off the ferries. Sadly," he added, "the debris was also from those who did not take the ferries and attempted to ford or float across the river. Too many deaths and loss has occurred at these crossings. So much of this tragedy could be avoided if people took time to properly secure their wagons and stock to the ferries, and patiently wait to cross at suitable locations."

Our company of ten gathered around Captain Reed as he continued to talk while he looked mainly at Captain Manus and his murmuring group of three families. "This is why we traveled on the north trail. It has been more difficult, but we avoided crossing the Platte River twice and cut at least three to four days off our trip." Captain Read continued as he pointed to the debris, "This ungodly feeling that has overcome this company is about the spirits of those who have come so far to only to lose so much. I will not let this happen to us."

He slowly looked over our company of ten and said, "If there is anyone who thinks they can preside over this company better than I, please speak now, and I will freely give up my post."

We all looked at Captain Reed with confidence and support.

Captain Reed walked over to Captain Manus and his group. "None of you have anything to say?"

They all looked down at the ground, unable to look Captain Reed in the eyes.

"This is a warning, Harvey. Get right with the Lord and get right with the company."

They said nothing as Captain Reed turned to us, tipped his hat, got back on his horse, and said as he rode off, "Get these wagons moving."

We traveled along the bluffs, still able to see the river on most of our travel. We could see large groups of wagons in the distance. They looked like little toys. There were great numbers of wagons near the ferry crossing. The river turned north and was now flowing north and south. We crossed many shallow ravines, climbed and descended many smaller hills until we descended once again to the river bottom where we followed the trail through a very narrow place between the cliffs and the river. Everyone traveled safely though this area.

We traveled another two miles and at four o'clock, we encamped about a mile from the ferry crossing under a large limestone formation. This formation had two giant outcrops: a smaller one in front of a larger one. There were more outcrops behind them to the north.

Captain Reed chose this location because the grass was good. Farther up the river, the stock coming across the river ate the grass to the ground.

We also had wood that we could easily gather along the river. Wood that drifted up on the banks. Captain Reed said not to drink, fish, or use this water because of all the dead animals along the river. Other than gathering firewood, we could not touch any clothes, blankets, or anything else that looked to have regular contact by people. The fear of illness still lingered in our minds.

We were however, allowed to go to the crossing and visit with some of the travelers crossing the river. We corralled the stock, unpacked the wagons, pitched our tents, did chores, and had time to go to the crossing. The youth company went about a mile upriver to the crossing. There was a ferry that had been constructed and seemed to be working well. Just like the ferry at home, it took a while to cross. Although it was mid-August, due to the heavy rains during the year, the ferrymen said the Platte River was still running higher than normal.

If we crossed at the ferry, it would take a little more than half-day for the ferry operators to cross a company our size. On the other side of the river were seven to eight companies our size, waiting to cross over to our side.

Just as Captain Reed said, there were others going further upriver to try to ford or float.

The ferry operators were doing a good job trying to avoid oxen and other stock that went swimming downriver. Most of the stock was able to swim to safety on either side of the river, but a few did not make it and drowned. There was a lot of confusion as people were trying to gather their stock from both sides of the river. This was an unfortunate and confusing mess.

We went a little more than a mile to where others were coming out of the river. We could tell immediately that this was no way to cross a river as deep and swift as the Platte River. While some came out with most of their provisions dry, others were coming out with the wagons nearly full of water. The mass disorganization of people trying to come out of the river was very troubling to watch. Women were crying while sorting through their wagons, throwing things out. The men were trying to separate out their oxen from others and deal with the constant arguments that came about because of this chaos. Others who had lost oxen were bartering with those who had enough to trade. I was sure grateful for Captain Reed and the decision to take the north trail.

After a couple hours, the youth company headed back to our wagons. When we arrived, the sight of our organized wagons, happy people being busy, making supper, and sitting around talking, was very welcome. We arrived at our wagons in time for supper of dumplings, dandelion greens, bread, and apple cobbler. Izzy and I told the others what we had seen and how sad it was.

Just then, we saw a broken wagon, barrels, and, I am not sure, but it looked like a body floating by, I hoped it was not what it appeared to be. We could do nothing but watch this awful sight. Others from our camp went to the river's edge, watched, and quietly said prayers.

I was so grateful we took the new north trail and stayed north of the Platte River our whole journey. I was glad Captain Reed was our captain and we did not have to wait and cross the Platte River with all that delay and confusion.

We made a fire, more to distract the mosquitos than for warmth, and sat around talking until it was time to go to bed. We had prayers and went to bed.

Thursday, August 21: Day 47

I woke up at four o'clock, did chores. Milk and eggs were up to normal again. We packed our tents, loaded wagons, and had breakfast of mush and cornbread. We finished packing, said prayers, and hit the trail.

Pa called us together and said that, because we were passing many people without oxen or stock, we might have to defend our stock. We were changing our formation. Pa would be with the lead wagon and oxen on the west side where the people had gathered near the river. Mama Julia would be on the second wagon, leading that team of oxen on the west side, and Rebecca on the third wagon, leading those oxen on the west side. James, Ben, Dottie, and I were with the stock on the west side, while Sam, Izzy, and Gabe were on the east side with the stock. Pa, James, Ben, and Sam had their revolvers and rifles in hand as we moved along the trail. Izzy was complaining she needed to arm herself, so Pa let her have her gardening hoe.

As we passed, many of the travelers were trying to gather their belongings along the river. Other people asked Pa to give or sale some of our stock. Pa and my brothers kept telling the people they were not for sale. Some of them were rude and started calling us names. Others looked like they wanted trouble, but seeing Pa and my brothers carrying rifles and Dragoon Revolvers, they controlled themselves and just called us names.

After traveling about two miles, the trail split from the river and we were free from insults and danger. It was hard to say no to such destitute people, but the stock we were protecting was not just ours, but belonged to the whole company of fifty and some belonged to the Church. We traveled another three miles and had a steady climb until we reached the top of a bluff. From this point, we could see long lines of wagons stretching for miles on the other side of the river. There was another long line of wagons waiting to cross the river what looked like about twenty miles ahead.

We traveled another five miles, traveled down the bluff, and crossed a shallow creek. Captain Walton asked James, Ben, and some other hunters to go secure meat. We traveled along the river bottom for another five miles and at four o'clock, we encamped at a nice location on the other side of a large bend in the trail. There was enough grass, wood, and water. We corralled the stock, did chores, unpacked and pitched tents, and had some free time.

Pa said I should gather the youth company and go fishing. So, we went fishing. We caught mostly catfish and walleye. We found we could secure our poles and could play while keeping an eye on our lines. By about six o'clock, we had caught about thirty-nine fish.

We returned just as James and Ben came into camp with eight out of twelve men packing antelope. James went to Captain Walton and asked if he and the other hunters could go out and hunt again in the morning. I heard James tell Captain Walton that it was best to hunt antelope in the morning before it got hot and while they were lying down. James told Captain Walton that, because antelope do not sweat, if they ran or got get hot, their sweat tainted the meat, and the meat would be tougher and not taste as good.

Captain Walton stood looking at James for a minute without saying a word. Then Captain Walton reached up, hit James in the shoulder, and said, chuckling, "This is why you are the hunter. Do as you wish and be safe."

James thanked him and came back to the wagons.

We all gathered. Well, seven families gathered with us and had a good feast. After supper, we had a big fire, talked while we kids played. We gathered and had prayers and went to bed.

CHAPTER 15
CONTROL ONLY THINGS YOU CAN CONTROL

Friday, August 22: Day 48

Pa had to wake me up at four o'clock. I was tired. I did my chores, packed our tents, and packed the wagons. Had breakfast of eggs, salt ham, and the rest of the cornbread. We had prayers and hit the trail at half-past six.

We traveled along the river bottom for about four miles, then climbed another bluff. On top of the bluff, we could see hundreds of wagons lining up to cross on the ferry just up the trail. We crossed ravines, and after another four miles, we descended on to the river bottom again.

The operators of this ferry were members of the Church, sent by Brother Young. There were some travelers who were not members of the Church and did not want to pay "Mormons" to cross the river. We hardly saw any debris along the river. A few fragments here and there, but not the death and loss we had seen a few days earlier.

We traveled the bottom until we came to the ferry crossing. We said hello to all the friendly travelers. Many were Church members. I talked to the couple of brethren working the ferry about fishing. They said it was mainly Walleye and Catfish. However, because of the heavy rains, some trout had swam down from the high country. They had caught only three in the last few months but said it was possible. I wanted to stay and visit, but if we stayed longer, we might have caused a holdup for those gathering as they came across on the ferry.

We continued, crossed a creek, and climbed another bluff.

The land we were crossing reminded me of the area we had crossed at the beginning of the week. Beautiful colors of soil and the ability to see for miles in all directions. This was a beautiful and solitary place. I wished we could live in this area.

We traveled another four miles and descended a steep sandy hill. Captain Reed said the scouts found a suitable place to encamp a little over a mile off the trail. We made a right turn and left our companion, the

Platte River, for good. *Thank you for taking care of us.*

We then followed the creek until we came to a clearing suitable for all the company and stock. After traveling sixteen miles, at three o'clock, we made our encampment. The creek was clean and cool, enough for the stock and us. There was plenty of firewood and very good grass. We placed wagons at the top of the canyon and at the bottom, creating a natural corral, allowing the stock to graze freely.

James and the hunters came into camp with another seven fresh antelope. That would be enough meat for the company for a couple of days.

As soon as we formed the wagons and were about to start chores, Sister Terry screamed, "Snakes. Snakes." She jumped into the wagon.

Nellie Terry, who was fifteen years old, came running towards our wagons screaming, "Snakes. Kill the snakes." She ran past Pa, James, and Sam and ran up to Izzy. "Izzy, please get rid of the snakes," Nellie said crying.

Izzy told her to calm down and quit screaming. Izzy walked towards our wagon and Pa met her holding her garden hoe. Pa smiled at her and asked if she needed any help.

Izzy rolled her eyes and shook her head. "Uh . . . no," she said walking away.

Pa held on to the hoe, looking at Izzy. "Kill them. Do not catch them. If they are bull snakes, let them be. Do not kill the bull snakes."

Izzy took the hoe and gave Pa her annoyed look. "Oh, alright. Be right back." She turned to Nellie. "Do you want to come?"

Nellie froze where she stood and just shook her head no.

Izzy laughed and went to work on ridding the camp of the snakes. Within no time, she was carrying two headless rattlesnakes. She said there were a couple more snakes, but those snakes were harmless.

Nellie stood there looking at Izzy holding the snakes. "How can you tell?"

Izzy chuckled. "You ask them, silly." Izzy walked to our last wagon, set the snakes on the back of the wagon, and began skinning and removing the meat.

Nellie walked back to her wagon, muttering to herself, "How do you ask them?"

We did our chores, unpacked the tents. We did not always sleep in the tents, but they needed to be set up for the women to do their thing, whatever that was. I was glad I did not need a tent to do my thing, whatever that might have been as well. Sometimes I just did not get some things in this life.

We unpacked our wagons and Captains Reed and Walton came riding up, looked at Izzy cleaning her rattlesnakes.

Captain Reed shook his head, chuckling. "We are staying here for a couple of days. We have good water, grass, and wood." He asked Pa if he could set up shop and do some wagon mending, if needed. He also asked us to gather some men and build a dam down the creek by the secluded bend so the women could bathe.

As they turned their horses, Captain Walton asked Izzy if he could buy the skins from her.

Izzy smiled and handed Captain Walton the skins. "No charge, sir. Thank you for all you do for us."

Captain Walton took the skins. "Thank you, young lady. You are very kind."

They both tipped their hats and rode off.

We all stood there with looks of surprise on our faces, staring at Izzy until she gave us that annoyed Izzy look. "I can be nice, too, you know." As she turned and walked away, she yelled, "Herk, Herk, come on. We are going hunting."

Pa asked James to go to Mr. Laroy and ask him if he could gather some men and start on the damn while we set up shop. Within a few minutes, Mr. Laroy came up with all the men except for Captain Manus and Brother Barker.

Mr. Laroy proudly exclaimed, "We are going to build a bully of a bathing hole."

Pa smiled. "Of course, you will, and after the women are done, we men need a bath, too."

Mr. Laroy chuckled with a mischievous grin on his face. "Indeed, we do, but why wait? Let us join them. It will be more fun."

Some of the brethren blushed as Pa and James laughed. Pa said, "Come now, Mr. Laroy, let us not cause temptation for our womenfolk."

Mr. Laroy laughed and the brethren blushed again as they walked down past the bend in the creek.

We finished unpacking the tools and set out to make fires to make charcoal. Once we had enough logs cut from tree fall, and a hole dug for the forge, we built fires at the head and the mouth of our canyon with guards at each end. This was to ensure Indians or travelers could not come into camp without an escort. Another reason was that we noticed bear tracks. Our fires would keep them away as well.

It was around half-past five. Most of our unpacking and setting up was completed. We had a fine dinner of antelope, bread, and berry cobbler. I prefer the back straps of the antelope, it is more tender and tasty. The youth company played games as we hooked up with some of the other kids in the whole company. We ran and played from the top of our canyon to the bottom many times. We enjoyed going to the top and talking to Brother Brown, who was standing guard, and teasing him by asking where his new lady friend went. He took it in stride, just laughed, and threw rocks at us when we came around. We felt a little sorry for Brother Brown. He was assigned guard duty the entire time we were there.

Around ten o'clock, we returned, sat around the fire with the grownups, and talked for a little while, then we had prayers and went to bed. It was nice to know we were not traveling the next day. Everyone needed a rest. In fact, even the mosquitos were giving us a break that night.

I stayed up a little longer, alone with my candle, writing and pondering on a poem I had recently memorized while walking: Longfellow's "Psalm of Life."

> *Life is real! Life is earnest!*
> *And the grave is not its goal;*
> *Dust thou art, to dust returnest,*
> *Was not spoken of the soul . . .*
> *Let us, then, be up and doing,*
> *With a heart for any fate;*
> *Still achieving, still pursuing,*
> *Learn to labor and to wait.*

Saturday, August 23: Day 49

I woke up at six o'clock, did chores, and went to help Pa and my brothers gather charcoal from the fires around the canyon. As we collected charcoal, we could see groups of women going down to the bathing pond. Some were carrying clothes to wash. This went on all day, and some women went two and three times with the little ones. Even Mother went down with Cate and James, Jr. All the people that came back from the pond had smiles and looks of refreshment as they returned to their wagons. The next day, it would be the men's turn, but until then, we had wagons to mend.

We had breakfast of eggs, bacon, and pancakes with butter and berry-spread. We had not had this much breakfast since we had left Kanesville. Looking around, it looked like some were so full they needed a nap, but duty never took breaks, and would not stop until the job was finished. We fired up the forge. Mr. Laroy was back at Pa's side, while my brothers received assistance from Brother Terry, Hart, and Mr. Bradshaw.

Brother Hart looked to be more of a hindrance than a help. Brother Hart was a college teacher, and he was always asking why things were done the way they were doing it. My brothers put up with him and, when they needed a break, they sent him on errands. Brother Hart did not mind running errands. He was willing to do anything that they asked him to do.

About halfway through the day, Nellie Terry came to the shop. We all thought she wanted to see her father, but it was not until Pa took a break, waiting for another wagon, that she approached Pa.

"Brother Killian, may I ask you a question?"

Pa gave her a puzzled look.

"Brother Killian, what did Izzy mean by 'I should ask a snake if it was harmful.' I am not a stupid girl, and I know snakes do not talk. Was she just being mean?"

Pa cleared his throat and put his tools down. "Well, Miss Terry, snakes do talk. Most snakes we have seen in this area are rattlesnakes and bull snakes. Bull snakes will chase you and could bite you, but they are not poisonous and do not talk. Rattlesnakes, on the other hand, are dangerous and could kill us, so they warn us if we get too close. Like us, they do not want to be hurt or killed, so if you get close, close enough to talk with them, they will rattle, giving you a warning. When you hear them rattle, you best back up and run away, and usually, the snake will go in the other direction. So, no, Izzy was not being mean. In her own way, if the snake talks, it is harmful."

Nellie stood there thinking. "Oh, all right. Izzy is one smart little girl."

Pa chuckled. "Yes, she is."

My brothers and I started laughing.

Ben blurted out, "If you get too close to Izzy, and you can hear her talking, you best back up and run away."

We all laughed.

Nellie chuckled and said, "I can see that. Now, if you will excuse me, have a fine day." She walked over to Brother Terry and kissed him on the cheek and left.

Another wagon rolled up and we went back to work.

People brought wagons and parts to the shop until about three o'clock, then people stopped coming. We did not disassemble the shop until we knew no one else needed our services. After Brother Hart, Charles, and I cleaned up the shop area and all the shavings and wood scraps, we put them into bags for later use on the trail. Pa dismissed me so I could lead the youth company on explorations.

I gathered up the youth company and we were ready to go exploring when Captain Walton announced that the bathing pond was available for all children twelve years old and younger. This ruined my ranks. I no longer had a company except for Hanna and Charles. Charles wanted to stay by the wagons so Hanna and I went exploring.

I grabbed my garden hoe and was about to take off when Hanna said she wanted her own garden hoe. We asked Dottie if we could take hers. Dotty said, "Yes," and warned Hanna it was a deadly weapon in the right hands. They both giggled and we went exploring.

We traveled up the south slope but found nothing of interest. Almost halfway down on the north slope, we noticed a shallow cave. I threw some rocks in to see if we could hear any rattles. We heard nothing, so it was safe to go in. Once inside, we found a few bones, some knapping shards, and a few nearly completed arrow and spearheads that had broken points. We pretended we were explorers.

I told her all about Jim Bridger, but she corrected me on about every fact I told her. Then she went on to tell me more about Mr. Bridger. After she finished her lesson on Jim Bridger, it was my turn to tell her all about Lewis and Clark. I told her that Grandpa Killian was on the expedition and that he had kept their journal. She looked at me with awe-struck eyes until I confessed that Grandpa made up this story. She started laughing and said that would be a fun way to learn history. Then she went on to tell me all about Lewis and Clark.

Hanna resembled a smaller version of her father, Brother Hart, always giving information on everything. Hanna asked me about Mother, Mama Julia, James, and why Izzy was so odd.

When she got on the topic of Izzy, I just chuckled. "She is just Izzy."

Hanna laughed and said, "Indeed, she is Izzy, and there are none like her."

I laughed. "Thank goodness."

We explored a little more around the cave, picked up some arrow and spearheads, then noticed that it was getting late, so we headed back with our garden hoes in hand.

When we returned, we told everyone about our adventure and showed them our treasures. Izzy asked if we found any snakes and we said no. Izzy looked disappointed, went back to her chair, and sat down, returning to sharpening her knife.

Hanna watched as Izzy spit on a stone and sharpened her knife. Hanna turned to me and whispered, "Thank goodness there is only one."

I just chuckled and sat down in my chair, and Hanna went back to her family.

While exploring, the men in our company made a big fire ring and had gathered enough wood for a couple of days. Soon, all the families were bringing food over to our long wagon tables.

I looked over to Mama Julia. "It looks like we are going to have another feast and dance, Mama Julia."

She nodded her head yes and whispered, "Look who else is joining us."

I looked over and to my surprise, it was Captain Manus, the Barkers, and the Pierce family.

Captain Manus called everyone together, thanked everyone for coming to gather, and asked Brother Pierce to say a prayer on the food. He did so and we all helped ourselves to beef, antelope, dandelion greens, and breads of many kinds. They lit the fire as we sat around eating. When all had enough supper, we cleaned our plates and those that had room in their stomachs helped themselves to several pies and cobblers.

After a little while, Mr. Laroy fired up his fiddle, accompanied by Brother Hart's guitar and Brother Carter's harmonica. It did not take long before people were laughing and dancing. What a good night this was. I did not have to ask Hanna to dance. She asked me. Maybe she knew I was still too shy to ask. Well, she really did not ask. She came over, grabbed my arm, and led me to the dance area. Herk still had no luck with Izzy, but danced with some of the other girls in the company.

As the music played, others started coming over just as they had a few weeks before. Some brought instruments and joined the band. It was interesting to me how these men, who did not know each other very well, let alone practiced, could create harmony, and keep tune with songs they were not familiar with until that moment. I reckoned harmony kept us together.

I looked towards Mother and Pa just in time to see the most disturbing sight I wished I had never seen or ever wanted to see. Pa walked over to Mother, reached out his hand to invite her to dance, and Mother slapped Pa's hand away, giving Pa a scowling look that would have sent most men to their grave. Pa put his hand on her shoulder and stood there. A few minutes later, Izzy grabbed Pa and led him to the dance area. I know Mother blamed Pa for Edward's death, but it was no one's fault. I know Mother wanted to stay with Grandmother and Grandpa Batchelor, but her place was with her family.

That look Mother gave Pa made my stomach upset. I walked over to the stock, shaking. I was very upset. I started talking to the stock and kind of praying to Heavenly Father. "I do not understand this life. How can Mother be so mean to someone like Pa? What would make Mother happy?" I walked around, trembling. "Why did not Pa let Mother stay with Grandmother and Grandpa Batchelor? What stops Pa from marrying Mama Julia? They look happy together. Other families seem to get along. Look at the Harts and the Terrys. Hanna has more than one mother. She has three and they all seem very happy. I do not understand."

I picked up a brush, walked over to one of our cows, and started brushing her. "I am still just a kid, but I am trying to be an adult. Do I have to understand these things before I become an adult? I just cannot get over the look Mother gave Pa. It was so mean and hurtful."

I started brushing the cow's other side. I thought maybe I should talk to Mother, but I was afraid she would give me that same glare she gave Pa. "I do not even want to talk to my mother or be around her after what I have seen. I will sleep with the stock. Why not? Unicornis always sleeps next to Izzy every night."

I turned to put the brush away and there was Nellie Terry, standing behind me. "How long have you been here?" I asked.

"I followed you over. I saw the same thing you did, and I heard everything you said."

I got mad. "That is none of your business. You should not have listened to me talking with our Heavenly Father."

Nellie walked over to me, "You were not talking to our Heavenly Father. What I heard was a young man whining about things he does not understand. Willy, I like you. You are a smart young man, but you are trying to control things you cannot control."

"What do you mean?" I asked.

"You want to change your mother. Well, guess what? You cannot change her. Only she can change herself. You want to change your father's situation with your mother and your Mama Julia, but you cannot do that either. You want everyone to be happy, but guess what? If Heavenly Father will not do that, then Willy Killian should not try. That is not how things work. Your happiness, Willy, will only come if you make yourself happy. If your happiness depends on others being happy, then you will never be happy.

"Willy, frustration comes when you do not have control of a situation or you cannot change things you wish you can. There are some things in life you cannot control or change, so do not try. You will only end up frustrated."

I just looked at her, listening as she continued.

"When my father was asked to take on another wife, it turned our home upside down. We cannot change God's plan. My mother told me to control only the things I had the ability to control, and right now, that must start with me, Nellie Terry's happiness. That is the only thing I can control. Leave the people changing to our Heavenly Father, not to Willy Killian. Do you understand what I am saying?"

"I think so."

Nellie took my hands and held them in hers, "Willy, if you want to make your mother and father and those around you happy, you have to first make Willy Killian happy and leave the rest to our Heavenly Father. If you do not, it will make you very, very unhappy, and that will make everyone around you very unhappy. Control only the things you can control. And what can you control?"

"So, what you are saying is, I, Willy Killian, can only control Willy Killian?"

She gave me a hug and said, "Let's go dance."

As we walked back to the dance area, she asked, "Does Izzy's bull really sleep next to her tent?"

"His name is Unicornis, and yes, he does."

Nellie chuckled. "Well, I guess that sister of yours is the only one I have met that can control more than just herself. What a sister you have."

I just looked at her and smiled. I enjoyed the rest of the night dancing and playing. I had a couple helpings of pie, played a while, then we gathered for prayer and went to bed.

I am sorry for whining, I will be more grownup and change only the things I can control . . . me, William Phillip Killian.

Sunday, August 24: Day 50

I woke up at six o'clock, did chores. Milk and eggs were more than average, which was a good sign. We loaded the shop tools and forge in the wagons, had prayers, and had breakfast of slices of beef, biscuits, and gravy.

After breakfast, we men went down to the bathing pond and gave ourselves a good washing and soaking. It felt good. Some kept their clothes on, washed their clothes, and then took them off to dry. I had never seen this done before. We stayed in the water for a couple hours just soaking and cleaning all the trail dust off.

After we dried off and changed into clean clothes, we headed back to our wagon for Sunday services. We went to the middle of the camp and listened to Brother Parker give a wonderful sermon from "Acts 9," the trail to Damascus. Saul converted and became Paul. Brother Parker made three points:

> *"1. The importance of true conversion. Saul was a persecutor of the saints, but his true conversion required the conversion and belief of those who he persecuted. Although they were already converts to Christianity, they needed to accept Saul's conversion and welcome him into the church.*
>
> *"2. We need to welcome all who experience true conversion. What if Saul/Paul was not accepted? What if the members of the church did not accept him into the church? The Apostle Paul was responsible for writing thirteen or fourteen books of the New Testament. Would those books have existed without the Apostle Paul? He traveled far converting thousands, setting up churches wherever he went. The Apostle Paul was very important in establishing and promoting the growth of the early church. Again, what would have happened if the members of the church did not welcome his conversion?*
>
> *"3. We never know who God sends through conversion. We do not know what God's plan is for each of us or know who we are in God's plan."*

We sang hymns, had prayers, and went back to our own wagons to prepare for the travels the next day. Had supper, did chores, double-

checked our wagons, had prayers, and went to bed.
	What a good visit in this canyon.

Monday, August 25: Day 51

I woke up at four o'clock, did chores, packed up the tents, and loaded the wagons. We had breakfast of mush and biscuits. Had prayers and hit the trail at half-past six.

We climbed out of the canyon and joined the old trail. The morning started cool, and we crossed a couple ravines and had good flat trail, dusty but good. We crossed a couple shallow creeks without any troubles. We traveled about six miles and about to go down off the bluff when a little old man in a cart, pulled by two mules, passed us making good time. He told us he was traveling alone. He said he started out with a few companions, but they had a falling out, so he was traveling alone. This cart business seemed to be the easiest of things on wheels. He did say, for safety, he tried to travel and encamp with others for safety.

Our company had to stop for a delay at the top of the bluff by a wagon that overturned in the first company of fifty. They did not distribute the load evenly in the wagon, which made it unbalanced. When it made a turn going down the hill, it overturned. No one was hurt, but there was some damage to the wagon and one of the wheels. They gathered up all the contents. Some food items, like flour and cornmeal were lost. They were trying to get it down the bluff on flat ground for repairs.

After about an hour, we made our descent and passed the accident sight. We also passed a grove of cedar trees along the edge of a ravine and made it to the bottom of the bluff. There were other items left or dropped by others all along the trail going down, mostly books. By the time we made it down, repairs on the wagon were complete and moved along. The trail was dusty and hot as we crossed a small creek. The stock took a couple licks and traveled on.

The land was colorful with red, grey, white, and brown soil, with a mix of green cedar trees and grey and greenish bushes. There were many small hills and ravines, which slowed our travel, but overall, it was beautiful country and easy travel. We had not seen any game but a few antelope in the distance. However, some hunters in the first company of fifty shot eight desert chickens. There were a few of crows or ravens. Because there were only two or three together at a time, I would have to say they were ravens. We crossed another creek and the stock grabbed a couple licks as we moved on. We traveled about six miles and passed a saleratus creek that looked and smelled bad.

We traveled another couple of miles and encamped at about five o'clock. There was no water, some grass, and the sagebrush provided wood for cooking. Because of the open area, we did not need to corral the stock. We unpacked and set up the tents and did chores. We camped by the point of a bluff and next to a horseshoe canyon formation about a mile away. It was still hot. The wind had blown constantly all day. Because of the wind, we did not have our bothersome companions, the mosquitos, bothering us. I did not miss them, but it did seem odd not to have them.

We had supper of stew, greens, bread, and sweetbread. After supper, we went exploring. We did not find anything of interest except for a spoon, part of a boot, pieces of broken barrels, books, and other items dropped or left behind. Gabe asked why this part of the trail was wider and trodden down more that the trail we had traveled on before.

I told the younger members of the youth company that travelers had used this trail for many years. The number of travelers had increased very much for the past six years. They asked why.

Hanna then corralled them together and explained, "From the eighteen-forties to eighteen-forty-five, explorers, trappers, and people going to Oregon and California to start a new life passed through this area."

Gabe asked about Indians.

Hanna smiled and said, "Of course, they came by here. They live here and have lived here a very long time." Hanna went on to explain, "In eighteen-forty-seven, some of the first members of our Church came past here to build the city of the Great Salt Lake, and that is where we are going." As we walked around, Hanna continued, "In eighteen-forty-nine, gold was discovered in California and then thousands of people came through here and are still traveling through here to go to the gold fields and to Oregon."

We headed back to our wagons, had prayers, and went to bed.

CHAPTER 16
INDEPENDENCE ROCK

Tuesday, August 26: Day 52

I woke up at four o'clock, did chores. Milk and eggs were still doing well. We packed our tents and wagons, had breakfast of salt bacon and biscuits, had prayers, and hit the trail at half-past six.

The morning was cool and the trail was sandy and rocky. We traveled a couple miles and went through what some called "Rock Avenue" and down a steep hill. The men and women walking next to the wagon brakes cautiously applied the brakes as we went down the hill. Close to the bottom, they took the brakes off and it gave the oxen momentum to make it up the sandy hill in front of us. The hill was steep and the sand and rocks made it harder. We reached the top and went down the other side.

The morning was still cool and we were seeing a couple snakes a safe distance away, warming themselves in the sun on the rocks. They were far enough away that we were unable to tell if they were bull snakes or rattlesnakes. We followed a shallow ridgeline down to the bottom and passed another alkali pond. We then followed the trail back up another small, but difficult sandy hill.

We followed the sandy, rocky trail, going down a small canyon. The stock could always smell good water long before we saw it. I could always tell when the stock smelled water because they began walking faster. A little after one o'clock, we made a turn into a small canyon and we could see Willow Springs about a half-mile down. We traveled down the hill to the springs, and we all had long, cool drinks of clean water. There was hardly any grass around. Others, before us grazed it down to the nubbin. The stock wandered for a little while, eating what they could find. We wanted to stay, but we knew we would have to climb that large sandy hill just ahead of us. We stayed for about an hour and began our climb.

We were the last ones to climb the sandy hill, so we watched and learned from the others going up. A slow, steady walk looked to be the best plan. It was our turn and we hit the trail. The trail was very sandy and, at times, we had to bring up oxen to double-team. As I was walking that slow, hard sandy climb, I had time to look around and concentrate on other things, like the giant anthills all around us. As the stock walked on or dragged their hoofs across the anthills, they opened the anthills up and hundreds of angry ants come running out. We tried to stay away from the angry pinchers. Believe me, they hurt!

We finally made it to the top, and we could see for miles ahead. Hanna pointed out the gap in the mountains ahead of us was Devil's Gate and Independence Rock. Since I knew she had never been in this place before, I asked her how she knew. She said it was because she was very smart.

Independence Rock

Brother Hart said, "Hanna knows because she heard Captain Reed tell us as we stopped at the top."

Hanna called out, "Pa, you are spoiling my story."

We chuckled as we moved on. We could see the Sweetwater River and Independence Rock and Devils Gate, but we knew it would be a day, maybe two, of hard sandy traveling before we got there.

Once we made it down the sandy bluff, we traveled down a deep steady ravine and up the other side. We were seeing dead animals along the trail as we traveled. The trail was getting better to travel. We went up another ravine and down the other side. At four o'clock, we encamped at a clear shallow creek. We had clean water.

The sagebrush made good fires for cooking and fires at each end of the corrals for light. I liked sagebrush fires because the bush had everything we needed for a fire. We could use the very thin sticks at the top to start fires, even after a rain. It had all the different sizes of sticks and branches to grow the fire from the beginning to a very large hot fire. The living plant burned as well. It smelled very good as we collected it, burned it, or traveled through it. I liked sagebrush.

The night would be very dark because of a waning moon. We pitched our tents, unpacked our wagons, did chores, and had supper of meat pies, cornbread, dandelion greens that we picked at Willow Springs because the greens were getting scarce, and honey. We all stayed near the wagons for the evening. There was not much around to explore. Too many dead stock nearby.

We later had prayers and went to bed.

Wednesday, August 27: Day 53

I woke up at four o'clock, did my chores. Milk was low and eggs were few. I needed to note that Cate's turtle Gerald was doing just fine. It had proved to be a good companion to Cate and little James. We packed the tents, packed the wagons, and had breakfast of pancakes and salt bacon. We finished packing, had prayers, gathered the stock, and hit the trail at half-past six.

The day started cool and the trail started good, but it became very sandy within a few miles. We crossed a dry creek bed, traveled for a little more than a mile, and crossed a shallow creek that fed into the creek we had been following. The sand had once again slowed our travels and made it very difficult for stock. We followed the creek but had to travel very slow, digging and pulling wagons out of the sand. By about eleven o'clock, the wind picked up again and caused additional difficulty. About four miles into our travels, we came across four wagons with oxen bones near the wagons. There were blacksmithing tools, shovels, picks, and other items left behind. They looked like these items were from the previous year's journeys or maybe a year before. Of course, we did not need any items and neither had anyone else who had traveled by that place.

We continued for about six miles and crossed what looked like a dried pond or lakebed with white alkali crust and sand under the crust. The wind whipped up this mixture. When it got in our eyes, it made our eyes sting. We did our best to keep the brim of our hats and bonnets down to keep the alkali sand out of our eyes. The sagebrush and other vegetation grew very low to the ground, so we did not have to worry about tripping as we walked. The alkali bed was only about a mile wide, and we came out into the heavy sandy trail again.

After traveling another few miles we turned left and came to our new friend that would take care of us, the Sweetwater River. I hoped she could help us like our old friend the Platte River. The Sweetwater River was not as big, but did look as if it had fish and another companion, the mosquito.

We found a place that had two large bends in the Sweetwater River, and at three o'clock, we encamped along the bend. The big bends created a natural corral for both companies of stock. The other sides of the river were cedar trees and the foothills of a mountain. The foothills were steep enough to prevent the stock from climbing. We had good water, little grass, and enough wood for cooking and fires at the corrals.

As we unloaded the wagons, I noticed about seventy-to-eighty Snake Indians riding and walking going east. We encamped about a mile from the trail. They traveled near us but did not stop. We later learned they were going to Fort Laramie to attend the treaty. I had always admired the Indians that seemed so at home in such a place where it looked that no one could live. I wondered if we could live in this area as they did. They did not have stock like we did, but they had the antelope, deer, and other animals, which appeared to be scarce in this area. They always appeared to have command of their surroundings. Interesting people.

We unloaded and pitched the tents, did chores, and the youth company went to the Sweetwater. We were surprised to see many catfish up and down the river. A little way down, there were shallow ponds full of reeds. As we walked towards the reeds, nearly a hundred small ducks flew up, circled around, came back, and landed out of sight.

Izzy told Unicornis to stay as she crept into the reeds. Within a few minutes, she came back and pulled on Hanna's dress. They whispered something, knelt down on the ground, and drew lines and circles. Then

Izzy and Hanna ran back to the wagons with Unicornis and returned with long pieces of string, leaving Unicornis at the wagons with Pa. We all asked what they were doing. They told us to be quiet and watch.

They went into the reeds and made a loud noise. The ducks flew off, circled, and returned. Izzy and Hanna came slowly out of the reeds, walking backwards and holding the ends of the string.

Hanna said, "Now!"

Hanna and Izzy pulled the string and the birds flew off again, but they pulled out two small ducks from the reeds.

"How did you do that," I asked.

Izzy said, "There are nests in there. We put a loop in the string and put it in the nest. When the ducks came back, they sat on the string and we caught them."

While Izzy, Hanna, Herk, and two other younger kids tried to catch ducks, Charles, I, and the others went catfish hunting. Within two hours, we had caught twenty-two fish, and the girls had caught eighteen birds.

We returned to the wagons and showed everyone our catch of the day. Everyone was in total awe at what we had brought back.

Pa said, "We have supper for tonight and tomorrow."

Brother Hart and everyone else were very happy at our accomplishment. Later, we heard the mothers comparing duck recipes. We had supper of ducks, fish dumplings, yucca roots, and raisin bread.

After supper, we went back to fishing and ducking. We were not as successful as on our first trip. Maybe the fish and ducks figured out what was going on. We brought back eight fish and no ducks.

We were about three miles away from Independence Rock. Hanna was going around to every wagon in the company, telling them about Independence Rock, the names that were on the rock, and the history of the travelers going to the rock. I was sure Hanna wanted to go over there, but it looked like there were at least a hundred wagons encamped at Independence Rock. I was sure the stock from the other wagons ate the grass down to the ground. We had prayers and then went to bed.

Thursday, August 28: Day 54

At a little before four o'clock, the voice of Hanna talking to Pa awakened me. As soon as I opened my eyes, she knelt under the wagon next to me.

"Do you know what we are going to do today?"

I rubbed my eyes, reaching for my suspenders. "Walking, like we do every day."

"No, silly. what we will see today?" Hanna said excitingly.

I knew what she wanted me to say, *Independence Rock*, so I kept avoiding the inevitable, "I . . . I reckon dirt, bushes, the sun, dust, ant hills, rocks, and maybe mosquitos?" I sat up to fasten my suspenders.

Hanna was getting irritated. "Well, of course, those things. Maybe not the mosquitos, but we were going to see Independence Rock! We are going to see the names of the many people who traveled through here. We will see the name of Mr. John Fremont and many other famous people, and maybe carve our name on the rock as well." She let out a very loud shriek of excitement.

All the sudden, we heard Izzy calling out from their tent, "Pa, shoot that varmint outside my tent making all that noise. That screech sounds like it is in pain, so put it out of its misery."

As I crawled out from under the wagon and stood up, Hanna said, "Izzy, it's just me, Hanna."

Izzy yelled out, "Pa, hurry, shoot it. It is beginning to talk."

Pa shook his head, looking at Hanna. "I am sorry, Hanna. They are not morning folks like you and I. I am looking forward to seeing Independence Rock and so will they, once they are up and moving."

Izzy yelled out, "Pa, there are more of them and one sounds like you. Shoot them. Shoot them."

Hanna looked over at me as I tried to find the wash bucket. "You are hopeless," she said and stomped back to her wagon.

"Wow, Independence Rock, that is exciting," I said to myself as I washed my face and finished getting dressed. I did my chores. Milk was low but eggs were good. We packed up the tents and blankets, packed the wagon, and had breakfast of eggs, ham, and biscuits. We finished packing the wagons, had prayers, gathered the stock, and hit the trail at half-past six.

The morning was cool and the trail was sandy as we headed for Independence Rock and beyond. We traveled almost two miles when we came onto Saleratus Lake. Some of the women gathered the powder to use in cooking and other uses. We had to be careful that the stock did not get into the lake or consume any of it. It would surely bloat the animals and kill them. It was interesting that the game in the area knew to stay clear, but animals unfamiliar with the area needed to learn the hard way.

We traveled another mile and there it was. We had our eyes on it for a couple days and now we were there. The company column stopped and we took the stock to the south side near the Sweetwater where there was some grass and good water. Brother Hart gave another lesson of the history of people that traveled through there. Izzy, Gabe, Herk, Hanna, and I ran around the rock, looking at names. We climbed on top and found more names. Some of the names that had the date carved in 1848 were starting to fade after three years.

We decided we wanted to put our initials in the rock, somewhere sheltered so they would last longer. We remembered seeing a small cave on the east side with a triangular entrance. We climbed down and ran over to find it. We all fit into the cave. I carved *W.P.K. 51* at the east entrance of the cave. Hanna also carved her *H.A.H. 51* next to mine on the right.

Izzy carved *IZZY* with a small circle by her name on the other side of mine near the back and close to the bottom. We asked her what the circle was for.

Izzy said, "It is a crown of course."

We helped put Gabe and Herk's initials below ours. Then we joined the many in the company that gathered in a cove just right of the cave and had an early lunch. We were interrupted by the sound of splashing in the river next to the rock. We jumped up and ran to the river and there were about twenty catfish rising, chasing bugs and smaller fish. They were causing a big commotion. We had enough fish and it was getting time to move on, or we would have tried to catch some. We went back to the cove and joined the others.

After about twenty minutes, Pa called us back to the wagons. As we headed back, I noticed Mama Julia coming from behind a boulder to the left of our cave. This boulder looked like it had fallen off the rock along time ago. The boulder had come to rest about three feet from Independence Rock. She did not see us as we followed up the dirt path between the boulder and Independence Rock. We found the name *GABBY* carved into the boulder, almost in the middle. We climbed down and went back to our wagons.

We crossed the Sweetwater River and continued for another six miles towards the giant V in the rock. I said to myself, "So, that is Devil's Gate." I wondered why a giant V in the rock could be a gate of the devil. I would have named it "Big V" or "Very Big V." I heard others call it, "The Twin Sisters," as well.

Oh, well, Devils Gate it is. Although I do not think that is an appropriate name.

As we traveled, a light rain joined us, but nothing to slow us down, only to make things a little muddy. We traveled about another two miles, and followed the trail through a narrow gap between the rocks on the south side of Devils Gate. This trail gap was wide enough to drive seven, maybe eight wagons side-by-side through the gap.

Captain Reed stood near the entrance of the narrow gap. It did not become clear why he stood there until we came to him. Captain Reed was standing next to a grave, making sure wagons and stock did not trample the grave. We passed through the gap and crossed a small creek.

As we looked back, the gap in Devils Gate was very narrow and the Sweetwater River flowed through it.

We traveled another three or four miles and at four o'clock, encamped along the Sweetwater. There was good grass, which was a welcome sight for the stock. There was good water and enough wood for cooking and for small fires throughout the night for the guards. There were cedar trees across the river if we needed wood, but I thought we had enough. The place we stopped had natural corrals for the stock. They could feed and water freely. We unpacked and set up the tents, unpacked the wagons, did chores, and had supper of duck, yucca roots, and apple cobbler.

After supper, the youth company, which now had seventeen members, went exploring. We all went together. However, we divided the company under two captains. I was one of the captains. I looked after ten kids. Charles Laroy was the other captain, and he looked after seven.

We were finding many items discarded by other people, either by mistake or on purpose. We were under strict instructions not to touch any clothing, blankets, or items worn by people. We found tools, like hammers, axes, shovels, hoes, sheep sheers, broken rifle stocks, stoves, chests, clothes, and books in abundance. We did not need anything, so we left them be.

It was starting to get dark. We headed back and went to our wagons. When we returned to camp, Pa called all of us together and pointed to the west. "Do you see that split in the mountain way off in the distance? The one that looks like a rifle rear sight? That is where we will stop tomorrow."

We all stood there looking at the landmark in the distance. It was always good to have landmarks to concentrate on as we were walking and our minds were napping.

We had prayers and went to bed.

Friday, August 29: Day 55

I woke up at four o'clock, did chores. Milk still down and eggs were good. Packed the tents and blankets, packed the wagons, and had breakfast of mush and cornbread. We finished packing the wagons, gathered the stock, had prayers, and hit the trail at half-past six.

The morning was cool with a slight breeze. The trail was sandy and very difficult. I was glad the stock had enough rest, water, and grass because the trail was difficult. If the trail would be like this all day, we would not go far. We traveled about four miles and the trail became worse. It was still sandy and now very bumpy. We were traveling up and down small hills all morning. The sand was dragging us down.

We said hello to a company going back to the States. They had about thirty wagons in three companies. They had only fifteen stock and two horses. They told us the trail would get better ahead. I hoped they were telling the truth.

As we continued, the trail remained sandy and difficult to travel. We came across another alkali lake and continued for another three miles. We made only thirteen miles, and at four o'clock, we encamped near the Sweetwater at the base of Split Rock. There was no grass and the scouts could not find any within our traveling distance. We did have good water with enough sticks to make fire for cooking. The sagebrush grew very low to the ground and the youth company ran around gathering dead sagebrush for cooking fires. Although the moon was still new, there was not enough little dead sagebrush to make fires tonight. There were a few cedars on the other side of the river and up the foothills. Pa said we did not need fires bad enough to destroy all vegetation. We corralled the stock near the Sweetwater, unpacked and set up tents and unpacked the wagons. I did my chores and we had supper of stew, bread, and berry cobbler.

We all stayed near our wagons, had prayers, and went to bed early.

Saturday, August 30: Day 56

Pa woke us up at four o'clock. I did my chores. Little milk and a few eggs. Packed up our tents, packed the wagons, and had mush, bacon, and biscuits. We had a heavy breakfast because Pa said we were going to have a long, hard day ahead. We finished packing our wagons, gathered the stock, had prayers, and hit the trail at half-past six.

The morning was cool. However, that did not last long. The sun soon became warm, then hot. We traveled about three miles and passed a company of saints with about two-hundred wagons. We learned they had camped there since Tuesday, fixing wagons and healing stock.

The trail was very sandy and difficult. We traveled another three miles, and I could see a few dead animals in different stages of decay. We followed the Sweetwater, going up and down ravines through the deep sand. At times, we had to double-team, which created delays. I saw a small group of antelope feeding in the distance.

We nooned close enough to the Sweetwater for the stock to get a few licks. The wind started to pick up, creating an already dusty trail even dustier. It stirred up a very fine dust. As we continued, we covered our mouths, noses, and wished we could do the same for the stock. About eight miles out, we parted from the Sweetwater and headed out into wide openness. There was a small mountain to the north and openness for miles to the south and ahead of us.

We continued and about two o'clock, the sky darkened and strong winds and rain came upon us. The rain was refreshing by keeping the dust down, but it made traveling a little harder. Mud coated the wheel rims, making it harder for the oxen. A few minutes later, the rain stopped and the wind let up a little, but did not stop.

It was now about three o'clock and I could not see anywhere close where we could stop. Mama Julia and Rebecca brought us bread, butter, with berry-spread. It was very welcome and soon lifted our spirits. We could see the Sweetwater, and after a mile and a very hard climb up a deep sandy hill, we came to the edge of the Sweetwater again.

We continued and the skies became cloudy but no rain clouds. This cooled us down a bit. After a while, I could see green in the distance. Captain Walton rode back to us and asked Pa to come up front. When Pa returned, he told us that Captain Reed thought it better to take the trail around the hills rather than attempt to cross the Sweetwater Three Crossings through narrow canyons. Pa said Captain Reed said the last time he crossed the Three Crossings, they lost a wagon and had damaged many others. We continued on the deep sandy trail.

Finally, after a few miles, the trail took us through a narrow gap and onto the hardest trail we had yet traveled. The trail climbed up a very steep and sandy hill. We double-teamed a few of the wagons. Some of the oxen were starting to stumble, and we immediately brought up reserves to help them out. We passed dead animals along this difficult sandy trail. After we traveled nearly three miles of the most difficult trail, we rounded a hill and could see snowcapped mountains in the far distance. We also set our eyes again on the beautiful Sweetwater River and plenty of grass. We finally climbed out of the sand.

At six o'clock and over twenty miles of hard traveling, we encamped on the Sweetwater. We found a place to let the stock water and graze freely without corralling. The water was good and there were enough sticks for cooking.

We did our chores, had supper of ham, beans, greens, and berry cobbler. Captain Walton informed us we were staying Sunday. After supper, we pretty much sat around and talked. Everyone was tired. We said prayers and went to bed.

CHAPTER 17
"ARE YOU ABANDON?"

Sunday, August 31: Day 57

We woke up at six o'clock, did chores. There was little milk and not many eggs. These last few days had been hard on man and beast. Finished my chores had breakfast of ham, biscuits, and gravy. We checked our wagons, but none needed repairs. We spent all morning tending to the stock. Many needed salve and wraps on their lower legs, as well as salve on their shoulders where the yokes had been rubbing. The sand was very damaging to these animals.

After lunch, we gathered for Sunday service. Brother Tucker from the first company of fifty gave a nice sermon on patience through adversity.

> *Proverbs 17:17:*
> *17 A friend loveth at all times, and a brother is born for adversity.*
> *2 Corinthians 4:16-18:*
> *16 For which cause we faint not; but though our outward man perish, yet the inward man is renewed day by day.*
> *17 For our light affliction, which is but for a moment, worketh for us a far more exceeding and eternal weight of glory;*
> *18 While we look not at the things which were seen, but at the things which were not seen: for the things which were seen were temporal; but the things which were not seen were eternal.*
> *James 1:2-4:*
> *2 My brethren, count it all joy when ye fall into diverse temptations;*
> *3 Knowing this, that the trying of your faith worketh*

patience.
4 But let patience have her perfect work, that ye may
be perfect and entire, wanting nothing.

While the adults spent time resting, reading, writing letters, and tending to the stock, the youth company went about trying to catch fish. We tried with rods and strings, but the river was shallow and the day was hot, so we went in after them. Most were small, about three to six inches. I did not know what type they were, but they looked good.

We put Charles's company about a mile up the river. Our company was at the other end. We walked towards each other, forcing the fish between us. Unicornis was a big help because he followed along behind us, scaring any fish that went through our company back to us. When we came together, we had fourteen fish and we were all very wet. We did this three more times and gathered up thirty-one fish. We also found black and red currant berries in abundance, and we gathered them up as well.

We cleaned the fish and brought them back to the wagons for those that wanted some fish. We had enough currants for everyone who wanted them. For supper, we had dumplings, water crest, cornbread, and currant berry cobbler. After supper, we did our chores, and the youth company went exploring. We also had three freight wagons pass our encampment. It seemed they were in a hurry because they did not stop to talk, only waved as they passed.

As it was getting darker, we went to our wagons, sat around, and visited. As we did, Captain Walton called all the men to a meeting. Pa came back and told us that Captain Reed received reports we will have to travel nearly twenty miles the next day in heavy sandy trails to find good grass and water.

"So, prepare and be stalwart, brothers and sisters," said Captain Walton. "We have done this before when we left the Platte after Fort Laramie, and we will do it again." We had prayers and went to bed.

Monday, September 1: Day 58

I woke up at four o'clock, did chores. We had more milk and eggs. Packed up the tents and wagons, had breakfast of mush and sweetbread. We finished packing the wagons, tended to the stock, applied salve, and wrap on the legs of the oxen that needed it. We had prayers, and hit the trail at half-past six.

The morning was cool as we started. The trail was sandy and traveling was slow. About three miles out, we could see the trail going up a medium-sized hill. If the trail was hard-packed, it would be an easy climb, but this was a very sandy trail. As we walked closer, we could see the first part of our column having a difficult time. Occasionally, they had to slow and have the men and women push the wagons. When we arrived, the wagons ahead of us churned the sand and the wheels sank deep. We went off the trail and made a new trail along the old trail. It was bumpier, but we did not sink down. Finally, we all made it to the top and continued along the sandy trail. Once on top, we could see another larger hill we needed to go up.

Whenever I saw difficulty in the trail ahead, I always thought of what Grandmother would say when we went wandering at home and lost the trail. "Oh well, what else are we going to do? Besides, we will never see this area again, so let's enjoy the trip." Then Grandmother would begin to whistle and we would join in.

So, when we had a hard trail, as usual, Sam and Ben would be first to see the difficult trail. They would breakout in a whistle. As soon as our eyes fixed on the difficult trail ahead, we would start whistling. Sometimes, even Pa would start the whistle and we would follow. I suppose whistling kept our mind off the hard walk, and it did help.

We traveled about a mile and went up the trail. Learning from our last climb, we went off the trail and found it easier. We had to watch out for large white rocks about the size of a loaf of bread, the low sagebrush, the prairie dog holes and mounds, and the anthills. We traveled about another mile and went down the hill, only to climb up another one. Once on top of the second hill, we could see some green.

Hanna came running back. "Hey, Willy, do you know what is ahead?"

Not caring, and wondering why she always had so much energy, I replied, "A spring with fresh water?"

"No, silly, it cannot be fresh water with all the white alkali around it. It is the Ice Sloughs. Sometimes, when you dig down about three or four feet, you can find ice."

I thought of how nice it would be if I could dig a hole, lay in it, and get away from the heat.

Hanna shouted, "Are you listening to me?"

"Yes. I am wondering how nice it would be to dig a hole to the ice, lay in it, and get away from the heat."

Hanna had to ruin my dream. "This late in the year, I am sure we will not be able to find ice. Just soggy alkali mud."

Then we heard Izzy's voice come from across the herd. "Hey, Hanna, we can still dig a hole and put you in it."

We chuckled. Hanna rolled her eyes, shook her head, and ran back to her wagon.

We traveled about two miles on sandy trails, but they were becoming packed down and easier to travel. We traveled through a couple sandy mounds with patches of taller sagebrush. We had to keep an eye out for rattlesnakes. Of course, this made Izzy excited as she ran to the wagon and got her hoe.

We came to the Ice Sloughs. Hanna was correct. They were just a muddy bog. We followed them for almost two miles and crossed what appeared to be the top of the slough. The ground was hard-packed and rocky, but easier than the sandy trail. As we traveled, the day was getting longer and the stock was bellowing of thirst. We were not stopping because there was nowhere we could stop that had water or grass. What would be the purpose of stopping? It would only delay our arriving at our destination.

Pa was dropping back more often to check on us. Gabe asked when we were stopping for noon lunch.

Pa picked him up and put him on Unicornis. "We are not stopping today, son. No place to stop and no water until this evening. Be strong and brave, and we will get there." Pa looked at all of us.

"We will, Pa. We will."

A little bit later, Mama Julia and Rebecca brought us honey-bread, and jerked buffalo, which Charles and I made.

I was noticing that the sagebrush was growing taller, and a lot more of them were growing everywhere. We crossed a dry streambed and continued up a medium-sized hill. The trail was rocky and sandy, but at least there was ground under the trail, unlike the sandy trails. The rocks shook the wagons as we moved along the trail.

As we came up a gradual bluff, we could see the Rocky Mountains far, far off in the distance. I could tell it was getting to be around five o'clock. The sun was high above the mountains in the distance and the day was at its hottest. We were keeping the brims of our hats down to keep the sun out of our eyes. Mama Julia brought us some bacon and large pieces of sweetbread. Of course, we had plenty of water. We always drank lots of water as we walked.

As we came to the edge of the bluff, I looked down to an impressive sight. I could see the trail turn and bend like a long ribbon. As I looked down the bluff, I could see a column of over a hundred white wagon bonnets following the long ribbon trail. There was a gap between companies filled with stock. I was grateful we were together. We had, for most part, traveled with health and safety. As inspiring as this view was, it looked like it was going to be a long time before we stopped. I was getting tired.

We traveled about two miles and went down a shallow canyon. The stock began to bellow. This was not a bellow of thirst. This was different. They could smell water, and they were letting us know it. The stock was picking up the pace. As we rounded the bottom of the canyon, we could see the green river bottom of the Sweetwater. We left the trail and traveled about a half-mile up the river where there was cleaner water and a little more grass.

Around half-past six and after nearly twenty-two miles, we encamped on the Sweetwater River. We had good water, grass, and wood. We had made it!

We corralled the stock on the Sweetwater where they could feed and water as needed. Many needed attention. Pa, my brothers, along with Brothers Hart, Pierce, and Carter, Mr. Bradshaw, and Mr. Laroy went around with salve and wrapped at least seventy oxen. Pulling the wagons through the sand was making sores from the yokes and were causing very bad rubs. Many were bleeding. They applied salve to the necks of most of the oxen, as well.

We unpacked and set up the tents, unpacked the wagons, and I did my chores. We had supper of a hash made with bacon, ham, eggs, and greens, and cornbread and currant cobbler. There was a half-moon with some light. Because of the hard trail, Pa put guards in rotation: one group from dusk to one o'clock, and the other from one o'clock to when we would wake up at four o'clock. We had seen bear tracks around where we had stopped. The constant cries of wolves and coyotes made Pa more watchful.

Captain Walton came and informed us that we would leave at the same time and travel for about eight miles to a canyon that had very good grass, water, and wood. The trail was sandy but not as bad as we had experienced the last few days. The stock needed rest and we could rest there.

Although it was late and I was tired of walking, I wanted to see what was down the trail. Izzy and Unicornis joined me. Soon, most of the youth company joined as we went down the river about a mile. We could tell many people had camped around that place because of all the items left behind, as well as the many, many fire rings and privy holes. I was glad our captains chose to camp upstream. The smell of privy holes was bad, and there were many of them around that area.

We headed back, had prayers, and went to bed.

Tuesday, September 2: Day 59

Pa woke me up a little before two and said the two replacement guards from the first company of fifty took sick. "William, Brother Ward has been on duty all night and said he will stay with you for the rest of the night."

"Of course, I will Pa." I finished getting dressed.

Pa said they had heard bears all night. He handed me his rifle and told me to be vigilant and careful. Then he gave me a hug and went back into the tent. Pa had already saddled Acer and walked with Acer to the corrals while I was getting dressed.

I was still trying to wake up when I greeted Brother Ward with a big yawn. "I bet you are tired after hard traveling and now staying up all night."

Brother Ward chuckled as he got off his horse. "Why, no, of course not. This was nothing compared to the march I took under General Washington as we kicked those English into the ocean."

I started laughing. "Oh, another storyteller. Well, Brother Ward, that must have been a very hard march, but it was schoolyard play compared to mine. I was the personal messenger for Captain Meriwether Lewis and Lieutenant William Clark. I had to run messages from Fort Clatsop all the way to President Jefferson in Washington, D.C. and then back." I paused, then added, "I mean Worshington, D.C."

Brother Ward laughed as he grabbed me, picking me up off my feet. He gave me a big hug. "Well, I'll be a blue-nosed gopher. I am bested at my own storytelling by a young master storyteller."

We laughed, and the rest of the night, we talked and rode around. We could hear a couple of bears calling out to each other in the distance, but nothing close. Sounds carried further than they did at home for some reason. I wondered why.

It did not take long for four o'clock to roll around. I gave Brother

Ward a hug and returned to our wagons to do my chores. Milk was low and no eggs because we had gathered them the night before for supper. Pa and my brothers went to tending the stock. We packed the tents and wagons, had breakfast of biscuits and gravy and salt bacon. We finished packing the wagons, said prayers, and hit the trail at half-past six.

The morning was cool as we followed the Sweetwater for about a mile and found a shallow and wide area to cross. We all crossed almost without any problems. The problems we did have were small. The team of oxen of one wagon got in the middle of the river and stopped. I reckoned the oxen liked the water on their legs and desired to stop. This held up the entire column until they were able to pull them to get them going. Once on the other side, they continued walking. The other trouble was a wagon that broke a couple spokes as they went down the embankment to the river. They quickly replaced the wheel and they rolled on.

We traveled along the Sweetwater, sometimes hugging the side because the trail was very narrow between the hills and the river. A couple times, we climbed the sandy hills out of the river bottom and came back down, which took time. The trail was sandy and we had to be careful along some edges. The people like Pa, James, Ben, and Sam, who walked with the oxen on the left side, had to make sure they pushed them over to hug the right side of the trail. We had a couple near-tragic events with oxen walking too close to the sandy edge. They lost their footing and almost went down into the river.

We continued until we came to the canyon, made a right turn, traveled for about a half-mile. At eleven o'clock, after nine miles, we encamped up the canyon. There was good grass, good water, and wood. When we arrived at the canyon, the first fifty stayed on the trail as we took our stock and wagons to the top of the canyon, around a bend where the grass and water were good. The first company of fifty followed up the canyon and had their stock near the bottom. Once again, we placed wagons around the bend at the top and at the bottom, with the column all along the canyon. This plan made it so we did not need guards. We all could get rest.

As soon as we unpacked the tents and the wagons, Pa said I could take a nap. I crawled under one of our wagons, put my hat over my face, and fell asleep. I slept for about an hour when I felt a stick poking in my ribs.

It was three-year-old little Abby Terry asking, "Cap'an, when are we going exploring?"

I rolled out from under the wagon and there was the whole company. I wondered who had put little Abby up to this. It did not matter. "I am up, so let us go exploring."

I looked over at Pa and he smiled, gave me a wink, and he went about treating the stock. Izzy and Unicornis did not come. Izzy was not feeling well. She was in the wagon with Mother.

We traveled up the left side of the canyon until we came to the top of our encampment. There was a small pool. We played around in the pool and headed back down the right side of the canyon. We did not find anything of interest, except a few rocks that looked exactly like wood. We continued down until, as we got to the end of the canyon, we spotted another column of about twenty wagons. We stood at the entrance of our canyon and waved.

The captain of the company came riding up and asked who we were and if we were abandoned. I answered that our company was up the canyon, and we were the youth company.

"Are you Mormons?" he asked.

"Yes, sir, we are. Well, most of us," I replied and asked, "Where are you folks headed?"

The captain said, "We are going to Oregon and most of us are from Ohio and West Virginia."

"Well, good luck and God Bless," I said.

The captain replied, smiling, "You as well, sir." He tipped his hat.

Of course, I had a big smile, and we all waved as the wagons passed.

We finished going down the hill, crossed the trail and to the river. We played around in the river for a while when we noticed dust rising around the bend. Soon, four freight wagons, each wagon pulled by eight mules, came to where we were playing. Once they noticed us, the lead rider stopped and asked if we were abandoned.

"No, sir, our company is resting up the canyon. We are the youth company."

He smiled and said, "Good. We do not have any room for all of you but we do have something if you want it." He rode to the third wagon, pulled out a bag, and returned. He got off his horse and opened the bag, "Hard rock candy."

"I am sorry, sir, but we have no money to pay you," I said.

"Nonsense. Come and take a piece."

The little ones went running up.

He started laughing. "Whoa, whoa, one at a time."

The men on the other wagons laughed.

When all of us got a piece of hard rock candy, I reached out my hand and thanked him."

He shook my hand. "Are you the captain of this company?"

"One of them, sir. Charles is the other."

He walked over and shook Charles's hand. "Keep up the good work. You are doing a fine job."

We all thanked him and waved as they started again. The man and the teamsters all waved and laughed as they rode off.

It was getting around five o'clock, so we headed back. Once we arrived, we told everyone of our experiences, showed them the rock wood we had found, and told about the candy the freighters gave us. The company dispersed and went to their own wagons. We all got ready for supper.

Izzy was running a fever, so Mama Julia took her down to the Sweetwater and started to bath her when she noticed about a dozen ticks on her. Some had already dug in. Mama Julia wrapped her up, brought her up to the wagons, and showed Pa. Pa and Mama Julia put salve on the ticks that went inside her skin.

Pa told James, "Run and tell Captains Walton and Reed, and have everyone checked for ticks."

Soon, everyone was at their own wagons and tents, checking for ticks. A few had some on them, but most, including myself did not have any ticks. No one except for Izzy and the two men that had taken sick the night before had ticks. Pa checked Unicornis, rubbed him down with saleratus ground to a power as a precaution. After our tick inspection, we had supper of ham and beans, bread, and current bread. We sat around the fire and talked.

Captain Walton came to Pa and asked if the oxen would be ready to travel Rocky Ridge the next day.

Pa said, "No, the sores are too deep. I would recommend we give them one more day."

A little while later, Captain Walton came back and said that Captain Reed agreed to stay one more day and asked if Pa and my brothers and a few others would examine every wagon to make sure the wagons were ready to cross Rocky Ridge. Pa said he would. Captain Walton thanked us and went back to his family.

I asked Pa if I could go to bed and he said yes. I got my blankets and crawled back under the wagon, said my own prayers, and went to sleep.

Wednesday, September 3: Day 60

I woke up at seven o'clock. Some of the others in the company were still sleeping. Although we did not travel very far the day before, the last few days of hard sandy traveling had been very difficult on man and beast. I did my chores. Milk and eggs were good. We had breakfast of pancakes, ham, and current bread.

After breakfast, Pa asked me to gather the youth company and go down to the Sweetwater and catch as many fish as we could. "If you manage to get some ducks, that would be good as well." He added, "Take my rifle. If you run into trouble, shoot in the air, and we will come to you."

As I went around gathering the youth company, Pa went around and gathered help to examine all the wagons. Captain Reed asked James and the other hunters to ride up the canyon and see what they could find. We all went our ways.

Izzy was still sick. She ate a little but mostly slept. Her fever was still with her, and Mama Julia would take her to the creek and bathe her to cool her down. I hoped Izzy would get better soon. We all missed her. I was sure she would get better.

The youth company went down to the Sweetwater, and we did the same attack plan on the fish as we did near Independence Rock. Charles went about a half mile down the river. When they were ready, we started walking towards each other. There were more fish and we were catching more of them. The size was about the same, five to seven inches, maybe a little bigger. After we made four passes, we had caught seventy-nine fish. We cleaned them and put them in bags. Five members of our company took them up to the encampment.

We sat on the banks of the Sweetwater when another company of wagons came by. These were members of the Church.

The captain stopped and I immediately told him, "We are not abandoned. Our company is up in the canyon."

The captain laughed. "It seems you have been asked these questions before. Who is your captain?"

"Brother E. D. Reed is our captain."

"Ah, yes, most of you are from Kanesville. Is there a blacksmith and cattleman with you by the name of Killian?"

"Yes, I am his son William."

The captain got off his horse and shook my hand. "I am Brother Carlisle, and I knew your father and grandfather in Nauvoo. If I had more time, I would ride up and visit them."

I told him, "Grandpa and Grandmother made the trip last year and they are doing well."

He told me to tell my father, "Hello from Terence Carlisle."

"I will, sir. God bless and see you again soon."

He got back on his horse, tipped his hat, and rode up to the front of his company. We waved as the long column passed us.

When they passed, the fish messengers came back and we sat and had a meeting on how we could catch ducks. They were not nesting, and we did not have the cover of reeds, so what could we do?

Hanna suggested that we get bread, small fishhooks, and string. "We tie the fishhooks to the string, make a bread ball around the hooks, and if the ducks take it, we can catch them like fish."

We voted on it and everyone said yes. Charles and Hanna ran back to camp to gather the duck-catching items. When they returned, we did as Hanna suggested. We put the floating bread hooks in the water. As soon as we did this, the fish ate the bread, and we caught fish. We took the fish off and put bread balls around the hook and tried it again.

This time Hanna, Charles, Herk, and Gabe snuck out to where the ducks were. When the ducks flew off, they put out the bread balls, along with other pieces of bread as bait, and hid in the grass. The ducks came back and started eating the bread. Each one caught a duck. We did this until the ducks figured out what was going on and did not come back. Before they figured it out, we had caught twenty-one ducks. We packed up the ducks and fish and headed back.

We noticed another group of wagons coming. It looked like about forty wagons. We had seen enough for the day and continued to our encampment.

When we returned, everyone in our company was amazed at the ducks we had caught. We gave the fish and the ducks to Captain Walton, and he gave them to Mama Julia and asked if she could organize the other women. He said, "Find the best solution for these items."

Mama looked at Rebecca and the other women in our company, and they all said yes.

The youth company sat around, plucked the ducks, and then went out to find more wood rocks. Around four o'clock, James and the others came back with three deer. They looked at our fish and ducks and asked who had shot the ducks and caught the fish.

Rebecca chuckled. "The youth company caught the fish and ducks. Maybe you need to go with them and learn how to hunt."

The women all laughed and the hunters went to the business of skinning and dressing the deer.

Other women of the whole company came and acquired what meat they needed for supper and for the trail. At six o'clock, we all sat down and had a good feast. We were all still a little tired and we knew what kind of trail the next day would bring. So, like our stock, we ate and rested.

Pa, my brothers, and I tended to the stock before we went to bed. Captains Reed and Walton rode up to inspect the stock. They looked them over and said ours were looking better than the stock of the first company of fifty. Although most still had open sores, they were healing well. Captain Reed said we had enough good grass there and, because he knew the trail ahead, he thought we should stay one more day. Captain Reed asked Pa and my brothers to set up shop again and mend any wagons that might need mending.

Pa looked at my brothers and said, "Let's unload the wagons, boys."

Captain Reed got on his horse, tipped his hat, and rode off. Captain Walton stayed and helped unload the wagons and set up shop.

Pa told me, "Run and tell everyone we were staying. And we need charcoal, so keep the fires going."

I went to each wagon and told them we were staying and we needed to keep fires going. As soon as I told the men, they immediately stopped what they were doing and went down to help Pa set up shop. The youth company went around collecting wood for the fires. I went to Captain Manus's wagon and told them we were staying. He was leaning on his wagon, talking the Brother Barker and Brother Pierce.

Captain Manus told me to come closer because he did not hear me. I went next to him and told him we were staying till the next day.

Captain Manus slapped me on the side of the head, knocking me to the ground. He yelled, "Listen, you worthless kid, who are you to give me orders? And who told you we are staying?"

I got up off the ground and pointed to Captain Walton, who was now walking towards us. "He did, sir."

Captain Walton walked over with a large stick in his hand. "What is the problem here, William?" asked Captain Walton.

Captain Manus started to reply, "Did you tell this brat to tell me—"

Captain Walton interrupted Captain Manus. "I am talking to young Brother Killian." He pointed the stick at Captain Manus's face.

I replied, "There is no problem here, sir. I am passing the word along to everyone like you asked me."

Captain Manus started to speak again, "But, I am the Capt—"

Captain Walton jabbed him in the chest with the stick. "Harvey, I do not know where your behavior is coming from. Maybe you should have stayed with your friends, the Law brothers and the Higbees and Fosters in Nauvoo. This is your last warning, Harvey. Next time you and your crew here," Captain Walton said pausing and looking over at the Barkers and Pierces, "upset, offend, or disrupt the harmony of this company, you will be removed and banished." Captain Walton looked down at me and asked if I was hurt.

I told him, "I am not."

Captain Walton turned to the three families. "I am going back to my wagon. I do not want to hear another word from any of you during our stay. Is that understood?"

Captain Manus started to say something when Captain Walton raised the stick again to his face. They all nodded yes.

Captain Walton put his hand on my shoulder. "Come on, Brother Killian. I will go with you and we will finish telling the others the good news."

As Captain Walton and I went around visiting each wagon, telling the other families we were staying, I mentioned to Captain Walton that Captain Manus was always nice to me back home when I would see him in church or in town. "Why is he acting so different now?"

Captain Walton said, "When you are around people all day every day, like we are on the trail, you often see people as they really are. Do you remember what Captain Reed told us at the beginning of our journey? 'Good and bad qualities will be revealed and intensified on the trail.' William, it is hard to hide your true self during hard and strenuous times for many weeks and months. Unfortunately, you are seeing them as they really are."

I then asked Captain Walton, about "The Laws, Higbees, and Fosters. Why did Captain Manus turn pale when you mentioned their names?"

Captain Walton told me that most everyone who lived in Nauvoo in 1846 was familiar with the Laws, Higbees, and Fosters, and with the newspaper whey had. Their newspaper was believed to have led to the death of the Prophet Joseph and his brother Hyrum. Some believe Captain Manus was involved in the newspaper that brought about the events leading up to the death of Brother Joseph and Hyrum."

"Oh," I said, "maybe his conscience is getting to him and that is why he is angry most of the time."

Captain Walton looked down at me, putting his hand on my shoulder. "That very well may be. That is a lot of wisdom for such a young man. That very well may be."

When we finished visiting all the families, Captain Walton said I should ask my Grandfather about the Law's, Higbees, Fosters and Captain Manus when I see him. "Your Grandfather was a high-ranking officer in the Nauvoo Legion and sheltered Joseph and Hyrum a few times at his home in Montrose, across the river from Nauvoo. Your Grandfather helped protect them. You should ask him. He knows more of what happened than most." Captain Walton shook my hand and he went back to his wagon.

As I walked back to our wagons, I thought, *Of all the made-up stories Grandpa would tell, he never mentioned the most important story, the true story of how he knew and helped the Prophet Joseph and Brother Hyrum.*

When I arrived at our wagons, I ran up to Pa and asked him about what Captain Walton had told me. Pa stood there looking at me, kind of stunned, then tears came to his eyes and he shook his head. "Not now, William. Not now." He walked away.

I did not expect that reaction. I had never seen Pa cry before. I was sorry I had mentioned anything.

It was almost half-past ten. We had prayers and went to bed. My left ear was still ringing from when Captain Manus knocked me to the ground, and my mind was wondering if I should ask Grandpa, or would he get upset like Pa.

Thursday, September 4: Day 61

I woke up at six o'clock, did my chores and Izzy's chores. The milk and eggs were back up to normal. The rest was doing well for everyone, including the animals. I helped Pa and my brothers tend to the stock. Most of the sores were healing well and they were walking around better. We still applied salve, wrapped many oxen legs, and put salve on where the yoke was rubbing sores. The day before, we had to cut the horses from the cattle because the horses were behaving ornery and pestering the cattle. The cattle could go a few days without water and good grass. They could eat most anything green. Horses were more particular on what they would eat. It was very hard on them without water and good grass, and they start becoming ornery. We noticed this towards the end of the day on Tuesday.

Towards the end of the trail, Sarah's horse Bell bit a cow on the ear when it came too close. We had to take her to the front and tie her to the wagon. The pigs were recovering and enjoying the mud in the small pond at the top of our canyon. The heat and the trail were very hard on them, but they were strong and determined to make it to the end. Chickens did not like the heat, either. We made an open pen for them in the grassy area. They liked the grass but preferred the dirt and dust. Gerald the turtle was doing fine as well. There were many horned lizards in the area. I hoped Cate did not catch one. I did not think Gerald wanted a companion. The dogs were in wonderful condition and were great to have along. The cat, well, it was a cat and, somehow, still with us.

We had breakfast of salt bacon and pancakes with butter and berry-spread. After breakfast, I helped Pa, my brothers, and the rest of the men in the shop. After lunch, Pa let me gather the youth group and go exploring.

I gathered up Charles and the group.

Hanna wanted to stay behind. She was worried about Izzy and wanted to be there for her. "She is very annoying, but she is like a sister and I cannot leave her," said Hanna.

Charles and I gathered up the youth company and headed up the creek. We were hearing the incredible sound of elk bugling up in the high country. We could not see any, but we could hear them. We went about a mile to another small pool. We noticed many bear tracks and some tracks that looked like a very big cat. We decided it would be safer if we headed back to the Sweetwater and did more fishing.

Before we left, each one of us filled our hats with currants, gooseberries, and other berries. We delivered our berries to our mothers and told them where we had found them. As we walked down, we noticed a small pond built at the end of our column and the women were washing clothes. We said, "Hello," and went on the Sweetwater. We had always felt safe at the Sweetwater, but now that most of the mothers were close, we felt even safer.

We decided to do more fishing, so we split up as we had done the day before and tried corralling the fish again. By two o'clock, we had another twenty-three fish. We took them up to camp.

James and some of the other hunters brought back nine desert chickens they had shot. We had a bite to eat and went back down to the river to go swimming. We found a shallow pool, fed by the current, but far enough from the main flow not to be dangerous. As we swam, two companies of wagons with about a hundred wagons in each company went by. We saw a freighter company with three freight wagons headed back to the States.

The captain came over. "You kids alright?" he asked.

We pointed to our mothers and the mothers waved.

The captain said, "That sure looks fun. Can we join?"

We all laughed and said yes.

The captain laughed and said, "We would like to, but we have to get moving."

We said good-bye and watched them ride down the river. They went about a mile and stopped, picketed the oxen and went swimming. They did not stay long and were back on the trail. We then lost sight of them.

We swam until about half-past four and headed back to the wagons, but we had to wait for another long column of wagons going west. There were about sixty wagons headed to Oregon. They were friendly and waved. Most everyone said they wanted to go swimming and they wished they were kids again. We smiled and waved. As their stock passed, we moved on. Their stock did not look very well at all. Some of the horses weaved as they walked, and the oxen had terrible sores. I was glad we had stopped.

When we arrived at our wagons, the shop was loaded and put away. I checked on Izzy. She was sleeping. Mama Julia said Hanna stayed with her most of the day. Izzy was trying to send Hanna away so she could have fun with us, but Hanna would not leave. Finally, after Izzy went to sleep again, Hanna went back to her family to get some rest.

I did my chores. There was more milk this afternoon. We had supper of fish, biscuits, greens, and berry pie. We were hearing elk bugles all afternoon and evening. It was a beautiful sound. This was the first time most in the company had heard an elk bugle call. Brother Hart said there was a river in Maryland named the Elk River, not because of the animal, but because Captain John Smith of 1608 drew a map of a river he had discovered and someone said his river map looked like an elk antler. So, it was named Elk River. However, elk did not live in Maryland or around that area.

We sat around a fire and talked and listened to the elk when Izzy came out of the wagon. She was hot with a fever. Pa took her to the pond and bathed her again. They came back and Izzy had a little bite to eat. She sat with Pa until she fell asleep again. About nine o'clock, we had prayers and went to bed. It was a warm night, but my grassy bed was cool.

CHAPTER 18
ROCKY TRAIL AND NEW LEADERSHIP

Friday, September 5: Day 62

I woke up at four o'clock, did chores. The grass and rest were good for our milk cows, and we had a good amount of milk and eggs. We packed up the tents and blankets, had breakfast of eggs, salt bacon, and biscuits. We finished packing the wagons. The rest and salve helped heal the sores on the oxen. We wrapped the legs and applied salve on the shoulders where the yokes rested, and we were ready to go. We yoked Unicornis to the second wagon so he could look ahead and see and be near Izzy. We had prayers and at half-past six, we hit the trail.

As we came out of the canyon, the trail was rocky, sandy, and slow. We traveled along the Sweetwater for about two miles and climbed out of the river bottom. We traveled along and around a sandy hill, went down a ravine, and climbed a steep sandy hill. This again was difficult on the oxen and wagons. The sole of my left boot came off and I ran on the hard sharp rocks to the wagon and fetched my other boots. I had worn my old boot to almost nothing. I lost the buttons before Fort Laramie.

We came to the top and looked at the trail ahead. There it was: Rocky Ridge. It looked as difficult as we heard it would be. We traveled down the steep sandy and rocky trail. The rocks were layered one on top of each other, overlapping, and the wheels of the wagons would fall between two and six inches. This was very hard on the wheels and the wagons. We could hear things falling in the wagons. There was not much we could do, but kept moving. We would have to rearrange the wagons later.

We came to the bottom of Rocky Ridge hill and waited until it was our company's turn. The first company of fifty made it up without any serious problems. Once our first company of ten made it to the top, we all learned how to climb the hill. Pa ordered all available oxen brought up. The horses were still in a cantankerous mood so they were no use. They took the oxen up to the bottom of Rocky Ridge, while Dotty, Gabe, and I returned to the remaining stock. Pa, Brother Ward, Brother Hart, and a couple other brethren stayed at the top to unhook the extra oxen teams. Mr. Laroy, Brother Pierce, and Brother Terry, along with six other brethren, stayed in the middle to offer any help pushing and steering the wagons. Mr. Bradshaw, Brother Carter, Brother Barker, Brother Stevens, and a couple other brethren stayed at the bottom to hook up the extra yoke of oxen. Captain Walton, Sam, Ben, and Charles, and other men from the companies helped run the oxen from the top down to the bottom to hook up again. Captain Manus stayed near the top so, as he said, he could, "Be captain over the company and watch."

The company ahead of us was almost half way and now it was our turn. Pa told us to bring the stock up on the right side of the trail as soon as our company started up the hill. The left side had big jagged rocky formations and it was too narrow for the stock. Mama Julia and Rebecca walked the young one up the hill while Izzy and Mother stayed in the wagon. Gerald was in a safe box in another box.

I looked up at that steep rough hill, took a deep breath, and said a small prayer to myself. I began to whistle and started up the trail. We continued hearing things falling inside wagons and, occasionally, something would fall off the wagons and someone would pick it up and return it to the owner. Wagons could not stop on this hill once we were in motion. It would be too hard for the oxen to start the climb again, especially on a hill like this. The system of men and oxen in stages was working very well.

All the while, I could hear Captain Walton yelling, "Come on, men, put your shoulder to the wheel. Push, push," urging us up the rocky hill as he did so many times before on the trail. By the time company in front of us made it up the hill, most of the men on the hill were whistling the same tune, a favorite trail hymn. The travel was slow and the trail was very hard on the wagons and oxen.

We made it more than halfway without problems. Captain Reed was at the top greeting people and tipped his hat and urging them on. As he stood there on his horse, watching, he noticed Captain Manus sitting on the large bolder on the other side of the trail. Captain Reed rode over to him.

I do not know what Captain Reed said, but Captain Manus walked down to the hill and helped push and steer the wagons uphill. We were at the top before most of our wagons. At the top, the sagebrush was growing very low to the ground and there was no grass, so we could not graze the stock. We corralled the stock, stood, and watched as each one of the wagons of our company. Once the last wagon made it to the top, they unhooked the oxen and returned them to the corral. They put the spare yokes in various wagons in our company of fifty. They put Cate and James Jr. back into the wagon. When we put everything away, we continued.

The trail was still very rocky and hard on the wagons. We went down the other side. The trail going down was not as rocky going up but still dangerous and hard on the wagons and oxen. We came to the bottom, crossed a dry creek, rolled on past a couple dry alkali ponds. After traveling a hard six miles, at one o'clock, we nooned at a flat place to have something to eat, rearrange the wagons, and check all the wheels and tires for any cracks. It was difficult to look at all the dead animals, broken wagons, and items left behind as we traveled. I was very grateful to my Heavenly Father that we had not suffered as much as others, and I prayed our blessing would continue.

After about an hour, we were back on the trail. We climbed another hill. This one was not as rocky and we traveled about two miles and came to a little stream. We stopped long enough for the stock to get a couple licks, then we continued. The trail was very rocky and sandy. The oxen were struggling as we went up and down ravines and climbed hills.

I could see a creek up ahead and I hoped we would stop there.

We traveled a few miles and came to Strawberry Creek, crossed over, and traveled about a mile upstream. At five o'clock, we found a place with good grass, good water, and some sticks for cooking. We unpacked and set up the tents, did chores, and I helped Pa and the others apply salve and wraps to the oxen. Except for the sores, they were still in very good condition.

We had supper of stew, bread, greens from the creek, and berry cobbler while listening to the choirs of elk bugles. Izzy was still running a fever and sleeping a lot. We went back to tending the stock until it was time for prayers and bed.

Saturday, September 6: Day 63

I woke up at four o'clock, did chores. Milk and eggs were at a good supply. I did Izzy's chores this day. She was still not feeling well. I hoped she got better soon. She was annoying at times, but she was my best friend, as well as my little sister. We packed the tents and wagons, tended to the stock with salve and wraps, had breakfast of ham, eggs, and cornbread. We finished packing.

Mother asked that Izzy have a bed in Rebecca's and James's wagon in case her sickness could spread to Cate and little James. Of course, that was not acceptable to Izzy. She wanted a bed in the tool wagon so she could look out the back to make sure that, "We were tending to the stock and not playing around or riding on the stock."

Gabe laughed. "Like you do all the time."

We laughed.

Izzy coughed and said, pointing to her eyes, "I am watching you."

Rebecca made a bed in the tool wagon and unyoked Unicornis. He walked to the back where he could see Izzy. We said prayers and hit the trail at half-past six.

The mornings were starting to become cooler. The trail was sandy and rocky, but travel was a little easier. We crossed a couple ravines and started a gradual climb. The sun was getting warmer, but not like when we crossed over those sandy trails the last few days. I was glad that was over. Within a few hours we crossed over Rock Creek. We noticed a large group of over two-hundred wagons, people busy working on wagons and washing clothes. It looked like the group from the Church that had passed us the previous day. My boots were not as worn in as my other ones and I was getting blisters.

We continued to climb. The trail became rockier and sandier, and that slowed our travels a bit. We crossed another deep creek ravine and had deep sand for about a mile until we came to another creek ravine. This one was not as steep, but we still had to be careful. As we traveled down the bluffs, we could see the Oregon Buttes to the south and the very high snowcapped mountains to our right. We could also see the Sweetwater once again. I believed we were about to make our encampment, but the area looked like a little city. There were hundreds of wagons for a couple miles up and down the river on both sides.

Sure enough, the word came down the line that we were continuing. I was hoping for a short day, but not this day.

We came to the Sweetwater and stopped long enough for the stock to get a few licks. We did not dare take drinks ourselves because of all the people above the river. We crossed the Sweetwater and continued down the trail. The trail was sandy and rocky, but we were still moving at a good pace. The sagebrush grew about six to eight inches from the ground. I could see taller ones out a ways by the alkali ponds and creeks. There were no trees or tall bushes and trail privacy was very difficult. I would have to wait until we reached our next encampment to find a privacy bush or tree.

There was a herd of elk, numbering about fifteen, running west to east towards the big mountain. When they got to the top of a bluff by the river, they scared up about fifty antelope that took off across the river and up a large hill.

As we traveled closer to the river, we could see trails made by deer, antelope, and elk headed toward the river. These animal trails were as deep as the ruts our wagon wheels were making. Some of them were at least four to six inches deep. They must have used the same trail for many years to have the trail so deep. We did not see any buffalo pies anymore, but we did see little round rabbit droppings everywhere, deer and elk droppings, and then the antelope piles. It seemed the antelope like to poop in the same place on the same pile. If I had not seen an antelope poop on a pile, I would not have believed it. There were these piles of antelope poop about a foot or more high and some were higher. Maybe it marked a territory. I did not know, but they were strange piles. Oh, the things I noticed when all I did was walk, and occasionally, push a cow or an ox. I was also noticing more horned lizards and mice running around. With the mice came hawks and golden eagles. I sometimes saw a hawk or an eagle every few miles, sitting on a large rock or flying above. And of course, there were the ravens.

It sure was hot and dry.

As we traveled, I saw we were entering a different area. The rocks in and around the trail were a greenish black. I picked one up and looked at it closely. The rock had many very thin layers. I could pick away at a layer with my knife, but it was difficult. It was a hard rock. If I held it in the sunlight a certain way, the rock had almost a silver shine with very tiny golden specks. I wondered if it was gold. No, I did not think it was. If it were gold, all the gold seekers would have come to this area and not traveled all the way to California seeking gold.

As Grandmother would say, "The gold seekers were jousting at windmills."

I missed Grandmother reading books to us. The way she read and her voice, she made the books come alive. When we went on our little adventures, she would always bring her basket filled with things to eat and a book to read. Sometimes, the book weighed more than we did, it seemed.

I was distracted from my daydreaming by Brother Hart over on a hill to my right. He was on his hands and knees. He was looking at these greenish black rocks sticking out of a hill. He went back to his wagon carrying a large piece of this layered rock.

The trail was good and quick. We traveled about two miles from an alkali pond on our left and about thirteen miles from our Strawberry Creek encampment when I started seeing graves. As we traveled closer to a landmark of two hills on either side of the trail, I was seeing more graves. The graves were easy to recognize, even if they had been there for a few years. They were mounds or sunken holes, most all the grave laid in an east and west direction. Some still had head markers and most did not. As we passed the taller hill on our left, we saw more graves along its northern foothill. I figured this was a good landmark for a grave if someone wanted to come back, or for others to seek on their travels. At least these people were not alone but had a fellowship of the dead. I could not imagine having to bury a loved one in such a lonely and uninhabited place.

A mile past the two hills, we dropped down onto the Sweetwater. At five o'clock, we stopped at a place along the river that had two separate horseshoe curves in the river, one for each company of fifty to corral the stock, to feed and water as needed. Although the water flowed southwest to northeast and we were upriver from the hundreds encamped. We did not know who or what was upstream. After we corralled the stock, each company of ten dug out watering holes. The watering holes were dug away from the main stream where water would pass through rocks, sod, and more rocks, like those that we made at home to make in the Missouri River, making sure we had clean water to drink.

After we made the watering holes, we unpacked and set up the tents, unpacked the wagons, and I did Izzy and my chores. Mama Julia took Izzy downriver to bathe her and cool her off. When they returned, she told Pa that Izzy had a rash all over her body and she was worried. Pa went to the wagon and applied a salve to help the itching.

After chores, we had supper of meat pie, greens from the river, bread, and glazed current cake. Izzy had a little to eat and went back to sleep. The youth company got together and we went exploring, but it was not the same without Izzy telling us what to do. As we explored, we found two types of bear tracks, big cat tracks, and all kinds of other animal tracks like antelope, deer, larger deer, or elk, and a few other tracks I could not recognize. We came back and told Pa about the bear tracks, and he wanted me to show him and Captain Walton.

I took them to the bear tracks. They knew one was black bear but did not know what the other one was, so they sent me to get Captain Reed.

When we returned, Captain Reed looked at the tracks and said, "This is not good. Grizzly bear." He pointed to the unidentified bear track. "Grizzly bear claws are longer, and toes are closer together and the grizzly does not have a wedge in their feet like the black bear print over here." Then he told us we were staying for the Sabbath.

We made fires at our wagons, as well as on the edges of the corrals. We all sat around the fire talking when we noticed Brother Hart going around to nearly each wagon, talking about the rock he had found. He came to our wagon and I was very interested in hearing about this black, green-layered rock. Brother Hart came and sat on the ground and held a rock in his hand. Pa brought him a seat.

He got up off the ground and sat in the seat and told us about the greenish, black rock around us. Brother Hart started, "About fourteen years ago, as I attended college in New York, I made friends with an English chap who lived in a poor area of the Manhattan Island. I would go home with him from time to time, and as we walked around where he lived, he showed me a big rocky mound. This rocky mound had layers and the color like this rock. Those giant rocky mounds had deep scrapes in the rock, always going the same direction, north to south. We would sit on this rock and try to identify what caused these scrapes. I had lost contact with my old school mate and forgot about that rock until today. The rock we have all around us here is the exact same rock my friend and I examined on the Manhattan Island. There were no big mountains like these in Manhattan, but it has the same rocks as we do here.

"What does this mean? I do not know There is some connection between the Rocky Mountains and Manhattan Island. William, maybe someday you might figure this out if you ask the right questions. Knowledge is all about asking the right questions. I believe, someday, our Heavenly Father will reveal some of these secrets when we are ready."

Brother Hart stood up, thanked us for listening, and left. He left us, me especially, wondering what he had just said. I thought he was going to tell us what made the rock or where it came from. He only left me with more questions. Brother Hart was no help at all. If this was what collage was like, I thought I would rather go fishing with Grandpa. I was very confused. There was so much to learn.

We sat around the fire, talking about what Brother Hart said, and I believed we were all confused. We said prayer and went to bed. I could not get the thought of those graves we passed out of my mind. I could not think of how it would be to leave a loved one out here in this lonely place. At least, these graves were not alone. They had each other.

Sunday, September 7: Day 64

Woke up at six o'clock, did chores. Milk and eggs were good again. I did Izzy's chores again. She was still sleeping. We tended the stock, applied salve, and rewrapped some of the bandages. Had breakfast of pancakes, salt bacon, and biscuits. I helped Pa and my brothers go around looking at wagons, especially the wheels and tires, making sure there were no cracks. We replaced a few spokes here and there, but overall, things looked good.

After lunch, we attended Sunday testimony services.

We came back and Izzy was still running a fever. Pa asked James, Brother Hart, and Brother Terry to help administer to Izzy. They gathered in the wagon and, after a few minutes, they came out. Brother Hart and Brother Terry came out looking at the ground and went to their wagons. Pa and James came out and did not say a word. Pa went down to the Sweetwater River and sat down.

Izzy climbed out of the wagon and went down to Pa. I heard her say, "Papa, it is alright. It will be alright."

Pa grabbed Izzy and hugged her. Pa was crying, I could tell by the way his body shook. This was the second time I had seen Pa cry. I hoped they were happy tears. All three of them, Pa, Izzy, and Unicornis, sat there for most of the afternoon with Pa holding Izzy the whole time. I was glad Izzy was up and feeling better.

We had a quiet afternoon, had supper of dumplings, greens from the river, and cinnamon bread rolls. Izzy came out and ate with us. She still had a rash, but was looking better. Captain Walton came and told Pa that he had assigned Captain Manus and Brother Barker to guard the stock.

Pa chuckled an uneasy chuckle, "Yes sir, it is nearly a full moon and good light tonight, I am sure they will do a fine job."

I could tell that Pa was uneasy about Captain Manus and Brother Barker guarding the stock, not because this was their first time as guards but who they were.

We had a quiet evening, said prayers, and went to bed.

Around three o'clock, a shot rang out!

We all got up and ran to see what had happened. It was almost a full moon and no clouds, so it was light enough to see. We ran towards the stock. Brother Barker was holding his rifle, shaking as he pointed across the river. "Bear . . . bear!"

Pa and James walked across the river and found one dead ox and one milk cow badly mauled, bellowing loudly, and in very bad shape.

Pa was very upset. "How could a bear drive two of the stock across the river without you hearing it? I can see one, but not two!"

Captain Manus came running over, asking what happened.

Pa angrily walked over to Captain Manus. "What do you mean what happened? You were supposed to be on guard. You tell me what happened!"

James walked over to where Captain Manus staked his horse, leaned down, and picked up a bottle of whiskey next to a blanket. "This is what happened."

Brother Barker said, stammering, "I . . . I think we must have fallen asleep."

Pa pulled his revolver from his belt.

James grabbed Pa's arm and took the revolver from Pa in one quick move.

Pa was trembling with anger. "My thirteen-year-old son is more responsible than the both of you and twice the man."

Captain Walton came running over, followed by Captain Reed, riding his horse bareback.

Captain Reed jumped from his horse, yelling, "What the hell is going on around here?"

Pa grabbed the bottle of whiskey from James, held it up, pointing it at the dead ox and the dying cow. "This is what is going on, by these two." He pointed at Captain Manus and Brother Barker."

Captain Reed walked across the river to the animals and yelled, "Whose milk cow is this?"

Captain Walton went over, looked at the animals, and said it belonged to the widow Sister Hill and her family in the second company of ten. The ox belonged to Brother Tomlin and his family in the first company of ten.

Captains Reed and Walton walked back across the river.

Captain Reed walked up to Captain Manus, yelling, "How many milk cows do you have, Harvey?"

Captain Manus replied, "One. This one here."

Captain Reed grabbed the rope from Captain Manus and handed it to

Captain Walton. "Not anymore. Ralph Barker, how many oxen do you have?"

Brother Barker said he had four, but two were in very bad shape.

"Show me," demanded Captain Reed.

Brother Barker took him around and showed him the four oxen.

"Elias," yelled Captain Reed. Pa quickly walked over to Captain Reed as Captain Reed demanded, "Which is the best one of these four?"

Pa walked over, looked over the oxen, and carefully pointed to one. "None of them are in good shape, but this one is the best one."

Captain Reed grabbed the ox by the nose and led it to Captain Walton. "Paul, take these to your families."

"Yes sir," said Captain Walton as he led the animals back to his area.

As Captain Walton led the animals away, Brother Barker almost started to cry and begged, "Please don't take my good ox. We cannot make it without a strong ox. We cannot make it."

Captain Reed gave him a scowl, shook his head, and walked back to the group. He yelled, "Luther Carter, where are you?"

Brother Carter came walking up quickly, strapping his suspenders. "Here I am, sir."

Captain Reed said, still yelling, "Luther, you are now the captain of this ten. From now on, these two families will be at least a mile behind the company at all times, whether we are traveling or stopped. If they come any closer, kill their oxen!" Captain Reed paused, looked around and yelled, "Bert Pierce, where are you?"

"Right here, sir," said Brother Pierce as he stepped forward.

"Do you want to join your friends or stay with the company?"

Brother Pierce quickly replied, "Stay with the company, sir."

Captain Reed walked over and grabbed him by the shirt and pulled him close and yelled, "Then get right with God!" He pushed him away, almost knocking him down.

Captain Reed walked back to his horse, jumped on its back, scowled as he scanned the surroundings again, shook his head, and yelled, "Why are we standing around here? Get this company moving!" He turned his horse towards James, pointing to the cow, and yelled, "Put that beast out of her misery." James walked across the river, still carrying Pa's revolver, fired a shot, and the cow was dead.

Monday, September 8: Day 65

Since we were all awake, I did chores. Milk and eggs were again good. I did Izzy's chores. Izzy was still not feeling well but her fever was gone and she was still very tired. We packed up the tents and tended to the stock. They looked like they were on the mend as well.

All morning, we could hear Sister Dawna Barker yelling at her husband and at Brother Manus. At one point, she slapped Brother Manus, calling him a very bad name. He just stood there and took it.

We had breakfast of mush and sweetbread. We said prayers and hit the trail at a little before six. As we headed out, the morning was much cooler as we started. The trail was rocky and sandy but good. We traveled uphill and, after about two miles, we came to the top of "South Pass."

I heard Hanna yelling back, "Hey, Willy, this is South Pass. Did you hear me, South Pass?"

I yelled back, "I know."

South Pass

At our left in the distance were the Oregon Buttes. Rising up close to the trail on our left was Pacific Butte. We looked over a vast, open area of very little trees, a lot of sagebrush, sand, and more sagebrush. I could see miles and miles in every direction of nothingness. It was beautiful.

Hanna came running back. "Hey, Willy, did you know that before we cross South Pass all the water flows east going to the Gulf of Mexico and to the Atlantic Ocean? Now, after we cross South Pass, all the water flows west going to the Pacific Ocean." Hanna let out her ear-piercing scream of excitement.

Just then, we heard a voice coming from the wagon. "What about the water we drink?" said Izzy in the classic sarcastic Izzy voice. "Which ocean does that go to?"

Hanna chuckled. "I can tell her majesty is doing better." Hanna looked into the wagon and asked Izzy if she needed anything.

Izzy replied, "No, but thank you anyway."

Hanna jumped on the wagon, gave Izzy a kiss on the forehead, jumped down, and ran back to her wagon.

There were items like plows, books, some clothing, and empty wooden chests, discarded by other wagons all around the area.

The farther we traveled from South Pass, the fewer greenish, black rocks did I see. The trail returned to white rocky and sandy dirt, and we were making a good pace. The sagebrush grew taller as we traveled down from South Pass. At one point in the trail, walls of tall sagebrush were almost as tall as the tops of the wagon boxes. Pacific Butte at our left was a beautiful mountain with large patches of cedar. Leafy trees were on the east side. As we rounded to the north side, patches of cedars were less abundant. I could see the trail make a ribbon path as the wagon's column wound up and over to where they disappeared in the blue sky. We traveled across a few more hills and ravines. After about six miles, we came to "Pacific Springs."

Hanna came running back. "Hey, Willy, do you know why they are called Pacific Springs?" Before I could answer, Hanna said, "Because it and all water from this point flows to the Pacific Ocean."

We heard Izzy call out, "What happens when it dries up? Where does it go then? To the Antarctic continent."

Hanna looked over to me with a puzzled look and said, "How did you know that? The Antarctic continent was discovered only thirty years ago."

I looked over to Hanna. "Hanna, you are not the only one who knows things around here."

Dotty and Gabe started laughing.

Hanna shook her head and ran back to her wagon. As she passed Pa,

Hanna said, "Your children are impossible."

As we came to Pacific Springs, I knew it flowed in the other direction, but to see it flowing opposite from the Sweetwater and the Platte was an odd sight. We traveled along Pacific Creek. We could see Pacific Peak at our left as we walked. As we crossed the creek, the stock grabbed a couple licks as we rolled on.

We traveled until four o'clock and stopped at a place called "Dry Sandy Creek." The name fit the creek because it was dry and full of sand. There was no water, no grass, and no wood, except for the sagebrush, which we used for fire for cooking. Sagebrush burns hot, fast, and leaves good coals for cooking. The day was warm but not hot, and the stock was doing fine.

We corralled the stock down in the creek bed, unpacked and set up the tents, and did chores. I again did Izzy's chores. She still had a rash from the tick bites but no fever, and was still really tired. We had supper of beef, cornbread, and cinnamon bread rolls. After supper, the youth company went exploring. We again found things others left behind or dropped. The best finds were always wooden spoons. The little ones could dig with them. We had to remind them constantly not to dig in the anthills. Almost daily, one more of the little ones came running along crying because they had ants hanging off them. It hurt when the ants bit them and left a bump that turned white and itchy.

We headed back, had a fire, and talked. Izzy came out and sat on Pa's lap. Although the exiled people were a mile away, occasionally, I could hear Sister Barker yelling. Captain Carter came over and said we would start having company prayers as the Church instructed us to do when we started our journey. We gathered and had prayers and went to bed.

Tuesday, September 9: Day 66

I woke up at four o'clock, did our chores. Milk was low, but the eggs were good. We packed up the tents and the wagons, tended to the stock, had breakfast of mush and left-over cinnamon bread rolls. Izzy came out for breakfast. Her rash turned red, and she had trouble keeping food in her stomach. I hoped she would get better soon. We gathered as a company, had prayers, and hit the trail at half-past six.

The trail was sandy but easy to travel. Occasionally, we came across a sand drift that caused the oxen to strain a bit, but overall, it was a good trail. We climbed a high sandy hill. The trail was rocky and sandy. Once on top, we could see for miles. We traveled about three miles. It was a little past half-past seven. Looking back, it looked like the exiled ones had not started.

It was a beautiful view from that place. I could see for miles in every direction. I hoped where we were going would look like this. I did miss the green trees, but every place has a beauty of its own.

We followed the trail off the hill and crossed a few ravines. The sun was getting hotter and the wind began to blow. We could see dark clouds ahead. We continued across another dry creek bed and climbed another sandy hill. When we came down the other side of the sandy hill, we came to the "parting of the ways." One trail would take us to Oregon and the other trail would take us to The Great Salt Lake City and to California. Three families with five wagons from Captain Reed's first company of ten parted and went on the Oregon Trail. I hoped they would meet up with other wagons and make it safely.

The trail was very dry. The thousands of wagons had turned the dirt into a very fine powder. Sometimes I could find a pocket of this powder and stomp my foot. A cloud of dust would rise, looking like smoke from a fire. It took a while for this powder to settle back down. I sometimes saw others stomping in this fine dirt powder. It sure made a mess, but it was fun.

We continued and the trail was good traveling until we came to a place where the trail climbed the side of a high bluff. We could not go around it because of a deep dry creek bed. As we traveled along the bluff, I could see some flat cone shaped mountains off to our left looking southward. They looked like someone took a knife and cut the tops off. The trail was hard to climb and made the wagons lean to the left. We needed to be very careful that the wagons did not tip. Fortunately, we had traveled trails like this and we knew what to do. As we rounded the bluff, we could see the Little Sandy Creek.

It began to rain, a hard rain, but it did not last long. As soon as it stopped, the air filled with the smell of sagebrush. Some said they did not like the smell. For me, it was one of the sweetest and best smells I had experienced. Except for the smell of Grandmother's house as she made bread and pies. The smell of sage was a very close second.

We traveled another few miles and I could see the multitude of rabbits coming out of their holes after the rain stopped. We came to the creek and stopped so the stock could get a couple licks, and we moved down the creek for about a mile. At four o'clock, we found a place that had good grass, good water, and we had enough wood around for our needs.

We made encampment, corralled the stock at the creek where they could freely graze and water. We unpacked and set up the tents, unpacked the wagons, did our chores, helped Pa care for the stock. The stock was tired and they enjoyed having their legs in the water.

We had supper of wild chicken, greens from the creek, and sweetbread. The happiness and harmony of our company had become much better in this short time. We finished caring for the stock, sat around a small fire. We gathered as a company and said prayers, and went to bed.

CHAPTER 19
IS THIS REAL? IT HURTS SO BAD

Wednesday, September 10: Day 67

I woke up at four o'clock, did our chores. Milk and eggs were good. As I packed up the tents, I found a scorpion and a strange looking bug that looked like a cricket, but it had a large red head and strips on the body. I was about to stomp on them when Mama Julia stopped me.

"They have a right to life, just as we do. Besides, they were here before we were."

I pushed them away with my boot and continued packing the tents and wagons. I helped Pa and my brothers tend to the stock. Had breakfast of ham and biscuits and berry-spread. We finished packing the wagons and gathered the stock, had company prayers, and hit the trail at half-past six.

We began our journey by crossing the Little Sandy River. The trail was sandy and rocky but good. The stock seemed rested and ready because their pace was a little quicker. The trail was flat for the most part, and traveling was quick, except for the rocks that shook the wagons. The oxen were moving without great strain and seemed to be doing well. Like the previous day, we sometimes came across a patch of deep drifting sand, but we traveled on without any problems. I was seeing more golden eagles.

We made six miles by nine o'clock and crossed the Big Sandy River. According to Hanna, the Big Sandy emptied into the Green River. I was sure she had heard Captain Reed telling people this information, then passed it on to us in the back so she looked smart. I liked Hanna, but sometimes she could be a pest. The crossing was a little harder because of the deep sandy banks going down and the same going up. This took a little time to get everyone across but everyone made it safely. The trail on this side was much like the trail on the other side of the Big Sandy, rocky, sandy, but easy to travel.

After traveling about three miles past the Big Sandy River, we started to get into small hills and a rockier trail. After we climbed a small hill, I could see another flat-top mountain. Brother Hart said this and the other flat-top mountain were ancient volcanoes. It was interesting that there were two close together. We crossed deep ravines, and within a short distance, we crossed another one, but the second one was not as deep.

The trail became harder and slower because the sand and the drifts came more often. We followed the Big Sandy, crossing more ravines, one very deep. We almost had a wagon tip, but we all knew what to watch for. I had noticed that, in this area, as well as other sandy areas, the trail cut deep into the ground. Some of the banks on each side of the trail were almost three feet high. I think that because the trail cut places where the snow and rain collected the sagebrush grew taller along these parts of the trail. Sometimes the deep trail and the tall sagebrush were almost six feet high.

Around two o'clock, Izzy said she was feeling better and wanted to be outside. She climbed out of the wagon and went to her position in the back. A little while later, she was riding Unicornis. Maybe the air would do her good. I hoped it would. I needed my little sister back.

The day was hot and the trail was sandy and rocky. We continued and crossed another deep ravine. When we came out of the ravine, I could see a clearing in the distance where Captain Reed led the first company wagons to stop. We headed to the river around a hill, the only high hill around.

I noticed Brother Pierce off the trail a short distance and bent down doing his duty, when all the sudden he started to yelling "Get away . . . get away!" He was running while trying to pull his trousers up from his knees, "Get away . . . get away!"

We could see a badger chasing him as he ran with great difficulty. As Brother Pierce got closer to the wagons, some of the men ran towards him and drove the badger away. As Brother Pierce was trying to catch his breath and finish getting dressed, some of the men started laughing and imitated him running.

This even made Brother Pierce laugh as he said, "You all would do the same if your bare behind was being tickled by sage brush, and a big 'ol badger wanted a bite of it."

We all laughed. Then one of the men noticed that Brother Pierce had dirtied his trousers and pointed it out to Brother Pierce.

"Now don't that just beat all," he said still laughing.

Sister Pierce met Brother Pierce by their wagon and handed him a clean pair of trousers and a drying cloth and pointed to the river. As Brother Pierce walked towards the river, he did a little dance jig, which made us all laugh again. We started down the trail, still laughing.

A few minutes later, Dottie noticed that Unicornis stopped and knelt down. As the company was moving, Dottie went to get Izzy and Unicornis. All of the sudden Dottie let out a loud scream, "No . . . no . . . no . . . Izzy! . . . No . . . No . . . Please, no!"

Pa ran past me faster than I had ever seen anyone run. I followed right behind. Pa got to Izzy, knelt down, and started hugging Izzy. Not a word, only a whimper came from Pa. After a few minutes, Pa lifted Izzy's lifeless body from Unicornis. Pa just knelt there holding Izzy tightly and cried. Mama Julia, Rebecca, and Sarah came running up with hands over their mouths crying. James helped mother from the wagon, and when they arrived, Mother fainted.

I stood there in disbelief. This could not happen. My little sister could not be dead. "She is not dead," I said to myself, crying. "She is not. She is not. She could not be." This really could not be happening. Not Izzy. It hurt so much, I could not take a breath as I walked around in circles trying to breathe. It took a while for me to get control of myself. I noticed Sam, Ben, and James helping Mother up. They took her back to the wagon where they put her back into her bed.

Soon the whole company of ten stopped their wagons and came running over. When they looked upon Pa holding Izzy's lifeless body, some dropped to their knees. Others stood there as Pa cried. Hanna held Herk, trying to comfort each other. Nellie came over and held me as we cried. Captains Reed and Walton came riding up, got off their horses, knelt down, comforted Pa, and caressed Izzy's head and hair. After a few minutes, they got up and spoke softly to Pa, told him and us how sorry they were. After standing there for a little while, they wiped their eyes, got back on their horses, and went back to their business.

Captains Reed and Walton gathered men from other companies and they came and corralled the stock while others staged our wagons. James, Ben, Sam, and I helped unload the wagons. It seemed a blur as I did some of my chores. Some of the sisters of other companies started the fires for supper. I noticed some men in the distance removing some planks and making a coffin for Izzy. I wanted to tell them to stop, please stop. It was not true, my little sister was not dead. It was all a bad dream. But I knew it was not a dream. It hurt so bad and I felt so numb.

After a while, Pa got up, still holding Izzy, walked to the wagons, and placed her in the wagon. Pa walked over to Mama Julia, Rebecca, and Sarah and said, "You know what to do. Please take care of my little girl." He walked away, still crying.

I noticed Pa surveying the land. He looked at the only high hill in the area. The hill was standing tall and all alone to the northwest. Pa walked to the edge of the bluff to the east as it looked east over the Big Sandy River. He gathered some large flat stones and placed them where he was standing. He came back, picked up a shovel, and walked back to the place where he placed the stones and began to dig. I wanted to ask if he needed some help, but I knew Pa wanted and needed to do this alone. Pa began to dig a final resting place for our princess.

James, noticing Pa was having difficulty digging in the hard rocky ground, grabbed a pick and walked over to Pa. They did not say a word. James handed Pa the pick and walked back to the wagons.

Captain Walton came and asked Rebecca for Izzy's birth name and birthdate.

Rebecca asked, "Can you put 'Our Princess' on the headboard?"

Captain Walton said they would, and it would be a headstone, not a board.

"Thank you," said Rebecca.

He gave her a hug and walked back to his wagons.

A small rain cloud came over and brought a light sprinkle of rain as I led the stock to the river to water. As I came to the river, I looked up to where Pa was digging. It was on a high cliff where the river cut through. I could see an eagle's nest in the cliff, close to where Pa was digging. Across the river, I noticed a small stream of water seeping out of the middle of the lower cliff face. With the gentle rain and a trickle of water out of the cliff, it felt like heaven and earth were weeping for my little sister.

Around half-past six, some of the sisters brought supper for us and we gathered around to eat. Mama Julia walked over to Pa. He shook his head, no.

Mama Julia walked back. "Your father is not hungry."

We were not hungry either, but James said we needed to eat because we would have to travel again the next day. We filled our plates of stew, biscuits, and cinnamon bread rolls.

After supper I asked Mama Julia what made Izzy die when she was starting to feel better. Mama Julia she did not know for sure but believed it was from Mountain Fever. She told me that Brother Brigham had

Mountain Fever when they entered the Great Salt Lake Valley. Because he was older and bigger it did not infect him like it would a little girl.

Around seven o'clock, the men brought the coffin. Some sisters had lined it in very fine cloth and had sewn flowers to the lining. Surprisingly, one of the sisters made a small crown out of needlepoint and sewed it in the cloth above her head. Some of the brethren brought over the grave marker. It was about two feet wide and three feet tall. Brother Hart pointed out that on the back of the marker were ripples, like on river and lake edges.

Pa came walking over, cleaned himself off, and changed his clothes. He went to the wagon and gently picked up Izzy, placed her in her coffin. Captain Carter, Mr. Laroy, Mr. Bradshaw, Brother's Hart, Terry, and Neal carried Izzy's little coffin to her final resting place.

Everyone in our company of nearly two-hundred gathered around as Captain Reed offered these words. "This is a very sad event that brings us together, here, in this Western Desert. Who knows what types of people passed through this desert valley over the many hundreds of years, or what had transpired here? We may never know, nor does that concern us now. What we do know is that on this spot is a very sanctified and holy piece of ground, which holds the precious body of one of our Heavenly Father's angels. This blessed spot will hold and protect her until the trumpet sounds, and she shall rise again to meet her Savior, and join again with her family and loved ones.

"Who knows why our Heavenly Father calls these precious little ones home. Perhaps it is as the Prophet Joseph taught, and there are some spirits that require only to be born and receive a body in order to progress in His eternal plan. Some might say Izzy was not ready for this world. Well, for the short time I knew Izzy, I submit this world was not ready for our Sister Izabella."

A soft laugh came from the crowd.

"The hurt of her loss will never go away. However, we must all accept and believe that we shall see our young Sister Isabella again.

"This was the second child taken from righteous and worthy parents. Our Heavenly Father's Plan of Salvation provides eternal comfort, but does little to ease this mortal pain of loss. We must look to our Savior in such times, for He shall help carry this burden.

"Brother Elias and Sister Irene, look to Him during this hard and difficult time, and He shall give you comfort.

"It is unfortunate that we cannot build a lasting monument in this harsh land to honor this cherished child, but we, her beloved family, and friends, we can and should be, her living monuments: monuments to her memory, goodness, and everything blessed about this child. My brothers and sisters all, live to be worthy monuments to her memory, and to each other, and never forget the happiness that she taught and brought to all of us. Amen."

Dirt was softly covered over her coffin, then were placed flat stones. They filled the hole up with dirt and placed additional flat stones on and around so no animal could disturb her resting place. They placed a stone marker at her head, which read:

Isabella Killian
Born April 19 1840
Died September 10, 1851
Rest in peace our Princess

Izzy's Gravesite

The moon was full and the creek below babbled her soothing sound. I imagined Heavenly Father receiving Izzy home.

We had company prayers and went to bed. I heard soft muffled crying through the night.

Was this a dream?

Thursday, September 11: Day 68

We woke up at four o'clock. No one said a word as we did our chores. We had milk and a couple of eggs. Had breakfast, packed the wagons, and walked over to Izzy's final resting place. We, as a family, said a prayer, and said good-bye. We hit the trail at half-past six.

As we were leaving, we noticed Unicornis stayed behind and stood next to Izzy's grave. Pa got on his horse and went to get him. Pa got off his horse and tried to get Unicornis moving. He would not move. Pa walked back to his horse and took out a brush from his saddlebag, walked back to Unicornis, and tenderly brushed him down. Pa then took off his hat and put his forehead against Unicornis' forehead for a few minutes, put his hat back on, got on his horse, and came back to the rest of us. We dropped down to the river bottom and that was the last we saw of both Izzy and Unicornis.

As we walked, I looked down at all the wagon ruts and footprints, thinking of Izzy and about Longfellow's "A Psalm of Life,"

And, departing, leave behind us footprints on the sands of time.

For such a little girl, she left some big footprints. I missed my sister. I did not understand so many things. Why Izzy? Why not someone who was always mean, like, well, you know? Did Brother Clayton lose a little sister on the journey? If he did or did not, how he could say, "Happy days. All is well." I was probably whining again, but it hurt and I did not understand why Izzy had to die. I missed my little sister. I knew I could not change it and had no control over it, but it still hurt.

I would just keep walking and have faith in my Heavenly Father's plan. That was all I could do. *I love you Izzy.*

Captain Walton told us there was a very long line of wagons that were waiting at the ferry crossing at the Green River. If we went that route, we would have to wait for two or three days. There was another crossing we could make further down the river. We would be taking the lower trail. We followed the Big Sandy until we crossed and came up to very barren and unique mud formations. The trail was sandy but good.

They found a place we could stop. There was no grass, no water, no wood. We made do. We corralled the stock, did chores, had supper, said prayers, and went to bed.

Friday, September 12: Day 69

I woke up at four o'clock, did chores. We had some milk and a few eggs. After we packed the wagons, had breakfast of mush and cornbread, we finished packing, said company prayers, and hit the trail at half-past six.

As we started our journey, we entered a small box canyon that appeared there was no way out. We followed the trail to the back of the canyon, around a large vertical mud wall. The trail went behind this mud wall, up and out of the small box canyon. The trail out was steep but everyone made it up and out safely. This box canyon was one of the most unique things I had experienced on the trail. I often wondered who and how scouts made and found these trails. I wanted to be a scout, only if Izzy was with me. I missed Izzy.

Once on top, the trail was sandy and slow. We followed the trail for a few miles and we could see the large cottonwood trees that lined the Green River. As we went down the bluff, the sagebrush grew very tall, some almost five feet high. We also noticed a herd of elk down by a bend in the river to our north. James and a couple hunters rode out.

We finally came to the Green River. There were many others up the river, crossing safely, but we did not want to wait. We went down about a mile and found a wide shallow place just before the river cut into some cliffs on our south side. We all crossed safely and traveled about a mile along the river. At three o'clock, we encamped at a big bend in the river where there was good grass, water, and wood. The company of fifty chose the north side of the bend, and we took the southern side of the bend. I was glad we had this side. There were islands and shallow areas to explore.

I could tell people had traveled through that area for many years. There were hundreds of tree stumps and a few trees still standing. There was an island upriver. I could tell from all the stumps that it had been full of trees at one time. Now there were only stumps. There was not a tree on the island. I was sure they would grow back.

As we came to our encampment, I could see the trail to the west as it climbed a high bluff. I reckoned we would be climbing that hill the next day.

We corralled the stock by the river so they could drink and eat freely. As we unpacked the tents and wagons, James and the hunters came back with six large elk. The meat was distributed and it was gratefully accepted. After we set up the tents and did our chores, I gathered the youth company and we went fishing. It was not the same without Izzy and Unicornis. We caught nineteen suckers and chubs.

Mama Julia and my sisters washed clothes. Later, they neatly packed all of Izzy's clothes and belongings in her sack. They did not know what to do with Izzy's treasures of shiny rocks, arrowheads, fish fossils, wood rocks, rattlesnake rattles, and other items she packed away since we had left Kanesville. They decided to pack them away as well. Sarah made the joking remark that all of Izzy's treasures might make the wagon lean to one side. They giggled, wiping their tears and tucked everything away.

Before supper, Mama Julia called all the men and boys of the family down to the river. We walked down and there were two chairs. Mama Julia told us to take off our shirts and sit in the chairs for haircuts. I could tell Pa was about to say no, but he looked at Mama Julia and he knew he had better do as told. Mama Julia and Rebecca gave us all haircuts then handed us soap, and told us to get in the river and bathe. When we got out of the river, the womenfolk were gone. On the banks were clean clothes. We dried off, changed into our clean clothes, and went for supper.

We had supper of elk, greens, and berry cobbler. After supper, we sat around the fire, talked, and the mosquitos visited us. We mostly talked about Izzy. We said company prayers and went to bed.

About one o'clock, two shots rang out and we all got up to see what was happening. The two guards from the second company of ten, Brothers Phelps and Andrus, killed a large black bear as it was trying to get one of the lame oxen. The bear did not injure the ox, except for a few scratches on his flank. The brethren were very proud. We all went back to bed while they skinned the quartered the bear.

Saturday, September 13: Day 70

We woke up at four o'clock, did chores, packed the tents, had breakfast of salt bacon, and pancakes. We said company prayers and hit the trail at half-past six. Once we left the river bottom, the trail again turned sandy. We came to a high bluff I had seen the day before. It was as big as it had looked, and sandy. The bluff stretched for miles so the only way to go was straight up. We made the steep sandy climb. Finally reached the top without accidents.

The trail was sandy, hilly, and we crossed many ravines that made traveling slow. As we traveled, the sun was hot. I could see the snowcaps of the Rocky Mountains to our left. They looked very high. I noticed antelope in the distance but nothing close. Occasionally, James would ride out to them, but once they had seen him, they would scatter. They were very fast and could run long distances before stopping. As I looked back towards the river, I could see the flat-top hill, or ancient volcano, that I had noticed before we dropped down and crossed the river. From this point, I could see for miles in every direction. Low rolling hills, grey sagebrush, and a greenish sagebrush covered the land. The only trees that grew were those along the rivers and streams. There were bluffs in every direction but far away. It was a beautiful place.

At about four o'clock, we encamped at a bend in the Blacks Fork River. The bend created a natural corral where stock could water and feed as needed. There was good grass, good water, and enough wood for cooking. We did chores, had supper of elk stew, greens, and bread.

We went exploring but found nothing of interest, except the same kinds of items and clothes left behind. Captain Carter informed us we would be staying for the Sabbath. We had company prayers and went to bed.

Blacks Fork River

Sunday, September 14: Day 71

I woke up at six o'clock. I did my chores. The milk was plenty and we had a few more eggs. One of Izzy's jobs, which was now mine, was putting feed in the coops. I usually did it anyway. She did not like the chickens, so she did not feed them very well. Another one of Izzy's chores was to help Pa grease all the wheels on the wagons. I wondered if Izzy really helped, because she never got grease on her hands. I reckoned Pa liked her company. We had company prayers and went about the day.

The mornings were cool. There was heavy dew on the ground. We started a fire to make charcoal and coals for cooking. We had breakfast of ham, biscuits, and gravy.

We spent most of the morning tending to the stock, applying salve to the oxen's shoulders and legs. We tried to keep them out of the water, but I reckoned the cool water felt good on their legs.

After lunch, we attended Sunday services. Brother Oldham gave a sermon.

> *2 Timothy 1:7 For God hath not given us the spirit of fear; but of power, and of love, and of a sound mind.*

It was a good sermon of not being afraid of who or what we were, and believing in our ability to perform the job or task assigned to us.

When we returned to our wagons, Mama Julia asked everyone, including Sarah and Isaac, to gather as a family. Once we gathered, Mama Julia told us about losing her husband and baby. I am not going to write about what all we talked about, except to say we cried a lot and laughed a lot. It did help us try to recover from losing Izzy. Mother joined us but did not say a word. It seemed she was with us in body only.

We had supper of the last of the elk, greens, and a berry pie. We sat around the fire, talking more, and healing more. Had company prayers and went to bed.

Monday, September 15: Day 72

I woke up at four o'clock, did my chores. Milk and eggs were good. Packed up the tents and wagons, and had breakfast of mush and cornbread. After breakfast, I helped Pa and my brothers gather the stock. There were two oxen in very bad shape. They belonged to Brother Hillsworth in the third company of ten. Pa sent me to get Brother Hillsworth. When we returned, Pa explained his oxen were in very bad shape and if he drove them, they would not make four miles. If we brought them along with the stock, they might make to our next stop, as long as there was grass and water. Brother Hillsworth said these were the only oxen he had. Pa told him he would lease him two of ours until his oxen healed or until we reached Zion. Brother Hillsworth said they did not have any money, but he would work something out later. Pa agreed and Ben handed him two healthy strong oxen. We had company prayers and hit the trail at half-past six.

The morning was cool, almost cold. The trail was rocky and sandy but easy to travel. About ten o'clock we crossed the Hams Fork River. It was an easy crossing and we were back on the same white, rocky, sandy trail. I noticed another bush growing abundantly. I ran up to Brother Hart and asked him about this bush. Brother Hart said he thought it was salt sage. It was a brighter green than the regular sagebrush. I was seeing this salt sage all around. I ran back and told Dottie and Gabe. They both gave me an absent stare. I did not think they were interested. Oh well, I thought it was good to know.

We followed the trail along the Blacks Fork River for about a mile and crossed near an island. The crossing went well again. The stock took a lick as we crossed. The trail, in some places, had deep sand, and the oxen were struggling as we traveled. We passed through a place with small hills on both sides of the trail. It reminded me of the hills with the graves before we crossed over South Pass, but I did not see any graves. The dirt was a greenish color in some places. We were traveling through some very interesting mud creations, and the greenish dirt was all around us. I wondered what made dirt red, grey, black, and now green. There were places I had seen yellow dirt, by the secret canyon, but there was not very much.

The trail was sandy and slow, becoming hillier as we traveled. We traveled up a small bluff and hit rocky ground. This made traveling faster and easier on the oxen. The oxen, walking in the sand, was very difficult for them. It pulled on the yoke and dug into their shoulders. It also slowly wore away their hoofs, especially the skin attached to the hoofs.

We traveled on rocky ground for about six miles. There were places where the trail cut through the high sandy mounds. Once cut through, it had stayed cut through. This was a very interesting area. Every time I started to wonder about what made these creations, I remembered Brother Hart talking about the greenish, black rock at South Pass and Manhattan. I got confused, stopped thinking about these things, and wanted to go fishing. I would just enjoy their differentness. The land had odd formations made from mud. It looked like the mud castles Izzy and I would make on the banks of the Missouri River near our ice shed.

We crossed many dry riverbeds: some were wide and some were narrow and they looked like water had not been there for a long time. We crossed another dry riverbed, but this one was deep and a couple wagons in the first company of fifty broke some spokes. Captain Reed called on some men to dig the banks of the riverbed down on both sides. It did not take long because the banks were sand, not rock. All the wagons crossed very easily. We were on flat ground with a good trail.

To the south, there was a high long bluff. As we got closer, I could see about four large bighorn sheep on the bluff. As we traveled closer to Church Butte, I could see more bighorn sheep. These were much bigger than the ones I had seen back home. They grouped between the high long bluff and Church Butte. It seemed there was not much to eat in the area, but they seemed to be doing fine. The Blacks Fork River appeared to be on the other side of the long high bluff.

As we came upon Church Butte, Captain Reed stopped for our daily nooning. I think he was allowing us curious ones to look around. I am glad he did. This stand-alone bluff was very intriguing. It was not as big as Independence Rock but seemed as high. There was no vegetation around the base to the bluff. The dirt on the bottom was a greenish grey, and then the dirt turned to a greyish brown, with another greenish grey layer about halfway up, with more greyish brown dirt. Near the top was another layer of greenish grey dirt with the top the greyish brown. All bluffs around there had the same color makeup. There were rock rings sticking out about six to twelve inches almost every five feet encircling the butte. As I walked around the base, there were many, many little caves. I threw a rock in each cave before I got in, making sure I did not hear a rattle. The rattle snakes in the area were smaller and a little reddish. I had not seen or heard any as I got into the shallow caves. Around the top were pinnacles just standing there, adding to the uniqueness of this bluff. After nearly an hour of exploring, we were back on the trail.

We came to the edge of the bluff and we could again see the Blacks Fork River. We went down the steep sandy bluff. The men and women by the wagon brakes had to use them as we went down to avoid pushing the yokes into the oxen. When we made it to the bottom, we came across another curious rock area. There were hundreds of thousands blackish rocks all around. They looked like the clinkers I would remove from the forge after burning coal. This was impossible because there was not a person or forge around the area big enough to make so many clinkers. Very, very, curious. Oh, the things I saw and noticed when I was walking and walking and walking and walking.

We traveled another mile and a half. At half-past three, we encamped at a grassy, marshy area that made a natural corral for the stock. Brother Hillsworth's oxen were still with us and doing well. We unpacked and set up the tents, unpacked the wagons, did chores. There were deer, antelope, and bighorn sheep in the distance along the river.

I could tell many others had stopped around the area. The grass was still good and there was still wood for fires, but there were many fire rings and items left. We had to be careful not to camp on the same spot others just used because of the waste left behind. Others did not properly take care of their waste or privy holes. Because everyone was using the same trail now, it was harder to find safe places to stop. The grass near the river was very short and looked to have a layer of alkali on the ground on the banks.

We had supper of desert chickens, cornbread with honey. After supper, the youth company went exploring a couple islands and cliffs in and along the Blacks Fork. We did not find anything on the islands but we noticed many birds that made holes in the cliffs for nests. They looked like those pesky swallows that annoyed us along the Platte. There were about a hundred or more birds in a small cliff area. There were five much bigger nests farther up. These nests were about as big as Cate. They built the large nests in big cracks in the cliff. We found some small black and gray feathers and large brown and white feathers. The big ones were keepers. We went back to our wagons, sat around the fire, talked, said company prayers, and went to bed.

CHAPTER 20
THE MOUNTAIN TOP – I MISS HOME

Tuesday, September 16: Day 73

I woke up at four o'clock, did chores, packed up the tents and wagons, helped Pa and my brothers salve up the stock. We had breakfast of salt bacon, and biscuits. We finished loading the wagons, gathered up the stock, gathered for prayers, and at half-past six, we hit the trail.

The day was cool, almost cold as we started out. The trail was rocky and sandy but good traveling. About a mile out, the trail became bumpy and we were crossing dry sandy ravines more often. There were some interesting mud and rock formations around there. We were going downhill and the oxen liked it because a slight downhill trail moved the yoke up and off sores. We traveled out of the bumpy trail back into sand. We traveled another mile and came out of the sand onto hard rocky and easy-to-travel trail until, once again, we were back into the bumpy, hilly road and ravines. After about four miles, we came to the Blacks Fork River crossing.

Ever since Chimney Rock, the creek and riverbeds were easier to cross because there was not a lot of vegetation along the banks. It was best to cross rivers and creeks where the path of the water made an outward bend next to an inward bend. The banks were next to the water, making it easier to get down to and out of the riverbed.

We had a delay as the company crossed the Blacks Fork River again. This time, we had a wagon in the first company of fifty loose a wheel. They quickly replaced the wheel and we were moving. The trail was sandy and rocky but traveled very quickly. We crossed a couple ravines, and after two miles, we crossed the Blacks Fork again, this time without problems. We nooned so the stock, especially the oxen, could get some grass and water.

The trail was sandy but not difficult until we traveled about two miles and went down a steep sandy bluff. A couple oxen in our first company of ten fell and the wagon's tree and yoke drove them into the sand, breaking the tree. The oxen managed to get up, and we did a short-term fix on the tree. Our oxen were becoming weaker because of this sand.

We came across some more very interesting mud and sand formations. On the bottom of some of these formations, the sand was a greenish color and as we went up, the color changed to grey, then red. It was very interesting. I wish we could have stopped there and explored.

We traveled into the bottomlands of the Blacks Fork. The trail became easier, still sandy, but a little better. We crossed another creek and Captain Carter informed us that we were close to Fort Bridger. I expected Hanna to come running back and tell us all about Mr. Jim Bridger, but ever since Izzy's death, Hanna had become quieter and not quite as fun. Herk hardly came around or joined the youth company. Everyone missed Izzy, and so did I.

We came out of the river bottom, and once again, traveled in sand. This sand was deeper and made traveling slow. We found ourselves among these mud formations. I could lose myself, exploring this area. I wondered how they formed into what they were this day. I pretended some giants made them. I was sure they were nice giants, not the mean giants Odysseus ran into in the story *The Odyssey* by Homer. I thought about many things when I walked all day.

We came off a bluff and crossed another creek. I could see the mountains to our left. They were beautiful and big! We crossed another creek and passed the first company of fifty as they repaired three of their wagons. Captain Reed moved on ahead of our company, waiting for the scouts to tell us where we were going to stop.

The trail was sandy and slow. We traveled another six miles, and we could see Fort Bridger. There were many, many wagons and Indian lodges around the fort. The Indians had many dogs and even more children. I could not make out what breed the dogs were. They looked to be a cross between wolves and bears because they were short and stoutly strong. I knew they could not make a wolf-and-bear dog, but that was what they looked like.

The fort had four buildings and a pen for the horses. They used mud and logs to make all the structures. This was a beautiful, grassy valley with good water in every direction. The mountains to the south looked beautiful, but almost unpassable. When I started to think of how we were going to go up and over those mountains, I got the itch-whistle and wanted to go fishing.

We traveled about a mile past the fort, crossed two small creeks, and at four o'clock, we encamped on the Blacks Fork River. The place had good grass, wood, and water. We found a place that looked like it was not used by others in a long time.

We corralled the stock, unpacked and set up the tents, unpacked the wagons, did chores. Rebecca, James, and Sam went to the fort to get some supplies.

Pa told Ben, Charles, and me to watch the stock while James and Sam were at the fort. "There are too many people around here to not look after the stock," Pa warned us.

After a little while, Rebecca, James, and Sam came back. They purchased some potatoes, fruit, fresh greens, and other items. Around six o'clock, the first company of fifty passed us and they stopped about a half-mile ahead of us to the north.

We had supper of beef stew, with potatoes and greens they got at the fort, and berry cobbler. We sat around the fire when a dozen Snake Indians came over looking at our horses. Pa and James talked to them and, after a while, the Indians came back with two robes and four bearskins. Pa handed them two of our good mixed-breed geldings. They shook hands and Pa came back, sat down, and covered himself with the robes and bearskins.

Pa looked around the fire at all of us. "I am warm. Too bad the rest of you did not have any horses to trade."

Rebecca and Dotty walked over, pushed Pa off his chair, and took his robes and skins. "Thanks, Pa."

We all laughed. Mama Julia said the little ones would sleep warm tonight. As the sun was setting, the mountains looked purple. They were beautiful.

We sat around the fire and talked, had company prayers, and went to bed.

Wednesday, September 17: Day 74

I woke up at four o'clock and the mornings were getting colder. I did my chores. Eggs and milk were good. Izzy's churning process was still working well. We loaded the tents, loaded the wagons, and had breakfast of mush and cornbread. I helped Pa and my brothers gather the stock, salve and wrap the oxen, and hitch up. Pa walked over to a freighter going to California and handed him a letter. Pa offered to give him some money, but the freighter refused and shook Pa's hand. We finished packing the wagons, gathered for prayers, and hit the trail at half-past six.

We left our encampment, crossed the Blacks Fork, and followed the trail going up a high bluff. We crossed a creek, traveled less than a mile, crossed another creek without difficulty, and started our gradual climb up. There was a very large sandy bluff in the distance, which served as a marker. The trail was rocky, sandy, and a little slow. We traveled about two miles and went up a sandy ravine. The ravine was bumpy and slow. We crossed over smaller ravines that fed into the ravine we were following, which made traveling slow. About three miles, we passed a medium-sized sand bluff with a few junipers and sagebrush. As we passed the small sandy bluff, areas of drifting sand were becoming more frequent, causing the oxen to strain as they pulled through them.

We were now in the shadows of the large sandy bluff we had first seen at the beginning of today's journey. The bluff was very big. We climbed the sandy trail going around the north side of the bluff. There seemed there were no trees that grew on top. A few cedars clumped in areas around the rim. As we rounded this giant bluff, we crossed over many small ravines and then a large ravine. The dirt on the south side of the trail was turning green. I scooped up a handful of this dirt to see if moss was the cause of the greenness. The dirt was dry, very dry, and sandy. I gave it more thought until I reached the point of thinking that made me want to go fishing, I let the dirt sift through my fingers. *I will think about it later.*

As the breeze whiffed the greenish dirt away, I noticed we were on the edge of a deep ravine. We carefully traveled down and managed to reach the other side without troubles. It seemed the ravine was a barrier, because the green dirt ended at the ravine. We were back to rocky, sandy, sagebrush trails, which shook the wagons every step we took. We followed the trail as it led us down from the base of the giant bluff. The sun was getting hotter. The mornings were cold and the days were hot. I wish I could have saved some of the cold for when it got hot.

We crossed over a shallow dry streambed and came to a shallow spring. We nooned at that place so the stock could get a few licks. We took the time to care for or trade out the oxen that needed it. Our midday stops from Kanesville to almost Fort Laramie were nice breaks, and most times unnecessary, but now they were very important. We checked on the oxen, changed them out, attended to sores, wrapped legs, and applied salve. We needed to be very careful with these strong gentle creatures. Our survival depended on it. It always made me sad when I saw a dead or dying ox or stock along the trail. And I had seen hundreds. Did the people who owned them take care of them? Or did they treat them as if they were some of the thousands of items discarded and destroyed along the way? We were doing our best to take care of the stock in our company, so we all could arrive safely.

I missed Izzy.

After our break, we were on the trail again, and after about four miles of difficult pebbly trails, we came to the edge of the bluff. We could see a creek below. We traveled down the high bluff. The trail was very sandy and pebbly with juniper trees all around. I overheard Mr. Bradshaw tell Mr. Laroy they should have picked the juniper berries and introduced our company to the spirits they could distill from them. They both laughed and a few brethren just chuckled and shook their heads. A wagon in the first company of fifty broke a back wheel. They set it upright and replaced the wheel. Nothing was broken that we could see.

We made it to the bottom and crossed Muddy Creek. We left the trail and went up the creek almost a mile and at four o'clock, we encamped along Muddy Creek. There was good grass, good water, and enough sticks for cooking. That night would be nearly a halfmoon and there would not be a lot of light. Captain Carter said the next day we would be at the Bear River and there would be plenty of wood. We would use the wood we had brought for fires on each end of the corrals. The Indians that traded Pa for the horses told him there were many bears, mountain lions, wolves, and coyotes in this area and we needed to watch for them.

We corralled the stock, unpacked and set up the tents, unpacked the wagons, did chores. Again, we attended to the stock, applying salve and wrapping, if necessary. Most of the yoke sores were callusing over. That was a very good sign. We had supper of dry buffalo dumplings, greens, and berry cobbler.

We did not do any exploring because of the predatory animals. That night was cold. We sat around the fire and talked, gathered for prayers, and went to bed.

Thursday, September 18: Day 75

I woke up at four o'clock and it was cold. I went to the wagon, put on another shirt under my coat. I did my chores. We had a few eggs and milk was good. We packed up the tents and wagons, had breakfast of salt pork, biscuits, and gravy. After breakfast, I helped Pa and my brothers with the oxen. Pa said some would be lucky to make it to the Bear River. Brother Hillsworth's oxen were coming along, but still weak. We salved up the legs and wrapped those that needed it. Caring for the oxen took a little longer that morning. We finished loading the wagons, had company prayers, and hit the trail at half-past six.

We backtracked to the main trail, which was sandy at first, then turned into good trails, easy to travel. We followed a canyon all that morning, occasionally catching water here and there. Of course, the stock grabbed a couple licks as we passed. After traveling about three miles, we started our upward climb. The climb was gradual but constant. Fortunately, the trail was good and the oxen pulled well without difficulty. After about a mile, the trail became steeper and the oxen were struggling. We noticed at least thirty or more dead animals on both sides of the trail in various forms of decomposition. Some were just bones while others looked to have died a few days before.

Towards the top, we brought oxen and horses up to help double-team. Too many oxen were wearing down. Once we reached the top, we took turns resting and looking at the wonderful view. It must have rained on the big mountains to the south because they were now snowcapped. The snowcapped mountains were a beautiful sight. I saw the vast beauty of the rolling hills to the east from which we came, and now the big snowcapped mountains to the south and rolling hills to the west. There was a green valley at the bottom of the hill on the north and south of the trail, with more mountains ahead of us. What a beautiful view. There were juniper trees lining the trail, along with little white lily flowers, tall purple thistle flowers, and little purple and yellow flowers amongst the sagebrush. There were current bushes and another grove of trees near the trail but I did not know what these trees were. These trees had a white bark and little round leaves.

They passed the word along that, at this point, the waters ahead of us flowed to the Great Salt Lake while the waters behind us flowed to the Colorado River. *Wow, the Colorado River*, I said to myself. I had never heard of it, but water on the other side flowed into it. *Maybe I should ask Hanna what the Colorado River was.*

The top of the trail

I did not need to ask. Brother Hart explained to us that all the rivers and streams from the Rocky Mountains, east of the point we were standing, flowed into the Colorado. The Colorado flowed all the way down to Mexico and then into the Pacific Ocean. Brother Hart said no one had ever explored the Colorado River, so he did not know that much about it. Brother Hart said we were standing about seven-thousand-six-hundred feet above sea level, a little over a mile above the Missouri River where we had lived in Kanesville. I was going to have to take his word for it. I knew how far a mile was to walk and that was very far up. This type of thinking was making me want to go fishing with Grandpa.

As I looked out at the vast openness and beauty of this area, I imagined this was what the Great Salt Lake Valley might look like. Suddenly, feelings overcame me. I missed the many green trees of home. Of course, that made me think of Izzy. I asked myself, "What if we had not left our home in Kanesville? My little sister would still be here. We were happy there." I wondered if Mother asked the same questions, and those questions made her sick.

I knew there were people back in Missouri and other places that wanted to hurt and even kill us, as they did to Mama Julia's family. I hoped we would find peace and security in Zion. I hoped the journey we and all the others were making would be worth the loss we had received. When I thought of those questions, my stomach became upset and I got tired and a little angry. Looking back towards the east, to where Izzy was buried, I could not but think that, someday, she would become no more than a thought, and her memory would fade as we faded, and no one would ever know she was there. *Oh, Izzy, why did you have to leave? Why did you have to die?* I missed my little sister. It hurt so much. Would I ever see the green trees of home again?

I needed to walk, work, stay busy, and make those thoughts go away. I needed to walk.

After our oxen, stock, and people rested, we started down. The trail was good, very pebbly in places. The men and women next to the wagon brakes need to make sure they did not apply too much brake, making an unnecessary tug on the oxen, but enough brake to keep it from pushing the oxen into the ground. If the wheels slipped too much on the gravel, they risked breaking a tire and losing a wheel.

After about two miles of slow, hard traveling down, we crossed a bend with big red boulders and red dirt that lined the trail. As we rounded a bend, I could see a valley with rolling hills behind the valley. Everyone made it safely to the bottom. We traveled along a small creek bed for about a mile and crossed the creek twice. The stock got a couple licks as we moved on. We continued gradually down a good trail. The soils turned from red to grey and to red and grey again as we traveled downhill.

We reached the bottom and came to Sulphur Creek. A very strong warning went out to everyone, making sure that neither man nor stock drank from this creek. People said it was poisonous. We had to drive the stock away with sticks. Apparently, there were tar springs within or around the creek that came out into the creek, making it very poisonous. I did see a rainbow-colored sheen on the water along the banks, which was always a bad sign.

We traveled a little over a mile, crossing Sulphur Creek, and came around a bend onto the beautiful valley of the Bear River. Big cottonwoods lined the river.

As we stopped, Pa motioned for me to check out the river. I found a path through the thorny wild roses that seemed to grow everywhere, I reached the river, and I could see fish rising to catch flies. I was excited to get to fishing. Maybe fishing would bring the youth company out again. We had not been together since Izzy had died. I headed back through the thorny roses, found a few berry bushes, and ate a couple as I headed back.

We traveled about a mile up the river and at four o'clock, we encamped at a place that had good grass, good water, and plenty of wood.

We unpacked and set up the tents, unpacked the wagons, did chores, and spent about two hours attending to the stock. We had supper of dry buffalo stew with potatoes, greens and glazed cinnamon bread rolls. I wished we had these cinnamon bread rolls more often. They were very good.

As we were eating, Captain Carter came and said we were staying there the next day. He asked Pa and my brothers to check after the wagons and make any repairs, if needed. Of course, said they would.

Captain Carter said he would round up help and he would pitch in as well. "Do you want Brother Hart's help? Or should I find him another job?" asked Captain Carter, speaking with a softer voice.

We all laughed and Pa told Captain Carter that Brother Hart was welcome to help any time.

Captain Carter laughed and stood there, not saying anything.

We went back to eating and Pa asked if he was hungry.

Captain Carter said, "I'm hungry, but not for stew."

Mama Julia stood up and said, "I better not get in trouble by spoiling your supper." She walked over to the oven in the fire, removed the lid, and took out a cinnamon bread roll, put some glaze on it, and handed it to him.

Captain Carter removed a handkerchief from his pocket and put it under the roll as he said, "I will not say a word." Captain Carter tipped his hat with a big smile and went back to his wagon eating his cinnamon bread roll.

We gathered as much wood as we could find and built a large fire so we could have charcoal the next day for the forge. The night cooled very quickly and, with no clouds in the sky, it was going to be a cold night. We gathered for prayers and went to bed.

Friday, September 19: Day 76
I woke up at six o'clock to a very cold morning. A heavy frost was on the ground. I did my chores. We only had one egg, but milk was good. We had to cover the chickens better with the cold nights. I helped Pa and

my brothers unload the tools and set up shop. We had breakfast of ham and hot cakes with berry-spread. We had company prayers, then Mr. Laroy and the brethren came to help. The most needed repairs were tightening and resetting tires and tightening wheel spokes. Charles and I helped with gathering charcoal and cleaning out the forge. The womenfolk were washing and mending clothes and cleaning out the wagons.

Cate and James Jr. were playing with Gerald when Cate said again, "Let it stretch its legs." That was a funny thing to say about a small turtle.

Around eleven o'clock, Pa asked Charles and me to gather the youth company and do a little fishing. Pa told me to take his rifle, in case we ran across any bears or moose. "Fire a shot in the air and not at the animal. If you shoot the animal, and you do not kill it, it will likely maul you to death. When we hear the shot, we will come running." Pa continued, "Tell the kids to make as much noise as possible, especially when moving through the willows. The worst thing you can do is sneak up or startle a bear or moose."

Charles asked if he could have a rifle, but Mr. Laroy immediately said no, laughing. "Now, Charles, do not be a ninny-whit. You need to learn how to shoot before you can carry a rifle."

Charles looked down and kicked a small rock. "Oh, alright."

We joined the youth company and went fishing.

We set our lines, then we older kids sat and talked about Izzy, just as Mama Julia did with us. Again, we talked, laughed, and cried. I did not fully understand, until now, how much they loved and missed Izzy.

"I reckoned Izzy was like an ornery, bossy, but fun sister," I said.

Hanna wiped the tears from her eyes. "No, Willy, Izzy was much more. Although Izzy gave everyone a hard time, she told everyone here, in private, how much she loved and appreciated us many times. Izzy loved us and we all loved Izzy."

That confession hit me hard, like a hammer on the anvil. It was a surprise to me and made me cry.

After our talk, we were back to our old fun youth company.

About two o'clock, we noticed James and five other hunters heading upriver on their horses. About that time, Sister Carter came over and gathered the fish we caught. I could recognize the trout but the other fish were new to me. Sister Carter pointed to a large calm pool away from the main river and told us to get in and stay in until we were clean. The pool was about two feet deep at the deepest place and it was warmer than the river. Of course, we obeyed and had a very fun time. We would get out every once in a while to eat berries and crest that grew everywhere around us and to get warm. Then we went back in the pool. We bigger kids looked after the smaller ones to make sure we were all safe. After about two hours, most of the kids were on the bank napping, while we older kids went back to fishing.

Around five o'clock, they called us back to the wagons to get ready for another fish supper and, hopefully, dancing. About the same time, James and the hunters came back with a black bear and two large moose on their travois. This would supply enough meat for the whole company for at least two, maybe three days. We all helped put the tools away and I did my chores.

Everyone in our company of ten, well now, eight, gathered around and had a great supper of fish, meat, potatoes, greens, and bread. After supper, we had pies and cobblers made of berries of different kinds.

After supper, the music started and the dancing began. Dotty danced with Herk and I danced with Hanna. We all enjoyed ourselves. Around ten o'clock, we gathered for prayers and went to bed. We all missed Izzy.

Saturday, September 20: Day 77

I woke up at four o'clock, did chores. We had a few eggs and milk. We packed up the tents and put them in the wagons, packed the wagons, tended to the stock. The day of rest and good grass restored many of the oxen. We salved and wrapped those that needed it and had breakfast of mush, biscuits, and raspberries. Mama Julia and the sisters picked enough raspberries and other berries to last many days. We had company prayers and hit the trail at half-past six.

We backtracked to the old trail and moved out of the river bottom. We were noticing many dead oxen, cattle, and horses. Not all these animals could have died of exhaustion. We could only suppose they drank the bad water from Sulphur Creek. Many of the animals had only the tender parts eaten out of them. No wonder we did not have any problems with bears or mountain lions. It looked like they had enough to eat.

The trail was good as we traveled and the morning was very cool. We followed a dry riverbed for a few miles, then we started climbing a sandy and rocky trail. The trail was now taking us up and down good-sized hills and ravines. We were hugging a hillside as we moved along. The trail was rocky and dusty, it shook the wagons hard, but we were lucky no one broke spokes or wheels.

We travelled about five miles, crossed two narrow and deep creeks. We stayed to the north of the riverbed, hugging the hillside. As the day warmed up, the trail became very dusty. I noticed different kinds of plants and very colorful blue, red, pink, white, and yellow flowers of various sizes as we traveled towards the mountains. Brother Hart said they were high desert plants. Some we could eat and some would hurt and could kill us.

Brother Hart stopped our column, bent down with his knife, and dug up a beautiful white lily flower with three predominant petals and red inside the flower. He brushed off the bulb and ate it. All of a sudden, his face turned red and he started heaving as if he was in pain. He fell on the ground, holding his stomach, and said, "Wrong one."

We all ran towards him and his wife was screaming, "Spit it out. Spit it out."

Brother Hart started laughing. "I am alright, just funning with you. This is your Sego Lily, and it is good for you. You can eat the whole plant."

Sister Hart picked up a small rock and threw it at him. It hit Brother Hart in the head as she yelled, "Do not do that again."

We all laughed.

Brother Hart stood up, rubbing the bump on his head and said, "I am sorry, but you should know there are deadly plants around here as well."

Brother Hart walked over to a plant with long spiny leaves, much like the yucca, but not as stiff, and it had a cluster of white flowers at the top. This was the "Death Camas."

Brother Hart dug the bulb up and held the plant and bulb in a handkerchief. "This plant can kill you. It is dangerous to touch. The Death Camas looks like the wild onion. They are easily confused and that confusion is deadly, so know your plants before you eat them. If you are not sure about a plant, it is a good idea to have someone near you. You can have them eat it and if they get sick, and . . . "

Sister Hart picked up another rock.

We all laughed as Brother Hart ran back to his position, throwing the plant and handkerchief on the ground.

We started the column again. We followed a creek and the sun became very warm. It was interesting how cold the day started and how hot it became in a short time. We traveled another five miles, and as we came around a bend in the creek, we noticed some grey round and pointed shapes ahead of us. They were a little like the mud formations we passed a few days before, but these were different. Each company stopped on the other side to look and allow their stock to grab a couple licks at the creek next to the trail. When we arrived, Brother Hart, still rubbing his head, pointed out the many rocks that made the structures. He said it looked like this place had been either an ancient riverbed or volcanic flow. I wanted to say giants made them but that would have been silly. *Who knows? They could have.*

We traveled about a half mile and as we rounded a mound, the trail opened into a very nice grass and watery area, stretching north and south. The trail headed south, so we headed north upriver for about a mile along the Yellow Creek where there would be good water, good grass, and plenty of wood. We were approaching a new moon in a few days and the nights were darker. With the threat of animals, like bears, mountain lions, coyotes, and wolves, we placed many fires around the corrals.

We unpacked and set up the tents, unpacked the wagons, did chores, and helped Pa and my brothers salve and wrap the stock. While we were tending to the stock, a large group of Snake Indians traveled by on the west side of the small mound west of our encampment. James could make out that they were going upriver for a few miles, looking for better hunting. They communicated to James that we should watch for mountain lions, bears, and wolfs.

We sat down for supper when Captain Carter came and said we would be staying for the next day's Sabbath. He also informed us that a baby was born in our first company of ten.

We had supper of moose, potatoes, greens, and a berry sweetbread. After supper, we unpacked the tools, in case we needed to do some mending the next day.

Brother Hart came around, informing us about the rocky formation we had just passed. As he pointed up the hill, he said, "That is the Needles."

As I looked up at the bumps, I wondered who named a bunch of bumpy rocks the Needles. Sure, there were some spires, but none looked like Grandmother's darning needles. One of the formations, about halfway up, looked like the head of one of those horned lizards with his mouth open, ready to eat a bug. Needles? More like bumps.

As the sun set, it became very cold again. Someone said we were seventy-one miles from the valley of the Great Salt Lake City. We made a nice fire and talked until we had company prayers and went to bed.

CHAPTER 21
GRANDMOTHERS KISSES

Sunday, September 21: Day 78

I woke up at seven o'clock. It was nice to sleep in. I did chores. Milk and eggs were very good. I helped Pa and my brothers tend to the stock. The sores were healing well and quickly. Another day of rest would do them well. We had breakfast of salt bacon and pancakes with butter and berry-spread.

I went to brush and walk Acer when a rude, ornery varmint, the badger, met me. It was not an adult badger but had an attitude bigger than its body. It must have smelled the blood from the oxen. As I walked towards it, it sat back with its front up, ready to charge. I had my bullwhip if he charged. I tried to shoo it away, but the more I tried to send it away, the more it hissed. I knew better than to turn around, which would be a guaranteed bite on the leg. I stood there and threw a couple rocks. It stood there hissing and challenging me. After about five minutes, this rude, ornery varmint ran into the sagebrush.

We gathered for company prayers.

The womenfolk went about cleaning and organizing the wagons while we went back to tending the stock. At one o'clock, we attended Sunday services where a Brother Wayne from the fifth company of ten in the first company talked about Proverbs 9: 8-12.

> *Proverbs 9: 8-12:*
>
> *8. Reprove not a scorner, lest he hate thee: rebuke a wise man, and he will love thee.*
>
> *9. Give instruction to a wise man, and he will be yet wiser: teach a just man, and he will increase in learning.*
>
> *10. The fear of the Lord is the beginning of wisdom: and the knowledge of the holy is understanding.*
>
> *11. For by me thy days shall be multiplied, and the years of thy life shall be increased.*

*12. If thou be wise, thou shalt be wise for thyself: but
if thou scornest, thou alone shalt bear it.*

After Sunday services, the youth company gathered, and we went exploring. The place we stopped at did not have any items left behind by others for us to look through. We walked back to the strange rock structures and climbed around them. Pa had sent Sam with a rifle to watch over us. We found nothing of interest but we did have fun digging around. We explored around until it was suppertime.

We had supper of moose dumplings, greens, bread with butter and berry-spread, and berry cobbler. We sat around the fire and talked about seeing Grandmother and Grandpa and what we would do after we settled in. I kept thinking about telling them about Izzy, how sad they would be. I thought about the Herbert's when they heard about Izzy and how very sad they would be as well.

The night was cold and we got together for company prayers and went to bed. The sun was setting earlier, so we were going to bed earlier.

Monday, September 22: Day 79

I woke up rested at four o'clock, did chores. Milk was up and we had a couple of eggs. We packed up the tents and blankets, packed up the wagons. Pa greased the wheels. When he got to the last wheel, Pa still held the bucket out as if Izzy was going to take the bucket and put it away. He looked over his shoulder at the bucket, took a heavy breath, walked over to the back of the wagon, and hung the bucket up on the hook.

We had breakfast of mush and cornbread, then gathered and salved the stock. The rest had done the stock well and it looked like Brother Hillsworth's oxen were going to make it. They could not pull wagons yet, but they would make it. We gathered for prayers and hit the trail at half-past six.

We traveled back to the main trail and started up a slow climb. The trail was rocky and dusty. I was glad it was cool because the climb would have been harder if it was hot. We climbed a few hills and dropped down to a small valley.

As I was looking up at the hill we were about to go over, Pa yelled, "Dotty, William, bring the up the strongest oxen."

Dotty and I cut twelve of the strongest ones out and took them to Pa and my brothers. They double-teamed the wagons. Once the wagons were on top, Pa, my brothers, and some of the other men brought them back and hooked them up to the wagons going up, like what we had done at Rocky Ridge. I was glad we went over Rocky Ridge. That experience was a practice for what was ahead of us. While the older men did this, the young men and the women took the wagons down to the staging area until the others were finished.

Everyone made it down safely. While at the top, I could see for miles in every direction. It was a beautiful view. I wish I could draw more than funny-looking pigs and cows. This would be a beautiful picture.

Once we rolled on again, we came across a clear cold spring. We took a couple licks and rolled on. The trail continued down as the day was warming up. The trail was good and travel was easy, but the rocky road shook the wagons as we rolled on.

After traveling about five miles, the trail finally leveled out. However, the trail was dusty and very rocky. We went up a side of a large steep hill and traveled along a small spring for a few miles. We came off the side of the hill onto a nice meadow with a spring to the north. I noticed some caves that the youth company would have liked to explore, but we were not stopping. We crossed Echo Creek and made a left turn. I could see the trail going down the canyon.

We traveled down the canyon. The trail was good and easy to travel. The mountain walls were high on both sides of us. We continued down, crossing the creek a couple times, and hugged the side of the mountain as we walked. This was a beautiful area with green grass and trees speckled among the red and grey rocks.

We came out from hugging the canyon walls and followed Echo Creek. It turned into wider areas with grass and good water. We were not close enough to the water, but the stock was doing fine. We continued until four o'clock, when we came to a canyon opening to our right. That would be a good stopping place.

The first company of fifty waited ahead on the trail until we went up the canyon, then they followed. There was a small cool creek, good grass, and some wood. We corralled the stock at the top and the bottom with wagons at the entrances on both sides. I could tell no one had ever camped in the area. It had fresh water. We would not have to worry about other people's waste.

We unpacked, set up the tents, unpacked the wagons, and did chores. I helped Pa and my brothers with the stock. There were only a few that had sores on their shoulders and a few with sores on their legs, but for the most part, they were doing very well.

As I helped Pa, the youth company came and stood waiting for me. Pa finally told me to go ahead and be safe. So, the youth company went exploring. We went up the canyon and did not see anything interesting, just more and higher hills. We asked Pa if we could go across the creek and look at the other side. Pa sent Sam with his rifle to watch over us. As we headed over, we met six freight wagons headed to California. We waved to one another as they moved on. We crossed the creek and explored around. Again, we found nothing of interest.

As we headed back, we met another group of eleven wagons going back to the States. They told us that they had left St. Louis in June and headed to California. They had made it to the Humboldt River in the desert, where Indians killed four of their companions and killed three oxen. They managed to make it back to the Great Salt Lake City where they purchased a couple oxen. Now they were headed back home to Owensboro, Kentucky. They wished us luck and as they left, they told Sam, "We're going to kill any Indian we see on the way home."

Sam warned them about doing that. He told them about the big treaty meeting at Fort Laramie and all the Indians we had seen, east of Fort Laramie.

They looked at each other and said, "Well, we would like to kill them anyway, but maybe we will not." They tipped their hats and continued up the trail.

We all went back to our wagons, had supper of stew, cornbread, and cinnamon bread rolls. We made a fire, visited until we gathered for prayer, and went to bed.

Tuesday, September 23: Day 80

I woke up at four o'clock and did chores; milk was good and had a couple eggs. The coyotes howled all night. A couple times, they sounded very close, but the guards said they had no troubles. We packed up tents and loaded the wagons. We had breakfast of mush, ham, and biscuits. Many of the other families were running short on food, so we shared what we could. The whole company was sharing. Together, we would make the next two or three days to the valley.

After breakfast, we tended to the stock. Overall, they were looking ready. We finished loading the wagons, gathered for prayers, and at half-past six, we hit the trail. We came out of our canyon and joined the main trail.

The trail was rough and difficult, but good for churning butter. We traveled along Echo Creek, crossed a small creek into a nice open meadow. As we traveled, the canyons began to narrow. Sheer red cliffs on the right side and high hills on the left. The very high red cliffs were made of red mud and small rounded river-type rocks. They were very interesting. We crossed the creek several times, some of the banks were very steep and difficult, but everyone crossed over safely. As we traveled, we could hear the wagons echo as we rolled on.

Of course, Hanna had to see if her echo carried, "Hey, Willy, can you hear me?" As her voice carried down the canyon, everyone could hear her.

"No, I cannot hear you," I replied.

There was a minute of silence, "How can you not hear me if you replied?"

The entire column laughed at her remark.

Hanna yelled, "Oh, be quiet, I am not talking to you anymore." Her echo carried through the canyon.

Another chuckle arose through the company.

The silence lasted only a few minutes. Hanna started up again, "Hey, Willy, my Pa said the red canyon walls were probably made of an ancient riverbed that ran through the canyon a long time ago."

I looked at the cliffs and imagined this place being a river. I was thinking what this would have looked like as a river and I forgot to reply.

"Willy," Hanna yelled, "are you listening to me?"

That snapped me out of my imagination dream. "Yes, I am listening. I am imagining what it would have been like if this were a river."

A voice came from far down the canyon, "Wet!"

Everyone started laughing because everyone was involved in our conversation in Echo Canyon.

About nine miles down, we crossed the creek a couple more times and stopped at a large grassy meadow so the stock could get a few licks and a couple blades of grass. We stopped by a red pebbly wall. Hanna, Charles, Gabe, and I, along with a few others, went exploring and chipping rocks out of the wall. The rocks were round like river rocks. We walked back to the wagons covered in red dirt from head to foot. We continued for a few hundred yards and we could see the mouth of the canyon and more mountains ahead.

We came out of Echo Canyon and followed the trail along the Weber

River. We passed many graves at the mouth of the canyon. Some looked to be recent. My thoughts immediately went to my little sister on the empty prairie. At least she was not alone. Izzy had Unicornis.

We traveled along the Weber River and came to what looked like the main river crossing. We went about a mile past the crossing to a large grassy area where a small creek flowed into the Weber River. The first company of fifty stopped and we went on until we passed them with space between our companies.

Weber River

Around four o'clock, we encamped next to the small creek and the Weber River. We had good grass, good clean water, enough wood for cooking and fires. It was almost a new moon and it would be very dark tonight. We corralled the stock along the Weber River. Pa instructed the guards to be watchful for bears, lions, and coyotes. Captain Walton asked James, Sam, and the other hunters to go upriver and see what they could find.

We unpacked and set up the tents, unpacked the wagons and did chores. I again helped Pa and my brothers tend to the stock. They were looking healthy and strong. The good and abundant grass and water was helping them very much.

After chores, the youth company went fishing. Our ranks spread out about a half-mile and, by six o'clock; we caught forty-four fish. James and the hunters came back with two large bull moose they had shot past the split in the cliffs that the river cut through. That was enough meat for Captain Reed's entire company.

As we sat down for supper, we heard a commotion going on in the companies above. The commotion continued down each company of ten until we heard a familiar voice behind the wagons, "What is for supper?"

We all jumped up. "Grandpa!"

Grandpa came around the wagon with horse reins in one hand and Sarah's hand in the other, followed by Isaac.

We all took turns hugging Grandpa and he hugged us back with his jolly laugh. Sam gave Grandpa his seat.

Pa said, "What are you doing here? How did you know we were here?"

"When we received the letter you sent with the freighter at Fort Bridger about Izzy, Grandmother said I had better come get you and bring you down safely. I did not know you were here. I thought I would find you by the Yellow River or around there. You have made good time."

Rebecca handed him a plate of moose and potatoes.

Grandpa gave Rebecca a kiss on the cheek. "This is fine, but I am disappointed there is no fish. Have I lost all my fishermen?"

Mama Julia brought him a couple trout filets.

"Now, that is what I am looking for. I knew I still had some fishermen," Grandpa said laughing. "So, tell me about the trip."

We talked as we sat around the fire. We went to company prayers and came back to the fires. The womenfolk went to bed and I wanted to stay up but Pa sent me to bed. I crawled to my own comfortable place under the wagon with my blankets. I could still hear Grandpa, Pa, and James talking.

I was falling asleep when I heard Pa tell Grandpa that he, James, and some of the other Brethren administered a Priesthood blessing to Izzy. Pa said that during the blessing, the Spirit of God told them Izzy was going to die. Pa and James started to cry.

Pa told Grandpa that Izzy knew it also. "After the blessing, Izzy got out of the wagon and walked over to me as I sat on the banks of the

Sweetwater. She sat on my lap and looked up at me. 'It is alright, Pa. It will be alright.' " Pa really started crying as he said to Grandpa, "She was trying to comfort me, Pa. Izzy was trying to comfort me."

I could hear Grandpa crying. I heard the women in the wagons crying.

Grandpa said in a loud, strong voice, "Be strong my Sons and Daughters of Zion. Our Izzy is walking with our Heavenly Father."

I cried myself to sleep.

Wednesday, September 24: Day 81

We woke up at four o'clock, started chores, remembering what I heard last night and listening to Pa and Grandpa crying. My stomach was sick again. I said to myself, "I cannot change it, so I will walk and walk and walk until I can feel better again. I know now that my depressed spirit will not stay if I am always busy."

We packed up the tents and wagons and had breakfast of fish, moose, and cornbread. We gathered for prayers. We hit the trail at half-past six.

We back-tracked to the main trail and forded the river. I believe that, because everyone was in a very guarded mood, everyone crossed safely. It was the quickest and most organized crossing yet. We traveled to the mouth of the canyon. After traveling about four miles of dusty and rocky trails, we started a gradual climb on a rock trail. The day was cool and the oxen were doing well.

We continued gradually climbing the mountain. After about three miles of climbing, we started down. The trail was rocky, dusty, and slow. We followed a steep ravine filled with small hills and shallow ravines. This constant up and down made travel slow and wore on the oxen. We passed groves of trees, mostly trees with white bark and small round leaves, like the ones on the hill before Sulphur Creek. I am sure Hanna would tell me what kind of tree they were. *Well, here she comes now.*

"Hey, Willy, do you know what kind of trees these are? Well, I will tell you. My pa says they call these trees money trees. They are called money trees because the leaves look like coins, but they are really called aspen." Hanna paused as she finely took a breath.

"Thank you. I was wondering about that."

"I thought you were, and I did not want you to think so hard that you would want to go fishing. With your grandfather around and all. It would be too tempting." Hanna laughed as she ran back to her wagon.

I looked over at Dotty and she just rolled her eyes and shook her head. I then looked over to Gabe. I think he was napping while he was walking.

We crossed a creek and continued down. The trail was difficult on the wagons as they jolted when they rolled. The oxen were doing better on rocky trails than sandy trails. The day was getting warmer, but thankfully, it was not hot. We came to a spring and followed it down a few miles, going up and down hills and across ravines.

At four o'clock and after traveling fifteen miles, we encamped at a place that had good grass, good water, and wood for fires.

We corralled the stock, unpacked and set up the tents, unpacked the wagons, did chores, and tended to the stock and wagons. Grandpa helped the brethren tend to the stock while Pa and my brothers went around mending wagons and tightening tires and spokes.

We had supper of moose stew, greens, and bread. We built a nice fire, sat around, and talked about our time in Kanesville.

Grandpa finally told Mama Julia what the Herbert brothers were really like, and how they gave to the needy. Grandpa told her they gave more than half of their yearly earnings to helping others. "Yes, they make quite a lot of money, but they give quite a lot away. For not being Christians, they are more Christian than most Christian people I have met."

Mama Julia and the sisters were ashamed about how they had treated them and how, when they get to the city, they would write and apologize.

Grandpa said that was not necessary. "The Herbert's know you are wonderful loving people, but you believed what they wanted you to believe."

We continued talking around the fire until we gathered for prayers. They asked Grandpa to give the prayer, which he did. I have always liked to hear Grandpa pray. He prays to Heavenly Father as if he knows Him. After prayers, we went to bed.

Thursday, September 25: Day 82

It was my birthday and I was fourteen years old. I woke up at four o'clock and did my chores. We had good milk and one egg. I did not think the chickens liked the bumpy trail. We loaded the tents in the wagons, loaded the wagons. We tended to the stock, ate breakfast of mush, salt bacon and cornbread.

We gathered and had prayers. After prayers, Captains Reed and Walton came to our company and visited with Grandpa and Pa. After they left, Pa and my brothers cut twelve of the strongest oxen from the herd and took them to the front of our company of fifty.

Captain Walton told everyone to have all their ropes and wheel chains ready. He said that once we started going over the most difficult parts of the trail, no one but the infirm and very small could be in wagons. "Infants are safer if the mothers carry them." Captain Walton wished us all Godspeed and said he would see us at the next encampment at Brother and Sister Killian's home.

We hit the trail at half-past six. The morning was very cold and it was dark.

We started on the trail, climbing the steepest part of the journey so far. The trail was very rocky and difficult. We crossed a few narrow deep ravines that jolted the wagons and the oxen. We had to push the wagons up a couple of the ravines. We crossed a creek and continued our climb. The trail, in some places, was very steep and we double-teamed and pushed the wagons up.

We came to a place where the trail was good and easy, but that did not last long. As we rounded a hill, we went up the side of the hill. Men tied ropes to the wagons and walked up along the hill. They held the ropes, making sure the wagons did not tip and roll down the steep hill.

At one point, we had delays because a wagon tree broke on the first company of fifty, but they repaired it quickly. Another delay happened when Captain Carter's wagon nearly tipped, but the men with the ropes brought it upright. When the wagon tipped, the yoke cut a deep wound into the left ox. We brought up another ox, yoked it up, and I took the injured ox back so Dottie and I could tend to it as we climbed.

As we climbed the summit and rounded a hill, we could see, for the first time, the valley of the Great Salt Lake. It was a beautiful sight. If we could have gotten away from the feelings of danger as we climbed the mountain, it would have been more beautiful: the red dirt, rocks, and large grey boulders, surrounded by knee-high green bushes and groves of money trees or aspen with their small, green, fluttering leaves. It was very beautiful. However, we did not have much time to take our eyes off the steep and dangerous trail. If we did, it could have been fatal.

We were now climbing down. We still needed to use ropes and chains to keep the wagons from tilting and to slow the wagons. At times, they used chains to lock the wheels to slow them down. The steep hill made using brakes useless and dangerous. When they chained the wheels, they needed to watch the tires very carefully so they did not break, lose a wheel, and send the wagon tumbling down the hill. Although we were in back with the stock, I could see the concentration and, sometimes, almost fear on the faces of the men as they pulled the wagons against the mountain while we climbed down. I marveled again at the harmony of these men as they safely glided the wagons along.

We came off the steep slope. The trail climbing down was a little easier. As we rounded a hill, we could see Little Mountain. We were almost there. We came to a spring and followed it until we crossed it, then we went around a hill, climbed one side, and went down the other. The trail going down was becoming easier. We should have nothing but butter in the churn.

As we traveled closer to the bottom of the mountain, we crossed many deep, narrow ravines, like the ones we met at the beginning of the day. These ravines were dangerous and slowed us down.

Finally, at almost four o'clock, we could see Grandmother's and Grandpa's house. Their house was across the creek on a small bluff looking over about a mile of rangeland for their stock. The stock ranged out of sight from travelers and out of danger from thieves. There were enough grassy areas for Captain Reed's company. Captain Reed rolled past and encamped on the southwest side, and Captain Walton encamped on the northeast side.

Grandmother and George were out waiting for us. It was so good to see them again. Grandmother came out and gave me a big hug, kissed me on my face about a hundred times, or so it seemed, and wished me happy birthday. Of course, everyone else in the family, as well as others, received the same treatment from Grandmother. It was a little embarrassing, but I did not care. We had made it!

George and a few hired hands killed a couple beef cattle for us. This, along with the moose meat we had would make a fine feast. This was a hard and tiresome day. Everyone was hungry and tired, not from the traveling, but from the stress of coming down the mountain.

We unpacked and set up the tents, unpacked the wagons, did chores and at six o'clock, we had a large fire in a very large area and ate supper. All the women had put together a feast.

As we ate and talked, Pa stood on the back of a wagon and called Captain Reed to come to the wagon. When Captain Reed came to the wagon, everyone stood up and cheered. Captain Reed tried to quiet the shouting and the thanks, but as he did, it only grew louder until he put his head down, untied the handkerchief from around his neck, and put it to his eyes.

The crowd quieted, and he regained self-possession and started to talk. He thanked everyone for supporting him and said he considered us all his friends. He said many other things, but I could not hear him very well. I was in the back by Grandmother and eating different kinds of pie. Captain Reed called up his captains of ten and everyone cheered. Then Captain Reed called up Captain Walton and gave him the wagon. Captain Walton talked for about five minutes and thanked everyone. Captain Walton called up his captains of ten and everyone cheered again.

Captain Reed got back on the wagon and said, "I know we are happy to be here, but our journey is not yet complete. We have one more day until we reach the valley. We have about six miles to travel before our journey is complete. Therefore, I want everyone ready to roll out by half-past six tomorrow morning."

The whole company went silent.

Captain Walton walked up to Captain Reed and whispered something to him. Captain Reed yelled out, "Excuse me, excuse me. I meant to say eight o'clock."

Everyone cheered and laughed.

Captain Reed called on Captain Walton to say company prayer. Captain Walton gave a fine prayer, mainly thanking our Heavenly Father for our safe arrival to this point.

After we said, "Amen," Captain Reed called out, "Mr. Laroy, let's get the music going."

Everyone cheered again, all the music makers gathered, and we had a great dance and celebration. We danced and had a good time until about eleven o'clock, then we went to bed.

Friday, September 26: Day 83

We woke up at six o'clock and did chores. We had some milk and no eggs. We were leaving two of our wagons and most of the stock in the area. We still had to drive thirty-seven stock, eleven horses, six pigs, and two donkeys. We were not responsible for cats, dogs, turkeys, chickens, or turtles. We had breakfast of ham, eggs, and biscuits with butter and berry-spread.

We gathered for prayers and prepared for our last day on the trail.

We hit the trail at eight o'clock.

We got back on the main trail and headed down the canyon following the creek. The trail was steep and rocky in most places. About a half-past nine, we came out of the canyon and entered the valley of the Great Salt Lake. We passed houses, farms, and many wagons, as we traveled down good roads. When we turned onto the main road, we had a gradual incline until we arrived at our final staging place.

The company met with the Presiding Bishop and relinquished our Church possessions. We said good-bye to everyone. We invited Mr. Laroy and Mr. Bradshaw and their family to stay with us until spring. They both said they wanted to keep moving. They promised to let us know when and where they landed. Everyone knew where we would be staying and could visit any time.

Pa met with Captain Reed and gave him a Colt Dragoon Revolver as a thank-you gift. Captain Reed thanked Pa for all he did and said, "We will be seeing each other very soon."

We climbed in the wagon, visited some shops, purchased some supplies, and headed back to Grandmother's and Grandpa's house.

CHAPTER 22
OCTOBER 1851

October 1851

    To catch up on the last couple of weeks. The Manus's and the Barker's made it safely five days after we arrived. Grandpa would perform the marriage ceremony for Sarah and Isaac in December. We would leave in the spring and travel about 150 miles south to settle a community. Looked like the Ward's, Thorston's, Gardner's, and others would be traveling with us. Grandmother and Grandpa would need to stay in Zion and help with managing stock and timber.

    The Treaty at Fort Laramie was moved to Horse Creek because of the number of Indians attending. The treaty created peace between the Indians fighting each other. The treaty also made the land north of the Platte River Indian land, and pioneers and settlers were not allowed to travel north of the Platte. The land south of the Platte River would be free from Indian troubles and safe for travel.

    I felt like I had lived an entire lifetime in one year. I would never forget 1851. I hoped it was truly worth the sacrifices and loss. As Brother Thorston taught us a little over a year ago, people would remember our lives, journeys, and experiences for a long time. If this was true, I hoped and prayed our descendants would remember who we were, and what we did, as we, today, remembered the descendants that came from the old country a little over a hundred years ago. I hoped they would take strength and pride, knowing they were descendants of a strong and dedicated people: Descendants of Pioneers.

William Phillip Killian

Epilog

Many historians have wondered why the death rate was so low on the trail in 1851 and went back up again in 1852. This book provides the answer. There were two events that happened in 1851. One was manmade: the Laramie Treaty, which prevented travel north of the Platte River. The other event was nature-made: it rained more often and washed the filth from the trail. From 1852 and on, people used the southern trail, and it did not rain as much. Therefore, the leading causes of death were cholera and dysentery.

Our family went on to settle communities in the Salt Lake Valley, central and southern Utah, as well as southeastern Idaho. Thank you, Grandmother and Grandpa, I miss you very much.

ABOUT THE AUTHOR

An interest in history and a knack for storytelling seems to be a part of Jeff's family legacy. Jeff was born and raised in Salt Lake County, Utah of strong pioneer ancestry. Jeff honorably served a mission for the Church of Jesus Christ of Latter-Day Saints and is an Eagle Scout. Carrying on his grandfather's tradition, Jeff enjoyed taking his son, and now grandson and granddaughter, on adventures exploring historical trails and landmarks. While on these adventures, he would tell stories of the people that passed through the area long ago. Jeff married his sweetheart Renee, a native Wyomingite, and they treasure living in Wyoming surrounded by family. He enjoys fishing and hunting in Wyoming and Alaska with family and friends. Jeff's interests include hands-on studies of the many historical, geological, and paleontological areas in Wyoming. While working with the American Indians in the Southwest, Jeff had the honor of being adopted into the Kachina Clan of the Hopi-Tewa. This provided him with an insight into the life of these native people, their unique history, traditions, ceremonies, and way of life, both past and present. This gave Jeff an understanding as to why they are a proud people.

Made in the USA
Las Vegas, NV
29 December 2021

39766447R10152